The Lifesaver

The Lifesaver

C.N. Steinhour

Hidden Shield Publishing
Sterling, VA

This is a work of fiction. All of the characters, organizations, places, and events portrayed in this novel are either products of the author's imagination or are used fictitiously. Any resemblance to actual persons, living or dead, is entirely coincidental.

The Lifesaver. Copyright © 2025 by C.N. Steinhour.
All rights reserved. No part of this text may be reproduced, scanned, or distributed in any printed or electronic form without permission, except as allowed under U.S. copyright law. For information, send correspondence to Hidden Shield Publishing, P.O. Box 651051, Sterling, VA 20165.
cnsteinhourbooks.com

Library of Congress Control Number: 2021908812

Edited by Gary Sunshine.
Cover design by Lena Yang.

Cover font is Caveat. Interior fonts are Adobe Garamond Pro, Caveat, Sharkscribble, Journal, and Ebrima.

BRIDGE OVER TROUBLED WATER
Words and Music by Paul Simon
Copyright © 1969 Paul Simon (BMI)
Copyright Renewed
International Copyright Secured All Rights Reserved
Used by Permission
Reprinted by Permission of Hal Leonard LLC

DR. STRANGELOVE OR: HOW I LEARNED TO STOP WORRYING AND LOVE THE BOMB
© 1963, renewed 1991 Columbia Pictures Industries, Inc.
All Rights Reserved.
Courtesy of Columbia Pictures

988 SUICIDE & CRISIS LIFELINE logo reprinted from
988lifeline.org

Second edition: July 2025

Publisher's Cataloging-In-Publication
(Provided by Cassidy Cataloguing Services, Inc.)

Names: Steinhour, C. N., author.
Title: The lifesaver / C.N. Steinhour.
Description: [Second edition]. | Sterling, VA : Hidden Shield Publishing, [2025] | Interest age level: 015-018.
Identifiers: ISBN: 9781737106838 (paperback) | 9781737106814 (ePub) | 9781737106821 (Kindle)
Subjects: LCSH: Teenage boys--Suicidal behavior--Fiction. | High school seniors--Fiction. | Friendship--Fiction. | Bullying--Fiction. | Sexual minorities--Fiction. | Self-perception--Fiction. | BISAC: YOUNG ADULT FICTION / Social Themes / Bullying. | YOUNG ADULT FICTION / Social Themes / Suicide.
Classification: LCC: PS3619.T476426 L54 2025 | DDC: 813/.6--dc23

To Mom,
for teaching me the piano

Content Notice

This book contains the following elements:
bullying, suicide, homophobia,
sexual assault, child abuse

1

"Run, Taylor!"

"Go!"

"Taylor, run!"

The cheers fill my ears as my feet pound across home plate. This was the best game I'd played all year: not only did I strike out the other team's best hitters, but I also popped a fly ball in the bottom of the seventh that landed way past their outfielders, allowing us to score three more runs and one more tally on our list of wins.

I look toward the stands, but I can't see anything through the blur of blue and white uniforms as my teammates crowd around me to pound me on the back. A gap appears and I spot my girlfriend, Ashley, standing on the front bleacher. I see her wave before my view is obstructed once more.

My best friend and fellow teammate, Drake, throws his arm around my shoulder. He's my height, with dark skin and the whitest smile I've ever seen, which he shows often. He yells something unintelligible in my ear.

"What?" I yell back.

"Coach wants to see you!"

I stand on my tiptoes and peer over the shoulders of my team members. Coach Barnes is hovering by the backstop with a man I don't recognize. When Coach sees me looking in their direction, he beckons me over. I make my way through the crowd and trot up to them. Coach claps me on the shoulder. I wince. He used to play professional football, back before he got middle-aged and grew a beer gut, and he hasn't quite figured out that high school baseball players aren't built the same as NFL linemen.

"Good game, Taylor," he says.

"Thanks, Coach."

"I want you to meet somebody." He waves a hand at the man standing next to him. "Avery Taylor, this is Ed Morris. He's here from the Major League Scouting Bureau. Ed, this is the kid I told you about. I wasn't lying when I told you he was good."

"Never doubted you for a second, Bill," Morris says. His grizzled face looks like it's seen its share of summers on the field. He stretches out his hand. I shake it nervously.

"How old are you, Mr. Taylor?" he asks.

"I'll be eighteen in July."

"You're graduating this year, correct?"

I exhale. "Fingers crossed!"

"Have you committed yet?"

"Sir?"

"Have you signed with any colleges yet?"

"No, sir. I've gotten a few offers, but I'm still deciding."

He considers me with a half-smile on his face. "Mr. Taylor, how fast do you think you threw today?"

I pulled out all the stops this game, so I know it had to have been pretty fast, but I don't want to guess too high and sound like a cocky bastard. I eye the radar gun in his hand. "I was hoping you could tell *me*, sir."

Coach Barnes answers for him. "You threw a ninety-five, Taylor," he says with an undercurrent of pride in his rough voice.

Ninety-five? That's the fastest I've ever thrown. Most high school pitchers don't even break ninety, and here I threw a ninety-five miles-per-hour fastball in front of a Major League scout. I can't believe it.

They both smile at my stunned facial expression. Morris continues. "I'm going to cut to the chase. We're searching for talent. From what I've seen today, I believe you have the talent we're looking for. I can't make any promises, but if I'm right, and if today is any indication of what we can expect to see from you, then we may just be looking at a frontrunner for the June draft."

He hands me a sheet of paper. I glance at it, but my thoughts are swirling too fast for me to read the writing.

"If you think you might want to play in the big leagues, then fill out this questionnaire and get it back to me. You don't have to fill it out right now. Go home; talk it over with your parents or your advisor, if you have one."

"It's your big chance to make something of yourself, Taylor," Coach growls as he gives me a meaningful look.

Morris holds something else out. "Here's my card. I look forward to hearing from you."

"Thank you, sir," I manage to spit out as I take the business card.

I shake his hand again, then head back toward the bleachers in a daze. I didn't know a scout would be at the game. It's probably better that I didn't; I most likely would have screwed up and embarrassed myself if I had known I was being evaluated for my career potential.

Ashley runs up and plants a big wet kiss on my lips. "You did great!"

She's really pretty—one of the hottest girls in the school—with blue-green eyes and dyed blond hair befitting a cheerleader. I know I'm lucky to be with her.

"Thanks." I beam down at her.

Drake appears by my side and says, "Hero of the day!" He's not as good at baseball as I am, but he doesn't hold it against me.

"So what did that guy want to talk about?" Ashley asks.

"He's a scout. He mentioned the draft."

"*What?*" Ashley says.

"No way!" says Drake.

I smile, but for some reason, I feel queasy inside.

"That's awesome, Avery." Ashley kisses me again.

"Do you wanna grab dinner?" I ask her, trying to shift the subject away from myself.

"Can't. My grandmother just flew in so I've got to spend quality time with her. I told her I'd be home right after the game ended, so I should probably go. Do you need a ride home?"

Before I can reply, Drake says, "He can ride with me."

"Okay. Thanks, Drake," Ashley says. She pecks me on the lips, then looks me in the eyes and says, "Call me."

"I will."

She flashes us one last brilliant smile before she turns and heads toward the parking lot.

Drake looks at me. "You ready to go?"

"Actually, I think I'll walk."

His eyebrows shoot up. "You sure? It's a long way."

"Yeah, it's cool. I've got some things I need to think about."

He shrugs. "Suit yourself."

The sun sets as I make my way home. I walk slowly, not only to enjoy the scenery, but to give myself time to think about my future

The Lifesaver

before I go home and have my future determined for me by my father. I know he would love nothing more than to see me go pro, but I'm not sure if that's really what I want. It sounds stupid, I know. I could have fame and fortune, why not go for it? The thing is, baseball has always been just a game to me, not a career path. I'm afraid that if I did it for a living, all the fun would be sucked out of it.

The problem, though, is that I have no idea what I would do instead. People are always asking me what my major will be and what I'm going to do after college, as if they expect all high school seniors to have their whole freaking lives planned out. The questions make me feel inadequate, so I just tell them my father's plans for me instead of admitting that I'll most likely end up begging for change on the streets due to my own lack of direction.

I take a shortcut through the woods, then follow the road until I come up to the river. As I walk across the bridge, pondering the practicality of joining the circus, I hear a splash nearby. Curious, I lean over the rail and peer down into the water. The streetlights are too far away for me to see anything clearly, but I think I see a large dark spot near the middle of the river. I squint. The way it's shaped, it almost looks like . . . a *body*?!

I sprint the rest of the way across the bridge and leap as fast as I can down the hill to the river's edge. As I get closer, I can see that the mysterious object is unmistakably a person. I throw my jacket on the ground and, without stopping to think, I plunge into the dark water.

Muscles strained from baseball scream in protest as I race to beat the current. The figure is floating just a few yards offshore. I slide an arm around it—him—and tug him back toward the reeds. His head dips beneath the water. I adjust my grip higher, struggling to keep us both afloat. This is nothing like they taught us in swim class.

Limbs shaking, I stumble out of the river and drag him up the embankment. As I drop to my knees beside him, I feel a spark of recognition: Tristan Chevalier. From my school, my grade. Way too young to die.

His skin has a sickening pallor and his lips are tinged with blue. I check his pulse and put my ear to his mouth. Nothing. No breath, no heartbeat.

My CPR training kicks in: I tilt his head back to clear the airway, then pound on his chest with the heels of my hands. Pump, pump, rest. Pump, pump, rest. I do this several times, then I put my mouth over his and force air into his lungs. After what feels like hours, even though it's probably only been a few minutes, he finally starts to cough. I turn him on his side so he can spit up the water (*So much water!*) from his lungs.

I check him over, but aside from the coughing, he doesn't appear to be hurt. I fall back on my heels and take long breaths to slow my rapid heartbeat. As I concentrate on breathing, I watch the color come back to his face. He's always been pale, but nothing like this. I brush his wet bangs off his forehead and out of his eyes. Without his hair in his face, I can see that his eyes are an astonishingly pale blue, like a lake that's frozen over. I don't know why I never noticed before; usually that's something you notice about a person. Maybe it's because his hair is always in his eyes, or maybe it's just that I never really looked at him before.

As I watch him splutter, I think about what I know about this kid, which isn't much. Even though we're in the same grade, I don't remember ever having a class with him. Mostly, I see him walking through the hallways with his head down, avoiding eye contact with other people. His dad is some sort of politician, but that doesn't seem to help Tristan make many friends. Rumor has it that he's gay, but I don't know how people would know that since he doesn't seem to talk to either boys or girls.

His lungs finally clear, he sits up and wraps his arms around his legs. I notice that he's not wearing a coat, even though it's March and still chilly outside; he's just wearing a loose, long-sleeve T-shirt over his blue jeans. I look around for my jacket and see it lying several feet away on the dead grass. I pick it up, brush it off, and walk back over to him. I attempt to put it around his shoulders, but he shrugs it off. *If he's not going to wear it, then I will.* I put it on, then sit cross-legged next to him. He doesn't say anything to me; he won't even meet my eyes.

I start to put two and two together. Loner high school student drowns in the river, at night, while fully clothed. This wasn't an accident.

I have to try to talk to him. Something tells me he won't be very forthcoming about his suicidal tendencies, but I can't just ignore the issue, either. I try to break the ice with some humor. "Do you always do crazy stunts at night, or do you do them during the day, too?"

Without looking up, he says, "Nighttime's usually the best time to avoid nosy people who butt into other people's business, but apparently that's not always the case. Are you always a lifeguard, or do you actually have a real job?"

Well, I didn't expect that. The kid has a smart mouth.

"Actually, I was a lifeguard once. Last summer. At the community center."

"Hmph."

Silence seeps into the air between us. I have to say something to distract him—and myself—from the cloud hanging above our heads.

"I wouldn't mind doing it again. Being a lifeguard, I mean.

Though most of the time I was bored out of my skull, I like the idea of helping people. Maybe I should consider being a police officer, or a firefighter, or—"

"Or a knight," he interrupts.

"What?"

"Yeah, you could ride around on a white steed and rescue damsels in distress and all that crap."

What is his problem? I just helped him and he's being such a jerk about it. Instead of getting worked up about it, though, I play along.

"Oh my God, I didn't think of that. I wonder where I would get a suit of armor from. I could go around and drink mead and enter jousting tournaments and sing love ballads to fair maidens. That would be badass."

At the word "sing," he seems to perk up a little. He peers up at me. "Do you sing?"

"Uh, no. Not well, anyway. Do you?"

"Yeah, a little. I mean, I used to. I haven't recently."

"Why'd you stop?"

He shrugs and picks at the blades of grass around his feet. *Maybe I shouldn't have asked.*

He seems to like music, so I say, "Do you play anything? Like, any instruments?"

"Yeah. I've played the piano since I was, like, six."

"You do? That's pretty cool." I never really thought of a piano as *cool*, but it's better than nothing, which is what I play. "What kind of music do you play?"

"Well, my piano teacher always makes me play the typical classical pieces. Chopin, Mozart, you know. My parents eat it up. But when they're not around, I mostly play classic rock."

"That's awesome, dude. I wish I could rock out on an instrument and have my own jam sessions, but I can't play anything."

"Oh, everybody can play something. The piano is like the easiest instrument in the world to learn. It's not rocket science."

"Then maybe you can teach me sometime." I don't really mean it, but it seems like something a friend would say. And I know that right now, he needs a friend.

"Yeah, maybe." The way he says it, I know *he* knows I don't really mean it. I feel ashamed.

"So what's really going on?" I finally ask.

"What do you mean?"

As if he doesn't know.

"I'm not stupid, Tristan. I don't believe you were out here alone in the middle of the night because you had a sudden urge to go swimming in freezing water."

"I didn't think you knew my name," he mumbles.

"Of course I do." I don't tell him it's because he's been the butt of tasteless locker room jokes the last few years. "We've been going to the same school since, what, ninth grade?"

"Eighth. We were in home ec together, remember?"

I rack my brain. I can barely remember that class, but now I vaguely recall a scrawny sandy-haired boy who always sat in the corner and never talked to anyone. He was a lot smaller then. He's still shorter than I am, though not by much. He's still skinny, too, but he's no longer the skin-and-bones figure I remember from middle school.

"Oh, yeah. Right. You've grown," I say lamely.

"So have you." I may just be imagining it, but it looks like he's blushing.

I quickly change the subject. "Are you nervous about exams?"

"I haven't thought much about them."

Of course he hasn't. He wasn't planning on surviving until the final exams.

"I am," I admit. Maybe if I'm honest with him, he'll open up. "If I don't ace my finals, I may be stuck taking summer school. Assuming my parents don't kill me first. I try to find time to study, but it's hard, what with baseball and fencing practice and—"

"*Fencing?*" he says.

"Yeah. What about it?"

"You mean like poking each other with tiny swords?"

"They're called sabers, but yeah. That's the general idea."

"Oh my God, you really do want to be a fucking knight. What a loser."

Did he seriously just call me a loser? Normally, I would punch him in the face, but that seems ridiculous considering I just saved his life. I think I see the corners of his mouth twitch, but it's hard to tell in the darkness.

"So what if I want to be a fucking knight?" I retort. "And if you call me a loser again, I'll cut you down with my battle-axe and throw you back in the river as fish food."

"Okay, Lancelot." He finally smiles.

He shivers, and I realize how cold it's become. If we don't get inside soon, we'll both probably come down with hypothermia.

"Come on, I'll walk you home," I say.

I scramble to my feet and reach out a hand to help him up, but he doesn't take it. He slowly stands up, wraps his arms around himself, then trudges up the hill without waiting to see if I'm following or not. I shake my head and walk after him. His legs are shorter than mine, so I catch up to him easily.

"Where do you live?" I ask.

"Around the corner."

He's not kidding—he literally lives the next street over from the river. I find myself wishing that it were farther, not only so there'd be more distance between him and the place of his attempted demise, but also so I could have more time to gauge his current emotional state. It looks like my time is up, though.

"Well, see you tomorrow," I call out as he steps onto his porch.

"Yeah, maybe," he replies without looking back.

I watch, feeling more than a little disturbed, as he disappears into the house. As I slowly walk home, I reflect on the events of the night.

He never thanked me for saving his life.

2

I sneak in through the back door to the kitchen, hoping that my parents don't see that I'm soaking wet. The kitchen is dark, and I can hear the faint sounds of a television coming from the living room on the other side of the house. I tiptoe through the hallway, then run up the stairs as quickly as I can.

"Avery?" my mother calls as I lock myself into the bathroom.

"Be down in a minute, Mom!"

I peel off my cold, wet clothes, then slip into the shower and turn the temperature way up. The scalding water stings and turns my skin pink, but I don't turn it back down. I need to get rid of the chill that has settled into my bones.

My fingers are pruned by the time I step out of the shower. I grab a towel to dry myself off, then use it to wipe the steam off the mirror. I examine my reflection. I don't look any different: I still have the same brown eyes, the same brown hair, the same everything. How can I look the same when I feel so different?

Within the short span of a couple of hours, I've experienced two potentially life-changing events. I know I'll have to tell my parents about the scout, but for some reason I'm reluctant to tell them about what happened at the bridge. I know that they would be proud of me if I told them that I had saved somebody's life, but I didn't do it for their pride, or for mine. Anyone would have done the same, if they had been in my place. I suppose that what's really nagging me is that I don't feel any closure. I saved him from the river, but did I really save him from himself? *Maybe I should have called an ambulance. Or the cops. Maybe I shouldn't have left him alone. What if he killed himself anyway after I left?*

A knock on the door brings me out of my dark meditation.

"Avery, honey? Everything alright?"

I try to sound normal. "Yeah, Mom. Be right out."

"Okay." She doesn't sound like she believes me. "Dinner's in the fridge."

"Okay, thanks."

I wait until I hear her footsteps disappear down the stairs, then I wrap my towel around my waist, collect my dripping uniform from the floor, and skip hurriedly to my bedroom down the hall. I close the door and turn on the light. My room looks like a small bomb went off: there are clothes in small piles on the floor and on my bed, textbooks strewn all over my desk, and some of my posters are even starting to fall off the walls. I let out a small sigh. *I really should clean my room.*

I hang up my jersey and pants in the closet to dry, then sift through the pile of clothes on my bed for something moderately clean to wear. Once dressed, I head back to the bathroom to retrieve my jacket. I pull the questionnaire out of the pocket and skim it over. The first part looks easy enough to fill out: name, address, school. But the questions get harder and harder. What college do I plan to attend? What draft round do I think I would be in? If I get drafted, how likely am I to sign? I don't know the answers to any of those questions. *Crap.*

Gripping the questionnaire in my hand, I make my way downstairs. Maybe I'll feel better after I've had something to eat. I go back into the kitchen, throw the light switch, and walk around the small island to get to the refrigerator. Our house was built in the 1970s, and the kitchen looks pretty much how I imagine it did back when the first owners moved in, except the linoleum countertops are peeling around the edges and the walnut-colored cabinets have turned a sickly whitish tinge. My mother frequently complains that if she had the money, she'd tear the whole thing down and start from scratch. There's no way we could afford a remodel, though, even with her working double shifts at the hospital on the weekends and my dad pulling in overtime at the plant. It's just as well; I kind of like it the way it is, even with the ugly old appliances.

I open the fridge and scrounge around until I pull out a covered casserole dish and a Gatorade. I put the dish into the microwave and set the timer, then rummage around in a couple of drawers until I find a pen. I grab the questionnaire and sit down at the little breakfast table at the end of the island. As I'm filling it out, my mother walks in from the hallway.

"What's that?" she asks as she eyes the piece of paper.

"A scout was at my game today. He wants me to fill out this questionnaire."

"A *scout?*"

I nod.

She bustles over to me and gives me a bear hug. "Ooh, wait till your father hears about this. *Jim!* Get in here!"

After a few seconds, my father appears in the hall in front of us. "What do you want, woman? Why are you yelling?"

My mom beams at me. "Well, tell him, Avery."

"A scout came to my game. He asked me to fill out this questionnaire."

He strides over to me. "Can I see it?"

I hand it to him. My mother peeks around his shoulder as he reads over the questions. When he gets to the bottom of the page, he says, "This is great news, Avery! It's about time they started recognizing your talent." He sets the paper back down in front of me and claps me on the shoulder. "You do your old man proud."

"Thanks," I mumble.

He pulls his phone out of his pocket.

"What are you doing?"

"Calling your uncle."

Before I can protest, he holds the phone up to his ear. "Paul? It's Jim. . . . No, your brother, Jim. . . . Guess who got picked up by a scout. . . ."

He wanders into the living room, off to brag about my exploits to everyone in his address book.

I repress a sigh and turn back to the questionnaire, trying to ignore my increasing discomfort and the fact that my mother is still hovering over me. I know that any second now, she's going to ask what's wrong, and I'll either have to lie or spill everything. At this point, I don't know which would be worse.

She bends down and kisses my hair. "I'm proud of you too, honey." Then she scurries off to celebrate with my dad.

I set the pen down. I lean back in my chair and stare up at the ceiling. I don't feel proud. Not at all.

3

"Where were you last night?" Ashley asks as I shove binders from my locker into my backpack.

I shrug. "My baseball game."

"I know *that*. I was there. I mean after. You were supposed to call me."

I close my locker and turn to face her. "I'm sorry. I was so beat after the game that I must have passed out right after I got home."

I don't know why I lie to her. I couldn't fall asleep because every time I closed my eyes, I'd see images of Tristan's blue lips and lifeless body all over again. I know a good boyfriend would be up-front and honest, but something tells me that Tristan wouldn't want me to go blabbing about what happened last night. Especially to Ashley, who keeps secrets the way a sieve holds water.

"Whatever," she says. "Are we still on for tomorrow night?"

Tomorrow night is the big bonfire the school hosts every year before the weather gets too warm. I promised Ashley a few weeks ago that I would take her and she hasn't let me forget it a day since.

With mock innocence, I ask, "What's tomorrow?"

She punches my arm.

"Of course we are." I grin. "I'll call you when I leave my house."

"You better call. Don't forget. Like you did last night."

I make a face at her. "Yes, dear."

She slugs me again, then kisses my cheek and flashes me a smile before heading off to class.

I watch her blond hair swish behind her as she walks around the corner, then I turn and head off in the opposite direction. I need to see if Tristan made it to school. I scan the hallways where I think he normally walks, but I don't see his sandy head in the crowd. I know the bell's about to ring, but I don't care. I'll make up some excuse for being late.

I go to the front office, which, as usual, is empty. The receptionist, Ms. Murray, never seems to be in her seat. I ring the bell on her desk repeatedly. She pokes her head out from behind the copy room door and gives me a suspicious look. "May I help you, Mr. Taylor?"

"Can you please tell me what class Tristan Chevalier is in?"

"Why?"

"He accidentally left his homework in my backpack yesterday, and I want to make sure he gets it before class starts."

"Well, class is starting right now. I suggest you go to class yourself before you're marked as tardy."

I'm starting to lose my patience. "I know class is starting right now. That's why I'd like to know where he is so I can drop off his homework before he gets an F."

She eyes me for a moment, then comes over and sits down at the computer. She taps on the keyboard and peers at the screen. "He's supposed to be in room 103 with Mr. Smith. However, I see a note here that he has an excused absence for today."

"He's not here?"

"Yes, Mr. Taylor. That is what 'absent' means. Now go to class, please."

"In that case, can you please let me know who the rest of his teachers are? So I can give him today's homework as well?"

She huffs. "Fine." She prints off his schedule and hands it over to me.

"Thank you for your assistance," I say through clenched teeth. I turn around and stalk out of the office. The bell rings as I walk through the empty hallways to my classroom.

I can't focus on anything the rest of the day. I'm so anxious to get out of class and check on Tristan that I can't sit still, and I snap two pencils from gripping them too hard. The students sitting nearest to me shoot me dirty looks—I'm sure my manic energy is distracting as hell—but I don't care. I have more important things to worry about at the moment.

Finally, the last bell rings. I jump out of my chair and head to room 103, not stopping to talk to anyone, not even Ashley. Mr. Smith looks surprised when I tell him I'm picking up homework for Tristan, especially since I'm not even in his class, but he doesn't question it; he just hands it over. I glance at Tristan's schedule and make my way to the next room on the list.

After baseball practice, I drive over to Tristan's house. I didn't notice it last night because it was dark and I was focused on getting him home safely, but now I can see just how impressive his house is. It's actually more like a mansion, with white pillars and everything, and the landscaping looks like something out of a magazine rather than real life. I let out a long, low whistle, then step out of my beat-up Honda and head up the curved driveway. I don't see any cars, but then, maybe they're in the four-car garage.

There are brass knockers on the front door, but I doubt anyone could hear them from the other side of the house. Glancing around, I spot a doorbell on the wall next to me. I press it three times, just to make sure.

After what feels like an eternity, Tristan opens the door. He looks bleary-eyed and miserable, but at least he's alive.

I breathe a sigh of relief. "Hey, man. I picked up your homework for you."

He looks startled. "Thanks," he mumbles as I hand him the worksheets.

"No problem," I mutter. I shift my weight, feeling awkward. I consider asking him how he's doing, but it's pretty obvious that he's not doing well. He's looking everywhere but at me and I know he just wants to go back inside, but I can't leave him alone like this.

"So. You gonna teach me to play the piano or what?"

He stares at me blankly for a few seconds; then he blinks and opens the door to let me in. As I kick off my shoes in the foyer, I look around. His house is huge and immaculate. I wonder if they have a maid. *Must be nice to be rich*, I think, but then I realize how stupid that sounds. If money made people happy, I wouldn't have dragged Tristan out of the river last night.

He walks over to a couple of French doors along the left wall and opens them up to reveal what I can only assume is the formal sitting room. I stop in the doorway, trying to take it all in. The whole room looks like it belongs in a museum instead of a house. There's a grandfather clock in the corner and several chairs are arranged throughout the room in neat semicircles. There's a china cabinet with various knickknacks against the back wall, and another cabinet near the doorway filled with really thick, boring-looking books. It must be just for show; the chairs don't look like they've ever been sat upon and the cabinets don't have any nicks or marks anywhere on them. The piece that really catches my eye, though, is the gigantic piano sitting right smack in the middle of the room. It's black, shiny, and sleek, and it must have cost a fortune. I almost expect an alarm to sound if I get near it.

Tristan lifts some sort of cover to expose the black and white keys underneath. He turns and sees me still standing in the doorway. He raises his eyebrows and gestures at the bench in front of the piano. They must come as a set because the bench matches the piano perfectly. Obviously, I'm supposed to sit, so I walk over and carefully lower myself down, hoping I don't scratch the finish. Tristan carelessly plops down next to me and I feel kind of stupid for being so cautious. I'm just not used to living in luxury, I guess.

This bench wasn't built for two people. Tristan's shoulder is up against mine; the closeness makes me slightly uncomfortable, but there's nowhere I can move without standing up or falling off. I don't want to hurt his feelings, so I stay put.

"I guess before we begin, I should ask what you already know. Can you read music?" he asks.

I shake my head. "Nope."

"Are you familiar with musical notes?"

"Negative."

"Okay. We'll just start at the beginning, then."

"Are we going to wear lederhosen and sing 'Do, Re, Mi'?"

He actually chuckles a little. "No, but I can show you how to play it, if you want. The lederhosen is purely optional." He points at what seems to me to be a random key. "This note is called A. The notes range from A to G, then they repeat again. See how some of the keys look the same?"

"They all look the same."

He shakes his head. "Look closer. Do you notice any patterns?"

I examine the keyboard. "Yes. There's only two black keys here, but three here. The same over here . . . and here . . . and here." I point them out.

"Good. That's because they're actually the same notes. Here, listen."

He presses one white key and sings in a clear, sweet voice, "*A.*" I look at him in surprise. He really does sing well. He either doesn't see my reaction or he chooses to ignore it. He presses a different key and sings, "*A,*" again, only this time it sounds higher. I think I see what he means. They sound like they go together.

"Like in the song. It brings you back to *do*," I say.

His lips curve upward in a brief smile. "Right."

I exhale. "Okay, so how do I know which ones are which?"

He points at a different white key. "Here. This one is called middle C. It's right before the two black keys in the middle of the keyboard. As long as you can find middle C, you can figure out the rest of the keyboard."

"Middle C, huh? Is it this one?" I hit it with my finger. Sound fills the room.

He nods. "You don't have to bang on it, you can just press it. The volume will depend on how hard you press. It can be tricky learning how to control it, but you'll get the hang of it. You want to hold your hand like this, though."

He gently grasps my wrist and pulls it upward. He molds my fingers until they're curved with just the fingertips touching the keys. Considering how standoffish he is, I'm surprised that he touches me so casually. Maybe he's not as antisocial as I thought.

"Pretend you're holding a baseball in your palm with your fingers curled around it. Keep your fingers curled over the keys, so the ball doesn't drop," he explains.

I smile. "Now you're speaking my language."

By the time the grandfather clock strikes six, we've gone over all the white keys, discussed C scales, and I can even play "Mary Had a Little Lamb" and part of "Do, Re, Mi." Tristan is a surprisingly patient teacher. He doesn't yell at me when I make mistakes like my coaches do, and he praises me when I do things correctly. It's not at all what I expected, considering how taciturn he was last night.

He looks over at the clock as the last chime dies away and sighs. "Jeanine—I mean, my stepmom—will be home any minute now. She'll kill me when she sees I'm not doing my homework." He gets up and walks over to the table where he left the worksheets I gave him. I grab my backpack and he follows me out to the foyer where my shoes are. "Thanks again, by the way, for bringing that over. I've been thinking to myself all day, if *only* I had homework to do on my *day off*. But once again, you came to my rescue." I can tell he's joking this time.

"That's what I do, remember? Rescue damsels in distress?" I tease as I slip on my shoes.

"Now I'm a fucking damsel?" He rolls his eyes. "I better not hear you singing love ballads outside my window tonight, Taylor."

I grin. "So will I see you at school tomorrow?"

"Yeah, maybe," he says again, but the corner of his mouth twitches up. I take that as a positive sign.

"Okay, good. See ya," I call over my shoulder as I skip down the steps. I feel his eyes on my back as I walk to my car. For the first time since the incident, I feel like some weight has lifted off my shoulders. I just hope he feels the same.

4

THE NEXT MORNING, after I've reassured Ashley that yes, I'm taking her to the bonfire tonight, I head over to room 103. I poke my head in and I'm relieved to see Tristan in the back of the room, taking books out of his backpack. Satisfied, I start to leave, but then Mr. Smith says in a loud voice from behind his desk, "Do you need something, Mr. Taylor?"

Tristan starts and turns around at the sound of my name. I can't leave now that he's seen me. I saunter up to him, ignoring Mr. Smith, who's peering at me over his glasses. *Why are adults always so suspicious?*

"Hey!" I say to Tristan.

"Hey . . . ," he says, as if he's not quite sure why I'd be talking to him.

Damn, is he suspicious of me too? I've got to do something about my image.

"So listen, I've got some free time after practice today. Would you want to show me the black keys after school?"

"Uhh... sure," he replies. I'm pretty sure Mr. Smith is listening to everything we say. He probably thinks we're talking about drugs. *Oh, well. He can think what he wants.*

"Okay, cool. I'll see you later."

The grandfather clock chimes six. I can't believe our session's over already. It took me a while to understand the concept of sharps and flats, but Tristan didn't seem to mind explaining it over and over until I got it. Maybe it's because it's Friday, but he seems to be in a better mood today. He's more relaxed, and I even get him to laugh once in a while at my stupid jokes. His laugh has an unexpected crystal-like quality to it.

"Our cook, Betty, is making lasagna tonight. Do you want to stay for dinner?" he asks as I get up and stretch. *Of course they have a cook.*

"That sounds delicious, but I can't. I promised Ashley I'd take her to the bonfire tonight."

"Oh. Okay." He looks disappointed.

I hesitate, then say, "You wanna go with us?"

I know Ashley will flip when she finds out that I asked Tristan to accompany us on our date, but it seems rude not to invite him.

"That's okay. I know better than to be a third wheel. Maybe some other time."

I'm grateful that he has more tact than I do. He probably just saved me from a huge blowout with my girlfriend.

"Sure. I'll see you around."

I pick Ashley up from her house at seven thirty. She's wearing a short, flowery dress that rides above her knees when she sits in the passenger seat. I place my hand on her left knee, then slide it up her leg. She bats my hand away. "Behave," she scolds, but I know she's not serious. I grin at her.

The school parking lot is nearly overflowing. I don't remember there being this big of a turnout in previous years. Maybe it's because the weather is actually nice, for once. It's still cool outside, though. I eye Ashley's bare legs. We better get a spot close to the fire, or else she's going to get cold and won't want to stay long.

I wrap an arm around her while we walk past the football field over to where the crowd is gathering. Ashley knows everyone, and they all know her. We have to stop every few steps for her to hug each "best friend." As far as I can tell, she has about two hundred of them. I like to think of myself as a popular guy, but Ashley seems to have her own gravitational pull. I don't really mind, but it can make it difficult to find alone time with her.

Finally, we get through to the inner circle of blankets and camp chairs. One perk of Ashley's popularity is that people make room for her. I spread out the tattered blanket I brought and she cuddles up next to me. I kiss her hair and she wraps her fingers in mine.

"So what did you do today?" I ask.

"Went to school," she says.

"Yeah, but after."

"Got ready."

"It took you three and a half hours to get ready?"

"Yes. Girls require prep time, you should know that."

"I'm glad I'm not a girl, then."

"I'm glad you're not a girl, too," she breathes in my ear.

I smile and steal a kiss, but she breaks it off before it gets too deep. She doesn't believe in overt public displays of affection.

"What about you?" she asks. "What did you do after school?"

"Learned to play the piano."

She laughs. "The piano?"

"Yeah, the piano."

"From who?"

"Tristan Chevalier."

"*What?*"

I turn to look at her. Her mouth is hanging open, like I just said something crazy.

"What?" I say.

"*Tristan Chevalier?*" she hisses, and looks around to see if anyone is listening.

"Yeah. So?"

"So? So he's gay."

"And . . . what? You think his gay cooties are gonna rub off on me? Besides, what makes you think he's gay?"

"He had an affair with Mr. Trawler, the choir teacher, last year. A *male* teacher." This is news to me. "And no," she continues, "I'm not concerned that he's going to rub off on you. But aren't you afraid he's gonna, like, hit on you or something?"

"No. No, I'm not. And even if he did, I think I can take care of myself."

"I still don't like it."

"Look, he's just teaching me the piano. That's it, okay?"

"The piano." She shakes her head and looks up at the sky as if asking God to grant her patience. "Sometimes I don't get you at all, Avery."

She settles back against me. Although our bodies are touching, I feel like a void has opened up between us.

5

My mother comes into the kitchen just as I'm finishing my bowl of cereal. "You're up early," she says.

I grunt.

"How was the bonfire?"

I grunt again.

"I'm glad you're so articulate, Avery," she says, her eyes twinkling. My mother's a morning person and it amuses her that I am not. "You sound like you need some coffee."

"C'nth," I mumble. She gives me a look and I know to swallow before I say anything else. "I have a match, remember?"

Coffee makes me jittery, and that's the last thing I need when I'm dueling someone with a saber.

"Oh, that's right. I'm sorry, sweetie, I forgot. I wish I could come watch you, but—"

"It's not a big deal, Mom. I get it." My mother's a nurse, so it's usually impossible for her to come to my sparring practice. I don't hold it against her, though. Not like my dad, who doesn't come even when he's not working at the plant. To him, anything besides baseball is an unwelcome distraction.

I throw my empty bowl in the sink and kiss her cheek, then grab my bag and head out the back door. I like to keep my Honda covered in the backyard, just in case. We don't live in the greatest area, and there have been a few incidents of vandalism and vehicle break-ins recently. Not that my car is in good condition anyway, but I have enough on my mind without having to deal with a busted windshield.

I pull up to the gym. It's in an old strip mall, between a mom-and-pop convenience store and a laundromat. I wrestle my bag out of the back seat and lug it inside. The gym is really just one big room that also serves as a dance studio. The back wall is lined with mirrors and dance bars, and along the side wall there are a few folding chairs for spectators. They're almost always empty, though. In the middle of the floor is a long, rectangular raised platform that our fencing instructor, Coach Doyle, constructed to serve as our *piste*. It doesn't compare to the electronic platforms the professionals use, but it's better than nothing.

Most of my teammates are already suited up and ready to go. I raise my hand in greeting as I walk across the gym toward the locker rooms. The men's locker room seems to have been added as an afterthought; there's only a handful of lockers and one bathroom stall. I change quickly into my uniform, then grab my saber and mask and head back out to the gym. I walk up to Coach Doyle, who's going over the roster on his clipboard. He's a short man, only about five seven, but he's lightning quick with a blade and can usually end a match before you've realized it's begun.

He glances up at me as I approach. "Taylor. Glad you could join us. You'll be first today. You're going against Thurston."

I look over at Brian Thurston, who, besides me, is the best in the class. He gives me a thumbs-up. This should be a good match.

I step onto the *piste* and turn to face Brian. I hear Coach shout, "*En garde!*"

We assume our fighting stances.

"*Prêt!*"

I raise my saber, but I'm not really ready. Mistake number one.

"*Allez!*"

Brian lunges. I try to parry, but I'm way too slow. I might as well have been standing still. I shake my head, trying to clear it.

We take our positions again at the starting line.

"*En garde! Prêt! Allez!*"

Brian lunges again. I block him, then take a swing. He blocks me easily. Then he strikes me again. *What is wrong with me today?*

By the time the match is over, I've been handily defeated by all of my opponents, even Timothy Sutton, who just joined our team a few weeks ago. For the first time, I'm glad that neither of my parents were here to watch.

Coach Doyle comes up to me afterward and says, "Taylor. Everything okay?"

The truth is, something Ashley said has been bothering me since the bonfire. About Tristan and the choir teacher. It just doesn't sound like something Tristan would do. And how did Ashley, who would never deign to even speak to Tristan, know about it when I didn't? But Coach Doyle can't help me with any of this, so I say, "Sorry, Coach. I guess my head wasn't in it today."

His frown lines deepen. "Anything I can do?"

"No, I'm fine. Really."

He claps me on the shoulder. "Okay."

After I change back into my clothes, I grab my things and leave without stopping to chat with anyone. I don't even notice it's pouring rain until I step out into the street. *Looks like the game is canceled.*

I pull my cell out of my pocket and turn it on. Sure enough, there's a text from Coach Barnes:

> No baseball today.

Secretly, I'm relieved. That gives me the rest of the day to figure stuff out. I know it's none of my business, but I want to find out more about Tristan's past. If Ashley was right and Tristan had a doomed romance with a teacher, then that might explain why he ended up in the river.

I drive to Tristan's house and peer out my window through the rain as I try to figure out what I'm going to say. *"Hi, Tristan. Tell me, did you have sex with an older man and then try to kill yourself?"* just doesn't sound right. I shake my head. *This is stupid.*

I open my car door anyway and sprint with my jacket over my head up to the porch. I ring the doorbell and wait several minutes, but nobody answers. He must not be home. *Damn.*

I pull out my phone again and text Ashley.

> Where are you?

She responds immediately.

> Home.

I type:

> Be right there.

Ashley greets me at the door. The rain hasn't let up yet and I'm soaked. She laughs when she sees me. "Hang on, I'll get a towel."

I wait in the entryway, trying not to drip over everything. Her little brother, Alex, walks by, his head buried in his LeapPad game.

"Hey, Alex," I say.

He doesn't even look up to acknowledge me. *Kids these days.*

Ashley witnesses this little interaction as she's coming down the stairs. She goes up to him and smacks him in the back of the head. "Don't be rude!" she scolds. She must not consider it rude to smack people in front of guests.

He rolls his eyes at her and mutters, "Hello, Avery." I see him stick his tongue out at her back as she turns toward me, but I choose not to say anything about it.

She hands me the towel. "So I guess baseball was canceled, huh?" she says as I dry my hair.

"Yup."

"Good. My grandmother's still visiting and I'm kinda sick of family right now. I'm dying to get out of here."

"That's fine. Have you eaten yet? I'm starving."

She shakes her head.

"Alright. I know a great place."

I sit down with my tray and she laughs. "*Two* Big Macs?"

I shrug as I open one of the cartons. "I told you I was starving."

"Yeah. You also told me you 'know a great place.'"

"This place *is* great," I say as I spread my arms wide. "Delicious food and lively atmosphere, all for the reasonable price of ten dollars. What's not to like?"

She rolls her eyes at me. I grin back at her.

"So how'd your match go this morning?" She's never attended any of my fencing matches. She claims she doesn't want to watch me get speared and bleed to death (as if that will ever happen), but I think she just doesn't want to get up so early on Saturdays. Still, it's nice that she cares enough to ask about it.

"Mmhh, not so good," I admit. "I didn't sleep so well last night, and I think it threw me off my game."

"That sucks. Will it hurt your rankings?"

I shrug. "Yeah, probably."

She gives me a funny look. "Doesn't that bother you?"

"I dunno. A little, I guess."

She smacks her hands down on the table, making me jump. "Avery, what's with you lately? You haven't been acting like yourself. You forgot to call me, you acted all weird at the bonfire, you don't care about losing your match, and you say you're learning the *piano*? From Tristan *Chevalier*?" She spits out his name like it's a dirty word.

It feels like everyone in McDonald's is staring at us. I try to keep my cool. "Look, Tristan's not such a bad guy."

"Avery, he fucked a *teacher*. Don't tell me that's not creepy."

Here we go.

"How do you know that?"

"Everyone knows that! Veronica Little saw them together in Mr. Trawler's room. That's why Mr. Trawler was let go. The school tried to keep it hush-hush so the parents wouldn't freak and take their kids out of school, but you know Veronica. She can't keep her mouth shut."

Sounds like somebody else I know, I'm tempted to say, but I bite my tongue.

"Hey, look, I'm sorry," I say instead, because I know that's what she wants to hear. "I guess I've been a little stressed lately. I'll try to make it up to you."

She relaxes back in her seat. With a seductive smile, she twirls a strand of hair around her finger. "Maybe you can make it up to me by picking me up for prom in a limo."

"*Prom?*" I say slowly, as if I've never heard the word before. "And what makes you think I'm taking you to prom?"

She punches my arm.

6

I watch as the sunlight slowly crawls across the ceiling of my room. I couldn't sleep. Again. Feeling restless, I jump out of bed, get dressed, and head out the door. I should probably go to church with my parents, but I don't want to hear about sinners right now. Besides, I told Drake that I'd go with him to see the new *Superman* flick, and the tickets are half-price before noon.

I park on the street in front of Drake's house and honk the horn. He opens the front door and yells something back into the house, then jogs to my car. He climbs in the passenger side and says, "*Vamos, amigo.*"

As I pull away from his house, he launches into a tirade about how his little sister used his English essay to make a papier-mâché elephant for school. I smile as I listen to him rant, glad for once that I'm an only child. He talks the entire way to the theater. I don't mind, because I don't feel much like talking.

The movie is action-packed and obnoxiously loud. I'm glad we went in the morning when there are fewer people, because Drake believes movies are interactive experiences rather than spectator events. His reactions are dramatic and he frequently shouts advice to the characters on the screen. It's pretty hilarious.

We grab lunch at Taco Bell afterward. As he drops into the seat across from me, he says, "So did you get everything all figured out?"

"What?" I ask, confused.

"The other day. You said you had some things to think about."

"Oh. Uhh, not really."

He peers at me. "Man, I thought Ashley was blowing things out of proportion again, but she's right. You *are* acting funny."

"She talked about me?"

He rolls his eyes. "Yeah, man, she won't shut *up* about you." He mimics Ashley's voice: "'Avery said this. Avery did that. Avery lost his match. Avery's learning the piano. Avery, Avery, Avery.' It's super annoying."

I choke on my taco. He reaches across the table and pounds my back as I cough.

"So what's going on?" he asks, after I've cleared my airway.

I shrug. "Nothing, really. I've just been stressed out, what with final exams and college looming in front of me and all that." *And dealing with a suicide attempt.*

He nods and says, "Yeah, I feel your pain." He's quiet for a few seconds, then asks, "So are you really learning the piano?"

"Yeah."

"What started that?"

"I dunno. Just thought I'd try something new, I guess."

"Good idea. Because your schedule isn't busy enough as it is. We wouldn't want you to get *bored*."

I chuckle.

"Is it true that Tristan Chevalier is teaching you?"

"Yes. Why?" I ask cautiously. I was reluctant to tell anyone else about my lessons after seeing Ashley's reaction, but since I did tell Ashley, everyone in the county probably knows by now anyway.

"No reason. Just curious. What's he like, anyway? He never talks to anyone at school."

"He's not a bad guy. He's actually a really good teacher. Better than most of the ones at school, anyway."

"Is he really gay?"

I feel defensive. "Does it matter?"

"Nah, it doesn't matter. Whatever floats his boat, doesn't bother me. I was just wondering if any of the rumors were true, that's all."

I shake my head. "I don't know. We don't talk about stuff like that."

He nods. "That's cool. If I were you, though, I wouldn't talk about Tristan to Ashley anymore. I don't know why, but it sounds like she really hates his guts."

I push my tray away. I don't feel very hungry anymore.

After I drop Drake off, I swing by Tristan's house. I'm still curious to find out if anything Ashley said was true, but not because I want to know the sordid details of his tryst with a schoolteacher. I just want to better understand why he tried to commit suicide. It had to have been really bad, whatever it was. I can't imagine wanting to off myself, for any reason. I still have no idea how I'm going to find out without seeming like a nosy prick, though. All I can do right now is wait and see if he brings it up.

He seems surprised to see me on his doorstep on a Sunday afternoon, but he lets me in without asking me why I'm there. I kick my shoes off in the foyer and say, "Hey, man. What're you up to?"

He shrugs. "Not much. My parents just gave me a new laptop,

kind of a consolation present since they'll be on a campaign trip the next couple of weeks and the guilt of leaving me alone was too much for them to bear. Not that they ever hear me complaining. I was just getting it set up."

"That's cool. What kind is it?"

"You want to see it?"

"Sure."

He leads me up the grand staircase and down the hall to his room. His room is smaller than I expected, given the size of the rest of his house. It's still bigger than mine, though. And it's messier than I expected, too—his bed is unmade and clothes and books are scattered on the floor. I was expecting to see the same spic-and-span tidiness as the rooms downstairs, but his room appears pretty typical for a teenager's. If they do have a maid, she's obviously never stepped foot in here. I wonder if it's his subtle form of rebellion against his parents' obsessiveness with cleanliness and order.

I walk in and look around. There's a wooden desk against the wall, big enough for his laptop but not much else, and a small matching bookcase across from it, next to the closet. I scan the titles of the books, and I recognize a few of them from our school reading lists. A twin bed with navy blue sheets sits against the back wall. The only thing that seems to be missing is the decorations on the walls. Most of my friends have posters or pictures lining their rooms like wallpaper, but the walls in Tristan's room are bare.

Tristan leans over his desk and types a few keystrokes on the laptop. I walk up behind him and look over his shoulder. The laptop is sleek with a huge vivid screen. It must have been expensive.

"Holy crap! Your parents gave you that just because they were going away for two weeks?"

"Yeah. Crazy, right?"

"Man." I shake my head in amazement. "Maybe *I* should go into politics."

"He doesn't get all his money from his job. He has a lot of investments, too. Hey, can you hand me that hard drive? It's on the dresser."

He points to a dresser behind me. I walk over and grab the drive, but something else on the dresser catches my eye: a Magic 8-Ball.

I pick it up with glee. "I haven't seen one of these since I was a kid."

"That thing is rigged. It never gives you a positive answer; it just comes back with, 'Very doubtful,' or some bullshit."

I hand him the drive. Then, with both hands, I shake the ball vigorously and say, "Oh, wise Magic 8-Ball, will I become a professional baseball player?"

A little triangle swims to the surface. I read it aloud: "Outlook not so good."

Tristan laughs. "I told you. Do you really want to be a baseball player?"

"I dunno. It's what my dad wants, but I haven't figured out what I want to do with my life yet." I look over his shoulder as he plugs the drive into the computer. A folder pops up with a bunch of files that appear to be songs. I scan the list of artists on the screen. I recognize almost all of them. The Beatles. Led Zeppelin. Boston. Queen. The list goes on and on. I laugh. "Your playlist looks like mine."

He looks back at me over his shoulder. "Really? I pegged you for a hip-hop fan."

"Why hip-hop?"

"Isn't that what everyone listens to these days?"

I shrug. "Not me. I prefer the classics."

"Huh. Go figure."

"What? Are you surprised we have something in common?"

"Yeah, a little."

"Why?"

"I dunno. I just don't have a lot in common with most people in my class, and I figured you were the same way."

"Well, that'll teach you to make assumptions about people."

He gives me a half-smile. "You're right. I stand corrected."

I hold out the ball. "Do you want to ask the all-knowing Magic 8-Ball about your future?"

"No." He turns his attention back to the laptop.

"Oh, do you already know what you're going to do after high school?"

He shakes his head.

"Well, what are you interested in?"

He shrugs.

"You don't like to talk about yourself much, do you?"

He sits down on the edge of the bed and looks at his feet. "No. Not really."

I pull out his desk chair and sit down to face him. "Well, that's not fair. How are we supposed to be friends if I don't know anything about you?"

He peers up at me. "Are we friends?"

"Don't be stupid. Of course we're friends. You think I'd invade your house like this all the time if we weren't?"

He blushes. "Well, what do you want to know?" From his tone, it sounds like he doesn't believe that there is anything about him that I'd find interesting. It's exactly the opposite, though; everything about this quiet, brooding kid is a complete mystery to me.

"I dunno. How does it feel to be a millionaire?"

He chuckles. "It's not all it's cracked up to be. Yeah, my parents are rich, but they spend their money on stupid things just to keep up

The Lifesaver

appearances. It kinda makes me sick, actually."

"Okay, next question."

"Wait a minute. Isn't it my turn to ask a question?"

I can't help feeling surprised, yet relieved, that he wants to play this game. "Alright. Shoot."

"What got you into fencing?"

"Do you really want to know?"

"Yeah, I do."

"Don't laugh, okay?"

"I won't laugh."

"You sure? 'Cause I seem to recall you making fun of me last time."

"I swear I won't laugh."

I give in. "Okay. I saw this movie when I was a kid, *The Princess Bride*. You know it?"

He nods.

"I thought that Spaniard guy, Inigo Montoya, was a total badass. So I got into fencing. It's nothing like the movie portrayed it, though."

As promised, he doesn't laugh. "That's cool. And you're right, Inigo Montoya is a badass," he says. He seems to mean it.

"Okay, my turn now." I take a deep breath. "What happened the other night? Why were you at the river?"

He avoids my eyes. "I was just out for a walk, and I fell in."

"You fell in?"

"Yeah, I fell."

I decide not to press the issue. I don't want to alienate him when he's just starting to come out of his shell. "Fine, whatever you say. Your turn now."

"Why do you want to learn the piano?"

"To impress the ladies, why else?" I say with a swagger.

He closes his eyes and shakes his head.

"Seriously, though." I frown as I think. "I've always wanted to learn how to play an instrument. I've always been jealous of the guys you see at school with their guitars, playing whatever song pops into their head like it's nothin'. I love music; I just never got around to learning how to play anything."

"What do you think of it so far?"

"I like it. You were right, it's not rocket science." Then I add, slyly, "It's a shame my piano teacher's such a dick."

Without missing a beat, he retorts, "You'd be a dick, too, if you had to deal with your dumb ass every day."

"Touché," I reply, grinning. He grins back. I'm secretly astonished that he's this easy to talk to and joke with. *Why doesn't he have more friends?*

"Do you have a piano at home?" he asks, interrupting my musings.

I shake my head. "No. The only instrument I have is an old recorder."

"Hmm. You'll need to practice in order to get good. You might want to consider getting a keyboard."

"How much do those cost?"

"I dunno. A couple hundred dollars, maybe?"

I whistle. "That's a little steep. Can't I just play on yours?"

He shrugs. "You can, if you want. I just figured you wouldn't want to keep coming over here."

"Well, how often do I need to practice?"

"Ideally, you'd want to practice every day, but that probably wouldn't work with all your baseball games and homework and stuff. You could probably get away with a few nights per week."

"Shit, are you serious?" I hadn't realized that a musical instrument would be such a big commitment.

"It doesn't have to be very long. Just a half hour or so. It's better to practice a little every day than a lot all at once. That's why a keyboard may not be a bad idea."

"I don't have two hundred dollars to spare, though. I guess I could swing by after baseball practice, if I'm free. Assuming that's okay with you."

He shrugs again. "It's fine by me. Though I don't know how long that will last. We may get sick of each other after the first week."

"Well, if you get sick of me, you're welcome to kick my ass out. Drake does it to me all the time."

"Drake Williams?"

"Yeah. Why? Do you know him?"

"No, not really. I know *of* him, of course. I've seen you two together a lot after school."

"Yeah, he's my best friend. We play baseball together."

"Huh. Birds of a feather, I guess," he mutters, as if thinking aloud to himself. He's silent for a moment, then he says, "It's your turn to ask a question."

"Oh. Right." I think for a second. "Okay, I've got one. It's kind of a personal question, though."

He looks apprehensive. "What is it?"

"I don't want you to take this the wrong way."

"Just ask, already."

"Are you gay?"

He tosses his hair out of his eyes. I've noticed he does that when he's irritated.

"I hate that word. It doesn't *mean* anything."

"What do you mean?"

"Well, humans can't be split into one category or another. We're more complicated than that. Like, would you say that Brad Pitt is unattractive? Even as a guy, you'd probably admit that he's a good-looking person."

"Yeah, but that doesn't mean I want to bone him," I argue.

"Do you want to bone every good-looking girl?"

I laugh. "I take what I can get."

He gives me a pointed look.

"Alright, fine. No, I don't want to sleep with every attractive girl I meet."

"Right. People are attracted to a variety of things: beauty, intelligence, ability to provide, whatever. It's not just about what gender you are or what they are, it's about what you see in that person. Besides," he adds with a smirk, "I bet you'd totally bone Brad Pitt."

7

Monday morning rolls around way too soon. I actually got some sleep last night, for once, but the positive effects of it are washed away when I look out the window and see that it's raining again. I just know that baseball practice will be canceled, which means that I don't have an excuse not to study for my upcoming math test. I don't know what I was thinking when I signed up for calculus. I guess I thought it would look good on my college applications, but I didn't take into account the fact that calculus is impossible for mortal minds to comprehend. It's too late to drop out now, though, so I just have to suck it up and hope that Ms. Prior takes pity on me and doesn't force me to skip graduation for summer school.

Sure enough, I get the inevitable cancellation text from Coach Barnes as I'm walking into my first period classroom. *Dammit.* I hate missing out on baseball, especially now that I've gotten the attention of a Major League scout. Now I feel even more pressure to practice and play well. Not that I don't want to practice, because I do—I love it. There's just more riding on it than before, and each day I'm not on the field is another day lost.

I silence my phone and turn my attention to Ms. Higgins as she begins her lecture on the rise of communism in Cuba. Most of the other students zone out immediately, but I actually enjoy history class. It's the only class in which I feel like I'm not just skating by—well, besides gym class, that is. It's a lot easier for me to remember who did what and when instead of trying to figure out what x and y equal or how many natural elements there are in the periodic table.

When she finishes her lecture, Ms. Higgins clears her throat and says, "For your homework tonight, I want you to pick a historical figure you've learned about this year that you would like to do a presentation on. The presentation will be a five-minute speech about the life of that individual and how they had an impact on society."

My stomach drops. *A speech?*

"The presentations will be two weeks from today, so start preparing now. Don't wait until the last minute, because they will count toward fifteen percent of your final grade."

Shit. There goes my A.

I can't give a five-minute speech. I doubt I could give a one-word speech. Even the thought of getting up in front of the class makes my palms sweat.

The bell rings, making me jump. With a heavy sense of foreboding, I close my history book and shuffle out of the classroom.

I head over to the locker room to get ready for gym class. I wind my way through the bodies and benches until I reach the back corner where my locker is. While I'm changing into my gym uniform, Mike Walsh, Jamaal Lewis, and Tom Polinski stroll in. The three of them are inseparable, and since I've been in the same class with them since freshmen year, they've dubbed me an honorary member of their pack.

The Lifesaver

Tom is undoubtedly the leader—he's got more brawn than brains, and Mike and Jamaal are the types to follow strength rather than cunning. I respect Tom, but I know better than to trust him to back me up unless it benefits him in some way. He's an alright guy, though. I may not follow him blindly wherever he goes, but the jabs he trades with Mike and Jamaal often leave me in stitches.

"Hey, fellas. What's happenin'?" I say.

"Hey, Taylor," they reply in unison as they drop their backpacks and go to work on opening the padlocks on their lockers.

"Taylor, I heard a scout was at your game," Jamaal says as he pulls his uniform out of his locker. He and Mike are of the same short stature, but where Mike is orange-haired and freckled, Jamaal has dark skin and very close-cropped black hair that nobody is allowed to touch.

"I can neither confirm nor deny the presence of a scout at my game. However, *if* said scout were at my game, he might have said that I am just the talent he is looking for."

"Oh yeah?" Jamaal says. "How many bases did you have to round before he told you that?"

Mike chimes in. "Don't be stupid, Jamaal. Taylor here is a pitcher. The question is, does he catch as well?"

The three of them laugh.

"You know, your baseball jokes are so original. You must be the next Abbott and Costello."

"Abbott and who?" Mike asks.

"Costello. You know, 'Who's on first?'"

"Who's on first?"

"Yes!" I can't help grinning at my own joke.

"Yes? Yes what?"

They look at me blankly.

I stare back at them in disbelief. "Come on! Who's on first, What's on second . . . How can you not know this?"

"What the fuck are you talking about?" Jamaal says. "I can't understand anything you're saying."

I shake my head. "Oh my God, I can't even talk to you right now. You guys have your heads so far up your asses, it's a wonder you can walk straight."

Mike scoffs. "This coming from the guy who thinks fencing is a sport."

"Hey. Fencing *is* a sport. It's in the Olympics, after all."

"Yeah, so is figure skating. Do you do that on the weekends too?"

"I would, if it meant being with girls in tights and short skirts all day. Have you seen some of the outfits they wear?"

Tom jumps in. "Speaking of short skirts, how 'bout those new cheerleader uniforms? When Ashley bends over, you can see almost up to her—"

"Knock it off. Girlfriends are off-limits."

"Nothing's off-limits," he replies.

"That's easy for you to say. You don't have a girlfriend. And with that nose, I doubt you'll get one anytime soon."

Mike and Jamaal laugh. Thankfully, Tom smiles. Although he's quick to dish out insults, he can be even quicker to take offense to one. "Okay, wise guy. No more talk about Ashley."

I breathe a small sigh of relief. "Okay. Thanks."

"Even if she is a slut."

I shake my head and close my locker. I shouldn't have said anything. Now they know what button to press to get a rise out of me. I'll probably spend the next hour listening to them speculate about Ashley's sexual prowess. That's the one thing I don't really like about being around them. I'm all for jokes and smack talk between friends, but sometimes they don't know when to leave well enough alone.

Tristan approaches me after school while I'm chatting with Ashley by my locker. She gives him a cold stare, as if he has no business talking to people in the hall.

"Hey," Tristan says.

"Hey, man," I reply, but Ashley says, "What do *you* want?"

I give her a sharp look. *What the hell is her problem?*

Tristan ignores her. He turns to me and says, "We doing lessons today?"

With some misgivings, I say, "Sorry, not today. I've got this calculus test tomorrow and I really need to study. I got a D on the last test and I'm screwed if I can't raise my grade."

"Do you need help?" he says. "I'm pretty good at math. I could show you how to do it, if you want."

"What, like tutor me?" I disregard Ashley's horrified expression.

He shrugs. "Sure."

I can't believe my good luck. Drake's just as useless at math as I am, and I've always been too nervous to ask the smart people in my class to tutor me because I don't want to look like an idiot. I don't mind Tristan teaching me, though, because he already knows I'm clueless and he doesn't seem to think any less of me for it.

"Cool," I say. Ashley looks angry, but I don't care.

"Well, that's settled, then," she says. "I'll see you later, Avery." She turns on her heel and huffs off.

I meet Tristan's eyes. He gives me a sardonic smile. "Think she likes me?"

"I'm sorry about her. I don't know what her deal is."

He shrugs. "I'm used to it. Come on, let's go."

We walk out to the parking lot. The rain has let up, but the air is thick with humidity and the pavement is shining. No chance the baseball field is dry.

I turn to Tristan and say, "You just want to follow me to my house?"

He nods. "Fine by me."

He stops by the driver's side of a silver BMW, which probably cost more than my house. I gape at him. "Dude, this is your *car*?"

He looks embarrassed. "Yeah."

"Wanna trade?"

"If you want to drive around looking like a preppy douchebag, be my guest."

"Why do you have it if you don't like it?"

"It wasn't my idea. I would have been fine with a used Civic or something, but my dad insisted that I drive this P.O.S. I guess he didn't want me to embarrass him in front of all his hot-shot lawyer and banker friends."

"Maybe he just wanted his son to have the best of the best."

"I'd rather he gave me what I want instead of what he wants. But I shouldn't complain too much. He didn't have to get me anything at all. I'd rather drive this than ride the bus with a bunch of assholes."

He opens the door and drops into the seat. I prop my hand on the roof to steady myself and peer inside. It still has that new car smell. The interior is a dark slate gray, with bucket leather seats, a navigation unit, and top-of-the-line speaker system. I shake my head in awe.

Tristan looks up at me and smiles. "Wipe that drool off your chin, Taylor."

I grin and step back so he can close the door. I walk back to my

The Lifesaver

Honda, which looks like a clown car compared to his brand-new BMW. I back out of the parking space, then look in my rearview mirror to make sure he's behind me. When he pulls up close to my rear bumper, I rev my engine. It sounds pitiful, like I knew it would. Through my mirror, I see him laugh. He revs his engine back at me, and his car gives a deep, throaty growl. I flip him off and he laughs again.

He follows me to my house and parks behind me on the street. I get out of my car and trot up to him before he climbs out of the seat. "You can park in the backyard. We have a problem with car thieves around here."

"Oh. Okay." He closes the door and drives his car up the driveway and around the side of the house to the backyard. I walk after him and pick up the car cover from where I left it on the patio. When he steps out, I hold up the car cover. He raises his eyebrows, but then he nods and grabs one end. We pull it over his hood and try to cover as much of the car as possible; it's too small to fit over the whole car, but at least it provides some protection from prying eyes.

"Do you really have that much of a problem?" he asks as I unlock the back door.

"Yeah. A couple of cars got stolen and we've had a few busted windows and break-ins. The police patrol our neighborhood a lot more now, but I still don't like parking out front."

We step into the kitchen and I turn on the light. I'm uncomfortably aware of how small everything looks compared to his big, spacious house. I go over to the fridge and say, "You want a Coke or anything?"

"Yeah, that's fine."

While I grab a couple of cans from the shelves, he looks over the magnets and pictures hanging on the outside of the fridge door. "Is this you?" he asks, smiling, as he points at an old picture of me from my Little League days. In the picture, I'm in my uniform, kneeling on the ground in the standard pose with my bat, grinning stupidly because I'd just lost my two front teeth the day before and wanted to show off the fact that I was one whole dollar richer.

"Yep," I say. "Back when I was a little pipsqueak."

"Nice hole in your teeth there."

"You should have seen the other guy." I hand him the Coke can and nod toward the hallway. "This way."

As he follows me up the stairs, he asks, "Do you have any brothers or sisters?"

"Nope. You're looking at the sole heir to this great estate. It's not a mansion like yours, but it'll do."

Genuinely, he replies, "I like your house."

I feel a little relieved to hear him say that. I know I shouldn't be ashamed of being less than wealthy, but it's hard not to feel self-conscious after seeing the opulence he's used to. It's good to know that he's not a snob, even though he is rich.

I open my bedroom door, then immediately kick myself for not having cleaned my room earlier like I told myself I would. "Sorry I'm such a slob."

He shakes his head. "Mine's not much better."

I pick up the pile of clothes from my bed and toss them into the closet. He perches himself on the edge of the bed and looks around. "So this is what your room looks like. I expected more pictures of baseball stars and half-naked supermodels."

I laugh. "No, I keep those under the bed."

I rifle through my backpack until I find my calculus textbook and notebook. I toss my backpack onto the floor and plop down next to Tristan.

"So what is your test on?" he asks.

"Differential equations," I groan.

"Oh, okay."

I gaze at him with relief. "You know how to do it?"

"Yeah, I do."

"Okay, good. Because I have no clue what I'm doing."

"That's alright. I'll show you."

Over the next two hours, Tristan patiently demonstrates how to derive equations and check them on my graphing calculator. When I don't get something, he rephrases his explanation or outlines the process step by step on a scrap piece of paper until I'm confident that I understand it.

After solving a particularly difficult problem with his help, I look up at him and say, "I wish you were in my class so you could translate for Ms. Prior. I swear, she gets up there and starts speaking in Greek or something because I just don't get it when she says it, but when you explain it, it makes sense. Have you thought about becoming a teacher?"

He shrugs. "No, I haven't really thought about it before."

"You should think about it. I think you'd be really good." Then I say, "*Although*, that would require you to talk to people every once in a while."

"Yeah, that might be a problem."

"Why don't you like talking to people?"

"Because I hate people."

"Why do you hate people so much?"

"Because they're all jerks. Why would I go out of my way to talk to people when all they do is treat me like shit?"

"What do you mean, they 'treat you like shit'?"

"Come on, Taylor. You know what people say about me. They

call me a faggot and a cocksucker and spread rumors and lies about me behind my back. Some of them don't even do it behind my back; they just tell me right to my face what a lowlife they think I am and use me as a punching bag whenever a teacher isn't looking. You really think that I would ever want to talk to any of those fuckers?"

My gut wrenches. I never realized how bad it was for him. Sure, I'd heard some of the jokes and gossip in the halls, but I didn't know he was being pushed around, too.

I try to reassure him. "Everyone's not like that."

"No, you're right," he snaps. "The rest of them just ignore me, as if I didn't exist at all."

He wraps his arms around his knees and glares at the wall away from me. With a sinking feeling, I realize that he's right. I've never seen anyone attempt to make a conversation with him or even say "hi" to him in the halls. I can see now why he was so suspicious of me at first. I'd have a hard time trusting people, too, if I were a target and nobody stood up for me.

I place a hand on his shoulder. "I don't ignore you."

He shakes his head and faces me again. It looks like his anger has dissipated already. His pale eyes meet mine as he softly replies, "No. You're different." The corner of his mouth twitches up. "*You* won't leave me the hell alone."

I drop my hand and scoff. "Excuse me? I believe *you're* the one who suggested this little tutoring session here."

"Well, it's a good thing I did, because I don't think you'd have a snowball's chance in hell of passing that test without me."

"You're probably right." I grin.

I hear a door slam, then the sound of footsteps coming up the stairs. My mother appears in the doorway. "Avery, whose car is that out back? Oh! Hello." She directs her warm smile at Tristan.

"Hey, Mom. This is my friend Tristan."

"Hi, Mrs. Taylor," Tristan chirps.

"Well, hello! I'm sorry, I didn't mean to interrupt the study session. What are you working on?"

"Tristan's helping me with my calculus class."

"Oh. Well, it's nice to see that you're making friends with smart people." She winks at Tristan.

"Hey, I'm smart," I protest.

She widens her eyes and says, a little too innocently, "I never said you weren't, sweetie."

Tristan laughs at our exchange.

"*Bye*, Mom," I say.

She points at me and says to Tristan, "You better keep an eye on this one, you hear?"

He laughs again and replies, "Will do, Mrs. Taylor."

She flashes us a dimpled grin before she disappears down the hall.

Tristan glances at his watch. "Crap. I should go. I have to meet my piano teacher in half an hour."

"Oh yeah, I forgot you were taking lessons, too. Didn't you say you'd been playing since you were six?"

"Yeah. So?"

"So don't you know everything there is to know by now?" If he's still taking lessons after twelve years, how long will it take me to get good?

"She's not really teaching me how to play. She brings me sheet music and then critiques how I play it. I guess you could call her a mentor more than a teacher."

"Huh. That sounds like an easy job. Why don't you just pay me and I'll critique you to your heart's content? I could even critique everything else you do as an added bonus. More bang for your buck."

He laughs. "Thanks, but no. My dad already does that for free." He stands and picks his backpack up from the floor.

"Speaking of free services, I feel kind of bad that you're paying someone else for piano lessons and here I am, mooching off you for the exact same thing. I'd understand if you wanted me to pay my share."

He stares at me a moment, then closes his eyes and shakes his head. "Just shut up, Taylor."

"What?" I ask, wide-eyed.

"You really think I'd *charge you*? We're friends, not fucking business associates."

I smile. "Well, okay, then."

He gestures toward my textbook. "You okay with all this?"

"Yeah, I think I'm good. Thanks."

"Okay. If you need anything, text me." He scribbles his cell number at the top of my notebook. I throw him a salute and he shoots me a smile before he turns and heads down the stairs.

I pick up my phone and add Tristan's number to my contacts list. Then I skim over the notes on the rest of the page; thankfully, the numbers and letters no longer look like hieroglyphics to me anymore. If all goes well during my test tomorrow, I may ask Tristan to tutor me on a regular basis. If he doesn't mind giving me free piano lessons, then he probably wouldn't mind walking me through my math homework. And besides, it would give me an excuse to keep an eye on him. If he's really as alone as he says he is, he may not be out of the woods yet.

8

THE TIME FOR MY CALCULUS TEST is finally here. After Tristan left, I stayed up late rereading my notes from our tutoring session. Lack of sleep probably won't work in my favor, but I'm hoping the extra study time will make it all worthwhile.

Ms. Prior hands me the test. I write my name at the top and take a deep breath. I read the first question, and I'm filled with relief that it's the same as one of the problems Tristan helped me solve. I write out the steps and the solution, then work my way through the rest of the test. The problems aren't nearly as difficult and confusing as I'd expected. When I'm done, I hand it over to Ms. Prior for her to review. She purses her lips while she looks it over, then writes "A" at the top and hands it back to me with a smile. "Well done, Avery," she whispers, so as not to disturb the other test takers.

I feel like whooping, but I restrain myself. I can't believe I got an A after I nearly failed my last test. This will definitely help raise my grade. I go back to my seat and wait impatiently for the bell to ring so I can go gloat to Tristan.

It finally rings and I hustle out of class to find him. I'm not sure where his locker is, but I think it's near Mr. Smith's classroom. Sure enough, I spot him a little ways down the hall from room 103, taking his jacket out of his locker. I saunter up to him and hold up my test. In a singsong voice, I crow, "Look who got an A!"

"Are you serious?" He grabs the test from my hand and scans it over. "That's awesome, Taylor." He hands it back to me and says, "I guess you're not as dumb as you look, after all."

"Yeah, guess not. Must be some of your smartness rubbed off on me."

Just then, Tom and Mike walk by. "Yo, Taylor!" Tom jeers. "I see you got a new girlfriend." He nods toward Tristan.

"Yeah. Your mom!" I call back.

They both laugh and keep walking.

Tristan looks like he just swallowed something bitter. "Are you friends with those guys?"

I shrug. "Yeah. We've been in a few classes together. They're funny, but they can be tool bags sometimes."

He shakes his head. "I don't get it."

"What?"

"How you can be friends with people like that."

"They'd say the same about you."

His lips tighten into a thin line.

I quickly try to explain. "Look, I'm not saying I approve of their behavior. I'm just saying that I'm not going to stop talking to them because they act like dickheads every now and then. I wouldn't have any friends if I held a grudge every time someone said something insulting to me."

"That's easy for you. People don't insult you the way they insult me. It's kind of hard to let it go when they call you names and you know they really mean it."

I open my mouth to reply, but Drake appears by my side and cuts me off. "Finally! I've been looking all over for you. We're gonna be late for practice."

I look at my watch. "Oh, shit! Sorry, Tristan, I gotta go. I'll catch you later." I don't want to end the conversation on such a negative note, but I don't have a choice.

He nods, looking unhappy.

As Drake and I walk down the hall, I glance back over my shoulder. Tristan's standing with his back against his locker and his hands in his pockets, contemplating his shoes. I'm disturbed by the haunted, unseeing expression on his face. I watch as he picks up his backpack, slings it over his shoulder, and walks slowly in the opposite direction as if he's carrying a much heavier burden than a few books and papers in his bag.

Neither Drake nor I feel like going home after practice, so we sit on the trunk of his car and shoot the shit as we watch the sun set over the baseball field.

"What were you and Tristan talking about?" he asks.

"Oh. I was bragging to him about how I got an A on my calculus test."

"You got an A on your calculus test?!"

I laugh. "Yeah, thanks to him. He helped me study."

"Huh. I need to get in on that action. My mom is straight up gonna murder me when she sees my report card."

"I can ask him, if you want. I don't think he'd mind helping the both of us."

"Sure. What's he up to now, anyway?"

I shrug. "I dunno. Should I text him?"

"Yeah, see if he wants to eat with us. I'm getting hungry."

I pull out my cell and text Tristan.

> Hey, it's Avery. What are you up to?

After a few seconds, my phone buzzes.

> Nothing. You?
>
> You want to get food with me and Drake?
>
> OK. When?
>
> Now. We'll come get you.
>
> OK.

I decide to leave my car in the parking lot and ride with Drake to dinner. I give him directions to Tristan's neighborhood, and his eyes widen when he sees the massive size of the houses along the street. When we park at the end of Tristan's driveway, Drake looks across me at the house and shakes his head in awe. "Man. Must be the life."

Tristan comes out the front door before I can even unbuckle my seat belt. He hops into the seat behind mine and shyly says, "Hey, guys." He looks a lot more cheerful now than he did when I last saw him in the hallway.

"Hey, Tristan." Drake flashes him a huge smile. I'm glad Drake is so friendly and nonjudgmental. Maybe hanging out with more people like him will convince Tristan that not everyone is a total asshole.

"So where are we going?" Tristan asks.

"I dunno. We haven't gotten that far yet," I admit.

"What about Red Robin? I could go for a hamburger," he says.

Drake and I look at each other and shrug.

"Sounds good to me," Drake says as he pulls away from the curb.

The Lifesaver

I slide into the booth next to Tristan and Drake sits down across from us. We order our drinks from the waitress, then Drake turns to Tristan and says, "So Avery tells me you're some sort of math genius."

Tristan blushes. "Uh, not really."

I nudge him with my elbow. "Come on, admit it. You know you're smart. Unfortunately for you, that means stupid people like us will bug you to give us all the answers."

"I didn't give you the answers. You figured out the answers yourself. I just gave you a push."

"Well, you can push me off a cliff if that means I'll pass my final exam," I retort.

Drake laughs and Tristan smiles.

"By the way, Drake here would like to be pushed too, if you don't mind dealing with two idiots instead of one."

Tristan shrugs. "No, I don't mind."

"Awesome," Drake says. His grin is infectious.

The waitress brings us our drinks and takes our order. We've all been here a million times, so none of us needs to look at the menu. After she disappears into the kitchen, Drake looks at me and Tristan and says, "So what's the story?"

We both stare at him. He holds out his hands and asks, in a tone that suggests he's dealing with morons, "How did you two meet?"

In the same tone of voice, I say, "What are you talking about? We go to the same school, dumbass."

He rolls his eyes. "You know what I mean. How did you become friends?"

I grab my glass and take a sip of water. *I'll let Tristan handle this one.*

Tristan gives me an appraising look. He answers, "We ran into each other near my house one day and we just sort of . . . *dove* into a conversation."

I snort into my water glass. The corner of his mouth turns up.

Drake looks between him and me suspiciously. He knows we're hiding something.

Tristan distracts him. "What about you? How do you know each other?"

"God, I've known this joker since the *second grade*. We were in T-ball together, and I tell you what . . ."

Drake launches into a long story about how he and I would raise hell and play pranks on our teammates. Tristan listens intently and laughs a lot at Drake's animated storytelling. I smile, relieved that my friends are hitting it off so well. If only I could get Ashley to like him, too, then my life would be so much easier.

We drop Tristan off at his house after dinner. Before he gets out of the car, he leans forward and says, "Thanks for inviting me. This was fun."

Drake says, "Yeah, man. We should do it again sometime."

Tristan looks over at me. "You coming over tomorrow?"

"Yep. I'll be there."

"Okay, cool." He smiles and tilts his chin up at Drake. "See you around, Drake."

"See ya," Drake replies.

Tristan gets out and walks up the long driveway. He turns and waves before he slips through the front door. I wave back, even though he probably can't see me in the dark.

Drake says, "You know, I just don't get it."

"What?"

"He seems like such a good dude. Why doesn't he have more friends?"

I gaze at the porch where he was standing a moment ago. "I don't know."

"I think he likes you."

"Well, sure. What's not to like?"

"No. I mean I think he *likes* you, likes you."

I look back at him sharply. "What makes you say that?"

He smirks. "I dunno. Just the way he looks at you sometimes."

I hadn't considered that Tristan may like me as more than a friend. *What if he does?* I don't want to lead him on, but I don't want to stop being friends with him just because he might have a crush on me.

"He knows I'm with Ashley. We're just friends, that's all," I tell Drake.

"Just be careful, okay? You don't want to break his heart."

I frown. He's right. That's the last thing I want to do.

9

"You've got *another* piano lesson?" Ashley says. "You just had one a couple days ago."

"So?" I say as I shove my jacket into my locker. It's too bulky to fit well, so I have to get creative with my packing skills.

"So I don't see why you need another one."

"How else am I supposed to get good?"

"Other people take music lessons, too, but they don't take them every day."

"It's not every day," I chide. She's so prone to exaggeration.

"It seems like it," she says.

"Why are you busting my chops? You do cheer practice after school. How is this any different?"

"I just don't see why you'd want to spend so much time with *him*." She won't even say his name now.

"He's my friend. Besides, it's just an hour or two. It's not like I'm not spending time with you."

"Oh, are you friends now? I thought he was just teaching you the piano."

"Yeah, we're friends. What's the big deal?"

"He's just weird, Avery."

"He's not weird! He's just quiet, that's all. Ask Drake. He'll tell you the same thing."

"Oh, I see. You're gonna pull Drake into this and make me look like the bad guy."

"What are you talking about? There's no good guy or bad guy! I just think you should let up on Tristan a little. I think you'd like him if you got to know him."

"Well, I don't like him, and I don't want to get to know him."

I shoot her an exasperated look. "Are you going to be like this every time I have a piano lesson?"

"Alright, fine. I don't care anymore. Do what you want."

I've been around the block enough to know that when a woman says, "Do what you want," she really means that you should immediately stop doing whatever it is that you're doing. I don't really want to stop my lessons—I'm actually enjoying playing the piano way more than I thought I would—but then again, I don't want to have a continually pissed-off girlfriend, either. Maybe I *should* take a break from lessons for a while. It would get Ashley off my back, and it would send Tristan the message that I'm not interested. That's assuming, of course, that a message is even necessary; I'm still not convinced that Tristan likes me that way. I already promised him I'd come to today's lesson, though. It would be pretty shitty of me to back out now. I guess I'll go to my lesson this afternoon and figure out what I'm going to do from there.

I spend first period trying not to stress out about my upcoming speech, but to no avail. Judgment day is less than two weeks away and I still haven't decided who I'm going to do a presentation on. *I'm so screwed.*

After history, I make my way to the locker room. Hopefully, gym class will help to relieve some of this tension. While I'm changing into my uniform, Tom, Mike, and Jamaal waltz in. I exchange friendly hand slaps with each of them and immediately start to feel better. Then Jamaal says, "Hey, Taylor, is it true you're hanging out with faggots now?"

My good feeling disappears. "Don't call him that."

"He's right," Mike says to Jamaal. "I believe the politically correct term is 'fudge packer.'"

They all laugh.

Exasperated, I say, "Why you gotta be like that? What has he ever done to you?"

"Just the fact that he exists at all is reason enough for me," Mike says as he exchanges malicious smiles with Tom and Jamaal.

I stare at them, dumbfounded. I'd understand trash-talking someone who did you wrong, but to go after someone just because? It boggles my mind.

I find my voice. "How can you be this way?"

They look at me as if I just said I'd been abducted by aliens. I've listened to them exchange derogatory japes about other people for years, and though I've never shared their sense of humor, I've never called them out on it, either. Now that I've seen the impact it's had on Tristan, though, I can't stay silent anymore.

"What's with you, Taylor? Why are you getting your panties in a bunch?" Mike says.

"I just don't see why you have to pick on people all the time."

"What? You gonna go home and cry to your mommy like a little bitch?"

"*Fuck* you!" I take a step toward Mike, but Tom slides between us and firmly presses his fingers to my chest. I know better than to move any farther.

From behind Tom, Mike yells, "Jesus, Taylor! Learn to take a fucking joke!"

"Hey now, take it easy," Tom says. "Let's all just take a step back and cool off a minute." He gives me a warning look as his voice drops. "You don't want to do anything you're going to regret."

I can hear the threat behind his words. If I take on one, I'll have to take on all of them. I can't afford to lose my temper like this. The baseball league has a zero-tolerance policy for fighting, and getting into a scuffle in the gym locker room with Coach Barnes next door isn't the smartest plan if I want to stay on the team. I back up slowly and shrug myself off.

Tom looks me in the eye and says, "You cool?"

"Yeah." I fake a smile as I lie. "I'm cool."

I'm still upset by the time lunch rolls around. The rest of gym class passed without incident, but even with the truce, it was pretty obvious that I was no longer considered part of their inner circle. It's just as well; if they insist on acting like first-class fuckheads, then I don't want to be associated with them. But since I was friends with them for so long, now I'm starting to doubt my own sense of integrity. It's not like today was the first time they had made offensive remarks— far from it. Does it make me a bad person that I didn't say anything before now? Does being friends with assholes make me an asshole, too? It makes me sick to think that other people might think I'm like them.

I decide to ask Drake. I know he'll be honest with me, even if it hurts my feelings. "Drake, am I an asshole?"

"Is this a question? Of course you're an asshole," he replies as he eats his sub.

"No, seriously. Am I? Like, do people think I'm a decent guy, or do they think I'm a jerk?"

"Well, I don't think you're a jerk. Isn't that what matters?"

I hadn't thought about it like that. The muscles in my neck gradually loosen. "Yeah. Thanks, Drake."

He nods and goes back to eating his sub. Between bites, he says, "You know who also doesn't think you're a jerk?"

"Who? Ashley?"

He shakes his head, then mumbles through a mouthful of bread, "Thisthen."

My first reaction is to feel relief. I don't want Tristan to think I'm like Tom and his crew, and, now that I think about it, I know that Drake's right—after all, Tristan already told me that I'm different from the other assholes. But my relief is quickly replaced by trepidation when I realize what he's implying. If Tristan likes me the way Drake thinks he does, then I'll have to tread carefully; otherwise, I may end up hurting him, and then I'll *really* feel like a jerk.

"Is something wrong?"

"Hmm?"

"You seem out of it. Is something the matter?" Tristan asks.

It shouldn't surprise me that he noticed that I've been distant throughout our piano lesson. I keep thinking back to what Drake said about breaking his heart, and I'm having difficulty trying to determine how friendly I can be before I cross the line into leading him on. Unfortunately, I've probably only succeeded in making him think I'm pissed off at him.

I shake my head. "I'm fine."

His brow wrinkles. "You sure? Anything you want to talk about?"

There are a million things I want to talk about. *Do you have feelings for me? Why did you lie about jumping into the river? Did you really have an affair with your choir teacher? Are you still suicidal?* I don't really know how to bring any of it up without freaking him out, though. Maybe I can find out if he likes me without asking him straight up about it.

"Honestly, I'm having woman trouble at the moment. Ashley isn't too happy that I'm spending all this time with you. I think she thinks you have a crush on me or something."

I watch his reaction closely. I think I see the faintest hint of color in his cheeks, but he answers smoothly, "I wondered why she was so snippy with me the other day. Look, if you'd rather spend time with your girlfriend, I'd totally understand."

His eyes are impassive. I consider him for a few seconds.

"Fuck it. She'll get over it," I declare.

The truth is that I enjoy hanging out with him, and I'm not going to let Ashley or stupid paranoia about romantic feelings get in the way of our friendship. If he does like me and it becomes a problem in the future, I'll just let him down gently. For now, though, I'm not going to worry about it. We'll cross that bridge when we get to it.

10

After school, I say goodbye to Ashley, then make my way over to Tristan's locker. Drake asked me when the three of us could get together to go over calculus, and I promised him I'd ask Tristan what his availability was later in the week. As I approach him, I immediately know something's wrong. He's standing in front of his open locker, staring at a piece of paper in his hand. His body is slumped and his face looks like he's just seen a ghost.

"What is it? What's wrong?" I ask.

"Nothing." He crumples the paper in his fist and slams his locker shut.

"I don't believe you. What's in your hand?"

"Don't worry about it."

I hold out my hand. "Let me see it."

He avoids my eyes as he deposits the wad in my outstretched palm. He leans back against the locker and looks down at his shoes. I smooth out the paper and read:

I HOPE YOU DIE FAG

"Oh my God!" I glance around, but nobody is looking in our direction. It appears that the perpetrator has fled. "How long has this been going on?"

He shrugs.

"Tristan, you have to report this!" I shake the paper at him.

"Report who?" he snaps. "They didn't exactly leave their name, and I seriously doubt Officer Gálvez is gonna dust for fingerprints."

Officer Gálvez is the school security guard, whose primary duty seems to be inspecting hall passes for potential fakes.

"Yeah, but you must have some idea who did it," I argue.

"What am I gonna say? That I *think* I know who did it, but I don't know for sure? And then they get into trouble even though I don't have any proof? They're just going to come after me if I say it's them."

"They can't just give you death threats and get away with it!"

"It's not a death threat. They're just *hoping* I die."

Exasperated, I stare at him. *We have to do something.*

I hear Drake's voice behind me. "Hey, guys. Uh-oh. What's going on? Everything okay?"

Tristan lifts his eyes and gives me a wary look. I consider him for a second, then turn around to face Drake. "Yeah. Everything's fine."

He looks doubtful, but he doesn't question me. "Okay. If you say so. You ready to go?"

I glance at Tristan. His eyes are downcast again. I can't leave him alone like this.

"Actually, I'm not going to practice today," I tell Drake.

Tristan looks up at me in surprise.

"What? Why not?" Drake says.

"There's something I've gotta take care of. Just tell Coach I had a family emergency or something."

"Hmm. He won't be happy about it."

"Don't worry about it. I'll deal with him later."

He hesitates, then says, "Okay. See you later. Don't forget." He points at us as he backs away. "We need to do some serious studying soon. I'm counting on you guys."

I roll my eyes. "Yes, we know. Go hit a home run for me."

He grins and turns away from us. Once he's out of hearing distance, I turn back to Tristan and say, "So. What are we going to do?"

"What are we going to do about what?"

"The note, dummy."

"There's no 'we.' This isn't your problem to deal with."

"It is now. If someone wants to mess with you, then they'll have to mess with me, too."

"Why? Are you really that anxious to get your ass kicked?"

"No, but that's what friends do. They stick together."

He sighs. "Taylor, I really don't think you know what you're getting into. It's best if you just walk away and let me handle it on my own."

"You shouldn't have to handle it on your own. What's the point of having friends if they don't have your back?"

"Well, I don't want my friends to get hurt, either."

"Don't worry about me. I can take a hit like a man. Speaking of which, you might want to sign up for some self-defense classes."

He smirks. "You want me to carry around a rape whistle, too?"

I shrug and grin. "Couldn't hurt."

He closes his eyes and shakes his head.

In a more serious tone, I say, "So how should we take care of this? It's your call."

He holds out his hand. "Let me see the note again."

I hand it over. He clenches his jaw as he rereads it. Then he pulls a lighter out of his pocket, flips it open and lights it, and holds the note to the flame. The light of the fire reflects in his ice-colored eyes as he watches the paper smolder between his fingers. He drops it to the ground with disgust and grinds it into the floor with his shoe.

"There." He flips the lighter closed. "I took care of it."

I cross my arms as I regard him. He glares back at me with a defiant expression on his face. I'm not sure which feeling is stronger: my irritation or my amusement. I raise an eyebrow. "Feel better?"

"Yes," he declares as he shoves his lighter back into his pocket.

I try to repress a smile. I narrow my eyes and say, "You think you're a little badass, don't you?"

He grins. "I have my moments."

I can't hold in my smile anymore. "Okay, pyro. Let's go."

Surprised, he asks, "Where are we going?"

"Anywhere you want. My schedule for this afternoon has unexpectedly opened up, so I'm at your disposal. Unless you have a more pressing engagement?"

"No. I don't have any plans."

"Okay. Let's get out of here, then."

I walk toward the exit. He falls into step beside me. Curious, I ask, "Do you smoke?" I don't remember ever smelling smoke around him, but some people are better at masking it than others.

"No, not really. I might smoke a cigarette every now and then when I'm in the mood for it, but I don't make a habit out of it. Why?"

"I was just surprised you just happened to have a lighter in your pocket."

"It's good to have one handy. You never know when you might need one."

"Like to set a fire in the school hallway, for example?"

"Exactly." His teeth flash in a smile.

Warily, I say, "You're not one of those people who likes to set buildings on fire just to watch them burn, are you?" With his questionable emotional stability, I'm a little concerned that he might pull a *Carrie* on all of us during prom.

He laughs. "No, I'm not a criminal. And in case you're wondering, I don't pull wings off flies or torture baby animals, either."

"Okay, good. I was a little worried there for a second."

"Come on, Taylor. You know me better than that."

Do I? I haven't known him long, and he's definitely one who keeps things close to the chest. Even if he were planning on taking his revenge by blowing up the school or something, he wouldn't tell me about it. I glance over at him. He's looking at his feet as he walks, so I can't read his facial expression. Despite his sharp tongue and obvious emotional issues, it's hard for me to imagine that this quiet, sensitive person who spends hours at a time patiently teaching me the piano or showing me how to do calculus could be dangerous. I make up my mind to trust him.

We step out into the parking lot. His car is parked near mine, way at the other end of the lot.

"Can you do me a favor?" I ask.

"Sure."

"You don't even know what it is yet."

"Okay, fine. The answer is 'no,' then."

I ignore him. "Can I drive your car?" I plead wistfully.

A smile spreads across his face. "You want to drive my car?"

"Please? Just this once?"

"Well . . . *okay*." He pulls his keys out of his jacket pocket and holds them up high. I stretch out my hand. "Just don't wreck it, okay?" he says as he drops them into my palm.

I grin like a kid in a candy store, then practically skip to the driver's side of his BMW. I press the unlock button on the remote

The Lifesaver

and the car gives a high-pitched *beep*. I toss my backpack into the back, then ease myself slowly into the driver's seat. The leather bucket seat hugs my body and makes me feel like I'm sitting in a racecar. I slide the seat back a notch and adjust the mirrors. I buckle my seat belt and insert the key into the ignition. I look over at Tristan, who's watching me from the passenger seat with his arms crossed and a wry smile upon his lips.

"Moment of truth!" I exclaim.

He rolls his eyes and replies, with as little enthusiasm as possible, "Whoopee."

I turn the ignition. The car comes to life with a satisfying rumble. I rev the engine a couple of times and whoop. "Yeeaahh, buddy!"

He shakes his head. "You're pathetic, you know that?"

"Just because you can't appreciate fine art when you see it doesn't make me pathetic."

He scoffs. "Fine art?"

I caress the steering wheel. "This car is a thing of beauty."

"Shall I leave you two alone, then?"

I laugh. "Maybe later. But right now, we're going to do whatever you want to do."

"Why is it up to me?"

"Because I'm the driver and I said so. So tell me where you want to go and I'll take us there."

"I don't want to go anywhere in particular."

I smile. "That's just where I wanted to go," I say as I peel out of the parking space.

"You're smoking crack! How is *E.T.* the best Spielberg film?" I say.

For the last forty-five minutes, we've been sitting in his car at the Sonic drive-in a few towns over, having a scholarly discussion about the history of motion pictures. I'd told him I'd gone to see *Superman* with Drake, and we quickly came to realize that, between the two of us, we've seen more movies than most people see in a lifetime.

"It's one of the best-selling films of all time!" Tristan argues as he dips a tater tot into his ketchup. I was reluctant to eat in the car, but Tristan assured me that he didn't care about spills.

"Yeah, so is *Jaws*!" I exclaim.

"*E.T.* is a timeless story about a kid who learns about friendship and selflessness. *Jaws* is about a killer shark."

"It's not just about a killer shark. It's about three different men who band together to save their town from a threat. It's an adventure movie."

"I'm not saying *Jaws* is bad. It's one of the greatest horror films of all time. I'm just saying it's not his best."

"Hmm. Okay, then. Best Tarantino film?"

"All of his movies are the same."

"What do you mean, they're 'all the same'?"

"They're all the same! He uses the same techniques and the same actors every time. If you've seen one of his movies, you've seen them all."

"I don't think that's true. You can't say *Pulp Fiction* is the same as *Inglourious Basterds*."

"Okay, I give you that one," he concedes. "But *Pulp Fiction* isn't much different from *Reservoir Dogs* or *Kill Bill*. There's a bunch of pointless dialogue and time jumps, and then a bunch of senseless violence."

I frown. "I dunno. I like *Pulp Fiction*."

"Of course you do."

"What is that supposed to mean?"

"Because every macho guy likes *Pulp Fiction*. You're all predictable."

"Oh, I'm predictable? Okay, then. What's my favorite movie?"

Without hesitation, he replies, "*The Godfather*."

Holy shit.

I set my jaw stubbornly. "Which one?"

He gives me a calculating look. "Part Two," he declares.

"Are you kidding me?" *Am I really that predictable?* I think with chagrin.

"Why? Did I get it right?" he says.

"No . . ."

He laughs. "I told you. Predictable."

"Alright, then. It's my turn to guess yours."

"Ooh, this oughta be good. I can't wait to hear this."

I rest my elbow on the back of the seat and chew on the tip of my thumb as I examine him. He sets his empty tater tot holder down on the center console and looks steadily back at me, as if we're in a Mexican standoff. His eyes don't give anything away, but a hint of a smile plays on his lips. I try to think about everything I know about him. As critical as he is, he probably prefers movies that have artistic value and can stand the test of time. I don't know enough indie or foreign films to hazard a guess on those, so hopefully it's not some obscure movie I've never heard of before. My best bet is a classic.

"Can I ask you one question?" I ask.

He thinks about it for a moment, then gives in. "Okay, fine. You can have one hint."

"Is it a Hitchcock film?"

He gives me a smug smile. "No."

"Okay. I'm going to go out on a limb here and say that you're a Kubrick fan."

His eyes widen. *Bingo.*

I point at him and declare, "*2001*."

"Wow. You're really close. *Dr. Strangelove*," he confesses.

"Ha! I knew it."

"How did you know I liked Kubrick?"

"Because you know your movies, and he's one of the best."

He smiles, pleased by the compliment.

I take a sip of my shake, then say, "You know, it's nice to be able to have a decent conversation about movies with someone. Ashley's favorite movie is *The Notebook*, so that tells you what I have to deal with."

He laughs. After a pause, he says, "Can I ask you something?"

"Yeah."

"What do you see in her? I mean besides the fact that she's pretty and she's a cheerleader."

"Well, what else is there?"

A look of disgust flits across his face.

"I'm just kidding," I assure him, smiling. "I'm not that superficial. I know she can be judgmental sometimes, but she's actually a really nice person once you get to know her. Like during spring break, my parents went up to Vermont to go to my mom's cousin's funeral. I came down with the flu while they were gone, and Ashley came over every day to make me soup and take care of me, even though she was supposed to go to the beach with her friends."

"Huh. She must really love you, then."

"Yeah, I guess so."

He smirks. "You guess so? You don't know?"

"No, I think she does."

"Do you love her?"

"Yeah, I do. I don't know yet if she's 'the one,' but I care about her a lot."

The Lifesaver

"Do you believe in that? That there's only one person for everybody?"

"I don't know. It doesn't sound very practical. What if the only person for you is in China or something?"

He laughs. "I guess if it's really meant to be, then you'll end up meeting somehow."

"Do you believe in it? You don't seem like the romantic type."

"I dunno. It's hard enough for me to imagine being in love with one person, much less multiple people."

"You've never been in love?" I think back to what Ashley said about his choir teacher.

"No. And I'm not sure if I ever want to be, either."

"Why?" I ask, surprised.

"Well, first off, they probably wouldn't love me anyway. But even if they did, they'd just end up getting hurt. I'm better off alone."

I sit there, stunned. There are so many things wrong with what he just said, I don't even know where to begin. Finally, I spit out, "That's a really negative thing to say about yourself."

He shrugs. "It's true."

"Why do you think you're better off alone?"

"I'm fucked up, Taylor. You don't even know *how* fucked up I am. Nobody wants to deal with my shit. And on the off chance that I did find somebody who wanted to be with me, they'd probably be treated the same way I am by those assholes who want to see me dead. I don't want to watch somebody I care about get hurt because of me."

I stare at him, not knowing the best way to respond. After a moment, I say, "We might be able to take care of one of your problems, at least."

"Which one?"

"The bullying."

"What are you suggesting? That we hire contract killers to take out my enemies?"

"Maybe not go to *that* extreme. Here, come on."

I get out of the car. He doesn't move; he just watches me with a confused expression on his face. I bend over and peer at him through the open door. "Let's go, slowpoke!"

He climbs out of the car. I walk toward the tree line behind the Sonic where the light of the streetlamps doesn't reach. He follows a few steps behind. When I get to the trees, I turn around to face him.

"Hit me," I say.

He folds his arms across his chest and scoffs. "What is this, *Fight Club*? I'm not going to hit you."

"Come on, hit me! You're gonna have to learn how to throw a punch if you want to stand a chance against the jerks who are out to get you. You can practice on me. So come on, give me your best shot." I wave my fingers in a come-get-me gesture.

"Fuck you." He turns around to leave, but I grab his arm. He glares at me and tries to pull away. "Let go."

"No. Not until you hit me."

"You're a dick."

"Yes, I'm a dick. That's why you should punch me in the face."

"I don't want to punch you anywhere."

"Why? Are you afraid you're gonna hurt your pretty little hand?"

"Leave me alone!"

He tries to pry my fingers off. I throw his arm back at him. The force sends him reeling a couple steps backward. He glares at me, then turns to walk away again. I push his back, not hard enough to knock him off balance, but just enough to provoke him.

"Taylor! Stop!" he scolds as he looks back over his shoulder.

"Or what? What are you gonna do about it?" I push him again, harder this time. He turns around and shoves my chest, but it doesn't affect me much. His heart must not have really been in it. "Good," I say. "Push me again."

"No!" He juts out his chin defiantly.

"Fine!"

I shove him as hard as I can. He falls backward and lands hard on his ass in the grass. He looks up at me wide-eyed in shock and anger and . . . fear? I gulp down the rock that's lodged itself in my throat. I hate doing this, but he's got to learn how to defend himself.

"Get up," I order.

He just sits there, frozen, looking at me like a hare caught in a trap. I stand over him with my fist clenched. "Get up and fight like a man!"

I must have hit a nerve, because his face goes pale and he starts to tremble. His lower lip quivers as he says, "Please . . . don't . . ."

An iron fist squeezes my heart. I drop to my knees in front of him. "Oh God, Tristan," I gasp. "I'm so sorry!"

He curls forward into a ball and buries his face in his arms. "I can't do it. I just can't."

I crawl over to sit beside him. "It's okay. We'll figure something else out," I say with more conviction than I feel.

He heaves a shuddering sigh.

I place a hand on his back. "Are you okay?"

He lifts his head and wipes the moisture off his cheek. "I'm spectacular. What do you think?"

In a low voice, I say, "You know I didn't mean it, don't you? Any of it."

He looks over at me. His eyelashes glisten with tears. He gives me a weak smile. "Yeah, I know," he mumbles.

"Good." I ruffle his hair, then get to my feet and hold out a hand to help him up. He takes it and allows me to drag him to his feet. He brushes the grass off the seat of his pants, then shoves his hands in his pockets and starts trudging back to the car with his head down. In a show of comradery, I drape an arm across his shoulders as I walk beside him. His mouth curves up in a small smile. "You know," I say conspiratorially in his ear, "a rape whistle *may* not be a bad investment."

He rolls his eyes and shrugs me off. "Shut up, Taylor," he grumbles, but I can tell he knows I'm just teasing.

When we reach his car, I stop and hold up the keys. "Do you want to drive?" I ask.

"No, you can."

"Are you sure?"

"Yeah. Since this is the only time you'll get to drive my car, you may as well make the most of it."

"What? I won't be able to drive it again?"

"No, because I'm trading it in for a Pinto tomorrow morning."

I laugh. "A Pinto?"

"It's better than this piece of crap."

"Are you sure you don't want a nice Volkswagen Beetle?"

"Yeah, 'cause that's what I need. More reasons for people to punch me."

"You could borrow my suit of armor. Then you wouldn't feel it when they punched you."

He crosses his arms and gives me a dubious look. "Please tell me you did not buy a suit of armor."

"So what if I did?"

He studies me hard, clearly trying to determine if I'm pulling his leg or not.

"Taylor."

"What?"

"You're kidding, right?"

"Why would I kid you about something like that? Of course you can borrow it."

His mouth drops open. "Are you fucking *serious*? You bought a suit of armor?"

I grin. "No, I didn't buy a suit of armor! This isn't the fifth century, Tristan."

He glares at me, but his mouth works like he's trying to restrain a smile. He holds out his hand. "That's it. Give me the goddamn keys."

"No." I turn on my heel and walk to the driver's side door. "You said I could drive, so I'm going to drive."

He walks over to the passenger's side. I shoot him a lopsided grin over the roof of the car as I open my door. He rolls his eyes back at me. We climb back into the car.

"So where to now?" I ask.

"What time is it?" He leans over to look at the clock on the dash.

"Eight ten."

"What time do you have to be home?"

"Nine."

"Should we head back, then?"

"Yeah, we probably should." I sigh as I turn on the car. I don't want to go home. If it were up to me, we'd drive around aimlessly and talk about movies and music all night long. There's a certain kind of freedom you get driving on the open road that you can't find anywhere else.

I take us back to the school parking lot. For some reason, it feels a lot smaller now. I park next to my car and turn off the engine. Reluctantly, I unbuckle my seat belt and climb out of the bucket seat.

Tristan walks around the front of the car with his hands in his pockets and watches as I pull my backpack out of the back seat.

"Do you want me to give you money for gas?" I ask as I shut the door.

"No. I don't want your money."

"You sure? I'm pretty sure I ate up half your tank driving us to Timbuktu and back."

"You covered dinner. That seems more than fair. Besides, it's not like I wasn't going to use that tank eventually."

"Okay. If you insist." I hold out my fist.

He pulls his right hand out of his pocket and bumps his fist against mine.

"I'll see you tomorrow." This time, I phrase it as a statement instead of a question.

I turn and walk to my car. As I unlock the door, Tristan calls, "Hey, Taylor."

I look over my shoulder. He leans against the roof of the BMW and says, "Thanks for hanging out with me tonight."

I smile. "Any time."

The second I walk through the front door, my father yells from the living room, "Son! Get in here."

Oh no.

I trudge in and see my father and mother sitting next to each other on the love seat, disapproval all over their faces. My father gestures toward the recliner across from them. "Sit down."

I have no choice but to obey.

My father is the first to speak. "Coach Barnes called." *Crap.* "He said that you missed practice today."

I stay silent. I should have thought up an alibi before walking into the house, but the thought never crossed my mind.

"Well?" he says.

"I did," I say reluctantly.

They both frown. "Did you know that a scout was coming today?" he asks.

My heart plummets to the pit of my stomach. "Another scout?"

"This is unacceptable," he says, leaning forward. "You think you're the only high school pitcher to get noticed by the League?"

"No, I—"

"Do you know how many players they look at each year? How many pitchers they pass over?"

"I know, but—"

"Filling out one questionnaire doesn't make you above everyone else. You have to work hard, you have to hustle. Scouts have a bunch of talented kids that they're looking at, and they don't have time to waste on slackers who are unreliable and don't respect the game."

"Dad, I missed *one* practice!"

"Yes! The most important one," he shouts.

My mother interjects. "Honey, why did you skip today?"

I'm not really prepared yet to field questions about what happened this afternoon. All the evidence is gone anyway. "A friend of mine needed help," I say uncertainly.

"Drake?" she asks.

"No. Tristan."

"Tristan? Who's Tristan?" my dad says.

"He's a friend. He's teaching me the piano."

"What?" Both of my parents look surprised by this revelation. I had never expressed any interest in the piano before, so I can see how it would seem to them to come out of left field. My mother's face alights into a smile, but my father looks even angrier than before.

"Is that what you were doing today? Playing the piano?" he demands.

"No."

"Then what were you doing?"

I could tell them what I was literally doing—that Tristan and I just drove around and talked all afternoon—but something tells me they wouldn't understand how that could trump a scout coming for the sole purpose of seeing me. How can I explain to them how the last few hours I've spent doing nothing may have meant everything?

"Providing moral support. He had a really bad day," I answer.

My mother's eyes are sympathetic, but my father doesn't seem to accept this as a good enough excuse. "We all have bad days," he grumbles. I know what he's thinking: he's having one right now.

"Well, what's done is done," my mother says with a resigned sigh. "Avery, you're going to call Coach Barnes and apologize to him. Make sure he knows how important this is to you."

"Okay, Mom."

I retreat upstairs and call him up on my cell phone. He gives me the same lecture as my dad, only with less compassion and understanding. I hang up, feeling like a degenerate. I throw myself on my bed and stare at the "Stairway to Heaven" poster on the wall.

My mother knocks on my door and walks in. "Did you talk to him?"

"Yeah, I did. He said he'd call around to see if he can get the scout back."

She breathes a sigh of relief as she sits on the edge of the bed behind me. "That's good."

I nod and look back at the poster.

She rubs my back. "Everything okay, sweetie?"

"I don't know." I've spent so much time focusing on Tristan's mental health lately, I haven't really stopped to evaluate how *I'm* handling it all.

"You want to talk about it?"

I sigh. "Not really." I wouldn't even know where to begin.

She nods and continues to rub my back. After a few seconds of silence, she asks, "Is Tristan okay?"

The poster turns blurry as mist fills my eyes. Shakily, I mumble, "I hope so."

11

Before school, I check in with Tristan at his locker before I head to my own. "Hey. How are you?" I ask.

"Fine," he replies unconvincingly as he hangs his jacket in his locker. He looks jumpy, as if he's nervous that another threatening note will materialize out of thin air in front of him.

I nod and say, with a straight face, "It's great to be fine."

Startled, he looks over at me. I give him a crooked smile and his face lights up. "*Dr. Strangelove?*" he asks.

"I may have watched it last night." Unsurprisingly, my insomnia kicked in again, so I ended up streaming movies to my computer most of the night.

"And?" he prompts.

I had seen bits and pieces of it before when I was younger, but last night was the first time I had watched it straight through. I didn't really appreciate it when I was a kid, probably because the jokes went over my head, but now that I'm older, I see how witty it is. I can see why Tristan likes it.

"It's no *Godfather*, but it's pretty good," I admit.

"Well, no, nothing's like *The Godfather*. Unless you count every other Mafia movie."

I laugh. "You know *The Godfather* puts all other Mafia movies to shame."

"Alright, Taylor, you win. *The Godfather* is the godfather of Mafia movies."

I shrug. "That's all I wanted to hear."

I grin at him and he smiles, too. He looks more relaxed now, and I feel more at ease as well.

"You stay out of trouble, Chevalier," I say, only half-joking, as I hold out my fist.

He smirks at my use of his surname. He bumps my fist and replies, "You too, *Avery*."

He may not have been fine when I first came up to him, but he seems to be fine now. It's funny, that quote. It's meant to be a joke, but, considering our circumstances, I think that being fine *is* pretty great.

"So what was that all about yesterday?" Drake asks during lunch.

"When?"

"Whaddya mean, 'when'? I mean when you skipped practice and asked me to cover for you because of some"—he curls his fingers as air quotes—"'family emergency.'"

"Oh. Yeah. Thanks for doing that, by the way. Did Coach give you a hard time?"

"Yeah, he did. I don't know why I stick my neck out for you when you won't even tell me what's going on."

"It's not about me. It's about Tristan."

"Yeah, I figured. When I saw you two in the hallway, I thought someone had died or something."

I debate how much to tell him. I know Tristan doesn't like his business being blasted around school, but this is one secret I don't think he should keep.

"He's being bullied, Drake," I say quietly.

Drake looks down at his tray. His Adam's apple bobs as he swallows. "Is it bad?"

"Yeah. It's bad. He got a threatening note in his locker yesterday. I figured he wouldn't want to be left alone after that."

"What did the note say?"

"'I hope you die, fag.'"

His head snaps up. "Jesus Christ! Are you shittin' me?"

"No."

"Does he know who sent it?"

"I think he knows, but he wouldn't tell me. He didn't want to tell any of the teachers, either. I wish I could walk him between classes to keep an eye on him, but there's just not enough time. His locker's on the other side of the school."

"Are you worried it's gonna be like Columbine? That one day he'll just snap and start shooting up the place?"

I shake my head vehemently. "No. He wouldn't do that."

"But how do you know?" Drake presses. "I mean, how well do you really know this guy? It's those quiet types you have to look out for."

"He's not quiet when he's with me."

"Yeah, but you've only been friends for a couple weeks. It's not like you and me, where we've known each other our whole lives."

I sigh. "Look, I just know, okay? He talks tough sometimes, but I really don't think he has a violent bone in his body. Like last night, I practically begged him to punch me in the face and he just couldn't take the shot."

He presses his lips together. His voice wavers as he says, "You asked him to punch you in the face?"

Despite my efforts to remain serious, my mouth smiles of its own accord. I look down at the table and mumble, "Yeah."

He busts a laugh. Then his eyebrows furrow together. "Hey, wait a minute! How come you never ask me to hit you?"

"I'm not a piñata! I was just trying to teach him some self-defense."

"Hmm. Do you think that *maybe* he didn't hit you because he likes you?"

Exasperated, I say, "Would you stop with all the romance bullcrap? You're making me fucking paranoid whenever I'm around him. It's not like that, okay? And besides, I don't think he'd hit me even if he hated my guts. I just don't think it's in him."

"Okay. Whatever you say, boss."

After school, Drake and I cut across the parking lot to go to the weight room. Coach Barnes insists that we spend the first twenty-five minutes of practice "building our strength," my least favorite activity. It's not that I mind working out, but I'd much rather be outside tossing a ball than inside tossing weights.

I glimpse the silver of Tristan's BMW on the other side of the lot, then something else catches my eye. Tristan's sitting on the ground next to the driver's side door with his head buried in his hands. I slow down, then I change direction and pick up the pace until I'm practically running. I don't turn around, but I hear Drake's footsteps behind me. When I get to Tristan, I drop to my knee in front of him. "Tristan? What is it? What happened?"

"I can't . . . I can't *take* this anymore, Taylor."

Behind him, the driver's side tire is completely flat. I can see at a glance that the rubber has been split open with something sharp. I look behind me, then under the car. They're all slashed. All four.

I sit down on the ground next to him. "Shhh. It's okay. We'll figure this out." I look up at Drake. He shakes his head with disbelief and concern.

I turn back to Tristan and nudge him with my elbow. "Hey, come on. Cheer up. It's not like you liked that car anyway."

He gives a strangled laugh. "No. It *is* pretty shitty."

Drake points at his watch. I nod.

"Listen, I have to go to practice. My parents nearly murdered me last night and I can't skip again. Do you want me to take you home after, or do you want me to get you a lift?"

"I guess I'll wait for you."

"Okay. Are you gonna wait in one of the classrooms, or—"

He shakes his head fiercely. "No. I'm not waiting there."

I examine him for a few seconds. He must really not want to go back in there alone, and I'm starting to agree that maybe he shouldn't. What if someone is waiting to jump him as soon as we leave?

"Alright. Come on, then."

The three of us walk over to the weight room. Tristan parks himself on the floor by the door. I set my backpack down next to him and follow Drake over to the rack of free weights. A couple of our teammates, Carter and Diego, are already there. As we approach, Carter nudges Diego and says, "Look who's here." He nods in Tristan's direction.

"Oh, God," Diego says. "Coach better make him leave. I don't want him checking me out all afternoon."

Drake retorts, "Like anyone would check out your pimply ass."

"Look, guys," I say more diplomatically, "he's only here because his car got trashed and he needs a ride home."

"Well, he better not be looking for a ride from me, that's all I have to say," Diego replies.

Before I can respond, Coach Barnes comes up. "Alright, ladies. Enough chitchat. Let's get to work."

As Carter and Diego walk away, Drake pulls me aside. "Hey. Maybe Tristan should wait for you somewhere else."

"Are you serious?" I hiss under my breath.

"If people already think he's gay, sitting around in the weight room watching the boys' baseball team work out ain't exactly gonna help his cause. Know what I'm sayin'?"

I glance over at Tristan. He's still sitting where I left him on the floor, looking in the direction of our catcher, Nick, where he's practicing squats. I sigh. Drake's logic makes sense, but I don't know how I'm going to explain it to Tristan in a way that won't upset him even more.

"Alright. I'll go talk to him."

Tristan frowns at me as I approach. I unfasten my keys from my belt loop and hand them out to him. "Here. You can take my car if you want. You don't have to wait around here for me all day."

"What? No. You don't have to give me your car."

"I'm not giving you my car, I'm just letting you borrow it for a couple hours. You'll just be bored sitting here."

"I don't mind."

I sigh. This is proving to be more difficult than I thought. "Tristan, I think you should take my car."

"You want me to leave?" Surprise and hurt fill his voice.

Reluctantly, I say, "I think it'd be better if you did. Some of the guys . . . well . . ." I trail off, feeling more than a little uncomfortable at the way this conversation is going.

He looks around the room, where I can only imagine my

teammates are watching and listening with bated breath. His face contorts with anger and disgust.

"Oh, I see," he snaps. "You don't want the homo around. Fine. I get it." He snatches the keys from my hand as he stands up, then grabs his backpack and tosses it over his shoulder.

"Tristan—" I try to grab his arm to stop him, but he shrugs me off and stalks away. I look up at the ceiling, feeling helpless. I seem to be fighting a losing battle. All I can do is pray that by the time practice is over, he—and my car—will still be in one piece.

"Tristan's pretty pissed at you, huh?" Drake says as we wait on the curb.

"He should be pissed! I shouldn't have run him off like that. He should be able to sit wherever he wants to sit," I say, feeling guilty and ashamed of myself.

"Avery, it's not your fault. Hell, you wouldn't have done it if I hadn't said anything. You were just trying to look out for him."

"Yeah, and look where that's got me. Now *I'm* the one without a car."

"He'll be back. Don't worry."

I glance at my watch. Practice ended over forty-five minutes ago, and there's still no sign of Tristan or my Honda. I have to do something to distract myself from this rising panic in my chest. Looking at my phone every thirty seconds to see if there's a text or missed call from him has gotten me exactly nowhere.

I gaze across the parking lot at his poor, out-of-commission BMW. "What do you think we should do about his car?"

"I have a jack. We could try to replace a tire," he says.

"That would still leave us with three flats. Maybe I should call AAA and get a tow truck."

"Shouldn't his parents deal with that?"

"They're out of town. I think our options are limited."

I go to my contacts list and make the call. Hopefully, Tristan will show up before the tow truck driver does. I don't want to have to explain why I'm towing a car that's not even mine to a house where nobody is home.

The bright yellow lights of the tow truck cut violently through the night as Tristan's BMW crawls up the ramp. I shield my eyes against the blinding flash, wishing that this shitty evening would be over, once and for all. Once the tow truck arrived, I told Drake he could bail and that I'd have the driver take me home. Drake argued with me at first, but I told him there was no sense in both of us being grounded for getting home late on a school night. After Drake left, I tried calling Tristan several times, but he never answered. Now I'm seriously worried that he and my car have disappeared for good.

As the tow truck driver hooks the last chain onto the BMW, a pair of headlights swings into the parking lot. I sigh as I stand up and brush the dust off my pants. The Honda pulls up in front of me. It doesn't look any better (or worse) than it did before, but it's a welcome sight nonetheless. Tristan steps out of the driver's side and walks around the front of the car. I can't decide if I should hug him or beat the living shit out of him, so I do neither. I just stand there, motionless.

He holds up a large McDonald's bag. "Here," he mutters. "I figured you'd be hungry."

I don't trust myself enough to respond without flying off the rails. Without a word, I take the bag from his hand. I open it and shove a few french fries into my mouth. I hadn't realized it until now, but he's right: I'm famished.

He looks over at the tow truck. "Did you call them?"

I nod as I chew.

With a shaky sigh, he says, "Avery, I'm sorry."

I didn't think "sorry" would cut it after all the grief he put me through, not just tonight but every night since I met him, but his earnestness and apparent contrition wash away all my anger.

I gulp down my food. "I'm sorry, too."

We don't say anything more to each other while we watch the tow truck driver make his final preparations. Once he's done, he walks over to us and exchanges information with Tristan while I finish my hamburger. The driver agrees to follow me back to Tristan's house and climbs back into his truck. Tristan hands me my keys and I settle into the driver's seat. I turn the engine back on, and the gas gauge on the dash catches my eye. I'm pretty sure I had a quarter tank this morning, but the arrow is now pointing at "full."

"Where did you go?" I ask as nonchalantly as possible.

"I just drove around."

He falls quiet again. He stares out the window at the passing streetlights while I drive and try to think of a way to break this heavy silence.

"Tristan, I wish I could take back what happened today. You shouldn't have had to deal with any of this, but then I had to go and make things worse."

He sighs. "I know you were just trying to help out your friends. It's fine. Really."

"What? No! I was trying to help *you* out."

He looks at me, his brow furrowed in confusion. I struggle to find the words to explain it. "If you had stayed, it only would have made people talk about you more. I was trying to *not* give them a reason to hurt you. But I ended up hurting you anyway. I shouldn't have asked you to leave. It was a shitty thing to do, and I'm sorry."

He mulls over my words. "So . . . you were trying to protect me?"

"Yeah, I guess. Yeah."

He shakes his head. "Wow. I did not get that at all. I thought you didn't want me around because you were afraid I was like some creepy Peeping Tom or something."

"No! Some of the other guys may think that, but I don't. I was fine with you hanging out until Drake had to open his big mouth and convinced me that it would be better for you if you went somewhere else. I never should've listened to him."

"No," he says with a sigh. "Maybe he was right. I don't need more reasons for people to call me a cocksucker."

"Why do people say all that stuff about you?"

"Why? You're asking *why* people call me names? Because they're fucking douchebags, that's why."

"Why don't you tell a teacher about it? Say you're being bullied?"

He scoffs. "Teachers can't do shit about it."

"You have to tell someone about your car, at least."

"Why?"

"So they can find out who did it! Get them to replace your tires."

"No. Besides, I already know who did it, and there's no way in hell they're gonna pay for my tires."

"Who was it?"

"I'm not going to tell you."

"Why not?"

"Because I know what you'd do! You'd go marching up to them and demand restitution or some bullcrap, and then they'd beat you senseless and I'd have to explain to your parents how their son ended up a paraplegic because of some goddamn hero complex."

I smile. "You know me too well."

His mouth quirks, but then he shakes his head. "I don't know what I'm going to do about the tires, though. I doubt any auto shops are open, and I don't have another car."

"You have a four-car garage but you don't have any cars?"

"No, I mean my parents have all the keys. I guess I'll have to wait until they get back home." He sighs. "I'm not looking forward to riding the bus again."

"I could drive you to school."

"What?" Clearly, the idea of carpooling had never crossed his mind. He glances at me and shakes his head again. "No, you've done enough for me already."

"It's not a big deal."

"It's out of your way!"

"Not really. I'm coming over to your house after school anyway."

"But don't you have practice?"

"That's true. If you don't mind waiting, you can stick around. Watch the show."

"Oh my God. I can't believe you just said that," he grumbles.

I smile. "Seriously, though. You can hang around if you want, or you could borrow my car again. As long as you remember to *pick me back up.*"

"I'm sorry I left you waiting so long."

"Well, it's a good thing you showed up when you did. Five more minutes and I would have called the cops and reported you for grand theft auto."

Alarmed, he looks over at me. "Really?"

"Okay, maybe not five minutes. Ten minutes, tops."

I park in front of Tristan's house and call my mom as the tow truck lowers the BMW onto the driveway. Luckily, she doesn't ask too many questions that would put me on the spot. Once the car is safely on the ground, I turn to Tristan and ask, "Are you gonna be okay by yourself?"

"Taylor, I'm fine. I'll see you tomorrow."

"Okay. I'll pick you up at six thirty. Cool?"

He hesitates. It's obvious that he's struggling to determine which he'd rather do: ride with me, thereby putting me out of my way; or ride the bus with people who in all likelihood will treat him like crap. To me, it seems like a no-brainer, but I can imagine that he doesn't want to feel like a charity case.

He comes to a decision. "Fine," he replies, but he doesn't sound thrilled. I swear, it's like pulling teeth to get him to let me help him. I don't know why, since he always seems willing to help me with stuff. Could it be pride? Or does he think he's not worth the trouble?

My mother's waiting for me in the kitchen when I get home. "Hi, hon. Did Tristan get home safely?"

"Yeah."

"What happened?"

"He got a flat tire." *Or four.*

"Oh, that's a shame. Did you help him fix it?"

"No, he didn't have a spare. I had to call AAA. I hope you don't mind."

"No. That's what it's there for. Though I wish you had called sooner. Your father would have come and helped."

"It's okay. We took care of it." We didn't really take care of it, but I don't think my father getting involved would have done much good. He's still bitter that I took off with Tristan yesterday, and I don't think he'd be too pleased to help the kid who potentially interfered with his son's future.

"Okay, well, it's a good thing you were around," she says.

You have no idea.

I yank the earbuds out of my ears. I thought that by playing classical music, I'd lull myself to sleep, but it's no good. I've been tossing and turning in bed for hours and I just can't seem to get comfortable.

I press the pause button and glance at the time on my phone. 12:51.

After a moment's deliberation, I text Tristan.

> You awake?

Almost immediately, my phone chirps.

> No.

I smile. I type back:

> Me neither.

I close my eyes and will my muscles to relax. After a minute, my phone chirps again.

> Good night, Taylor.

> Good night, Tristan.

I set my phone back on the nightstand. I close my eyes again, and before long, I slip into a fitful dream where I'm in the river, but the water is too dark and swift, and the harder I try to swim, the farther I drift away from shore.

12

At six thirty, I pull into Tristan's driveway behind the heap that used to be his car. The whole house is dark. I honk my horn and wait, but the door never opens. *Crap.*

I pull out my cell and call him. It rings several times. I'm about to hang up when I hear his voice on the other end of the line. "Hello?" he says groggily.

"Get your ass up. We have to go to school."

"Shit . . . ," he mutters under his breath. I hear rustling in the background, then he says, still half-asleep, "Okay. I'll be right down."

A few minutes later, he stumbles out the door and trudges to my car. He moves like the walking dead. He slumps into the passenger seat, leans his head against the headrest, and closes his eyes. *And I thought* I *was bad in the morning.*

I stifle a laugh. "Long night?"

With his eyes still closed, he says, "I couldn't sleep. Some asshole kept texting me."

"I hate it when that happens," I say as I reverse out of the driveway.

His mouth twitches, then he rests his head against the window and falls asleep. I drive the rest of the way to school in silence.

When we get to school, I throw the car into park and look over at him. "Tristan."

No response.

I shake his shoulder. "Tristan, wake up."

"Five more minutes," he grumbles.

"Aren't you anxious to start another fun-filled day at Springfield High?"

"Fuck off."

"Come on, Tristan. If I can do it, you can do it. Get up."

He groans. We grab our bags and head across the parking lot. Both of us are dragging. I don't know how we're going to make it through our classes today.

Drake is loitering by the entrance. I'm not surprised; he makes a point of spending as little time inside the school as possible. He grins when he sees us. "Well, look who the cat dragged in! I see both of you made it home in one piece."

I yawn as I nod. Tristan looks like he's about to fall over.

"Good, good. Well, don't let me hold you up."

Tristan starts to walk inside. I'm about to follow, but Drake grabs my arm. "Everything okay?" he mutters.

"Yeah. I think so," I whisper.

"Okay." He thumps my back as I walk away.

I catch up to Tristan and accompany him to his locker. I'm not going to take a chance on him not making it to class.

"You don't need to follow me around all day," he mutters as he fumbles with the padlock.

"I'm just making sure you don't pass out in the hallway and block traffic."

He stuffs his coat in the locker and slams the door. "Alright. Let's go."

As we're weaving our way through the sea of students, something rams into my side. I throw a dirty look over my shoulder at whatever rude person didn't even apologize for running into me. I'm disappointed and angry, though not terribly surprised, to see that it was Mike. He glances back and sneers at me.

"Watch where you're going, fuckface," I snap.

He doesn't answer; he just laughs and keeps going.

Fuming, I turn and continue walking toward room 103. Tristan frowns. "What was that all about?" he asks as he falls back in line next to me.

"Let's just say that Mike and I don't see eye to eye."

"Are you not friends anymore?" he asks, surprised.

"No. I have better things to do than hang out with scuzzballs like him and Jamaal Lewis."

He stops in the doorway of his class. I pull my keys off my belt loop and hold them out. "Don't wreck it, okay?" I say in a threatening tone as I repeat his words back to him.

He smirks as he takes the keys from my hand. "I'll try not to."

"And don't forget to pick me back up."

"Jesus, Taylor. You're such a *worrier*. You'd think I'd left you at school or something," he says as he turns and goes inside the classroom.

I smile, then rush through the throngs to get to my locker before the bell rings.

The last several nights of sleeplessness are definitely starting to take their toll. I sludge through the morning as best I can, but all I really want to do is go back to bed. Even gym class wasn't enough to get my blood pumping again. I was a little worried the incident with Mike in the hallway would be the start of something bigger, but he spent all of second period ignoring me. I'm grateful; the last thing I need is more drama.

During lunch break, I resist the urge to take a nap and seek out Officer Gálvez instead. Since Tristan obviously won't tell anyone about what's going on, it's time I took matters into my own hands. I find Gálvez near the front office, berating a couple of freshmen for having the audacity to use the vending machine in the teachers' lounge. After he lets them off with a warning, he turns to me and says, "Let me see your hall pass, Taylor."

I ignore him. "I want to file a report."

"What kind of report?"

I glance around. There's no one in the hallway but us, but I still don't feel comfortable talking about this in such a public spot. "Can we talk somewhere else?"

He stares at me a moment, then nods his head toward the teachers' lounge. "This way."

He follows me into the lounge and closes the door behind him. The lounge is laughably small—my guess is that it used to be a janitorial closet at one point. There's only room for a small table, three chairs, and the forbidden vending machine. I sit in one of the chairs and he sits down across from me.

"So what's going on?" he asks.

"Yesterday, somebody slashed all the tires on Tristan Chevalier's car."

At hearing Tristan's name, he bows his head and rubs his eyes. This must not be the first time he's had to deal with Tristan.

"Do you know who?" he asks as he continues to rub his eyes.

"No. I think Tristan does, though."

"Have you asked him?"

"Yes. He wouldn't tell me. I was hoping you could look at the security footage, or . . ."

I stop. Officer Gálvez is shaking his head.

"There isn't any footage," he says.

"What do you mean? Why not? There's cameras in the parking lot, there has to be some—"

"The cameras don't record anything, Taylor. The school doesn't have the money or the resources to set up a surveillance system."

"You mean they're fake?"

"The cameras are real. And they still provide deterrence."

"Tell that to Tristan's car!"

"If Tristan knows who did it, he might be able to press charges for vandalism. Have him come to me and I'll help him get in touch with the local police department. They'll do an investigation, but I'm afraid that without proof, they may not be able to do much about it."

"No. Tristan won't press charges." I sigh. "He doesn't even know I'm here."

He regards me sympathetically. "Here's what I'll do: I'll write it up and put it in my file. That way, if Tristan or his family wants to press charges, there's at least some evidence that it happened on school grounds. Unfortunately, there's not much else I can do unless Tristan comes forward himself."

"What about in the future? What if whoever it was decides the tires weren't enough?"

"I'll keep an eye on him."

"With what? Your stupid cameras?"

"Cut me some slack, Taylor. If the school has no money, it has no money. I do the best I can with what I've got to work with. I'm only one security guard in a school full of students, and I can't be everywhere at once. That being said, if you see anything or hear anything, let me know. I don't want to see anyone get hurt any more than you do."

I sigh. I know I shouldn't direct my anger at him. I just hate this feeling of helplessness all the time.

He must see the worry on my face, because he says, "It'll be okay, Taylor."

That's the first lie he's told me.

My Honda is already in the parking lot when I get out of practice. Tristan's leaning against the trunk, looking down at his shoes. He's always looking at his shoes, though, so I can't tell from a distance what kind of mood he's in. "Hey," I say as I come to a stop in front of him.

He doesn't look up. "Did you tell Officer Gálvez about my car?"

"Yes, I did."

"Why?"

"Because I knew you wouldn't."

"If you knew I wouldn't want you to, then why did you do it?"

"Because I think you're wrong. If you don't speak up about this, it's only going to get worse."

"How can it possibly get worse?" He lifts his head and glares at me.

"They could take a knife to you instead of your tires," I say.

"And you think Officer Gálvez is gonna stop that from happening?"

"Yes, if you told him who's been bullying you."

"I've always been bullied, Taylor!" he shouts. "Ever since I was a kid, I've been kicked around and called names. And you know what I've learned from all that? Nobody gives a shit! They just watch it happen. Nobody cares what happens to me. I could disappear tomorrow and nobody would even notice."

"How can you say that? I just gave you *my keys* to *my car* so you wouldn't have to ride the bus! I bring you your homework, I skip baseball practice to hang out with you, I call a fucking tow truck to tow your car home. Don't say nobody cares, because that's bullshit and you know it!"

After a few seconds of stunned silence, he hangs his head. "You're right," he mumbles. "I'm sorry. I guess I'm just not used to this 'friend' thing."

I feel a stab of pity for him. I've never had trouble making friends, so I'd always taken it for granted that what I do matters to people. It must be hard living on the other side of the social spectrum.

"It's okay," I say. "Come on, let's go get something to eat. I'm starving."

13

Saturday is finally here, and I'm so glad I can put this shit week behind me. My fencing practice this morning went way better than I expected, and the ground is dry enough that our baseball game is still on as planned. I pull into the parking lot at school and my spirits rise even higher when I see Ashley's Toyota. Hopefully, she'll be free after the game to spend some quality time with me. I feel like we've been out of sync lately, and I want to get back to the way things were, before my life became exceedingly complicated.

I seek her out before the game. She's waiting for me in the stands with Drake's girlfriend of the week, Kima. I give Ashley a peck on the lips and say, "Hey, baby. Thanks for coming."

"Of course I came! I wouldn't want to miss a performance by my future Major Leagues star."

"Don't get your hopes up. I haven't been drafted yet."

"No, but it looks like your chances just went up. Look." She points toward a group of six men lined up along the backstop. All of them are holding clipboards and radar guns. *Scouts.*

"Oh my God!" I say.

"'Oh my God' is right!" she says. "This is so exciting! I can't believe I'm dating a celebrity."

My nerves immediately go on edge. After the fiasco of missing practice, I thought the scouts would have given up on me. Now it's like I've been shoved under a microscope. If I don't do well today, they might just write me off as a fluke and I'll never hear from them again. On the one hand, it might be a relief to not have to worry about crowds and cameras and reporters. But on the other? How would I explain to my dad that I couldn't hack it?

"Alright. Here I go. Wish me luck."

"Good luck! Don't screw up!" she calls after me as I walk toward the field.

Not helping, Ashley.

Coach Barnes greets me as I approach. "Taylor. I suppose you noticed those scouts over there."

"Yes, sir."

"Well, they came to see you, so I expect you to play your hardest today. Some of them came a long way. Let's make it worth their while, huh?"

"Yes, sir."

"That's my boy." He claps me on the shoulder, then walks toward the group of scouts, presumably to butter them up. As I nervously watch him go, Drake appears by my side.

"I see you've got a fan club over there," he says, smiling.

"What am I gonna do, Drake?" I moan.

His eyes widen. "You're gonna do what you always do. You're gonna go up on that mound and you're gonna kick some serious ass."

"How can I kick ass with a bunch of scouts breathing down my neck?"

"Don't worry about the scouts. The scouts don't matter. All that matters is that you get up there and you show those Fairview clowns that they ain't got nothin' on the Springfield Cardinals."

I smile. Drake always says the right thing to put things into perspective.

"You're right," I say. "Let's go show those pansies who they're dealing with."

Miraculously, I don't embarrass myself too badly. The scouts seem impressed enough because after the game, they thrust a bunch of questionnaires and business cards into my hand. I plaster a fake smile on my face as I shake hands and exchange pleasantries with all of them, wishing the whole time that I were anywhere else but here. After I've said goodbye for the sixth time, I shove the cards and papers into my pockets and make my way over to Ashley. She wraps her arms around my neck and kisses me soundly. "You were amazing!" she says. "There's no way you won't get drafted."

"Yeah," I mumble.

Her brow creases. "What's wrong?"

I sigh. "I don't know. I guess I'm just not sure if this is what I want, you know?"

She loosens her hold on my neck. "Avery, how can you not want this? I thought this was your dream, to play baseball."

"I mean, yeah, it'd be nice to get paid to play, but . . ."

"But what?" She's giving me that look again—the one that clearly says I've lost it.

"Never mind." I pull her tighter against me and press my lips to her forehead. I breathe in the sweet coconut scent of her hair. She always smells so good.

"Let's get out of here, huh?" I murmur. "We can drive around, get lost . . . What do you say?"

Her lips curve into a sexy smile. She stands on her tiptoes and presses herself against all the right spots.

"I say that sounds perfect."

An afternoon with Ashley is a much-needed diversion, but even the best things in life aren't enough to delay the inevitable. After I drop her off, I go home and pull out the questionnaires and business cards from my pockets and line them up one by one on the dining room table. The questionnaires are along the same lines as the one I filled out before, only each of these is imprinted with the logo of a different team.

My dad struts in and peers over my shoulder. "More scouts?" he asks eagerly.

"Yeah," I reply, with much less enthusiasm.

He gives me a critical look. "You don't seem very excited."

I sigh. "I dunno, Dad. Are you sure this is what you want me to do? I mean, you've always said I should go to college, and—"

"And you should go to college. But college can wait a few years, after you've had some time on the field and earned a salary that can help pay for it."

"What if I don't want to play baseball?"

By the look he gives me, I may as well have said I wanted to be a ballerina.

"What do you mean, you 'don't want to play baseball'? You were *born* to play baseball."

"Dad, I—"

"Avery, you have a gift! A gift that can take you places that most people can only dream about! And here you are, talking about throwing all that away." He shakes his head in disappointment.

"I'm not throwing it away, Dad! I just mean I'm not sure what I want to do right now, okay?"

He points a finger at me. "Now listen to me. This is a once-in-a-lifetime opportunity, and I'm not going to watch my only son squander away his future because he's 'not sure.' You better think long and hard before you tell me that there's something better out there besides baseball."

He stalks out of the room. I sigh heavily.

Well, that went well.

14

This is hopeless.

I shut my history textbook and rub my eyes, feeling nervous and stressed out. I've finally finished writing up my speech for tomorrow, but I don't know why I even bothered. I won't be able to deliver it anyway. *I need a break.*

I look up at Tristan, who's sitting on the other end of his bed with his laptop on his lap. He chews on his lower lip as he concentrates on the computer screen.

"What are you looking at?" I ask.

"Hmm? Oh, I was just looking up this university that my dad wants me to go to."

"Really? Which one?"

"Cornell."

"Cornell? Isn't that an Ivy League school?"

"Yeah. He wanted me to go to Harvard like he did, but I told him he could go fuck himself. There's no way I'm going to that stuck-up, elitist institution. Cornell doesn't look much different, but at least it's not Harvard."

"Did you get accepted to Cornell?" I ask, surprised.

"Yeah," he says dismissively.

"Tristan."

He looks up at me.

I hold out my palms in disbelief. "You got accepted to an *Ivy League school*. Aren't you at least a little excited?"

He sighs. "I don't know. My dad's really excited about it, which is a red flag right there. Usually the things he wants are the exact opposite of the things I want."

"Well, where do you want to go?"

"Honestly, I have no idea. My dad made me apply to a bunch of places, but I don't know if I even want to go to college. It's probably just going to be more of the same bullshit as high school, only more expensive."

"I think you should go. Maybe not to Cornell, but I think you should go somewhere. Most places require a college degree in order to get a job."

"I don't know what degree I would get."

"I still think you should look into teaching. You're really good at it."

"Yes, because that's my dream. To stay in high school forever."

"You don't have to teach high school. You could teach elementary school, or college. Or you could teach piano professionally. Charge people for lessons."

He stares pensively at the computer screen. After a moment, he looks up again and asks, "What college are you going to?"

"Umm . . . I may not go to college," I admit with embarrassment.

"What the hell? You were just getting on my case about not going to college, and now you're saying you're not going?"

"I just said I *might* not go. People seem to think I have a good shot at being drafted."

"Drafted? Drafted for what?"

"For the Major Leagues, what else?"

His eyebrows rise. "Are you serious?"

"Yeah."

"Wow. I didn't realize you were that good."

"Yeah, I guess so. My dad likes to tell people that I could throw a curveball before I could walk."

"Huh. Is that what you want to do?"

"I still don't know. My dad's pressuring me to. He nearly blew a gasket last night when I told him I wasn't sure if I was destined to be the next Babe Ruth. But even if I wanted to play ball, I should probably choose a college in case it doesn't work out. I just don't know which one I should pick."

"Did you apply to any?"

"Yeah. I got accepted to USC, Middleton, and Arizona State. They all offered me athletic scholarships, but I don't know which one would be best. If I knew what degree I'd want, I could probably choose based on the classes they offer, but I'm just not sure what I want to do."

"Well, what are you interested in?"

"I don't know. That's the problem. The only thing I'm good at is sports."

"That's not true. You're good with people. You said yourself that you liked the idea of helping people. Why not be a police officer or something?"

"Hmm, I don't know if I'm cut out for that. When it came down to it, I don't think I could shoot somebody."

"Yeah, I guess there is that risk. What about a doctor?"

I shake my head. "My mom's a nurse, so I know how hard it is working crazy hours and dealing with victims of drunk driving and stuff like that. I don't know if I could deal with that every day."

"Well, you don't have to work in the ER to be a doctor. There are other kinds of doctors. Like dentists."

"Eww, and deal with people's nasty-ass teeth? No, thanks."

He laughs. "You could be a psychiatrist. Or a psychologist. They're doctors, but they don't deal with blood and guts. All you have to do is listen to people talk for an hour and then you write them a prescription for some ADD meds and you get paid beaucoup bucks for it."

I grin. "That sounds easy enough."

"I'm oversimplifying, of course. I think you could do it, though. You're good at listening."

"So what's the difference between a psychiatrist and a psychologist?"

"Psychiatrists are medical doctors that can prescribe drugs. Psychologists have doctoral degrees, but they're not medical doctors so they can't issue the drugs themselves; they have to refer you to a psychiatrist for that. But they provide counseling to people who have mental illnesses or other issues."

"How do you know all this? I swear, you're like a walking encyclopedia."

He smiles. "I may not talk much, but that doesn't mean I don't listen."

"Maybe *you* should be a psychologist, then."

"I have enough issues of my own to deal with than to listen to other people's problems."

"You listen to my problems," I protest.

"Yes, because your problems are *so challenging*. Let's see, should I get paid a ton of money to do something I love? No, I think I'd rather deal with other people's shit for a living."

I smirk. "Well, when you put it like that . . ."

He grins back.

I hesitate, then ask, "Do you really think I should go pro? Is it really that obvious and I'm just overthinking things?"

His face turns serious as he replies, "It's up to you, Taylor. You're the only one who can make that decision. Not me, not your dad, not anybody. Just you. You should do what makes *you* happy, because it's your life and you're the one who has to live it."

"What if I don't know what will make me happy?"

"Well, then I guess you're out of luck. You'll just be miserable the rest of your days."

"That's uplifting."

"I'm just kidding. It's not like it's the end of the world if you don't know what you want to do the second you graduate from high school. Most people go through a few jobs before they find their calling—or, if not their calling, at least a job that pays the bills without making them want to blow their brains out every day."

"I guess that's true. Of course, that's assuming I'll even graduate. At this rate, *I'll* be the one who's stuck in high school forever."

"What d'you mean? I thought you were doing better in calculus."

"It's not calculus I'm worried about. I have this presentation tomorrow for history and I'm pretty sure I'm going to bomb it."

"Why do you think you're going to bomb it?"

"Because I have horrible stage fright. I get up in front of a crowd and my body basically shuts down. Did you know that most people are more afraid of public speaking than they are of death?"

"Well, that's understandable. Between the two, death is definitely the lesser of two evils."

I glower at him. "Thank you, Tristan. That helps a lot."

"Any time," he replies, smiling. Then he says, "Why don't you practice? Pretend I'm the class and you're giving your presentation to me."

I study him for a minute, then give in. "Okay."

He closes his laptop and sets it on the bed beside him.

I look at my notes and start reading aloud. "In 1917, Joseph Stalin—"

"Not like that. You have to practice like it's the real thing." He points toward the wall across from him. "Go stand at the front of the class."

"Oh, are you my history teacher now, too?" I tease as I slide off his bed and saunter across the room.

"Yes," he declares. "I'm a man of many talents."

"Is one of those talents the ability to fast-forward through time so my presentation is already behind me?"

He sighs. "Unfortunately, time travel is beyond my abilities."

"Damn."

I stare down at my notes. My hand is already trembling. If I'm this nervous in front of one person I trust, how am I supposed to keep my cool in front of a whole classroom full of people who would love to see me make a jackass out of myself?

"I don't know if I can do this. I just know that when I get up there, I'm going to freeze up and look like a friggin' idiot."

"You need to calm down. Try to relax." As an afterthought, he says, "They say if you picture the audience naked, you won't feel so anxious."

I look up at him and raise an eyebrow. "You're saying I should picture you naked?" *He walked into that one.*

His face turns a brilliant shade of pink. "W-what? N-no! That's not . . ."

I can't help but laugh at his obvious discomfort. "Dude, I'm just messin' with you!"

His cheeks still flushed, he grumbles, "Fuck you, Taylor."

I laugh again.

"Ohh-kay. Back to business," I say as I turn my attention back to my notes. My hand isn't shaking anymore.

I read through my lines, trying to keep my voice from quavering. Even though it's just him observing me, I'm still unnerved by the feeling of eyes upon me as I read through my presentation. I feel like my whole worth is being judged based on how many *umm*s and *ahh*s spill out of my mouth. Tristan is the perfect listener, though—he doesn't laugh or fidget, and he gives me his full attention. I know I won't be so lucky to have a room full of people like him tomorrow.

After what feels like an eternity, I finally get to the end of my speech. I exhale and look up from my notes nervously.

"Is that it?" he asks.

"Yeah."

"I thought it'd be longer."

"Seriously? That was like pulling teeth out."

"You were only up there for five minutes."

"Yeah. Five minutes of torture."

"You didn't do too bad. You hesitated a lot, but that will go away when you become more confident."

"I don't think that's ever going to happen."

"Sure, it will. It'll get easier with time."

"I don't have time. My presentation is tomorrow. If I'm this nervous in front of you, I'm going to be a train wreck tomorrow when I have to do it for real. I can't just pretend to be sick that day, either, because it's a major part of my grade. What am I going to do?"

"You'll just have to learn how to face your fears."

"Face my fears," I mutter as I walk back over to the bed. I sit down next to him and lean back against the wall. He shifts his body around so he's facing me. "Have you ever had to face any of your fears?" I ask.

He shrugs. "Sure. Everybody does, at some point. Well, maybe not *all* their fears. You don't really come across axe murderers every day."

Curious, I ask, "What are you afraid of?"

"Umm . . . ," he hums as he thinks. "I'm afraid of spiders, which, I'm sorry to say, I've had to face many times. And I'm afraid of water, which—"

"Wait. I'm sorry, did you just say you're afraid of *water*?"

"Yeah."

"You mean like the ocean? Like sharks and barracudas and stuff?"

"Well, yeah, I guess those, too."

I shake my head, not understanding how someone could possibly be afraid of water. Confused, I ask, "So how do you get clean?"

He rolls his eyes. "Jesus, Taylor, you're too literal. I'm not afraid of the *shower*. It's just that I can't swim, so—"

"What do you mean, you 'can't swim'?"

"I mean I can't swim."

"Didn't your parents take you to the pool or beach when you were little?"

"Sure, they did. I just never went in past my knees."

I shake my head in disbelief. "God, no wonder you drowned!

The Lifesaver

You can't go through life not knowing how to swim! It's an essential survival skill."

"Well, I'm probably too old to learn now."

"Don't be ridiculous. You're teaching me the piano. I'll teach you to swim. Quid pro quo."

"Oh yeah? Where are you going to teach me? I don't really want other people to see me flail around in the water like a four-year-old."

I think for a moment. "I've got connections at the community center. I bet I can get us in there before they open to the public."

He considers me for a few seconds, then shrugs. "Okay. Let's do it."

The next morning, I pick Tristan up from his house and drive him over to the community center before school. We arrive an hour and a half before they open, which should give us plenty of time to cover the basics before the first customers arrive. I ring the buzzer and Jeremy, the manager, lets us in. He was my boss back when I was a lifeguard here, and we hit it off immediately. When I dropped by and asked if we could use the pool in the mornings for private lessons, he didn't even bat an eye. All he said was, "Just don't pee in it, okay?"

Tristan's never been here before, so I give him a short tour. The facility isn't very big, but it has an Olympic-sized pool and a decent racquetball court. I hold the door to the locker room open for him. He looks nervous.

I throw my bag onto the bench in the center row of lockers. "We don't have to lock this stuff up. Jeremy's the only one here besides us, and he won't steal our stuff. He's probably asleep in his office anyway."

Tristan nods and disappears into the next row over. I guess I shouldn't be surprised that he's too shy to change in front of other people.

As I'm stuffing my shirt into my bag, Tristan reappears in front of me in his swim trunks. On his chest, there's a small drawing of what looks to be a shield near his heart. The shield is divided into red and white quadrants, with a star down the middle. I stop fiddling with my bag to gape at him.

"You have a tattoo?" I exclaim.

He looks down at his chest. "Uh, yeah. Why?"

"I dunno. You just don't seem the type, that's all."

He blushes a little. "I got it when I left my mom's house to go live with my dad. It's my dad's family crest."

"Huh. Well, that's . . . pretty awesome."

His cheeks turn redder. I resume shoving clothes into my bag.

He changes the subject. "So how are we going to do this?"

"What do you mean?"

"Are you going to make me wear those stupid floatie things on my arms?"

I try to look as serious as possible as I reply, "That was the plan, yeah. Is there a problem?"

His mouth drops open. "Are you fucking kidding me?"

I can't help but laugh. "*Yes*, I'm kidding you! Although that would make an excellent yearbook photo, don't you think?"

"Shut up," he mutters.

We head out to the pool area and I grab the lifesaver and a couple of pool noodles from the supply cabinet. I wave a pool noodle at him and wink. "Floaties," I explain.

He chuckles and shakes his head.

I hop into the shallow end and beckon for him to follow. Instead of just jumping in, he sits down on the edge of the pool and slowly eases himself into the water. He looks apprehensive, like he's expecting a shark to grab his leg and pull him under. I roll my eyes. "Tristan, would you relax? I'm not going to let anything happen to you. I promise."

He nods and wades over to where I'm standing in the middle of the pool.

I smile. "Good." I push the lifesaver toward him. "Here, lay across this and push off the ground with your feet."

He does what I ask. I move over to his side, intending to hold him afloat, but then I stop short. White lines are crisscrossed all across his back. *Scars.*

"What happened to your back?" I blurt out.

He immediately stands up and backs away a couple of steps. He wraps his arms around himself and stands there silently. I stare at him, but he won't meet my eyes; he just looks down into the water.

"Hey," I murmur. "I'm sorry. I didn't mean to make you feel uncomfortable. You don't have to tell me if you don't want to."

"No, it's . . . it's okay," he says. "Remember how I said that I used to live with my mom?"

I nod.

"Well, she ended up marrying this *asshole* who didn't think I acted like a boy should. He punished me. A lot. Said he would *make a man out of me.*"

He looks up as he spits out the last few words. I'm startled to see that his pale blue eyes are full of seething hatred. The sudden realization hits me that this is the reason he cowered when I tried to goad him into taking a swing at me. I feel disgusted with myself. This is not how I wanted our first swim lesson to go at all.

I gulp. "So what happened to him?" I ask, almost afraid to hear the answer.

He tosses his hair out of his eyes. "Child Protective Services found out and they sent me to live with my real dad. The police sent *him* to jail. Good riddance."

"What about your mom?"

He barks a sharp, derisive laugh. "She was able to convince Protective Services and the police that she didn't know anything about it. But she knew. How could she not? But she let him do it anyway." He looks back down at the water. "I guess she just loved him more than she loved me."

"Jesus. I'm really sorry." I don't know what else to say.

He shakes his head. "It doesn't matter."

"It does matter," I argue. "It matters to me."

He straightens his body and looks at me again. I'm relieved to see that his eyes are calmer now.

I clear my throat. "So. I think we've dealt with enough heavy shit for one day. Now grab the floatie."

15

I park behind the school, but I don't make a move to get out. My presentation is first period and the sooner I get out of the car, the sooner my execution begins. I drum my fingers on the steering wheel, trying to ignore the butterflies while I rehearse my speech in my head.

Tristan takes off his seat belt and looks over at me. "Everything okay over there?" he asks.

"Yeah. Well, no, not really. I feel like I'm about to walk the plank."

"Don't worry. You've got this." Last night, he insisted that I practice over and over until I knew all the words by heart.

I exhale heavily. "Alright. Let's go."

We get out of the car and walk into the school. Before we go our separate ways, he says, "Tell me how it goes, alright?"

"Yeah. See you on the other side."

He smiles and turns down the hall to the left. I make my way down the right hall toward my locker. Ashley's already there, waiting for me.

"Hey." My voice sounds thin.

"Hey," she says. "You okay?"

"Yeah, I'm just freaking out a little. I have to give a speech this morning."

"Oh. Stage fright again?"

"Yeah."

"Hmm. Well, just pretend that everybody's naked."

I laugh loudly, remembering Tristan's facial expression from last night.

She smiles. "Are you doing anything after practice tonight?"

"I've got my piano lesson, but after that, nada."

At the mention of piano lessons, she purses her lips. To head off another fight, I say, "Do you want to go out for pizza after?"

"Will Tristan be joining us?"

I'm not stupid enough to even entertain that thought. "Nope. Just you and me, baby."

Her sunny smile returns. "Well, in that case, pizza sounds great."

"Okay. I'll text you when I'm on my way."

"Okay." She looks at her phone. "Ugh, I'm going to be late. You better get a move on."

Crap. I slam my locker shut, give her a quick peck on the lips, and rush to my classroom.

The presentations take up the entire class period. I was hoping Ms. Higgins would go in reverse alphabetical order this time so I could get it over with, but no such luck. I feel my blood pressure skyrocket every time someone sits back down after giving his or her speech because I know that at any second, my name could be called. I find it difficult to pay attention to what each person is saying because I'm so anxious about my own presentation. *Maybe they won't pay any attention to me, either.*

"Avery Taylor," Ms. Higgins calls.

My palms start to sweat as I walk up to the front of the class. I open my notebook to the page where I wrote down my speech, and I do a double take. In red ink, there's a note scrawled at the top of the page that wasn't there before:

You'll do fine. Good luck!
—T

How did he . . . ? I try to think back to when he might have taken my notebook without me seeing. He must have grabbed it when I was showering off after our swim lesson. I feel a sudden surge of affection for him. While trying to contain a smile, I begin my speech.

After practice, I head over to the parking lot. Tristan's already there, leaning against the trunk of my car with his hands in his pockets. I stroll up and lean against the trunk next to him.

He looks at me expectantly, but I don't say anything. I keep my eyes forward and try my best to maintain a neutral expression.

"So?" he asks.

"So what?"

"How'd it go?"

I shrug. It's so easy to torment him.

"Well, what'd you get?"

"B-plus," I reply, as if it were no big thing. Truthfully, though, without Tristan's help and the extra boost of confidence his note gave me, I probably would have failed.

"*B-plus?*" he exclaims.

I nod.

"Fuckin' A!"

My face breaks out into a huge smile as he gives me a high-five. "Thanks for your help, man. I totally would have bombed it if not for you."

He tosses his hair out of his eyes, but his cheeks turn pink. "Whatever. Let's get out of here."

"So what the hell are the foot pedals for?" I finally ask.

"Oh," says Tristan, "don't worry about those just yet. They're for more *advanced* students."

"Are you saying I'm too slow to figure out how to use a pedal? I'll have you know that I've been driving go-karts since I was five. I'm pretty sure I know how to use one."

"You want to use the pedals? Fine. Go ahead, step on one. See what happens."

He crosses his arms and smirks at me. I regard him suspiciously. I feel like this is a trick.

"The piano won't move, will it?"

"I don't know. You figure it out, since you're so smart."

"Okay, jackass. I will."

I examine the three brass pedals. *Which one should I start with?* I decide to go for the right one, since that's the closest to a gas pedal. Tristan shifts to the right to give me more room. Slowly, I ease my foot down onto the pedal. Nothing happens.

"Well, that was exciting," Tristan says.

I ignore him and try the other two pedals. Still nothing.

Okay, then. What happens if I press a key?

I hold down the left pedal and press middle C. It sounds muted somehow. I lift the pedal and press the key again. The volume goes up. *Huh.*

I move to the next pedal and press C again. It doesn't sound muted this time; in fact, it doesn't sound different at all.

I glance over at Tristan. He's watching me with a curious half-smile on his face. I feel like he's silently encouraging me to figure it out, like a puzzle. My pride wouldn't let me ask him for help anyway, since I acted so cocky before.

I try it the opposite way: I hold the key down, then step on the pedal. Still no difference. *Is it broken?* I wonder.

I decide to come back to it later. I move to the right pedal and try the key again. Like the center pedal, it doesn't make a noticeable difference. It doesn't seem likely that two pedals would be broken, especially considering how expensive the piano is. I must be missing something.

Determined now, I step on the right pedal. I hold down C and listen carefully. As the note starts to fade, I raise my finger and I'm surprised to find that the note continues to play even after I release the key. I hit C and quickly let go. The note hangs in the air. Out of the corner of my eye, I see Tristan smile. *Ha!*

I go back to the center pedal and tap C. The note stops as soon as I take my finger off the key. I guess I shouldn't be surprised that it doesn't act the same way as the right pedal—what would be the point?—but it's still frustrating that I can't figure out what the center pedal is for.

In a soft voice, barely more than a whisper, Tristan says, "Try pressing the key first."

I take his advice and press C, then step on the pedal. I release the key and the note continues to play. I look up at him and grin triumphantly.

"So what does each pedal do?" he asks.

"The left one makes it quieter, the right one holds the note, and the middle one holds the note after you press it."

He beams. "Good job!"

"So what's the point of the middle pedal?"

"Honestly, you hardly ever use it. Only a handful of composers include it in their songs. It's designed to hold some notes but not others. Here, listen."

I swivel my legs out of the way so he can reach the center pedal. He reaches across me and holds down a chord on my side of the keyboard, then moves his hands to his side and plays a few short notes. The low chord he played continues to sound as background accompaniment to the quick high notes.

Inspiration hits me. I have to be careful in how I execute my plan, though. "Ooh, let me try." I scoot toward the middle of the bench.

"Okay." He slides to the right to give me room.

I scoot just a fraction more and try to take up as much space as I can on the bench without making him suspicious. I hit a chord on the left, then lean to the right and crowd into his personal space while trying to make it seem unintentional. He scoots farther away from me to give me more room. Still in instructor mode, he says, "See? It's a cool effect, but you don't usually need it. The only pedal I use frequently is the right one."

I smile inwardly. "The right one, huh? Okay, I'll try that one."

I scoot farther to the right. He's balanced precariously on the edge of the bench now. I step on the pedal, then lean forcefully into Tristan's side as I move my hands to the rightmost keys. He lets out a strangled yelp as he falls off the side of the bench. I bust out laughing.

"Oh my God, you should have seen your face!" I wheeze.

His cheeks are flushed with embarrassment. "Asshole," he grumbles as he climbs back onto the bench.

"Come on. You have to admit, that was a little funny."

Reluctantly, he admits, "Yeah, it was a little funny." Then he says, "Though not as funny as this." Before I can react, he shoves my shoulder. I wave wildly to catch my balance, but it's not enough to stop my momentum. I fall to the floor with a thump. He leans over the side of the bench and smiles wickedly down at me. "Yeah, how does it feel now, bitch?"

"What the hell? *Now* you push me? I *begged* you to push me the other day and you wouldn't."

"You were expecting it then," he says with a cheeky grin.

"You're a sneaky little bastard, aren't you? I'm gonna have to keep my eye on you."

He reaches a hand down to help me up. I go to sit back down on the bench, but then I notice a big scratch on the finish. I look down at my pants. My keys are dangling from my belt loop—they must have scratched the bench when I slid off.

"Holy shit!" I say as I rub my finger over the scratch.

Tristan's eyebrows shoot up. "What is that from?"

"I think it was my keys. I'm sorry, I didn't even think about them."

"What are you sorry for? *I* pushed *you*."

"Yeah, but I was asking for it. I should have taken off my keys before I sat down. Now I feel like a douchebag. Is there something I can do to fix it?"

"Don't worry about it."

"Won't you get in trouble, though?"

"I doubt it. I'm the only one who plays the piano, so I doubt my parents would even notice. But even if they did, I wouldn't care. Their furniture could use some breaking in. Make it look like someone actually uses it."

Perplexed, I sit back down next to him. "How did you turn out this way? It's like you're the exact opposite of your parents."

He shrugs. "How do any of us turn out the way we do?"

"Yeah, but you have their genes and you were brought up by them.

You'd think you'd have something in common with them."

"I didn't come to live with my dad until last year. I guess I have more in common with my mom."

"Oh, really? Like what?"

"Well, she likes music, for one. She's the one who started me on piano lessons, though she may have done that so somebody else would look after me for an hour. Being around kids wasn't her strong suit. Or other people, for that matter. I think that's one of the main reasons my mom and dad broke up."

"Why do you say that?"

"Dad wanted a wife who could be the perfect hostess and help him schmooze with the bigwigs at his campaign functions, but she couldn't do it. She hated small talk, and she knew they were all liars and crooks anyway. She saw through all their bullshit and called them out on it. She and my dad always got into fights whenever they went to parties together. Eventually, my dad left her and she got even worse. She didn't trust anybody, until *Dale* came along. I don't know what he said or did to convince her that he was a good guy, but it was all downhill for me after he moved in. I guess she saved her trust for the wrong person."

"Do you still talk to her?"

"No. She's never called me, and I've never called her. We're better off that way."

"Maybe you should call her. She's still your family."

"No, she's not. We may have the same blood, but that doesn't mean we're family. Not anymore, at least."

I give him a half-smile. "I'm guessing you got your stubbornness from her too, huh?"

He grins sheepishly. "Yeah, I guess so." Then he nods at me and says, "You take after your mom, too."

"How do you know that?"

"I met her, remember?"

"You saw her for like ten seconds!"

"Yeah, but I could tell. She has your smile. Or you have hers, I should say. And the way she talks, she sounds like you."

"I hope that's a good thing."

"It is."

The grandfather clock chimes six behind us.

"I should get going," I say. "I promised Ashley I'd take her out for pizza tonight."

"Oh, okay." Then he adds, with a sardonic smile, "Tell her I said 'hi.'"

I laugh. "I will."

Ashley's sitting on her driveway watching her brother, Alex, play with sidewalk chalk when I pull up in front of her house. I roll down my window and catcall. "Lookin' for a ride, sweet thing?"

She grins at me, then picks Alex up underneath his arms and carries him to the front door. He struggles and whines, but she ignores him. She deposits him in the foyer and orders, "Go find Mom." She closes the door in his scowling face, then jogs to my car and hops in the passenger seat.

She kisses me and says, "Hey, you."

"Heya back." I smile at her as I put the car in drive.

"How'd your speech go today?" she asks.

I shrug. "It could've been worse."

"That's good, I guess. At least you got it over with."

"Yeah. I feel like I can finally relax again."

"How was your lesson?"

The question is innocent enough, but there's an undercurrent in her voice that sets off alarm bells in my head. I try to sound cheerful as I reply, "It was fine. Tristan says 'hi,' by the way."

"Ugh. He's such a jerk."

"How is he a jerk? He was being nice!"

"No, he wasn't, and you know it."

I sigh. "Let's not talk about Tristan anymore, okay?"

She looks like she's about to argue, but she says, "Okay." After a brooding pause, her face brightens. "So guess what! My parents put in the deposit for NYU. It's official!"

"Really? That's awesome." Although I'm happy for her, I feel a twinge of envy. Both of her parents attended New York University, so there was never any question in Ashley's mind where she wanted to go. That's one of the traits I admire most about her: she always knows exactly who she is and what she wants. I wish I were that sure of myself. Maybe I should just put my options on a dartboard, close my eyes, and let chance take me where it wants me to go.

We pull up outside Tony's Pizza. I get out of my car and open Ashley's door for her. She shoots me a dazzling smile as she steps out. "Well, thank you, kind sir."

I give her a chivalrous bow. "My lady."

She grabs my hand and we walk inside. Tony's is a hole-in-the-wall pizza joint that's run by (you guessed it) a guy named Tony. He's the first generation from an immigrant family from Sicily, so the pizza is as close to authentic as you can get. The whole restaurant is a medley of reds, but instead of being garish, it gives it a cozy feel. There are only a few tables and a handful of stools at the bar, but there's a carry-out counter for people who are too impatient to wait for a table. Lucky for us, a booth opens up right as we walk in.

The waiter appears and we order a couple of Cokes and a large pepperoni pizza. Like most guys, he lets his eyes linger on Ashley a little too long. After he walks away, Ashley clears her throat and looks down at the table. "You know, we haven't really talked about what's going to happen after we graduate."

Uh-oh. I'm not sure if I'm ready for this conversation yet. I've been avoiding thinking about what's going to happen to our relationship when Ashley packs her bags for the Big Apple and I end up God-knows-where. Although I enjoy being with her, I can't really see us continuing a long-distance relationship, especially considering all the male attention she receives. It's not that I don't trust Ashley, because I do. I just don't want to be "that guy"—the loser boyfriend who holds her back from having fun and enjoying the full college experience.

"Do we have to talk about it now?" I ask.

She bites her lip. "We're going to have to talk about it eventually."

"You won't be going off to college until August. That's four months away. I don't think we need to make any decisions today. Why don't we just take our time and see where we stand at the end of the summer?"

She ponders my suggestion for a few seconds, then nods. "Okay."

I reach across the table to hold her hand. "Have you picked out your prom dress yet?" I know that any mention of prom will lift her spirits.

As if on cue, her eyes light up and she starts chattering excitedly about dresses and shoes and getting her hair done. I smile at her, glad that I can make her happy, at least for the time being.

16

I can't believe it's been a whole month since the incident under the bridge. Even though the sun is setting later, it feels like each day is shorter than the last as the end of the school year approaches. It's probably due to the fact that my schedule is even busier than before, what with swim lessons, school, baseball practice, fencing practice, piano lessons, homework, and now regular interviews with scouts. Not to mention squeezing in time for my girlfriend. There are seriously not enough hours in the day.

    I shouldn't complain too much, though. My grades have improved now that Tristan is helping me with my schoolwork, and the morning swim sessions help keep me in shape. You'd think that getting up so early every day would kill me, but actually, I don't mind it. Part of it may be that I've been sleeping better recently, but mostly it's because teaching Tristan how to swim makes me feel like I'm actually accomplishing something worthwhile. Plus, it's fun hanging out and listening to him talk. It's amazing that someone who spends his days not speaking could have so much to say. It's as if throughout

The Lifesaver

his life, he saved up all his words and he's just now getting around to spending them. Sometimes, we'll get so caught up in a deep philosophical discussion about whether we're alone in the universe or why armadillos exist that I have to remind myself that we're on a schedule and we can't just sit around and bullshit all day, even though I may want to.

I still drive him to school, even though he replaced his tires a while back. It didn't take much to convince him to leave his car at home to keep it out of the line of fire. He'd never admit it, but I think he cares about it more than he lets on because it was a gift from his dad. The only times he drives it to school now are the days when he has his own piano lesson, but those are few and far between. On those days, he parks behind the church across the street from the school and walks over. So far, nobody has messed with his vehicle, and I'm hoping it stays that way.

The evenings are the worst part of my day. When I get home after my piano lesson or dinner with Ashley, there's almost always another home visit with a scout for which I have to dress up in my own house and pretend like there's nothing in this great wide world I'd rather do than play for whatever team they're representing. Most of the time I pull it off, but sometimes my dad will give me a piercing look and I know that I'm not conveying the proper enthusiasm. I guess I can cross *actor* off my list of potential career goals.

The one day a week when I can stop and breathe is Sunday. That's the day when I have no practice, no interviews, and no obligations. Well, almost none. I decided to throw on my Sunday best and meet my parents at the church this morning for the eleven o'clock service. It had been a while since I'd gone, and I was starting to feel like a bad son.

Throughout the service, I sit quietly and try not to doze off while the pastor talks about the sanctity of marriage and the family unit. I don't feel like any of it applies to me—I still have several years before I have to worry about all that.

A loud chirp emanates from my pocket. The people in the row in front of me turn and shoot daggers out of their eyes as I pull my phone out and fumble with the mute button. Sheepishly, I mouth the word "sorry" to them, then read the screen. It's a text from Tristan.

I'm bored. You want to grab lunch?

OK. Give me 30.

After the service is over, I jump out of my seat and turn to my mom. "I gotta go. I'll see you later."

"Where are you off to in such a hurry?" she asks.

"I'm going to lunch with Tristan."

"No, you're going to spend time with your mother and me," my father says. "It's Sunday. You should be with family."

"Oh, let him go spend time with his friends," she says. "He doesn't want to hang around a couple of old farts like us."

Before my dad can argue, I kiss her cheek and say, "Thanks, Mom. I'll be home for dinner."

"Okay, sweetie."

My father juts his chin and glares at us, but he doesn't say anything more. I squeeze my way past the churchgoers standing in the entrance, then hop in my car and drive over to Tristan's house.

When Tristan opens the door, he looks me up and down and a big smirk stretches across his face. He crosses his arms and leans against the doorframe. "Well, this is a surprise! If I'd known we were going on a date, I'd have worn my pearls."

I look down at my clothes and laugh. "You did say you wanted to go to lunch together."

"True. But don't think for a minute that you're getting past first base without bringing me some fucking flowers first."

I roar with laughter. He grins as he steps out onto the porch and closes the door behind him.

"I just got out of church," I explain as we walk back to my car.

"Which church do you go to?"

"First Baptist."

"Huh. That's the one my family goes to."

"Really? I don't remember ever seeing you there," I say as I climb into the driver's seat.

"Oh, I stopped going years ago." He plops down into the passenger's seat and buckles his seat belt.

"Why?" I turn the radio down before it blasts our eardrums out.

"There's no point," he says as we head down the street. "I'm not even sure if I believe in God. But even if I did, I don't see a reason to waste any of my time worshipping Him when He's never answered any of my prayers."

"What do you pray for?"

"I don't pray anymore. I used to pray for Him to strike my stepfather down with a bolt of lightning, but that never happened."

"Maybe He sent Child Protective Services instead."

"No, that was my neighbor. She saw him hit me in the backyard and reported it."

"Well, your stepdad was taken away. Doesn't that count for something?"

"Not really. My life didn't get much better after he left."

It didn't? I would think that being removed from a violent household would be a huge improvement in his life. He must have had more unanswered prayers besides justice against his abusive stepfather. Concerned, I ask, "Is your life better now?"

"Some parts of it are," he admits. "I don't think that has anything to do with some higher power, though. If God really cared about me, He wouldn't let assholes like Brandon Stover beat me up."

It doesn't surprise me to hear that Brandon is one of the people who push Tristan around. He's a big thug who thinks it's funny to lock freshmen inside their lockers.

I glance over at Tristan. He's staring moodily out his window. I feel conflicted; I want to assure him that it's all part of God's plan, but I don't know if I really believe in that myself. Why would God's plan involve so much suffering?

Tristan continues. "At church, they tell you to keep faith. That God works in mysterious ways. That it'll all work out in the end. But what about the people it *doesn't* work out for? Haiti is one of the most religious places in the world and an earthquake annihilated them. Why would God allow that to happen to His most devoted followers?"

"I guess maybe so they could be with Him in Heaven?"

He scoffs. "Heaven. Where all your wishes come true and you can be with God for all eternity. Sounds like a fairy tale, if you ask me."

"I don't know. I like to think that there's *something* waiting for us after this life. It's hard to think that we only get one shot and then nothing."

"I'd prefer nothing over having fruity wings and playing on harps all day."

I laugh. "You could always go to Hell."

"Haven't you noticed? We're already *in* Hell. Hell isn't a bunch of fire and demons with pitchforks—it's called 'high school.'"

I was hoping things had gotten better for him over the last few weeks. He hasn't received any more threatening notes or had his property vandalized, and he seems to be much happier in general. But his words and tone of voice make me worried that it's all been an act for my benefit. In a low voice, I ask, "Is it still that bad?"

He looks over at me. "It can be," he says quietly. "You've seen what I have to put up with. But I do have to say that since you and I started hanging out together, it's been more . . . tolerable."

I breathe a sigh of relief. "Okay, good. I was afraid I was just annoying you."

"Well, you are rather annoying."

"But in a good way, right?" I flash him a smile.

"Yes. In a good way," he concedes.

"So where do you want to go?"

"Umm . . . Chipotle?"

"Yeah, that sounds good."

I drive us over to the Chipotle in the middle of town. We grab our food from the counter, then sit down at one of the small metal tables near the window. As I unwrap my burrito, I notice a group of four girls about our age sitting at the table next to us. They keep glancing over at Tristan and whispering and giggling amongst themselves. Tristan's completely oblivious, though; he's too focused on his lunch to notice them. I'm about to give him a heads-up that he's the center of female attention, but then his cell phone rings in his pocket. He pulls it out and groans as he looks at the screen. "Sorry, it's my dad."

I shake my head. "Nah, it's cool. Take it."

He puts his phone to his ear and says, "Hey, Dad." For the most part, it's a one-way conversation. Tristan's only contributions are an occasional "uh huh" and "okay." After a minute or so, he says, "Okay, bye."

He hangs up and says, "My dad's on his way home from a business trip."

I open my mouth to ask for more details, but I'm interrupted by a pretty brunette at the next table. "Excuse me," she says as she bats her eyes at Tristan. "Can I borrow your cell phone real quick?"

I catch on immediately—I've used this trick before. I smile, fold my arms, and lean back in my chair to watch the show.

"Uhh . . . sure," he replies uncertainly. He holds it out to her.

She accepts it and flashes him a brilliant smile. "Thanks. I'll give it right back."

Her fingers fly over the screen. She holds it up to her ear and all her friends watch her with breathless anticipation. A cell phone rings in her purse. She pulls it out and says, "Oh, *there* it is! I thought I lost it." All the girls at the table laugh. She holds Tristan's phone out to him. "Thanks. Now you have my number in case you ever want to find my phone again."

It looks like he's too confused to move. I reach out quickly and take the phone from her hand. "No, thank *you*," I say with a wink and a smile.

She and her friends grin at us as they stand up as one and sashay out of the restaurant. After they walk out the door, Tristan says, "What the hell was that all about?"

"What do you mean?" I ask as I hand him his phone.

"Why did she give me her number?"

"Whaddya mean, 'why'? She wants to hook up with you, dumbass! You should call her."

"But why me?"

"'Cause she thinks you're hot!"

He looks stunned. "What?"

Amused, I say, "Tristan, let me explain something to you. Girls don't give out their numbers freely to every guy. Well, most girls, anyway. They only give their numbers to hot guys and assholes. Since you're not an asshole, that kind of narrows it down, doesn't it?"

He looks back down at his phone. "She thinks I'm hot?" It looks like he's having difficulty processing this information.

"Man, you really need to get out more often. I can't believe that's the first number you've scored. Chicks dig that elf look."

His mouth drops open. He leans forward and hisses, "Are you saying I look like a fucking *elf*?"

"Yeah." I grin. "With those eyes and that chin, you totally look like one. All you need is the pointy ears. Then we could call you Legolas."

"Jesus Christ. I can't even begin to describe how much I hate you right now," he grumbles as he folds his arms across his chest and looks away from me.

I laugh. "Why do you hate me? I'm trying to pay you a compliment!"

"No, you're not. You're making fun of me."

"Well, yeah. I was kidding about the Legolas thing. But you have to know that you're a good-looking guy. That's probably one of the reasons people are mean to you. They're jealous. Of that, and because you're rich and live in a palace."

He looks down at the table and furrows his eyebrows as he thinks over what I said. After a moment, he says, "I don't know. I don't think that's why people are mean to me. I think they just don't like me because I'm different."

"Well, I like you *because* you're different. So that shows you how much they know."

His face relaxes and his mouth turns up in a reluctant smile. "Okay, fine. I don't hate you anymore." He shoves his phone back into his pocket.

"So. You gonna call her?"

"No."

"Why not?"

"Because I have no interest in calling someone who gave me their number at a Chipotle."

"Why not? At least you know you have similar tastes in food."

"Yes. That's the foundation of a strong relationship right there."

"It could be. Who knows what else you might have in common?"

He shakes his head, then says, "Why do you want me to call her so bad?"

"It's not really that I want you to call her specifically. I just think you should give people a chance more often."

He sighs. "I don't know what I would say. You know I don't feel comfortable talking to people."

"You're talking to me right now."

"Yeah, but you're not people."

I laugh. "Okay, then what am I? And don't say, 'An elf.'"

He smiles. "Actually, I was going to say, 'An idiot.'"

"Oh, thanks, that's much better."

"I'm just kidding. You're not an idiot, even if you are a jock."

"You think I'm a jock?"

"Taylor, you're wearing a *varsity jacket*. Of course you're a jock."

"I know." I sigh. "'Jock' just sounds so negative, like all I care about is sports."

"Well, don't you?"

"It's not *all* I care about. I may like baseball, but it's not my life. Sometimes I wish it was—it would make living with my dad easier."

"Is he still giving you a hard time?"

"He hasn't brought it up again, but I know what he's thinking. I see it on his face every time I'm around him, like he thinks there's something wrong with me." I rest my chin on my hand and stare out the window. "I dunno. Maybe there *is* something wrong with me."

"Avery, there's nothing wrong with you. You don't want to be just another athlete. I get it."

I look back at him. He put into a few words what I've been trying to express to myself for weeks. I nod. "Yeah. That's exactly it."

He gives me a small, sympathetic smile. Then he asks, "When's your next game?"

"Next Sunday. Normally, we play on Saturdays, but we don't have one this Saturday 'cause of prom."

"What time does it start?"

"Ten thirty."

"I might come check it out, then."

"You like baseball?" I ask, surprised. Since I've known him, he's never expressed any interest in sports.

"I don't *dislike* it," he says. "I can't play for shit, but I don't mind catching a game now and then. I'm interested to see if you're as great as people say you are, or if they're just boosting your ego."

"You think they might be overestimating my abilities?" I ask, smiling.

"Probably. You could do with someone on the sidelines to take you down a peg or two, in case your head gets too inflated."

"What, like an anti-cheerleader?" I grin at the mental image spurred by the words "Tristan" and "cheerleader."

He smiles. "Exactly."

"So are you really going to come?"

"Of course." He shrugs, as if it's a given.

"Cool. Thanks." I'm glad to know that someone besides Ashley is willing to provide me with moral support at my games. I hate looking into the stands and seeing only strangers.

Tristan crumples his burrito wrapper into a ball and drops it on his tray. "So what do you want to do now?"

"I dunno. You want to go see a movie?"

He smirks. "You sure this isn't a date? 'Cause it sure sounds like a date."

"Go ahead, yuk it up. You want me to go home and change?"

He laughs. "I'm just messing with you. I don't care what you look like. You could go around in a pink feather boa and I wouldn't give a shit."

"I've got one of those at home, too. Should I go get it?"

"No, we might miss the movie."

"Oh, so you *do* want to go see a movie."

"Yeah, I want to go see a movie. Duh." He pulls his phone back out of his pocket and taps a few times on the screen. "Hey, look!" He turns the phone around to show me the display. "*Full Metal Jacket*'s playing at the Regal!"

Sure enough, two showings are listed for *Full Metal Jacket*: one at 1:45 p.m. and one at 7:00 p.m. The last time I saw it was years ago, but I remember it being good. I look at my watch. 1:28.

"Shit, we better get going!" I exclaim.

The Regal is right up the street, so we make it in time to find our seats before the previews begin. Unsurprisingly, they shoved us into the smallest theater, the one they reserve for arthouse movies and foreign flicks. It's just us and a group of three guys in the back who look to be in their late twenties. There must not be a big demand for old Vietnam War films.

The movie starts, and we're immediately thrown into the Marines' barber shop where the recruits are getting their heads shaved in preparation for boot camp. I can't help but smile at the looks on the recruits' faces as their hair falls in clumps to the floor. I shaved my head once and it was a disaster. Drake laughed when he saw me and called me a skinhead. After that, I grew it out and never looked back.

The scene changes, and it's the infamous boot camp sequence. The guys in the back of the theater laugh as the drill instructor, a loudmouth hard-ass named Hartman, lays into each private in turn. It's been a while since I've seen the movie, but I remember laughing just like them at the outrageous insults that pour out of Hartman's mouth. Now, though, I'm not laughing. The longer the scene goes on, the more I feel sick to my stomach.

Hartman picks a private from the lineup and dubs him Gomer Pyle. He gets up in his face and yells at him about sucking dicks. The guys in the back of the theater howl with laughter.

I glance over at Tristan. His mouth is twisted in a grimace. I shift uncomfortably in my seat. I can't help but wonder how many times Tristan's been at the receiving end of equally vicious taunts.

Reluctantly, I watch as the drill sergeant continues his relentless assault on Private Pyle. The only relief from the barrage of insults is when another private by the name of Joker tries to mentor Pyle and help him through the difficult obstacles of PT training, but even that tentative friendship is short-lived. I rub my hand down my face as Joker bows to peer pressure and attacks Pyle when he's asleep in his bed, hitting him over and over again with a club he made out of a towel and a bar of soap.

Why did Tristan want to see this movie? I wonder.

Finally, it's the inevitable showdown between Pyle, Hartman, and Joker in the bathroom. Even though I already know what happens, I feel a terrible sense of foreboding as Pyle raises a loaded rifle and points it at Hartman.

I look over at Tristan. He's leaning forward slightly in his chair, and there's a hunger on his face that disturbs me. Hartman hurls more insults at Pyle until a sound of a gunshot silences his screams.

The corner of Tristan's mouth turns up in a small, satisfied smile. I don't want to look at him anymore; I'm too afraid to know what he's thinking. I look back up at the screen, but what I see now doesn't make me feel any better. Pyle points his rifle at Joker. Joker holds his hands up and tries to soothe him. It works . . . almost. Instead of shooting Joker, Pyle sits down on the toilet and puts the rifle into his own mouth. Internally, I scream with Joker as he yells, "*NO!*"

Pyle pulls the trigger. His head slumps back as blood and brain matter spray all over the white tile walls.

I feel like I'm going to throw up. "I'll be right back," I mutter to Tristan, then hurriedly make my way out of the theater and across the hall to the bathroom. I rush to the nearest sink and grip the edge of the counter as I cough and choke, trying to clear the bile in the back of my throat. I turn on the faucet and splash cold water on my face. I do it once more, then raise my head and gasp for air. My reflection stares hauntingly back at me from the mirror. My eyes are bloodshot and water is dripping off the tips of my hair and running down my chin onto my shirt.

Get a hold of yourself, I scold.

I take a deep, shuddering breath, then look around for paper towels. Unfortunately, I only see an electronic hand dryer. I don't really feel like putting my face under it, so I go into a nearby stall and grab a bunch of toilet paper instead. I wipe my face and shirt off as best I can, then return to the mirror and examine my reflection. My eyes are still red and the collar of my shirt is damp, but I'm hoping they won't be noticeable in the dark theater.

Feeling anxious, I return to my seat. Tristan leans over and whispers, "Are you okay?"

I nod and whisper back, "Yeah. Just had to take a piss."

The rest of the movie follows Joker as he makes his way through

The Lifesaver

Vietnam as a combat correspondent. I worry the edge of my thumbnail with my teeth as I look up at the screen and try to get back into the story. Every now and then, Tristan chuckles at a satirical line—he's obviously interested in what's going on, but my brain isn't registering most of it. I feel a sense of relief as the end credits begin to play.

Tristan looks over at me and gestures toward the exit with his head. I nod and follow him out of the theater.

As we walk back to my car, Tristan says, "That was cool. I like watching classic movies on the big screen."

I shove my hands in my pockets. "Yeah, me too."

He shoots me a sharp look. "You okay?"

"Yeah, I'm fine."

"What's wrong?"

"Nothing." I unlock the door and slide into my seat.

His brow furrows as he sits down and shuts the door. "Did you not like the movie?"

"Some of it was difficult to watch," I admit.

"Well, yeah. It's a war movie. It's supposed to be difficult to watch."

I examine him carefully as I ask, "Why do you like it?"

He shrugs. "It's well made. I agree that it can be hard to watch sometimes, but that's why I like Kubrick so much. He doesn't hold anything back. You ever see *A Clockwork Orange*? Now *that* shit is really fucked up."

"But I didn't think you liked violence."

"I don't. But that doesn't mean all violence is unjustified or wrong. Like at the end, when he killed the girl. It was the right thing to do."

"Why? Because she killed his friend?"

"No. Because she was suffering. He put her out of her misery."

"What about the drill instructor? Was that the right thing to do?"

"What do you mean?"

"Did he deserve to die?"

"I think he was stupid and was asking for it. You don't yell at somebody who's got a gun pointed at you. Joker handled it the right way."

"He didn't stop Pyle from killing himself."

"Well, no. But there wasn't anything he could have done about that."

"Yes, there is," I argue. "He shouldn't have beaten him up. If he had stood up for him, maybe Pyle wouldn't have snapped."

He looks at me skeptically. "That's a big 'maybe.' Pyle seemed a little out there from the start. It may not have made any difference."

"I think it would have. Pyle asked Joker for help because he knew he needed someone to look out for him. But instead, Joker betrayed him. It was a dick move, and it cost him a private's life."

"Are you saying that it's Joker's fault that Pyle went batshit crazy?" He looks at me like he can't quite believe what he's hearing. Even I have to admit that it would be a stretch to pin Pyle's mental instability on Joker.

"I dunno. I guess what I'm saying is that he should have done everything in his power to stop it from getting to that point. He saw what was happening. He knew Pyle was losing it. But he didn't do anything about it."

"What could he have done?"

Feeling frustrated, I exclaim, "I don't know! Reported it up the chain! Protected him from Hartman! Stood watch over him so he wouldn't get beaten up in his sleep!"

He peers at me curiously. "Why are you getting so worked up about this? It's just a movie."

I sigh. "I don't know. I guess it got me thinking about you and the shit you put up with. I don't want to be like Joker and wait until it's too late."

"Is that what you're worried about? That I'm going to grab a rifle and go on a shooting spree?"

I gaze out the window. I don't think that he'd hurt other people, but that doesn't prevent him from hurting himself. How can I tell him that my deepest fear is seeing *his* blood splattered on the bathroom walls?

He raises his voice. "Taylor, I'm not a homicidal maniac! I can't even throw a punch! How do you expect me to be able to shoot somebody?"

"It's not other people I'm worried about." I look over and meet his eyes.

His lips tighten into a thin line. "Look. If I wanted to kill myself, there's not a hell of a lot you or anybody else could do to stop me. So don't worry about it."

He may be right, but that won't stop me from trying to keep him back from the ledge. The hard part is figuring out how close to the ledge he really is. I decide to finally ask the question that's been nagging me ever since I met him. "*Do* you want to kill yourself?"

He smirks. "At this moment? Not particularly, no."

"I mean, do you ever want to kill yourself?"

He rolls his eyes. "Jesus, Taylor! Just drop it already! I swear, if this is how you react every time you watch a movie, I'll never go see a movie with you again."

I sigh. He didn't really answer my question, and it doesn't appear like he's going to, either. I give in, for now. "Alright, fine." Then I say, "But just so you know, I would never betray you like that. Ever."

His face softens. "Yeah, I know."

"Okay, good." I turn on the engine and head out of the parking lot. "So where to now?"

He glances at his watch. "Actually, I should probably go home soon. My dad will be back any minute now and he said he wanted to talk to me about"—he wiggles his fingers and drops his voice into a deep, mystical tone—"*my future.*"

I laugh. "And what future might that be?"

"Fuck knows. He probably just wants to give me another lecture about not going to Cornell."

"You're not going to Cornell?"

"No. I decided I'm going to stay here and take online courses for my undergrad."

"Tristan, are you sure you want to do that? We're talking about Cornell here."

"Jesus, you too? You sound just like my dad. I'm not trying to be president of the United States or anything. I just want to get a piece of paper that'll allow me to get a job. My dad doesn't need to spend half his salary on Cornell when I could just as easily get the same degree from Strayer."

"I figured you'd want to get the hell out of here and start fresh. Nobody would know you. You could make new friends and get away from all the bullshit."

"There's just going to be bullshit there, too. I've been ostracized all my life. You think Cornell would be any different?"

"It could be, if you made an effort to talk to people."

"So it's my fault that people treat me like shit?"

"No! I'm just saying that you can't make friends without talking to people first. At least at Cornell, you'd have a roommate and then you'd be forced to talk to them. Staying alone in your dad's house all the time won't help you make more friends."

"Nobody wants me as a roommate. They'd only end up murdering me in my sleep."

"What are you talking about? I think you'd be an awesome roommate."

"You do?" He looks surprised.

"Yeah. You're cool and you're funny and you're not anal retentive about cleanliness or anything like that. I'd room with you."

His eyes light up. "Really?"

"Yeah. You're one of my best friends. I think it'd be fun."

He looks at me hopefully for a second, then shakes his head and gives me a sad smile. "It wouldn't work out."

"What d'you mean? Why not?"

"Because we'd just end up getting on each other's nerves. The quickest way to end a friendship is to live with that person. You learn about all their little annoying habits, and you start fighting about stupid crap like who left the towel on the floor or who took the garbage out last."

"You're really a glass-half-empty person, aren't you? Yeah, we might want to strangle each other every now and then, but that doesn't mean we'd end up hating each other. I roomed with Drake every summer for baseball camp and we made it through okay. We fought sometimes, but we'd always make up afterward because we realized that our friendship was more important to us than the little things that don't matter."

He thinks for a moment, then shakes his head. "Well, I'm still not going to Cornell. Not unless you go, too, because you're the only person I'd even consider rooming with." As an afterthought, he says, "Well, maybe Drake, too."

I laugh. "I wish I were smart enough to get into Cornell. Then I wouldn't need to bug you all the time for help on my homework."

"You know I don't mind helping you. And don't say you're not smart, 'cause you are. You may not be Einstein when it comes to higher math, but who cares? You're street smart, and in a lot of ways that's better than being book smart."

"Hmm. Maybe I should have included that on my college applications: 'Has street smarts.' Then they'd all be begging me to come to their school. Even Cornell."

He laughs. "You could still put it on your résumé."

I smile. "True."

I pull into his driveway behind a Mercedes-Benz. It looks like his dad is already home.

He sighs. "I'm not looking forward to this. I guess I should just go in and get it over with."

"Yeah. Good luck."

He smiles at me. "Thanks for today. I had a good time."

"Yeah, me too. Even though I freaked out a little."

He laughs. "That's okay. Next time, we'll go see a Muppet movie or something."

I chuckle. "Okay. Sounds good."

He opens the door and starts to climb out of the car.

"What? No good-night kiss?" I ask with feigned indignation.

He stops and bows his head, then looks over his shoulder at me. His mouth turns up in a wry smile. "Fuck you, Taylor."

He gets out of the car and closes the door behind him. He walks over to the porch and looks back as I reverse out of the driveway. I wave to him as I start to drive down the street. He must not be able to see me because he doesn't wave back; he just turns away and goes back inside the fortress he calls home.

17

"How did it go yesterday, with your dad?" I ask Tristan as we walk out to the pool.

"He said the same thing you did: that I shouldn't be cooped up in the house all day, and that I should get out more and"—he mimics his dad's deep voice—"'broaden my horizons.'"

"And what did you say?"

"I gave him a guilt trip and said he just wanted me to go to Cornell so he wouldn't have to see me anymore. It worked, too. Now he says he doesn't want me going somewhere so far from home."

"Tristan!" I scold.

"What?" He sees the disapproval on my face and says, "Oh, like you never laid a guilt trip on your parents."

I shake my head. "So is he okay with you doing Strayer instead?"

He sighs. "No. He said that I had a choice: I could either go to college and keep my laptop, or I could take online classes without it. I don't really want to take eighteen hours of classes at the library, so

I told him I'd keep my laptop and go to the community college. He wasn't happy about that, but a deal's a deal."

"Do you want to go to community college?"

"Yeah, I don't mind. I can live at home and not worry about roommates or meal plans or not being able to drive my car. I'll just go to class for a couple hours at a time, and then I can do whatever I want the rest of the day."

I cross my arms and give him a shrewd look. "You're somethin' else, you know that?"

His eyes widen innocently, but a sly smile plays upon his lips as he says, "Why? What do you mean?"

"You knew from the start that your dad would never let you go to Strayer. I bet you just told him that bit about online classes so he'd give in and allow you to go to community college instead of Cornell."

"That's not true. Online classes would have been my first choice. But yeah, I knew that would never fly. So I went with plan B instead. It's called 'compromise.'"

"No, it's called 'strategy.' You're too smart for your own good, you know."

He grins cheekily at me. "I know."

I smile and shake my head, then assume my instructor role. "Okay, so today I want you to practice holding your breath underwater. The longer you can hold your breath, the better chance of survival you'll have."

"Why can't I practice holding my breath above the water?"

"Because holding your breath underwater is different. The water presses on your lungs and makes it harder. You're never going to be a good swimmer if you can't keep your head under the water for more than two seconds."

"I don't like going under the water."

"It's okay, I'll be right here with you. I'll even do it with you, if you want. Why don't we bet on it? I'll bet you five bucks that I can hold my breath longer."

He scoffs. "I'm not taking that bet. I know you can hold yours longer."

"Okay, then. Why don't you practice so someday, you *can* take that bet? I know you'd just love it if you could show me up and put me in my place."

"Hmm. I *would* like to smack that cocky grin off your face."

"See? Alright, let me go get us some goggles."

"What do we need goggles for?"

"I want you to watch me count the seconds on my fingers so you know how long you've been under. And I want to be able to see you to make sure you're doing okay."

"Oh. Okay."

I rummage through the supply closet and pull out a couple of pairs of goggles. I walk back over to him and hold out the purple pair. "Here you go."

"Can I have the blue ones?"

"No. They're mine."

"Jerk."

We put on our goggles and step into the pool. He follows me until we're chest-deep in the water. I turn around to face him. "You ready?" I ask.

"Yeah."

"Okay. One . . . two . . . three . . ."

We both take a deep breath. I submerge myself under the water and wait, but Tristan stays standing with his head above the water. I surface again.

"What the hell?" I say.

He laughs. "I was just seeing how long it'd take you to figure it out." He holds up his fingers and smugly declares, "Seven seconds."

"Oh, who's the jerk now?" I say as I splash water in his face.

His mouth drops open. "I know you did not just do that."

"Oh, and what if I did?"

He splashes me back.

"You wanna start somethin', punk? You're messing with the wrong—"

A wall of water hits me in the face. He stands there and grins at me while I cough and spit.

Once I recover, I give him a villainous smile. He laughs and backs up quickly as I stalk menacingly toward him, his eyes bright from the thrill of the chase. When I get close enough to reach him, he takes a breath and drops under the water. I'm too surprised to keep count, but he stays under for a while. I cross my arms and wait for him to resurface. He comes back up and brushes the damp hair from his forehead. "How was that?" he asks.

"Good!" I beam at him. "You wanna do it again?"

"Yeah. Together this time."

"Okay."

I count to three and we both go under.

Drake announces, "So I decided to go to UT Austin."

I drop my fork onto my tray. "When did you decide this?"

"Just now. I was eating this nasty barbecue sandwich and I thought, 'Hey, I know where they have good barbecue: Texas.'"

I laugh. "Food is pretty important."

"The most important factor, in my book."

"Are you seriously going?"

"Yeah. My mom sent the deposit last night."

"Wow. Just wow. I can't believe you're leaving me. What the hell am I gonna do without you?"

"Cry, I expect."

"I just might cry. First Ashley and now you? Even Tristan knows what he's going to do. I feel like such a slacker."

"Where is Tristan going?"

"He's going to the community college."

"Oh. Well, he'll still be here, then."

"I know, but that's not the point. The deadline for deposits is next week and I still haven't made up my mind what I want to do."

"You could come to UT with me."

"I didn't apply to UT."

"So? You could still come. You could live in my dorm room and I could give you a water bottle and some food pellets and you'd be set."

I laugh.

"What are you so worried about, anyway?" he says. "You know that whatever you do is gonna be fine. You'll play baseball and the ladies will love you and you'll be the coolest cat around. Oh no, wait, that's me. Never mind, you're screwed no matter where you go."

"I guess you're right. It doesn't matter, as long as I have my best friend. Wait, I *won't* have my best friend! God *damn* you, Drake!"

He shrugs as he picks up his sandwich to take another bite. "Hey. Gotta cut the cord sometime."

"Why don't *you* play something, for a change?" I say as I rub my fingers over my eyes. For the last hour and a half, Tristan's been making me practice sight-reading sheet music and the little dots on the page are starting to blur together. I'd been hoping that my lesson would help me to forget about the fact that everyone around me is jumping ship, but no luck. Now I just feel lonely and burned out.

Tristan looks down at the keys and chews his bottom lip as he thinks. "Okay. Give me some room."

I stand up and step to the side of the piano. He scoots to the middle of the bench and positions his hands over the keys. He starts to play and I watch his fingers carefully, prepared to take mental notes that will help me enhance my own piano-playing skills. His fingers fly too quickly for me to keep up, though, so I give up trying to learn and just marvel at how easy he makes it look.

After a few bars, I recognize the song: "Bridge over Troubled Water." I don't know if he chose it because he likes to play it or if he chose it for me, as an inside joke, because of how we met. I open my mouth to ask him if there's some hidden meaning behind his song of choice, but then I see the look on his face and I stop short. I move toward the back of the piano so I'm across from him, where I can see him more clearly. His eyes are closed (*How can he play when he can't see the keys?*) and there's an intensity in his expression that captivates me. I imagine that this is how fine artists look when creating a masterpiece.

I close my eyes, too, trying to hear what he hears. The variation he's playing is intricate and I wonder if he memorized it from somewhere else or if it's his own creation. The sound carries me like a wave: at first, the music is delicate and soft, but then the volume gradually swells and it lifts me with it, up and up, until it feels like I'm soaring through the clouds. By the time he gets to the powerful final chorus, I have a lump in my throat and it feels like my heart will burst through my chest. When he hits the last triumphant note, I open my eyes and see that he's watching me, just as I was watching him earlier. His pale eyes meet mine and I hold his gaze until after the long last note has faded away completely. It feels like he just told me another deep, emotional secret.

I clear my throat. "Wow. That was really beautiful, Tristan."

He blushes. He seems embarrassed but pleased by the compliment.

"You should be a concert pianist."

He tosses his hair irritably. "That's what my dad always says. But he doesn't understand that I don't want the limelight like he does. Being the center of attention isn't really my thing, if you hadn't noticed."

"Then what is your thing?"

"This." He gestures at the piano. "But that doesn't mean I want to share it with everyone."

"But you shared it with me," I say in a low voice. I was right. In a way, he did tell me a secret.

"Yes," he whispers, avoiding my eyes. "I shared it with you."

18

I climb onto the bench across from Drake at the lunch table. He eyes my tray with disgust. "I can't believe you eat those things," he says.

"I don't know what you're talking about. Fish sticks are delicious."

"Not at this school, they're not. How do you even know if they're fish?"

I shrug. "I don't. It adds an element of intrigue to my lunch."

He wrinkles his nose as I take a big bite out of my fish stick. I smirk at him as I chew.

"You're disgusting, you know that? I don't know how Ashley puts up with you."

"I bribe her. For instance, she wants me to take her to prom in a limo on Saturday. That'll earn me at least three weeks of fish stick privileges."

"Did you already reserve one? You probably won't get one if you haven't."

"Yeah, I made the reservation a while back. I just have to

remember to call the guy to tell him where to meet us."

"That's good. You'd never hear the end of it if you couldn't get one."

"Yeah, Ashley's not one to forget about stuff like that."

"Speaking of forgetting promises, I seem to remember you and Tristan promising to teach me some calculus. Do you think we could meet up after school to go over some stuff?"

It's been raining since this morning, so our baseball practice was canceled. I already made plans with Tristan to squeeze in some piano practice before his own piano teacher arrived, but now that Drake mentions it, I do remember that we'd promised him a tutoring session. Feigning reluctance, I say, "Yeah, I guess I could skip my piano lesson just this once to accommodate my best friend. But you'll owe me."

"Here we go. What do you want? More fish stick privileges?"

"Mmm, steak and lobster dinner sounds better."

"What are you, my girlfriend? I'm not buying you steak *or* lobster. Now Tristan, on the other hand, I might buy *him* steak and lobster if I get an A on my final."

"You and me both."

"Good. The kid could use some more meat on his bones."

"He looks a lot healthier now than he used to."

"No doubt."

I pop another stick into my mouth. "So where should we meet?"

"We can go to my place. You wanna just meet there?"

"Sure, that works for me. I'll talk to Tristan to make sure he's cool with it."

After the last bell rings, I seek out Tristan by his locker. He smiles when he sees me. "Hey! What's up?" he says.

"Well, you're in a good mood," I observe.

"It's Thursday, which means tomorrow will be Friday and then I don't have to come back to school until Monday."

"Uh-huh. Sounds logical to me." I smile. "So Drake was wondering if you'd want to go over to his house this afternoon so we could study for calculus."

"Umm . . . I'm okay with it if you are."

"Yeah, I told him he'd have to buy us both steak and lobster dinners and he said, 'Sure, no problem.'"

"I'm sure he did." He shuts his locker. "You ready to go?"

"No, I've still got to pick up my textbook."

We head over to the other end of the school. Ashley's standing by my locker, waiting for me. Her eyes narrow when she sees Tristan.

"Hey there," I say to her as I fiddle with the padlock.

"Hey. Where are you off to?"

"We're gonna meet up with Drake to study. You going to cheer practice?"

"Yeah, in a few minutes. I just wanted to see you first. Did you get the limo for Saturday?"

"You'll just have to wait and see."

She pouts. I shrug on my jacket and turn to face her.

"Well, I better get going," she says. She steps forward and slides her hands up my chest and around my neck. Pulling me to her, she kisses me, but not in the quick, chaste manner that she normally uses in public; instead, she parts her lips and caresses my tongue with hers. I open my eyes in surprise. *What is she doing? This isn't like her.*

She pulls back and looks up at me through hooded eyes. "Love you," she murmurs.

Bewildered, I answer automatically, "Love you, too."

She grins and steps back.

I glance over at Tristan. He's looking away from us, but I can tell that his jaw is clenched.

She gives him a smug look as she walks by him. "Tristan," she says.

Suddenly, I feel angry with her. *Why does she have to be so mean?*

He meets her eyes and retorts, in the same disdainful tone, "Ashley."

When she disappears around the corner, I sigh. For some reason, I feel the urge to apologize for her behavior. "I'm sorry," I mutter.

"For what?" he asks.

"I dunno. For the way she treats you. I keep telling her to back off, but she doesn't listen."

"Don't worry about it. It's not your fault."

"No, but I still feel bad."

"Don't. Just forget about it."

I exhale. "Okay. Come on, let's go meet up with Drake."

Tristan follows me over to Drake's house. Drake and I are way past the point where we need to announce ourselves, so I just walk inside without knocking. Drake comes out of the kitchen to the right of us, eating a PB&J. "'Ey, guythe." He swallows. "Make yourselves at home."

We kick off our shoes and follow him into the kitchen. He opens the pantry and hands me a bag of chips and a jar of salsa, then pulls three 7UPs out of the fridge and gives them to Tristan. We carry our spoils down the hall to Drake's room. Unlike Tristan's room, the walls of Drake's bedroom are plastered from floor to ceiling with posters and pictures ranging from family photos to cutouts of swimsuit models. Despite having multiple plastic organization bins in his closet and along the walls, his room is in constant disarray. I know it drives his mother nuts, but I don't mind it. It's a homey kind of chaos.

Drake dumps the contents of his backpack onto his bed. I open mine and grab my calculus book and notes. Tristan doesn't even bother opening his; he must know it all in his head.

Tristan sits between me and Drake on the bed. He says to Drake, "Okay, so what do you need help on?"

"All of it," Drake replies.

Tristan smiles. "We won't be able to cover a year's worth of school in one afternoon, but we can go over the major stuff. Do you still have your midterm test?"

"Uh, no. I think I threw it away so my mom wouldn't see it."

"That's okay, I think I've got mine." Tristan opens his backpack and pulls out a binder. He flips through it until he finds a test paper. I can see an A written at the top. "We can go over the questions that were on the midterm today and see how you feel after that."

"Okay, sounds like a plan," Drake says.

I lean closer so I can copy the problems onto a blank piece of paper in my notebook. Tristan angles the test toward Drake so he can write the problems down, but it makes it harder for me to see. I lean forward more and he tilts the test farther away from me. I narrow my eyes into an accusatory glare. He throws a sideways glance at me and gives me a mischievous grin, then lowers the test again so I can see the problems. I smile and shake my head as I scribble in my notebook.

We spend the next two hours poring over the midterm questions. Drake gets frustrated easily and frequently bursts out things like, "What's the point of learning this? We're never gonna *use* it," and, "Why do we have to do it by hand? That's what computers are for." His constant bitching doesn't faze Tristan, though. I'm amazed that he can keep his cool; if I were sitting next to Drake, I'd have smacked him a long time ago. Occasionally, Tristan's eyes meet mine when Drake goes off on one of his rants and I roll my eyes dramatically or mime impressions of Drake to make him smile. By the time

Tristan has to go home for his piano lesson, I'm exhausted from listening to them.

Tristan grabs his backpack and says to Drake, "I think we've made a lot of progress today. We can meet again tomorrow, if you want, to go over the stuff we've learned since the midterm."

"Yeah, that sounds good. Thanks a lot for doing this. I'm sorry I'm such a pain in the ass."

Tristan laughs. "It's no problem." He looks at me. "You still picking me up tomorrow morning?"

"Yup. Bright and early."

"Okay." He grins. "Bye, Drake."

He walks down the hall, slips on his shoes, and throws us a wave as he steps outside.

Drake turns to me and asks, "What's tomorrow morning?"

"Oh. We're going swimming at the community center before school."

"What? Why on earth would you get up that early to go swimming? Why not just go after school?"

"I don't have time after school." I don't want to embarrass Tristan by telling other people that he doesn't know something as basic as how to swim. The last thing he needs is another reason for people to make fun of him.

"What time does the community center open?" Drake asks.

"Six thirty."

"That doesn't make any sense. School starts at seven."

"Yeah, I know. We go before they open."

"Seriously? Does it cost anything?"

"No, the manager knows me. He's cool with it."

"Hmm. Does Ashley know?"

"No. Why?"

"Just wondering. Are you going to tell her?"

I think back to how she acted this afternoon around Tristan, and I decide that telling her I'm spending my mornings with him in addition to my afternoons is not going to improve her feelings toward him.

I shake my head. "No. Not unless she asks. It's not like she needs to know what I do every second of the day."

"I don't know, man. You know it's just gonna bite you in the ass if she finds out that you're spending so much time with Tristan instead of her."

"Well, if she wants to get up at four thirty in the morning to go swimming with me, then she's welcome to. But you and I both know that that's never going to happen."

"I think you're missing the point. She doesn't want you to spend time with Tristan at all."

"Why should she care, though? I don't like some of her friends, but I don't give her shit for hanging out with them."

"You might if they wanted to be more than friends."

"I don't know, I—wait, what? What are you saying?"

"Come on, Avery. Do I really need to spell it out for you?"

"What?"

"Look, I've said it before and I'll say it again. Tristan. Likes. You." He enunciates each word as if I'm hard of hearing.

"Did he tell you that?" I ask, shocked.

"He doesn't need to! It's like you come in the room and he lights up like a goddamn Christmas tree. And don't pretend you haven't noticed that puppy dog look he gives you whenever you get near him."

To be honest, I had noticed a subtle shift in our friendship since he played "Bridge over Troubled Water" for me—a shift that we've both acknowledged but don't talk about. For that brief moment, I felt like there were no walls between us. Would Tristan have let his guard down for someone he didn't have feelings for? I don't want to dwell on it. If I admit to myself that Tristan has most likely fallen for me, then our friendship will only end in heartache, and I don't want that to happen.

Aloud, I say to Drake, "We've been over this. We're just friends, nothing more."

"To you, maybe. But to him? The more time you spend with him, the more you might get his hopes up."

"He knows I'm not gay."

"That doesn't stop you from flirting with him."

My mouth drops open. "*What?* I never . . . I don't know what you . . ."

He rolls his eyes. "God, Avery, just admit it. You're a flirt, you always have been."

"How am I possibly a flirt?"

"You bat those big brown eyes and flash that goofy-ass grin of yours and people fall all over themselves for you. It's disgusting, really."

"And you're just telling me this *now*? After all the years you've known me? I thought we were friends!"

He shrugs. "I figured you already knew. I must have underestimated how clueless you were."

"Well, crap. Maybe I really am clueless. I had no idea I came across that way to people. Do I flirt with you?"

"You try, but it doesn't work on me. I can see through your bullshit a mile away."

"Huh. I guess I need to work on that. I don't want to lead people on."

"Exactly my point."

"Well, I'm not going to stop hanging out with Tristan. I'll just try not to blink or smile anymore, in case he gets the wrong idea."

Drake laughs. "Good plan."

19

Tristan trots out his front door and slides into the passenger seat. Without preamble, I say, "Can I ask you something? And I want you to answer honestly."

He eyes me warily as he buckles his seat belt. "What is it?"

"Am I a flirt?"

He barks a laugh. "Yes."

"Dammit!" I exclaim as I hit the steering wheel. I shake my head and put the car in drive.

He smiles and asks, "So what prompted this?"

"Just Drake. He told me I was a flirt and I needed a second opinion."

"Yes, you're a flirt. But I won't hold that against you."

"Okay, good. Because I don't know when I'm flirting, so I don't know if I'm able to control it. I feel like I have a disability."

"Do you want me to follow you around and let you know when you're flirting? I could put a shock collar on you and zap you whenever you use a corny pickup line or something."

"Yeah, that might work. Shock therapy is always fun."

"Spoken like a true psychiatrist. You may have a future in it yet."

I laugh. "So am I like the harmless flirt that people joke about, or am I the creepy guy that nobody wants to invite to parties?"

"Well, that depends. How many parties have you been invited to this year?"

"Uhh . . . not many," I reply with chagrin.

"Hmm. That's not a good sign," he admits.

"Maybe I should conduct a poll during prom tomorrow. Give everyone a piece of paper that says, 'Is Avery Taylor a creep?' and count how many yeses and nos I get back."

"Ooh, that'd be an interesting experiment. Though you better be careful where you choose to hand them out. You'll get way more nos if you stand by the punch bowl than if you stand by the door to the girls' bathroom."

He grins at me while I throw my head back and guffaw.

"So I'm guessing you're not going to prom?" I say after I've recovered from my mirth.

"What gave you that idea?"

I shoot him a surprised look. "You're going?"

"Psshht. *Hell*, no."

I smile and shake my head. "Don't you want to show your kids and grandkids your prom pictures? I bet you'd look dashing in a powder blue tux."

"That's assuming I'll ever have kids and grandkids. And even if I did, I don't think they'd want to see my stupid prom pictures."

"You don't want kids?" I ask, surprised.

"I don't know. Maybe if I met the right person. Though I don't know what kind of dad I'd turn out to be. I don't have the best role models to work from."

"I think you'd be a good father. You have more patience than I'll ever have, that's for sure. And since you don't have the best role models, you can use them to determine what *not* to do with your kids."

"I guess that's true. It scares me to think that I might turn into my father someday. Or worse, my stepfather."

"You won't," I assure him.

We pull into the parking lot at the community center. I grab our bags from the trunk and carry them inside to the locker room. I hand Tristan his bag and he disappears into the next row.

"So what about you?" I hear his voice call over the lockers. "Are you looking forward to a bunch of miniature Taylors running around?"

"Hopefully not anytime soon, but yeah, I'd like to have a few rugrats to carry on the family name. I'm the last male in my family; all my cousins are girls."

"How many do you want?"

"I dunno. Five or six? I feel like I should have a few backups in case the first one turns out to be a little shithead."

He laughs. "And how does Ashley feel about that?"

"We haven't talked about it," I admit as he walks around the corner.

He stops at the end of the row and looks at me in surprise. "What? Really?"

I shrug as I stuff my shirt into my bag. "We haven't really talked about our future yet. I told her that we should wait until the end of the summer to have 'the talk.'"

"I thought you guys had been together for a long time."

"We have. Well, if you consider a year to be a long time. But we're only in high school. It's not like the old days when people got married at sixteen, thank God. We've got time to figure all that stuff out."

"I guess so," he says, as if he doesn't really believe it. "It just seems to me that you should find out sooner rather than later if she even wants the same things you do. If you think you might want to settle down and have kids someday, but she wants to be an independent woman who lives for her career, you're both just wasting your time."

"I don't think it's wasting time to be with someone you like to be with. If it's not meant to be, we'll just enjoy it while it lasts."

"Yeah, but meanwhile, you could be missing out on the love of your life."

He's got me there. I tilt my head and meet his gaze while I try to think of a counterargument. He must know I can't come up with one, because after a few seconds he nods toward the door to the pool. "Shall we swim?"

Drake meets me outside of my classroom after school. "We still on for meeting with Tristan this afternoon?"

Coach Barnes decided to take pity on us and not make us practice in the mire that is our field, so now we've got the whole afternoon to study.

"Yep. I told him we'd meet him at his locker," I say.

"Okay, cool."

We head over to the other side of the school. As we turn the corner, Drake stops in his tracks and says, "Shit," under his breath. I stop too when I see what he sees: Brandon Stover has Tristan pinned up against a locker.

Brandon sneers. "Where's Mr. Trawler, huh? I'm betting you were the girl in the relationship."

A deep, burning rage consumes me. Drake tries to grab my arm but I shrug him off and stride over to them. As I approach, Brandon shoves Tristan's chest and jeers, "What's wrong, faggot?"

Tristan winces as his back hits the padlock. Then Brandon punches him in the stomach. Tristan bowls over and cries out in pain.

Something snaps within me. I grab Brandon by the neck and haul him away from Tristan, then start wailing on him with my fists. He tries to hit me back and gets in a good punch or two, but I barely register them. I just keep punching his face over and over until he falls down, and then I punch some more. I feel hands pulling at my arms, trying to tug me off of Brandon, but I fight them off, too. I want to beat him to a bloody pulp.

Somebody hoists me up and drags me a few feet away. I realize that it's Drake and Mr. Smith, Tristan's teacher. Brandon sits up and spits blood out of his mouth. "*Fag*," he hisses at me.

I lunge at him again, but Drake has his arms wrapped around me and I can't go anywhere.

"*Enough!* Both of you!" Mr. Smith says. "Mr. Stover, you're coming with me. Williams, Chevalier, I suggest you take Mr. Taylor home and get him cleaned up."

Brandon gapes at Mr. Smith. "What? You're not giving him detention?"

The look Mr. Smith gives him could freeze steel. "The consequences of Mr. Taylor's actions are none of your concern. I will deal with him appropriately."

He helps Brandon to his feet, then grips his arm and leads him away. Brandon throws a menacing glare over his shoulder at the three of us as Mr. Smith escorts him down the hall.

My mom comes into the kitchen and halts when she sees me, Drake, and Tristan sitting at the table. "Avery, what happened to your face?"

"Got in a fight," I mumble. I know I'm in for it now.

"Avery! What have I told you about fighting?"

"It wasn't his fault, Mrs. Taylor," Drake pipes up. "Some jackass was pushing Tristan around. Avery put him in his place."

"Yeah, Mrs. Taylor. You should be proud. Avery was a real knight in shining armor," Tristan says. He smirks at me.

"Well," she says, her expression softening as she looks at Tristan, "hopefully, it won't happen again." She comes over and examines my wounds. "Hmm, it doesn't look too bad. You'll have a black eye tomorrow, that's for sure. I'll get you some Neosporin and some ice packs."

She rummages around in the freezer and the kitchen drawers and deposits the supplies on the table in front of me, then heads to her room to change out of her scrubs. I groan as I place an ice pack against my eye. I think she's right; I will have a black eye. Tristan grabs the Neosporin bottle and squeezes some onto his finger. He applies it to the cut on my eyebrow with a half-smile on his face.

Drake loudly clears his throat. *Ahem.* Well, I better get going." He gets up and grabs his backpack.

I look up at him in surprise. "I thought you wanted to go over calculus."

"That's okay. I think your head has gone through enough abuse for one afternoon. We can meet up some other time."

My mom reenters and sees him standing with his backpack in his hand. "Aren't you staying for dinner, Drake?"

"Nah, tonight's family night at Uno's. Thanks anyway, Mrs. Taylor. See ya, Avery. Bye, Tristan." He walks out the door.

My mom turns to Tristan and asks, "Will you be having dinner with us, Tristan?"

"Uh, sure. My parents are out of town so I'm kind of on my own tonight anyway."

"Good." She beams. "Because I'm making my famous green chile stew."

"That was really good, Mrs. Taylor," Tristan says as he helps me clear the table.

"Thank you, Tristan. I'm glad someone appreciates my cooking." She looks pointedly at my dad, who pretends not to see her.

"So, Tristan. You got a last name?" my dad asks gruffly.

"Yeah. I mean, 'yes.' My last name is Chevalier."

"Chevalier, huh? Now where have I heard that name before?"

"You've probably seen my dad's commercials. He's a senator. In the state senate."

"*Franklin* Chevalier?"

"The one and only."

"No offense, kid, but your dad's a moron."

"Jim!" my mother scolds, but Tristan just laughs.

"None taken," he replies.

"So what are you two up to this evening?" my mother asks, trying to change the subject.

Tristan and I look at each other. "My parents just got a big-screen TV," he says. "Seventy-eight-inch. You wanna check it out?"

"Sure!" I say.

I head to the bathroom to brush my teeth. My dad follows me and says, "Son, can I talk to you for a second?"

Uh-oh. I don't know what he wants to talk about, but he only calls me "son" when I'm in trouble.

He pulls me into his bedroom and closes the door. He crosses his arms and scowls. "What happened today?"

I should have known I wouldn't get away with it completely. I try to sound as nonchalant as possible as I say, "I got in a little fight, but it's no big deal. I wasn't suspended or anything."

"No, it's a very big deal. You *know* that the baseball team has zero tolerance for fighting. What were you thinking?"

"Dad, I didn't have a choice! Tristan was in trouble and he needed backup."

"That's what this was about?"

"Yeah, Dad. He needed help and—"

"Avery, you need to let people fight their own battles. You can't afford to get into trouble like this."

Indignantly, I reply, "I figured you'd be proud of me for sticking up for my friends."

"Not when it's your life on the line."

I want to argue with him, but I see his point. At the time, I thought I was doing the right thing, but in retrospect, maybe I should have handled it differently by going to get a teacher or Officer Gálvez instead of putting myself in harm's way and jeopardizing my career. On the other hand, if I *had* gone to search for help, there's no guarantee that I would have found someone, and what would have happened to Tristan then? I don't even want to think about that. I'd rather be reckless and stupid than see Tristan in a hospital. *Or a morgue*, my brain whispers.

"I'm sorry, Dad," I say, even though I don't truly feel sorry. "I'll try not to get into any more fights."

"See that you don't."

I try not to sound exasperated as I say, "Okay."

I turn to leave but then he says, "Wait a minute, son. I'm not done talking to you yet."

He's not?

I turn back around to face him. In a low voice, he asks, "How well do you know this kid?"

Surprised, I say, "Who? Tristan?"

"I recognize his name, and not from his dad's stupid commercials, either. Something to do with an incident with a teacher last year."

The Lifesaver

I grit my teeth. *What does that have to do with anything?* I decide to feign ignorance. "I don't know anything about that."

"Well, let's just say it wasn't something you want to be a part of."

I gulp down the anger that has flared up again inside me. "Who cares what happened a year ago? He's my friend."

"Some things don't go away over time. Some things follow you no matter where you go."

"So you're saying I shouldn't be friends with Tristan anymore? Is that what you're saying?" I ask, my voice rising.

"I just want to help you make the right decisions. Who you associate with can have a lasting impact on your future. Remember that."

"I'll take my chances," I retort. I turn on my heel and stalk out of the room.

He doesn't follow.

I go back to the kitchen and find Tristan and my mother laughing about something. His clear, crystal laugh mixes well with her light, jingly one. *At least one of my parents likes him.*

I march up to Tristan and mutter in his ear, "Let's get out of here."

He gives me a searching look, then nods.

"Thanks again for dinner, Mrs. Taylor. It was nice seeing you again," he says over his shoulder as I push him out the door.

"You too, sweetie. Drive carefully," I hear her call after us.

20

I DRIVE, WAY TOO FAST, over to Tristan's house. He doesn't say anything the whole way, but he keeps shooting me concerned looks.

He holds the front door open for me and I walk through without saying anything. I kick off my shoes as he turns off the alarm. He finally breaks the silence. "Your mom's really nice."

"Yeah, she is," I admit.

"Your dad's quite a character, though."

I sigh. "I'm sorry about him. He's not the most tactful person in the world."

Tristan shrugs. "It's no problem."

I don't want him to know that my dad doesn't want us to be friends. I want to forget about it. To distract myself, I look around. "So where's this monster TV you were talking about?"

He leads me toward the back of the house to a big den-looking area. There's a wraparound leather couch that looks like it could fit fifteen people comfortably, and there are shelves and shelves full of DVDs and Blu-Rays lining the walls. Just like he said, there's a huge

TV hanging from the wall in front of the couch, and right underneath it . . .

"Holy crap! How many game consoles do you have?"

"Uh, just about all of them."

I walk up to get a closer look. "You have the original Nintendo?"

"Yeah. It was a gift." His voice sounds strained. I look over at him and see that his arms are crossed over his chest. He looks uncomfortable.

"You okay?" I ask.

He shakes himself and responds, a little too brightly, "Yeah, I'm fine." Then he walks over to a cabinet that I hadn't noticed before and opens it up. "Wanna drink?"

The cabinet is chock-full of liquor.

I gape at the rows of bottles. I've had alcohol a few times before at weddings and other family functions, but there were always adults around to supervise. "Are you serious?" I ask, my mouth hanging open.

"Yeah. My dad's got tons of this stuff. The cook keeps it stocked. My parents will never notice."

I know we shouldn't. I *tell* myself that we shouldn't, but the temptation to drown my feelings in a bottle is too strong.

"Okay," I say. "What you got?"

"So you're saying that if I point the gun at the middle, I'll get the duck every time?" I ask. We're playing *Duck Hunt*, and it's the Best. Game. Ever.

Tristan's sitting cross-legged on the floor in front of the couch, surrounded by Nintendo cartridges. He nods as he takes another swallow of Jack Daniel's. We gave up on glasses and started drinking straight from the bottle a long time ago. More efficient that way.

I don't believe him. I have to try it out. I scoot forward in my seat until I'm perched on the edge of the couch. I point the controller at what I judge to be the middle of the screen and pull the trigger. I miss.

"It didn't work!" I accuse him.

He giggles. "I said the *middle*, not the *side*. Here, I'll show you."

He gets up from the floor with some difficulty and falls gracelessly onto the couch next to me. He grabs the controller from my hand and waves it in the general direction of the television. He pulls the trigger and misses, too.

"*Curses!*" he shouts, and I laugh until tears stream down my face. It feels so good to laugh.

"Ohh, Jesus," I wheeze. "This was a good idea, Tristan. This is just what I needed."

"Yeah, you were acting kinda weird after dinner. What's up with that?"

"Oh, just my dad. Being a jerk."

"He wasn't being a jerk. He was telling the truth. My dad *is* a moron."

"No, not that. He pulled me aside after dinner and basically said I shouldn't hang out with you anymore."

"What? Why?"

"I dunno. Thinks you're a bad influence or something."

"Well," he says as he hands me the bottle, "can't argue with that."

I laugh and take another swig.

What the hell is that noise?

Groggily, I open my eyes and see that the TV is still on. The game has reverted back to the main menu and the theme song is playing on repeat. It makes my head hurt.

Something heavy is weighing on my side. I blink a few times and see that Tristan has passed out, his head slumped against my shoulder. The controller is still in his hand. We both must have fallen asleep mid-game.

I look around for the remote. I finally spot it on the coffee table by my feet. I'm reluctant to wake Tristan up, but I can't take the annoying beeping of the game anymore. I slowly lean forward, careful not to jostle him too much. He sort of groans and tilts his head the other way so it's propped up by the couch. He never even opens his eyes. It takes a few attempts, but I'm able to grab the remote without falling off the couch. I can't really see the buttons, but thankfully the second one I press is the mute button. I close my eyes and fall back into the cushion. Tristan groans again and lays his head back on my shoulder. His warm breath tickles my neck. Suddenly, I don't feel tired anymore; instead, I feel hyper-alert, as if all the nerves in my body are standing on edge. My heart is racing and I'm finding it difficult to breathe. Tristan stirs, and I stop breathing completely. He lifts his head and our eyes meet. The light of the TV makes his pale skin glow and he looks otherworldly, like an angel or a ghost. His eyes are luminous and close—very close—to my own. A little voice inside my head tells me that I should back away, but that sounds wrong. It has to be wrong, when everything in my body is telling me that we need to be closer. Much, much closer . . .

I open my eyes. The light burns, so I immediately shut them again. *Why is it so bright?* I squint and see that it's just the daylight coming through the window. I wonder what time it is.

My head feels like a log that survived the chopping block. I rub my hands down my face. I must have drunk waaayyy too much last night.

It occurs to me that I'm lying on the floor. Gingerly, I sit up. A blanket slides off my chest and pools in my lap. *Funny. I don't remember getting a blanket.* I look around the room, taking in the damage. It's not too bad; there are bottles and games scattered everywhere, but aside from that, I don't see any spills or destroyed furniture. I don't see Tristan, either. My stomach drops.

Oh God. Tristan . . .

Hazy memories flash to the surface: memories of Tristan's lips, his hands, his heat . . . it's all a blur. I can't remember much. Suddenly scared, I throw the blanket off. My pants are still on. *Thank Christ.*

I cradle my head in my hands, trying desperately to recall what happened, but it's no good. Parts of last night have probably been erased from my mind forever. I wonder how much Tristan remembers. *Oh no. Holy shit.*

Feeling woozy, I fumble with the couch and pull myself to my feet. The bathroom door down the hall looks open. I pad down there and peek inside, but no one's there. He must have gone upstairs.

The ticking of the grandfather clock follows me as I make my way up the grand staircase. When I get to the top of the stairs, I peer down the hall to where his bedroom is. A little strip of light shines between the door and the frame. I tiptoe up to it. I don't know why I feel compelled to keep quiet. Maybe I'm afraid of waking him up, or maybe I just don't want to disturb the stillness of the house. I knock softly on the door and say, just as quietly, "Tristan?"

He doesn't answer.

My gut tightens further into a ball as my fingers close around the doorknob. I'm not sure if I want to open this door to find out what's on the other side. What if he doesn't remember anything? Can I just move on and pretend like it was all just a strange dream? Or worse, what if he remembers everything? It seems highly unlikely that we'd be able to laugh it off and go back to the way things were. Not if he really has feelings for me. How many lines did I cross last night? Do I even want to know?

Well, there's no going back now. I have to try to talk to him if I'm going to have any chance of setting things right between us. I take a deep breath, then cautiously open the door and step inside.

It's empty.

I stop in the middle of the room and look at the unmade bed and books scattered on the floor, feeling lost and confused. My knees falter, and I sink onto the edge of the bed to stare at the lines of shadows on the carpet. I can't believe he just took off and left me alone in his house without saying anything, especially after what happened between us. I'm surprised by how much it hurts.

Jesus, you sound like a girl, I scold myself.

I'm tempted to laugh, but it comes out like a groan. Of all people, I was Tristan Chevalier's one-night stand.

21

I try to sneak in through the back door, but my mother's already in the kitchen.

"Avery James Taylor!" she yells. "Where. Have. You. Been?"

"Sorry, Mom," I mumble. "Tristan and I fell asleep playing video games."

I know I must reek of alcohol. I try to keep my distance from her, but it's no good. "Were you drinking?" she asks in a low, threatening voice.

I sigh heavily. "Yes. Unfortunately."

She glares at me, then sighs, too. "I suppose I should be grateful that you didn't try to drive home last night."

"Mom, I'm not stupid."

"Hmph. That's a matter of opinion," she replies, but her eyes twinkle when she says it. She looks me up and down. "You look like hell. And your eye is black, just as I thought. I'll let you use some of my cover-up tonight."

Tonight? Shit!

I forgot about prom.

I straighten my tux nervously and pray for the pain relievers to kick in while I wait for Ashley to open the door. My headache hasn't gone away, no matter how many pills I've choked down. It'll be a miracle if I can get through this night in one piece.

To make matters worse, it isn't Ashley who opens the door—it's her father. Mr. Devens is a short man with a short temper, and I've always felt a little uncomfortable in his presence. As we wait for Ashley, he gives me the obligatory speech about curfew and appropriate behavior and treating his daughter with respect, followed by a detailed outline of what he's going to do to me if I don't abide by the rules he so graciously provided. As he threatens to hunt me down if I step one toe out of line, I cross my fingers and hope to God he never finds out about what I've done.

When he gets to the part about a shovel, Ashley comes down the stairs and saves me from his tirade. She's wearing a stunning rose-colored gown that matches her lipstick, and her blond hair is swept into a fancy updo, with curly tendrils cascading down to graze the nape of her neck. It hurts my heart to see how beautiful she looks. *She deserves better*, my conscience chides. I try to swallow my unease and focus on smiling for the camera.

After her parents have taken the required ten thousand pictures of us standing in front of the fireplace, and the stairs, and the front door, we finally make our escape. Ashley squeals ecstatically when I open the limo door for her. She scoots over and gives me a big kiss on the lips as I sit down next to her. I try not to think of the last lips I kissed.

"Thank you, Avery! You're the best boyfriend ever," she gushes.

I try my best to smile back at her, but it comes out more like a grimace. She doesn't notice, though; she's too busy playing with all of the switches on the control panel next to her seat.

I look up and see a mirror above me. I pull it down and check out my eye. The cover-up seems to have helped hide the ugly bruise as well as the bags under my eyes.

"What are you doing?" she asks.

I flip the mirror back up. "Nothing."

She peers closer at my face. "Are you wearing makeup?"

I don't like where this is going. "Yeah. I have a black eye and I figured you wouldn't want me to look like a piece of meat in your prom pictures."

"Where'd you get a black eye from?"

"Brandon Stover."

"*Ugh*. He's an asshole."

"Yeah, he is."

"Well, I hope you gave better than you got."

"Yeah, I did."

"Good." She kisses me again.

I relax a little. Lucky for me, she never asked what started the fight.

The limo pulls up outside the hotel, and we're immediately bombarded by Ashley's friends. I inch my way out of the mob and make my way over to Drake, who's hanging by the entrance. "I see you remembered the limo," he says by way of greeting.

"Yeah. She won't talk about anything else the next few days."

"How you doin'?" He peers at my eye.

"I've been better," I admit. "I'm so fucking hung over. Hopefully, the music won't be too loud."

He blares a laugh, making my head ring. "So you and Tristan partied it up last night after I left, huh?"

"*Shhh!* Keep it down." I look frantically over in Ashley's direction. Thankfully, she's too far away to hear us.

I look back at Drake. He's regarding me in a peculiar way.

"What?" I say.

He opens his mouth as if to say something, then seems to think better of it and closes it again. He shakes his head. "Nothing. Come on, let's go retrieve our womenfolk."

The music *is* too loud, but I grit my teeth and bear it for Ashley's sake. She insists on dancing to every song. I don't know how she has the energy.

A slow song comes on, so I grab her waist and she wraps her arms around my neck. She rests her cheek against my chest while we pivot in slow circles in one spot on the dance floor. As the song plays, I find myself instinctively focusing my ears on the piano accompaniment in the background. I wonder if Tristan knows how to play it.

It's as if Ashley read my mind. "How are the piano lessons going?"

"Good, I guess," I reply slowly. I get the feeling that I'm walking into a trap.

"Maybe you should play for me sometime."

"I'm not that good yet. Besides, I don't have a piano."

She looks up at me. "Then where do you practice?"

"Tristan's house," I say without thinking.

She stops swaying. I stop, too.

"You go to his *house*?"

Unease boils into the familiar anger. "Yeah, I go to his house. So what?"

"Avery! Are you insane? People might start to talk about you."

I drop my hands from her side. "People like you, perhaps?" I hiss. She releases my neck.

"I'm sick of this! You judge him, but you don't even know him! You think you know everything there is to know, but you know nothing."

"I know enough!" she snaps. "I know that he's a pervert. You don't need friends like that, Avery."

"You don't know what I need."

"Well, in that case, why don't you just dump me and get it over with?" she says with angry tears in her eyes.

"That's the best idea you've had yet. We're done."

With my hands balled into fists, I brush past her and storm out of the dance hall.

22

I WAKE UP the next morning to find three new text messages from Ashley:

> I'm sorry.
> You ok?
> Call me.

I delete them all.

I head downstairs. My mother's already left for work, but my father is sitting in the kitchen reading the paper. He's the only person I know who doesn't get his news from the internet.

I pour myself some cereal and sit across the table from him. He eyes me over his paper. "How was the dance?"

"I don't want to talk about it."

"That good, huh?"

I don't return his smile.

"Your mother told me you came home in a taxi. What happened to the limo?"

I don't really want to admit that, like an asshole, I dumped my girlfriend on prom night, but I won't be able to keep it a secret for long anyway, so I say, "Ashley and I broke up last night. I let her take the limo home and I got a cab."

His eyebrows shoot to the top of his head. "You broke up? Why?"

"I dunno, Dad. It just wasn't working out."

His mouth works as if he doesn't know what to say. Finally, he says, "Well, that's a shame. She's a nice girl."

I grimace. What can I say to that?

He must notice my discomfort, because he clears his throat and changes the subject. "So today's the big game, right? Are you psyched?"

"Yeah, I suppose. Are you coming?"

"I wish I could, but I've got to head over to the plant. Got a call that there's a malfunctioning lever that needs attention."

If it's that important, why aren't you there now instead of reading the paper? I think. I know better than to say it out loud, though.

"Do you think there will be more scouts today?" he asks.

"Probably," I grumble.

He must have noticed my tone, because he shakes his head in disapproval. "I don't know why you're not more excited about this. Most people would love to be in your shoes."

He's not wrong. At first, my teammates were thrilled about being able to showcase their skills in front of so many scouts, but now I can see the envy and resentment in their eyes whenever they look at me. Drake seems to be the only one who doesn't take it personally that the scouts don't shower him with attention, probably because he sees how stressful being in the spotlight is for me.

"Dad, don't you think I should go to college? I mean, what if I get hurt and can't play anymore? I won't be able to do anything without a college degree."

"Nobody's saying you can't get a degree, Avery. You can still take classes in the off-season."

"What if I don't get drafted, though? Shouldn't I register for fall semester just in case? The deadline for deposits is this Thursday."

"If you don't go to college, we'll have to forfeit the deposit."

"Does it matter? If I don't go, my signing bonus will cover it."

He considers me over his paper. "Alright. Which college?"

Shoot. I'd spent so much time arguing my point, I hadn't stopped to think about which college I should attend.

"Umm . . . Middleton?" Middleton's still about an hour away, but it's a lot closer to home than any of the other colleges I got accepted to.

"Middleton isn't a Division One school," he says.

"Well, it doesn't matter, does it? I'm probably not going there anyway."

"Now, son, you really need to think about this—"

"Just put in the deposit, okay?"

I hear a car horn honk outside. It must be Drake. I toss my bowl into the sink, then rush to the front door. As I grab my bag from the floor, I hear my father's voice behind me. "Good luck today. Make me proud."

"Whatever," I mutter. I slam the door behind me.

I'm so irritated with my father right now. His disapproval of my choices lately is really starting to wear me down. He criticized my friendship with Tristan, he obviously doesn't understand how I could break up with a "nice girl" like Ashley, he doesn't get why I'd even consider another future besides baseball. And now he tells me to "make him proud," as if the only way to make him proud is to play well at the game—a game he claims he's too busy to even watch.

I climb into the passenger seat of Drake's Mitsubishi. As he pulls away from my house, he glances over at me and his eyebrows furrow together. "You okay?"

I shake my head. "Just my dad. He's disappointed that I'm not meeting all of his expectations. Like he ever meets any of mine."

"Well, that's family. Can't live with 'em, can't kill 'em." Then he asks the inevitable question. "So what the hell happened between you and Ashley last night? It's like everything's fine one minute, then I turn around and you're gone and Ashley's crying, saying something about breaking up."

"Yeah. We broke up."

"Dude. Why?"

I lean back against the headrest and look out the window. "She was badmouthing Tristan again and I lost my cool. I just don't get what her deal is with him."

"Are you gonna try to get back together?"

I shake my head. "No. It wasn't going to last anyway. It was only a matter of time before we broke up." I sigh. "The ironic part of all this is that I think Tristan's avoiding me, too."

Drake's jaw drops. "What? Why? What did you do?"

I rub my hands down my face. I don't want to explain to my best friend that I'm a sack of shit who betrayed his girlfriend and possibly lost a friend by acting like a complete idiot. I can't even explain what happened to myself. So I just mutter, "I don't know. He ditched me after you left Friday and he hasn't talked to me since."

"Well, you're just pissing everybody off, aren't you?"

I groan.

"If it's any consolation, I'm not pissed off at you."

"The day's not over yet," I grumble.

"Taylor, you want to explain to me what the hell happened to your face?" Coach Barnes growls. I'm no longer hiding behind my mother's cover-up, so it'd be impossible for him not to notice the cuts on my face or the fact that the cheekbone under my eye has turned a sickly greenish purple.

I know I have to be careful in how I answer. It would be stupid to pretend I didn't get into a fight, but the rules are pretty clear: you fight, you're out.

"I'm sorry, Coach," I say. "I didn't mean to get into a fight, but I didn't have a choice. It was either that or let him beat me up."

"Who threw the first punch?"

"He did." Technically, Brandon hit Tristan first, not me, but I won't bother Coach with the little details.

"You know you could get kicked off the team for this?"

"Yeah, I know," I mumble.

He looks me over, obviously weighing his options: kick me off the team now and risk losing the game, or overlook my infraction and risk having his team think that he won't enforce the rules.

"Alright, Taylor," he says. "You're still on the team. A man has a right to defend himself. But if you're smart, you won't let yourself get backed into a corner more than once. Understand?"

"Yes, sir. Thank you, Coach."

"Alright. Go warm up."

I walk over to where Drake is stretching by the backstop. The rest of the team sneaks glares at my eye. I turn my back to them while I scan the faces in the crowd. I don't really know who I'm looking for. I don't expect Ashley to show after the way I treated her last night, and I know it's too much to hope that my parents suddenly decide to quit their jobs to come watch me play. Drake sees my expression and sympathizes. "Parents couldn't come again, huh? Sorry, man."

I swallow my disappointment and try to get my head into the game. I've never been so reluctant to take the mound, or so relieved when the last inning is over.

After I've made the customary rounds with the scouts, I rejoin my teammates in the middle of the field. While they're arguing over where to go for the team lunch, Drake nudges me and whispers loudly in my ear, "Look who's here. Eight o'clock."

I glance over my shoulder and see Tristan leaning against the backstop. I stare at him in disbelief. I know he promised that he'd come to the game, but after what happened the other night . . .

I know this is going to be super awkward, but I have to talk to him. I can't avoid this.

I jog up to him. "Hey."

"Hey," he says back. He doesn't meet my eyes.

"Thanks for coming."

"I said I would. You did really good. Congrats."

"Thanks."

Awkward silence.

I try my hardest to sound casual. "So what happened yesterday? I woke up and you were gone."

"Oh. I was at my therapist's."

My heart drops. He needed to see a therapist after . . . after that night?

"I didn't know you saw a therapist."

He shrugs. "My parents force me to. I go every Saturday."

"Oh." I don't know why I never thought about it before. A therapist is probably the best thing for him, considering all the stuff he's gone through. "So what do you talk about?"

"She tries to get me to talk about my *feelings*, while I try to catch up on my sleep."

"You don't think it helps to talk about stuff with someone?" I'm a little perturbed that he's not taking advantage of the support system his parents have provided, especially considering that night by the river. I try not to think about it too much, but the thought always lingers in the back of my mind: *What if he's still suicidal?*

"Maybe with someone I trust," he says. "I just don't feel comfortable spilling all my deep dark secrets to someone on my dad's payroll."

"Well, maybe you should try it and see what happens. You can't go through life not trusting anybody. She's a professional. It's her job to help you work through your problems."

"It's not like I don't tell her anything. I just don't tell her everything."

"Well, what *do* you talk about?"

"I dunno. School. Parents. The usual."

"Do you talk about me?"

He blushes a little. "Maybe."

I choke back a laugh. "Well, that's a 'yes.' What did you tell her about me?"

He scuffs at the dirt with his shoe. "I told her I was teaching you the piano, and you were teaching me to swim. I told her I was coming to your baseball game today."

"Did you tell her about Friday?" I blurt. I kick myself. *Stupid.*

He freezes. "What about Friday?"

Attempting to play it off, I say, "I don't know. Anything."

He resumes digging a line into the dirt. "Yes, I told her about Friday. How you punched Brandon so hard I swear he blacked out for a second. That was awesome, by the way. And how we hung out at my house. She didn't approve of our underage drinking, but I don't give a shit."

"Will she tell your parents we stole their liquor?" I ask, suddenly alarmed.

He laughs. "No, that's the beauty of it. She can't tell them anything. Patient confidentiality and all that."

I exhale, relieved. "Anything else?"

"What else is there?" His expression is inscrutable. Maybe he honestly doesn't remember. Or he doesn't want to remember. Either way, it looks like that subject is closed. "So how was prom?" he asks.

I groan. "'Horrible' is probably an understatement. I was so hung over from our night of revelry that I felt like I was going to puke the whole time."

He laughs.

"And . . ." I hesitate. "I broke it off with Ashley."

He raises his eyebrows. "You did?"

"Yeah. In the middle of the dance floor, too. It was kind of a shitty way to do it, but things had been rocky for a while and I just couldn't take her bullshit anymore."

Tristan looks like he's attempting very hard to appear somber. "I'm sorry to hear that," he says, his voice shaking.

I peer at him suspiciously. "Are you?"

He breaks down and laughs loudly. "Honestly? No, I'm not sorry. I didn't want to say anything before, but Ashley can be a real bitch."

I can't help smiling a little.

"Yo, Avery! Time to go!" Drake yells from across the field.

I hold up an index finger. He nods.

I turn back to Tristan. "We still on for swimming tomorrow morning?"

"Yeah, of course."

"Okay, cool. See ya then."

I trot across the field with an extra spring in my step.

23

Tristan's voice carries over from the next row of lockers. "Do you think Brandon will be at school today?"

"I'm guessing no," I reply as I take off my shoes. "He probably got suspended for a couple of days, at least. Mr. Smith looked pretty pissed at him."

"Do you think he'll come after you when he gets back to school?"

"I don't know. I don't know Brandon that well. He might try to take revenge, or he might just avoid me since I humiliated him so badly."

Tristan comes around the corner and sits on the bench in front of my bag. "I just hope he leaves us alone," he mutters.

"Me too," I say with a sigh. "If I get into another fight, I'll get kicked off the baseball team."

"What? Are you serious?"

"Yeah. Coach Barnes flipped out when he saw my black eye. We're not supposed to get into fights because it's unsportsmanlike, but I told him that it was self-defense and he let it slide. I don't think he'll give me a pass a second time, though."

"Holy shit! Would that hurt your chances of being drafted?"

I push my bag onto the floor and sit down next to him. "I dunno. Maybe."

"Christ, Avery. I didn't want you to put your future on the line just for me. You should've let me deal with Brandon on my own."

I give him a reproachful look. "Like I would really stand by and let Brandon beat you up. Come on, Tristan."

"But now you're a target, too."

I shrug. "If he comes after me, I'll just ask him to punch me where Coach Barnes can't see the bruises."

He frowns. "That's not funny. He wouldn't be punching you at all if it weren't for me."

"Don't go taking the blame here. It's not your fault that Brandon is a worthless piece of shit. You didn't ask for him to hit you."

"I'd rather he hit me than you," he grumbles. His mouth twists as his eyes linger over my bruises and cuts.

"What's wrong? You don't like my face this way? I thought it made me look like a badass."

The corner of his mouth turns up as he gently tilts my cheek with his fingers. "Yes," he says as he examines my bruise. He drops his hand and declares, "You're one dangerous motherfucker."

"Damn straight." I smile. "Now let's go play with floaties."

We head out to the pool, and I throw the lifesaver and pool noodles into the water. Tristan jumps into the shallow end without hesitation. I guess he finally realized that three feet of water won't hurt him. I dip my toe into the water and call out, "Is it safe?"

He rolls his eyes. "Very funny."

I grin and hop into the pool. "Today, we'll go over treading water.

Swimming's all well and good, but if you're lost at sea, you're just going to wear yourself out faster by swimming around. Sometimes your best bet is to stay where you are and wait for help to find you. But to tread water, you need to be deeper. Follow me."

I grab the lifesaver and tow it over to the wall. He follows me as I grip the wall with one hand and move along it toward the deep end. I stop when our feet can no longer touch the ground and look over at him. His knuckles are white and his eyes are wide and fearful as he hangs on to the edge.

"Just relax," I say. "The worst thing you can do in the water is panic."

He gulps. "Okay."

"Okay, good. Now, there are a few ways to tread water. I'll show you the easiest way and then we'll work our way up from there."

I demonstrate different kinds of kicks and he practices each one with me, first while holding the wall and then without the wall. I keep the lifesaver within his reach just in case, but I'm pleased to see that he doesn't try to grab it, even though he's obviously still anxious about being in so deep.

After a while, he starts to show signs of fatigue. "Do you need a break?" I ask.

He grabs the wall and exhales a sigh of relief. "Yeah, if you don't mind."

"Sure." I toss the lifesaver onto the platform, then crawl along the wall to the ladder next to the diving board. When I reach the top of the ladder, I step to the side so he can climb out. I stretch my arms above my head to loosen up my muscles. Even though we've been coming here almost every day, my body still can't get used to getting up this early.

Without warning, Tristan shoves my back. I shout as I hit the water, swallowing some. I cough it up and wipe the water out of my eyes. "Ohh, that was a *big* mistake, buddy! You're gonna get it."

"You have to catch me first!" he calls as he trots along the platform's edge toward the shallow end.

"No running in the pool area," I scold him in my best authoritative lifeguard voice.

He rolls his eyes at me, then hops into the pool. I hum the *Jaws* theme as I swim toward him, watching his body language to anticipate which way he'll go. As I get closer, he lunges to his right. I just barely miss him. He splashes me in the face. I dive under the water and grab his foot. It's slippery, but I'm able to hold on as he tries to kick me off. I come up out of the water, still holding on to his foot. Instead of trying to get away, he reaches for my shoulders and shoves me back under the water. I let go of his foot and grab his wrists instead. I pull his hands off my shoulders and surface again. Still holding on to his wrists so he can't escape, I shake my head vigorously, like a wet dog. He laughs as the water droplets from my hair hit him in the face. I grin at him and he smiles back at me breathlessly. Then he leans forward and kisses me on the mouth. I stiffen in surprise. Before I've had time to register this turn of events, he breaks away.

"Sorry," he mutters, avoiding my eyes. My thoughts swirl through my brain as he slips out of my grasp and climbs out of the pool. Confused, I watch him disappear into the locker room. *What the hell just happened?*

I walk into the locker room and stop in the doorway. He's under one of the showerheads across the room, but it doesn't look like he's cleaning himself off. He's just standing in his swim trunks under the water with his arms wrapped around himself. I slowly approach, not knowing what to say. As I get closer, the scars across his back catch my eye and my heart goes out to him. I reach out and grip his shoulder. He doesn't turn around at my touch; instead, he seems to shrink inside himself even more.

"I'm really sorry," he chokes. "I'm such an idiot."

He sounds so angry with himself. Doesn't he see that there's nothing to be angry about?

"Tristan . . . ," I murmur. I gently trace one of the scars near his shoulder with my fingertip.

He shudders.

I step forward and press my lips to the back of his neck. I hear his sharp intake of breath. He trembles as I kiss along the back and side of his neck up to just under his ear. The hot water is pouring on my hair and down my face, but I don't care. I can taste the chlorine and sweat and water on his skin.

A door creaks.

Shit! I jump back and hop over to the shower stall at the end of the row. I throw on the water and try my best to look casual.

Jeremy's voice calls out, "Opening time in five minutes, guys."

The door closes again.

My skin tingles as I wait a few more seconds. Tristan's frozen with his head bent toward the drain, but I think he's watching me out of the corner of his eye. I wipe the back of my hand across my forehead and go, "Whew."

He bites his lip and starts to shake. After a few seconds, he can't contain it anymore, and he leans his hands against the wall, laughing harder than I've ever seen him laugh before. I join in, and our laughter reverberates around the locker room walls.

24

"So how are we going to handle this?"

"What do you mean?"

"Well, I'm not sure if I want anyone to know about this just yet," Tristan admits.

I get it. I'm not sure I want the whole world to know about us, either. I look down at our hands, which somehow became connected on the drive to school. "Um . . ." I let go of him, trying to regain some sense. "What if you go in first and I follow? People probably won't say anything if we don't walk together."

"Sure." He picks up his bag and reaches for the door.

"Hey, wait."

He stops and looks back at me, his hand still on the door handle.

God. Are we really doing this?

I glance around the parking lot. Nobody is looking in our direction, and they're all so far away that I doubt they could see into the car anyway. I quickly lean across the center console and touch my lips to his. "See you later," I whisper.

Even in the shadows, his cheeks are bright red. He gets out and walks to the school with his head bowed. I wait until he's halfway across the parking lot before I go out after him.

As usual, Drake is leaning against the wall next to the door. "Hey, Tristan," he calls as Tristan passes.

Tristan continues walking, but I hear him say shyly, "Hey, Drake."

Drake spots me and saunters up. "Good morning, sunshine. What's with you?"

"Nothing. Why?"

"You look too damn happy to be at school on a Monday morning."

I should have known he'd notice something was different. Normally, I'm a grouch in the morning, but right now I'm having trouble wiping this stupid grin off my face. "I dunno. Just in a good mood, I guess."

"Well, if I were you, I'd turn that smile down a few notches before getting to your locker. Ashley's waiting for you, and she won't be too happy to see that you're not completely devastated by your breakup."

Immediately, my smile falters. I hadn't anticipated that Ashley would want to talk to me after the way I treated her this weekend. I figured she'd just avoid me and say bad things about me behind my back. "Okay. Thanks for the heads-up."

I approach my locker the way a man approaches the executioner's block. Sure enough, she's standing there with her arms crossed, accusing me with her blue-green eyes. "Did you get my texts?"

I sigh as I open my locker. "Yes. I did."

"Well, why didn't you call me back?"

"We broke up, Ashley. Remember?"

Her eyes fall. "Look, I'm sorry about what I said. I didn't really mean it when I said we should break up. I was just upset."

"I know you were upset. I was upset, too. I don't like it when you put people down like that."

"I know." She hesitates, then says, "I think it's really good that you're learning the piano. And it is nice of Tristan to teach you."

My book slips out of my hand. I pick it up and close my locker. "Thank you," I say robotically.

She gives me a tentative smile. "So do you want to go out to dinner tonight?"

I sigh again. "Ashley . . ."

"What?" She looks at me wide-eyed.

I try to think of a way to let her down gently, but everything I come up with sounds harsh. "I just want to be friends," I finish.

"Yeah, okay," she replies shakily. Tears form in her eyes and she nods. "That's cool. I think I need some time to think about us, too."

The bell rings before I can explain that I don't need time to think; I've already made my choice.

Over the next couple of weeks, Tristan and I maintain our routine. Only now, there's an element of secretiveness and suspense to it. It's kind of thrilling, actually, like we're fugitives on the run.

After our close call in the locker room, we reached a silent, mutual agreement that we would keep it strictly business while at the community center. I try to keep my distance from him, but it's difficult sometimes when he looks up at me through his eyelashes and gives me a small secretive smile, as if he can read my thoughts.

It's the car ride to school that I look forward to, when we're in the dark and there's no one around, and we can laugh and talk about anything that's on our minds. When we get to school, I park in the very back of the parking lot, under the trees where there's the smallest chance of being seen. Every day, I look around to make sure the coast is clear and then kiss him goodbye before we go in separately. And

The Lifesaver

every day, our kisses get longer and deeper, and it gets harder and harder for me to watch him get out of my car and leave me behind.

During school, we avoid each other, which is relatively easy to do since we don't share any classes. I wish it were like the old days, when I was free to visit with him whenever I wanted and I didn't have to worry about arousing suspicions, but that was back when we had nothing to hide. I still walk by his locker in the afternoons before practice just to check on him, especially now that Brandon is back at school, but he hasn't looked upset or disturbed any of the times I've gone by; in fact, he looks quite the opposite. Every time I pass, I say his name in greeting, and he smiles at the floor as he replies, "*Avery*," and it's enough to assure me that I have nothing to worry about. Sometimes I wonder if this is just the calm before the storm. Whenever I see Brandon in the halls, he gives me a deadly stare, and I stare right back. There's no way I'd ever let him know that he scares me a little. The day that I show weakness to Brandon is the day that Tristan becomes a lamb before the slaughter, and I'm not going to let that happen.

The time after baseball practice is undoubtedly my favorite part of the day. No matter how shitty my day was, when I see Tristan leaning against my car, waiting for me, it never fails to bring a smile to my face. I drive him to his house, which used to seem like a cold, clean castle to me, but now it feels like home. Although I'd love to take advantage of the big empty house all to ourselves, Tristan insists that I continue my piano lessons like before. I've come a long way—I can read sheet music now, and my playing sounds more like music rather than disjointed, senseless noise.

For today's session, I suggested that we take turns playing one song apiece. Whereas the songs I choose are short and simple, his are lengthy and complex (although, I have to admit, his songs would probably be a lot shorter if I didn't keep distracting him with kisses). I love to listen to him play. He's so talented, and I'm always interested to see what he'll decide on next.

It's his turn now, and the song he's playing is unfamiliar to me. The melody is sweet, and the notes seem to flow into one another. After he hits the last note, he lifts his hands from the keys with a flourish.

"I liked that one. What's it called?" I ask.

"'Heaven Can Wait,' by Meat Loaf. Well, Jim Steinman wrote it, actually. My mom and I used to sing it together when I was little. It's one of the few good memories I have of when I lived with her."

"Why don't you sing it for me?"

"I don't like to sing anymore."

That's right. He mentioned that the night we met. "Why don't you like to sing?"

He looks down at the keyboard and wraps his arms around his waist. With a half-hearted shrug, he says, "I dunno. Just doesn't interest me, I guess."

I stare at him, but he refuses to meet my eyes.

"Bullshit," I declare.

He looks up at me, startled.

"You know what I think? I think you love to sing. You're good at it, too. Does it have anything to do with your choir teacher?"

His face turns white, then red. "I don't know what you're talking about."

"Don't lie to me, Tristan. You know exactly what I'm talking about."

"No, I don't know. Enlighten me."

"Well, Ashley told me—"

"Oh, *Ashley* told you," he sneers. "I thought you were better than that, listening to the filthy gossip Ashley and all her little friends spread around school."

I suck in a short, sharp breath. *That hurt.*

"I didn't say I believed her! I just want to know the truth."

"The truth? The truth is that it isn't any of your business!"

"Oh, really? I think it is my business. If something happened to you that caused you to stop doing something you love, I want to know about it so I can help you deal with it."

"You don't have to help me deal with anything," he shouts. "You think I'm like this helpless child who constantly needs a babysitter, but I'm not."

"Tristan—" I begin, but he cuts me off.

"You know what? I think you should leave."

Drake lies across his bed and watches me pace around his room. He lazily tosses a baseball up in the air and catches it in his mitt while I rant. After Tristan kicked me out, I drove straight over to Drake's. I had to vent to somebody, and he was the only person I could think of who could provide unbiased advice.

"I just don't get it. You'd think that after I saved him from an ass-beating, he'd trust me a little," I gripe.

"What do you want to know so bad?"

I shake my head. "That's not the point," I say as I spin his desk chair around and sit down to face him.

"Then what is the point?"

"The point is that he's so . . . *aargh* . . ." I clench my teeth while I mime putting my hands around his neck. *"Aggravating!"*

Drake just sits there and smirks at me.

"What's so funny?" I demand.

"You. In love."

The world comes to a screeching halt. My mouth drops open.

"What did you just say?" I splutter.

"Aw, come on, man, don't give me that! A blind man could see that you two fools are crazy for each other."

I gape at him, speechless.

Drake must see the horror on my face, because he quickly tries to reassure me. "Look, I won't tell anybody if you don't want me to. It's your business. Though God knows what he sees in *you*."

I stare off into space during dinner, trying to sort out the jumble of thoughts and emotions that are consuming me. Drake's words are still ringing in my ears. *Am I in love with Tristan?*

"Hello? Earth to Avery?"

I jump. "What?"

My mother smiles at my bewilderment. "I said, 'How was your day?'"

"Oh. Uh . . ." I can't tell her the truth: that I had a fight with my secret boyfriend, whom I may or may not be in love with. She wouldn't believe me anyway. I can't even believe it, myself; it sounds too preposterous. "Fine," I reply.

"That's informative." She smiles. "Anything you want to talk about?"

Good. A question I can answer truthfully. "No."

"You sure you're okay, sweetie?" she asks, but my father cuts in before I can answer.

"Let him be, Mary. He said he was fine." For once, I'm grateful for my dad's disinterest in my feelings.

She purses her lips in disapproval, but she doesn't ask me any more questions about my day. To my chagrin, she asks me a question that hits closer to home. "I haven't seen Tristan around lately. Are you still friends?"

My heart starts pounding. I try to keep my expression as neutral as possible. "Yeah."

"That's good. He seems like a nice young man."

I shoot a glance at my father. He clenches his jaw, but he doesn't contradict her.

I clear my throat. "May I be excused?"

Her eyebrows furrow. "You hardly ate anything."

"I'm not very hungry."

"Well, that's a first!" she says with a laugh. Then she says, "Are you sure you're okay?"

"I'm fine, Mom!"

"Mary!"

She raises her hands in surrender. "Okay, okay! I'm just checking."

I head upstairs to my room and shut the door. I dump my English book on the bed and try to decipher my reading assignment, but it's no use—my brain won't process the writing on the page. I reread the same sentence four times before I realize that none of the words have sunk in. I can't focus on anything else with Tristan weighing heavily on my mind. I have to figure out my feelings toward him before I can figure out whatever the hell the metaphors mean in Henry James's writing.

I slump back onto the pillow and stare at the ceiling. Even though my body is still, it feels like I'm on the Tilt-A-Whirl at the amusement park. Everything seems so upside down. I thought I knew what love was, but now I'm not so sure. Ashley and I were together for months before we said, "I love you," and even then, it felt more like a duty to say it due to the natural progression of our relationship rather than the burning passion that you hear about in songs. I liked Ashley a lot, and for a while I thought I did love her, but the fact that I don't feel brokenhearted now that we've split up is definitely a sign that I wasn't as head over heels for her as I had led myself to believe.

So what is this thing with Tristan? Everything happened so fast, and I haven't let myself stop to think about what it really means. If I'm not in love with him, then what the hell am I doing? Until recently, I'd never had any reason to doubt my own sexuality. Like any other guy, I'd check out the hot girls in the hallways at school and fantasize about hooking up with *Sports Illustrated* swimsuit models. But I can't deny that Tristan gets under my skin. When he fixes me with his pale blue eyes and he gives me that smile that he saves only for me, I find myself wanting him just as much as, and maybe even more than, I've ever wanted any girl. Does that mean I'm bisexual? How many guys must I be attracted to before I'm no longer straight? I just don't know. After several minutes of internal debate, I give up on trying to categorize myself and focus on how I feel about him.

What if I am . . . ? I'm almost too afraid to finish the thought. How could I fall for another guy? That isn't the kind of future I had hoped for. My plan was to settle down with a beautiful woman, have kids, and have a normal, happy life. Being with somebody my own sex doesn't fit in with that picture. Sure, it's possible for same-sex couples to get married. Maybe even adopt. But it's certainly not the norm, and I can't imagine that everyone I care about would be supportive of that. Not to mention that I'd probably be subjected to ridicule and prejudice on a daily basis. It would be difficult. Very difficult. Is that really what I want for myself, and for my family?

But I don't know why I'm even thinking about a future with Tristan when I don't even know if he wants to be with me anymore. He kicked me out of his house, which usually isn't a good sign. I know I should try to make up with him, but the truth is that I'm angry with him, too. I've done so much for him and he still doesn't trust me enough to talk to me. *I'm just trying to help him. Why does he have to be so stubborn?*

I sigh. I've been mulling things over for an hour and I don't feel like I'm any closer to discovering the truth about Tristan or myself. Reluctantly, I pick up my English book, flip back to page ninety-seven, and start reading from the beginning all over again.

25

I wake up early and text Tristan.

> Swim today?

I drum my fingers impatiently on the bed while I wait for his response. After a few minutes, my phone buzzes. I pick it up and squint at the screen.

> No.

I set my jaw. *I guess he needs some space.* I feel frustrated and disappointed, but I also feel a little relief. Some distance between us might help to give me the perspective I need to figure out what I really want.

I drive to school by myself and go straight to my locker. As I'm pulling binders out of my backpack, Mr. Smith walks up. "Mr. Taylor. Do you have a minute?"

Crap. Is he going to give me detention after all? I close my locker and follow him to his classroom.

"Shut the door, please," he says.

The Lifesaver

I close the door, then sit on one of the desks at the front of the class.

"I've been meaning to talk to you about Mr. Chevalier."

I eye him warily.

"I wanted to say that I appreciate your taking an interest in his well-being. Although I don't condone violence, I admit that your interference in Mr. Stover and Mr. Chevalier's confrontation likely prevented what could have been an even uglier situation. As I'm sure you are aware, Mr. Chevalier does not have many friends. Truth be told, I was concerned about him at the beginning of the year. But I believe that your friendship has helped him to become more self-confident and to take an interest in class. Whatever you're doing, keep it up. He needs people like you to look out for him and to show him that they care."

I swallow the lump that has risen in my throat. "Yes, sir. Thank you."

Tristan opens the door at that moment. He freezes when he sees me sitting on the desk.

As I look at him standing in the doorway, frowning at me, I make up my mind. I walk up to him and steer him out of the classroom. "We need to talk," I mutter under my breath.

He still looks mad at me, but he doesn't protest. He allows me to lead him into the bathroom. I check under the stall doors to make sure that we're alone, then I turn to face him. He crosses his arms and tosses his hair out of his eyes. "What do you want, Avery?"

I take three long strides to bridge the gap between us. I grab his face with both my hands and kiss him, hard. He seems taken aback at first, but then he responds with a passion I've never experienced before. He grabs my hair in both his fists and kisses me deeply and insistently, pressing his body against mine. Desire courses through me, and the intensity of it takes me by surprise. I would love nothing more than to stay right here, locked in his feverish embrace, forever, but I have to remind myself that this isn't the reason I dragged him in here. I know that this is, without a doubt, the least romantic setting I could have picked, but I have to tell him now, before the bell rings and we have to go back to reality. Reluctantly, I tear my lips away from his.

Still holding his face in my hands, I look into his eyes. He looks as exhilarated as I feel. His blue eyes are shining and his cheeks are flushed. I shake his head once and say, "Listen to me. Are you listening?"

He nods quickly, wide-eyed.

Clearly, and without any reservation, I say, "I love you."

He inhales sharply. His lower lip starts to quiver.

"I love you, too," he whispers as the bell rings.

I spend the rest of the morning in a daze. All the stress from finals and baseball and college just disappears, and it feels like I'm floating on a cloud. *He loves me.*

Drake snaps his fingers in front of my face. I jump.

"What?" I say as I take another bite of my cardboard cafeteria pizza.

"Snap out of it. You look like a twitterpated zombie."

I laugh. "What the hell does that mean?"

"You know what I'm talking about. Don't deny it. So when are you going to tell him?"

"Tell who what?"

He shakes his head. "God, you're so fucking hopeless. Both of you are."

"Are you just going to keep speaking in riddles all day, or are you actually going to get to a point eventually?"

"You know what? Forget I said anything. It's none of my business anyway. But if you want to keep secrets from me, you're gonna have to work on your poker face. I can read you like a book."

I scowl at him. I don't know why I'm so reluctant to tell Drake that he nailed it on the head. Maybe it's because I'm sick of him being right all the time. Or I'm afraid that if I admit it to one person, then I'll have to admit it to everybody and I'm just not ready for that yet.

After school, I make my way over to Tristan's locker. He blushes and looks away when he sees me. As casually as possible, I hold out a folded piece of paper and say, "Here. I forgot to give you this earlier."

Bemused, he takes the piece of paper from my hand and unfolds it to read it.

Meet me outside your house at 6#. I love you.

He looks up at me quickly, his eyes wide.

"Well, see you around," I say as I walk past him.

I glance back over my shoulder. He reads the note again, then, with a secretive smile, he folds the paper hurriedly and stuffs it into his pocket.

When I get home, I pull out our old cooler from the hall closet and lug it into the kitchen. I've been trying to come up with ideas for taking Tristan out on a date, but it's difficult because restaurants and all the other normal spots are public places, which wouldn't be conducive to keeping our relationship a secret. I finally decided on a picnic, which sounds cheesy, but at least it would provide some privacy.

My mother comes through the door as I'm making sandwiches. "What are you doing?" she asks.

"I've decided I can't take it anymore, so I'm running away from home."

"Hmm, that's nice. Don't forget your jacket." She smiles.

I smile back. "No, I'm just gonna meet up with Tristan to study. I told him I'd bring refreshments." *A little white lie never hurt anybody.*

"Oh, okay. Tell him 'hi' for me."

"Will do."

I throw the sandwiches into the cooler and close the lid. I grab the handle and open the back door to leave, but my mother's voice stops me. "Forgetting something?"

I turn around, confused. She nods at my backpack on the floor by the counter.

"Oh. Right. Thanks." I grab it and she gives me a smile as I shut the door behind me.

I park in front of Tristan's house right before six. Just as the clock ticks over, Tristan opens the door and trots down the steps. He walks hurriedly to my car and jumps in.

"Where are we going?" he asks, out of breath.

"You'll see." I hand him the aux cord as I pull away from the curb. "You wanna pick something?"

He searches his phone for a moment, then settles on Bob Seger. As "Night Moves" begins to play, I turn up the volume, then reach over and grab his hand. He blushes and looks out the window. I sing and he hums softly along with the music while I drive.

I take him across town, past all the shopping centers and the police station and the library, until we come to an old neighborhood full of small houses that were built in the mid-1900s. Many of them have fallen into disrepair, but there are several whose owners still care enough to make them look habitable. I pull up in front of a ranch-style house at the end of a cul-de-sac and turn off the engine.

The house has dark wood siding that looks like it could stand to be replaced, and the roof is missing several shingles. An old tattered American flag hangs limply by the front door. The grass is slightly overgrown, and faded children's toys litter the yard.

Tristan gives me a confused look. I nod toward the house and say, "That's where I was born. In that house."

He raises his eyebrows and looks back at the house. "You were born there? Not in the hospital?"

I shake my head. "No. My mom was on bed rest at home for most of her pregnancy. She had a high risk of miscarriage, so the doctors told her she couldn't walk or do anything except lie down the last several weeks. She went into labor early, and by the time the ambulance came, it was too late. I'd already been born. They were able to patch her up, but they told her she couldn't have any more kids after that. I think it broke her heart because she always wanted a big family."

He swallows and says, "I wish I had a mom like that. I don't think my mom even wanted me. I think she had me so my dad would stick around, but he left her anyway."

"What about Jeanine? What is she like?"

He shrugs. "She's okay. I'm probably not as nice to her as I should be. I think she tries, but to me, she's just my dad's wife."

I kiss the back of his hand, then say, "My mom likes you, you know. I told her I was meeting you and she said to make sure I told you 'hi' for her."

"Did you tell her about us?" he asks, surprised.

"No," I admit. "I haven't told anyone. Though Drake knows anyway. He's too damn observant. He asked me at lunch today when I was going to tell you how I feel about you."

He sits forward in his seat. "Are you serious?"

"I'm dead serious. It wasn't even four hours after I told you that he asked me about it. It's like he could read my mind."

"Well, what did you tell him?"

"I played dumb. It's not like I could just announce out loud to him in a crowded cafeteria that yes, I'd kissed you and told you I loved you in the guys' bathroom just this morning."

"Are you going to tell him?"

"I dunno. I might eventually. It's weird, though. I've slept over at his house so many times, I just . . ." I trail off, not sure how to finish the sentence.

He sighs and rests back in his seat. "Yeah, I know what you mean. People always think I have an ulterior motive for everything I do."

"Well, don't you?"

His mouth twitches. "If I do, I'll let you know."

I grin and start the engine. He watches my childhood home get smaller in the sideview mirror as I drive down the street.

When we get to the main intersection, I turn the opposite direction of the way we came. Tristan looks over at me, but I don't explain where we're going. After a few minutes, I point out the window at an old brick building with a handful of trailers next to it. "That's where Drake and I went to elementary school."

"You went to Woodlawn?"

"Yep. The Woodlawn Woodchucks."

He laughs. "The *Woodchucks*? That's lame."

"What were you?"

"Shit, I don't remember. I went to Jefferson. So you and Drake have been going to the same school since elementary?"

"Yeah. We moved into our house right after I finished the sixth grade. Drake's family moved to the same neighborhood a couple weeks later, so we ended up going to the same middle school and high school, too. Funny how things work out like that sometimes."

"Why are you showing me all this?" he asks curiously.

"Do I need a reason to take a trip down memory lane with my sweetheart?"

He wrinkles his nose. "Don't call me that. It makes me sound like a chick."

"Okay, then. What should I call you? Pumpkin? Sugar lips? Boo bear?"

"Stop. You're gonna make me puke."

"Whatever you say, stud muffin."

"*Stud muffin*? That's it. Turn around. I want to go home."

"No. You're my hostage for this evening."

"Oh, really? You gonna tie me up so I can't escape?"

"Mmm. Sounds kinky. I'm game if you are."

His mouth drops open. I can't help but laugh at the mixture of shock and embarrassment on his face. "Hold on, I need a picture of this. That look on your face is priceless."

He flushes and shakes his head. "Shut up, Taylor."

"Oh, so now I'm 'Taylor' again? You must really be mad at me."

"I'm not mad at you. I'm just amazed that one person can be so obnoxious."

"You know you love it."

"You keep telling yourself that." After a moment, he asks, "Does it bother you when I call you 'Taylor'?"

I shrug. "No, not really. I think it's funny when you do. You can call me whatever you want. Even 'stud muffin.'"

"Thanks, but I think I'll pass on that one."

I grin. "I do like it when you say my name, though. My first name, that is."

"Alright. Avery." A thrill runs down the base of my spine as he sounds out my name. "I'll only call you 'Taylor' on special occasions."

I flash him a smile. "Sounds good."

I turn onto a side street that winds its way for several miles through the forest. I always loved driving down this street when I was a kid, especially in autumn when all the leaves changed color and they fell from the trees like rain on a blustery day. Right now, though, the trees are bright green with their spring foliage. At the end of the street, the trees open up to reveal a little park. I pull into a parking space next to a small playground. It looks just as I remember it, except the wood on the jungle gym has darkened over time and one of the chains on the swing set has broken. Beyond the playground, there's a field with a baseball diamond and a handful of benches at one end and a couple of goalposts way down at the other end. The park is deserted, as I'd hoped.

"You hungry?" I ask as I unbuckle my seat belt.

His brow furrows. "Yeah, I guess so."

"Good." I smile and get out of the car.

I walk around to the trunk and pull out the cooler and blanket. He laughs when he sees them. "A picnic? Are you serious?"

"Sure. Why not?" I grin as I slam the trunk shut.

"Damn, I left my sundress and parasol at home."

"That's okay. I won't tell anyone."

He follows me over to the baseball field. I spread the blanket out on the pitcher's mound and sit down cross-legged on top of it. He sits beside me and watches as I pull out the food and drinks from the cooler.

"So what possessed you to do all this?" he asks.

"Actually, you can thank Mr. Smith. It was his idea."

"Mr. Smith told you to take me on a picnic?"

"Not in so many words, no. But he told me that I should show you that I care about you, and I figured you'd rather I gave you food than diamond earrings."

"He said that?"

"Yeah. I think he cares about you, too, in that strict, no-nonsense, old-fashioned way of his." I hand him a sandwich and a water bottle. "Sorry, we didn't have champagne."

He chuckles. "That's okay. I've sworn off drinking since our game night a few weeks ago."

"Yeah, me too. I'm not anxious to relive that hangover anytime soon."

We watch the sun set over the tops of the trees as we eat our sandwiches. The sky turns a soft orange, then slowly deepens into a dark pink followed by purple. I'm relieved that it turned out to be such a beautiful evening. Something tells me my idea for a picnic wouldn't have gone over nearly as well if it had started raining.

Tristan watches a flock of geese fly overhead. "How did you know about this place?" he asks.

"This is where I first learned how to play baseball. Drake and I used to come here every weekend for Little League practice. It looks just like it used to, only smaller." I point toward the playground. "And that's where I had my first kiss. Tracy Long. I was six and she was seven. I'd fallen off the swing and I was just bawling. I was a little wimp then. I don't even know where my dad was—he was probably off talking with some of his buddies and not even paying attention to me. But Tracy came up and kissed me on the lips, and I immediately stopped crying. I told myself I would grow up to marry her, but the next day I saw her kiss Kyle Gragson and so I wrote her off for good."

Tristan laughs. "Have you had a lot of girlfriends?" Normally, that's a loaded question, but the way he asks, it doesn't sound like he's trying to bait me; he sounds genuinely curious.

I shrug. "A few. Ashley was the longest. Most of my relationships ended after a couple months because they thought I wasn't serious enough. It's not that I didn't like them, it's just that I didn't feel the need to tattoo their names on my arm or exchange vials of blood with them. They just didn't get that."

He smirks. "How shallow of you."

"I know." I sigh. "I'm so ashamed."

"Well, if it makes you feel any better, I don't want a vial of your blood."

"Dammit! Now you tell me. That was going to be my next gift to you."

He laughs. He pulls his knees up to his chest and wraps his arms around his legs. "Any more interesting stories about this place?"

I smile as I slide closer to him. I caress his cheek with my thumb. "We can make some," I say, then I kiss him softly on the mouth. He closes his eyes and parts his lips, causing my pulse to quicken. I slide my arm around him as he slowly rotates his body toward mine. Although this sweet embrace is nothing like the desperate, frenzied one we shared this morning, that doesn't make my desire any less intense.

My phone buzzes in my pocket, ruining the moment. "Goddamn it!" I sigh, exasperated. I shoot him an apologetic look and pull my phone out of my pocket. I squint at the screen. It's a text from Coach Doyle:

Match postponed until 9:30.

"Who is it?" Tristan asks.

"It's my fencing instructor. Apparently, our match tomorrow got pushed back an hour."

"What time does it start?"

"Nine thirty."

"In the morning?"

"Yeah."

"Do you mind if I come and watch?"

My heart leaps. None of my friends or significant others have ever come to watch my fencing matches. But then I remember what Tristan told me about Saturdays. "Don't you have therapy during that time?"

He shrugs. "I'm supposed to, but I can skip it."

The selfish part of me wants him to blow off his therapist to spend time with me, but I don't want him to stop going to his sessions, either. Not if they have the slightest chance of giving him some peace of mind about his past. "I don't know, Tristan. I don't want you to stop going because of me."

"It's just one session. Despite what my therapist might think, I can survive one Saturday without her."

I spend a few seconds weighing the pros and cons. *One Saturday can't hurt.* "Well, okay. But I want you to promise me something."

"What is it?"

"I want you to try to talk to your therapist. I think she could really help you."

He rolls his eyes. "There you go again, thinking I'm a damsel in distress."

I smile. "Want me to sing you a love ballad?"

"No."

I laugh.

"Seriously, though," I say as I look into his eyes. "I know you're keeping things from me."

He opens his mouth to protest, but I hold up my hands and say, "And that's okay. I don't need to know." I heave a sigh. "I'm really sorry about yesterday. I shouldn't have pressured you to tell me things you don't want to tell me. I hope you feel comfortable enough to talk to me about anything, but I understand if there's some things you just don't want to discuss."

He bites his lip, then says, "I'm sorry, too. I overreacted. I shouldn't have kicked you out."

I give him a lopsided smile. "It's okay. Next time, you can just say, 'Shut the fuck up, Taylor,' and I'll leave you alone."

"Okay." He smiles shyly.

I resume a more serious tone. "Listen. I know you don't want to hear this, but I have to say it anyway. All those things you don't want to talk about? It's not good to keep it bottled up inside. If you don't want to tell me about it, that's fine, but you should tell *someone*. And the best person to tell is your therapist."

"I don't know, Avery. You know how hard it is for me to talk to people besides you."

"I know, but I want you to try. That's what your parents are paying her for. You don't have to do all this on your own, you know."

He frowns as he examines my face. He must see the pleading in my eyes, because, finally, he whispers, "Okay."

"You promise?"

"I promise."

I smile and lean forward to kiss his downturned mouth. Somewhat reluctantly, he kisses me back. I can tell he's not pleased that I'm pressuring him to come clean. I don't feel guilty, though. He may not agree with me, but I honestly believe it's in his best interest to discuss his issues with someone who has experience in dealing with things like that. With any luck, he'll come to see it that way, too, and then he'll forgive me.

26

Here we go.

I take a deep breath, then grab my saber, tuck my mask under my arm, and make my way out to the gym. Tristan's sitting alone on one of the folding chairs along the side wall, watching my teammates get warmed up. He smirks when he spots me. I feel the blood rise to my face as I walk up to him. *Maybe this was a bad idea.* It's one thing to look like this when everyone's dressed the same, but now I am uncomfortably aware of how lame our uniforms must look to him.

"You look like a droog," he says as he looks me up and down.

I glance over at the mirror. With the all-white uniform and the way the *lamé* tapers over the crotch, I can totally see why he'd think I look like the futuristic teen miscreants from *A Clockwork Orange*. I laugh a little, embarrassed. "I never thought about it before, but yeah, I guess I do."

I look back down at him. He tilts his head, then says, with a sensual half-smile on his lips, "It's kind of hot, actually."

My jaw goes slack. That is literally the last thing I expected to come out of his mouth. After a couple of seconds, I recover enough to tease, "Just wait until you see me with my mask on. Then you won't be able to keep your hands off me."

"If it really is you. If you're all wearing masks, I won't be able to tell you apart. Who knows? I could end up going home with Brutus over there." He nods toward Brian Thurston, who dwarfs everyone else on the team.

"You better not! Okay, new rule: no going home with anyone wearing a mask."

"Hmmm. I guess I can live with that." He smiles.

"Okay." I smile back, then slide my mask over my head.

He grins wider and nods. "Oh yeah. That's much better."

I kick his foot and he laughs.

"Taylor," Coach calls from behind me. "Waiting on you."

I give Tristan a thumbs-up, then trot over to get in line with the rest of the team. As Coach goes over the order in which we'll duel, I feel a twinge of anxiety. *What if I mess up?* I try to push the thought away, but it clings to the back of my mind.

Throughout the match, I try to keep my attention on my opponent, but I'm so self-conscious with Tristan watching that I don't do nearly as well as I'd hoped. I'm not the worst on the team, but I'm definitely not at the top of the list, either. Afterward, I shake hands with all my sparring partners, then walk back over to Tristan, feeling defeated. I take my mask off and wipe the sweat from my brow. He bites his lip as if he's thinking something but doesn't want to say it out loud.

"What?" I ask, dreading what his answer might be. I don't think I could take it if he told me how disappointing my performance was.

He flushes and shakes his head. "Nothing."

The Lifesaver

"What is it?"

"You just . . . look really good."

As his words sink in, a slow smile spreads across my face. "You are totally digging this outfit, aren't you?"

"It's not just that. You standing there with your hair all wet, and the way you moved up there . . ." He sounds almost frustrated as he gestures at me, then at the platform. "You just look like a million bucks, is all."

"The way I *moved*?" I groan. "I was horrible."

"What are you talking about? I thought you did great!"

"I definitely didn't do great. Normally, I'm in the top two or three, but I just wasn't feeling it today. I think I was nervous because you're here."

Surprised, he asks, "Why were you nervous?"

"I dunno. I just didn't want to screw up in front of you."

He scoffs. "You know I can't do this shit. Even if you came in last, I'd still be impressed." With real admiration in his voice, he says, "I can't believe how quickly you move. It's like watching a snake fight."

Warmth seeps through my body like honey at the unexpected compliment.

Just then, Coach Doyle comes up to us. "Good effort today, Taylor."

"Thanks, Coach."

He looks at Tristan and asks, "Is this a new recruit?"

I smile at the thought. "No. He's just here to watch. He hadn't seen fencing before."

"I hope you'll consider it. We could always use more people." He stretches out his hand. "Patrick Doyle. I'm one of the instructors here."

Tristan shakes his hand. "Tristan Chevalier."

"Oh, a knight!"

Stupefied, we both gape at him. In a low voice, Tristan says, "What?"

"Chevalier," Coach says, as if it were obvious. "The French word for 'knight.'"

Tristan and I look at each other. He looks absolutely horrorstruck by this revelation. I start laughing, and then I can't stop. He glares at me as I double over from laughter. "Shut up, Avery," he mutters, but that only makes me laugh harder. Coach looks between us, obviously bewildered by our extreme reactions to hearing Tristan's namesake.

I wipe the tears from my eyes and say to Tristan, "Ohhh my God. I'm glad you came today. That was totally worth it."

Tristan insists on attending my baseball game as well, even though I assured him I wouldn't mind if he'd rather do something else besides sit through all my sporting events. His eyes widen when he sees the ten or so men lined up behind the backstop. "Are those all scouts?"

"Yeah, looks like it."

"Wow. You're practically famous."

"Don't worry, I won't let it go to my head. I'll only sign autographs after the game."

He doesn't laugh; he doesn't even crack a smile. He just continues looking at the scouts with a slightly worried expression on his face.

"You okay?"

He seems to snap out of it. "Yeah, I'm fine."

"Okay. I'll come find you after."

"Okay. Break a leg. Or whatever you jocks say to each other."

He heads over to the bleachers and I make my way onto the field. I try to quell my nervousness while I stretch. You'd think I'd be used to the scouts by now, but I guess old habits die hard.

The Lifesaver

The game goes by pretty quickly. After I shake hands with the players, the scouts descend on me like buzzards. By the time I'm able to make my escape, everyone else has gone home. I find Tristan sitting cross-legged on the grass underneath the bleachers, gazing toward the trees. I sit next to him, but he doesn't look at me.

"You did good," he says, but he sounds far away.

"Thanks."

I wait, but he doesn't say anything more.

"Are you okay?"

"Yeah." He smiles at me, but it doesn't reach his eyes.

"What is it? What's wrong?"

He sighs and looks back at the tree line. "Why are you with me, Avery?"

"What do you mean?"

"You're so good at everything you do. You're an amazing athlete, and you're funny and gorgeous and you're the nicest person on the planet. You could seriously have any girl you wanted." He shakes his head and looks down at his lap. "I just don't see why you're with me."

I give him a half-smile. "I don't know. Maybe I wanted to try something different, for a change."

He looks stricken. My stomach falls.

"Oh my God, Tristan, I'm just kidding! You know it's not like that. I'm with you because I love you, not because I decided one day to see if the grass was greener on the other side! I may be curious, but I'm not *that* curious."

He doesn't look at me, but the corner of his mouth turns up. "You're not curious?" he says as he picks at the blades of grass in front of his lap.

My heart trips, then thuds harder than before. I lean in close to nuzzle his ear. "Okay," I murmur, "maybe I'm a *little* curious."

He smiles.

I turn his chin so he's looking at me. "But that's not the reason I'm with you. You got that?"

"Yeah," he says softly. "I got it."

27

Ashley approaches me before first period. "Hi." It's the first word she's spoken to me since I rejected her.

"Hi . . ." I don't know what she wants, but whatever it is, it doesn't bode well for me.

"I was hoping you'd want to go get a cup of coffee with me after school today."

"Can't. I've got practice."

"I know, but after."

I take a deep breath to prepare to let her down gently, but she cuts me off. "You told me you wanted to be friends. Were you lying when you said that?"

The weight of remorse presses heavily on my shoulders as her wounded eyes bore into me. I shouldn't treat her so coldly. Even though we're not a couple anymore, it would be cruel to act as though I never cared about her. *Maybe we can still be friends.*

"No," I say. "I wasn't lying. Coffee sounds great." Tristan has his piano lesson today anyway, so I don't see any harm in it.

Her face lights up. "Cool. Let me know when you get out and I'll meet you at Starbucks."

"That works. I'll see you then."

After practice, I text Ashley, then drive over to the Starbucks. By the time I get there, she's already inside waiting for me at a table near the back. She's changed into a flattering blue dress that she knows I like, and she's done something with her makeup to bring out her eyes. It makes me uncomfortable to think that she's trying to impress me, but I don't call her out on it.

"I ordered you a caramel macchiato," she says as she hands me a cup.

"Thanks," I say, surprised that she remembered my favorite drink. I pull out my wallet and thumb through the bills.

"Don't worry about it. It's on me."

I furrow my eyebrows. "You sure?"

"Yeah, I dragged you out here."

"Oh. Thanks." I shove my wallet back into my pocket.

"You're welcome." She sips at her coffee.

"So how've you been?" I've been avoiding her for so long, I'm not sure if she's enjoying her newfound freedom or if she's spent the last few weeks holed up in her room, crying. I hope it's not the latter.

She shrugs a little. "I'm okay," she says, but I can hear a hint of sadness in her voice. "I've been really busy, actually. My parents are preparing this big graduation party for me, so I've been helping them get ready for that, and I've been spending a lot of time practicing for our final cheer competition next week. On top of studying for finals, of course."

"Yeah, I can't believe they start next week. I feel like this semester just flew by."

"Yeah, I know. Can you imagine how quickly the summer will go by? And then we'll be off at college. Or at least I will be. Have you heard anything more about the draft?"

"It starts next month. I put in a deposit for Middleton, though, in case it doesn't work out."

"That's a good idea. Do you know what you want to study?"

"I haven't made up my mind yet. I may look into their psychology program. Find out what makes people tick."

"Really? I didn't know you were interested in psychology."

I shrug. "Well, it's either that or underwater basket weaving. I'll probably just flip a coin when it comes time to choose my major."

She smiles. "You never change, do you?"

"I don't know about that. I feel like a lot has changed this year." I swirl my straw around my cup as I mutter, "I'm surprised I can even recognize myself in the mirror."

Her smile dims. "Yeah, you're right. Some things have changed, at least."

I need to steer the conversation away from myself. "What about you? What do you want as your major?"

"I'm thinking about business with a concentration in marketing. You can use that just about anywhere."

"I think that'd be good for you. You're good at promoting stuff."

She blushes at the compliment. "Thanks. I hope so." She looks down at the cup in her hand. "Are you seeing anyone?" she asks, keeping her eyes trained on the lid.

I'm tempted to tell her the truth, but I know I can't. If I told her, that would pretty much guarantee the end of our friendship, and then the whole world would know about my relationship with Tristan before the first bell rang tomorrow morning.

"I'm not interested in having another girlfriend right now."

Technically, it's not a lie. "What about you? You probably had a long line of suitors waiting to snatch you up. Am I right?" I ask with a crooked smile.

She chuckles. "I did have a couple of guys ask for my number. I turned them down, though. Right now, they'd just be a rebound, and I don't need any of that drama. I figured I'll just wait until college before I enter the dating scene again."

I nod. "Makes sense."

She gives me a wistful smile. "I miss you."

I know I have to be careful in how I reply. I don't want to give her false hope.

"We had some good times together," I admit.

"Yeah, we did." She drains her cup, then says, "You ready?"

"Yeah."

We throw our cups away and walk out to the parking lot. Her car is next to the entrance, so I stand by and watch her unlock her door. She turns around and gives me a hug. "Thanks for meeting me," she whispers in my ear, then pecks me on the cheek. Before she gets in her car, she says, "Maybe you, me, and Drake can go bowling sometime."

"Yeah, that'd be cool."

"Okay." She smiles. "I'll see you later, Avery."

"Bye."

I stop by my driver's side door, and she waves as she drives by. I lift my hand in return, then exhale slowly. *That wasn't so bad.*

Hopefully, tonight gave her a sense of closure, so we can both move on with the next chapter in our lives.

"I think I'm ready for my first concert, don't you?" I finally made it through "Piano Man" without screwing up once and I'm feeling pretty damn good about myself.

Tristan smirks. "You want to give a concert?"

"Yeah. You can be my stage manager. We'll charge a hundred bucks a seat and make a ton of money. It's foolproof!"

"And what makes you think people would want to come see you?"

"Isn't it obvious? With my God-given talent and devastatingly good looks, people will be lining up for miles. I'll be the biggest sex icon to tickle the ivories. Well, except Mozart. I hear he was hot stuff."

"Oh my God, you're ridiculous."

"You say that now, but just you wait. We'll see who's laughing when the money starts rolling in. Though we'll need to hire some bouncers to keep the ladies from rushing the stage when I start to play. I might be able to ward them off for a little while, but all bets are off once the panties start flying."

He shakes his head. "You never change, do you?"

"Why does everyone keep saying that?"

"What do you mean?"

"Ashley said the same thing last night."

Instantly, Tristan's smile disappears. His face turns ashen. "You were with Ashley last night?"

"Yeah, we went to Starbucks. Why? Are you jealous?" I ask, surprised. After all we've been through, it never occurred to me that Tristan might still be jealous of Ashley.

He swallows. "No," he answers, but I can tell that he's lying. I kick myself for having been so callous.

"Don't worry, nothing happened. We just had coffee, that's all. She's just a friend."

"She's not just a friend. She's your ex-girlfriend!"

"Yes, but that doesn't mean I'm gonna get back together with her."

He frowns and looks at the wall away from me. *Does he not believe me?*

I sigh. "Tristan, why do you think I broke up with her?"

"I don't know," he mumbles to the wall. "She's pretty and she's popular and she obviously likes you."

I roll my eyes and nudge him with my shoulder. "I broke up with her for *you*, dummy."

His head swivels back around. "What?"

"Yeah. At prom, we got into a fight over you. Basically, it was you or her and I chose you. And *then*, two days later, you and I got together. You think that was just coincidence?"

His mouth hangs open. "You mean, that morning at the pool . . . you were *planning* on making a move on me?"

"Well, no," I admit. "That was kind of a spur-of-the-moment thing. I guess I was hoping we would get together eventually, but then you kissed me and I knew that that was my chance."

He shakes his head in disbelief. "I thought I'd totally blown it when I kissed you. I thought for sure that you'd never want to see me again. I had no idea you felt the same way about me."

"Honestly, I didn't know it either until that weekend. I didn't really figure it out until Saturday morning, when I woke up and you were gone and I realized how much I cared that you had left me without saying goodbye."

"I'm sorry. You looked so peaceful, I didn't want to disturb you."

"It's okay. I forgave you as soon as I saw you at my baseball game. That meant a lot to me that you showed up."

"I said I would."

"I know you did. But still, I appreciate it." I kiss his cheek, then say, "So no hard feelings? About Ashley?"

He gives me a small smile. "No. I guess not." Then he says, "But just so you know, I don't care if she *is* a girl. If she tries to take you away from me, I'll kick her fucking ass."

28

Ashley's waiting for me by my locker Friday morning. Since our coffee outing, she's become a familiar sight in the hallways at school. It almost feels like it used to, back before we hooked up, when we were just good friends.

"Hey," I say.

She smiles. "Hey! Are you and Drake doing anything tonight?"

"I dunno. Why?"

"You said you might want to go bowling sometime. I was thinking we could go tonight, say around eight? If you don't have anything else going on, that is."

"Umm . . ." I thought Ashley was just being friendly when she suggested going bowling the other night; I didn't know she was really serious about it. I'd rather be with Tristan, but I can't keep blowing Ashley off if I want to maintain our friendship. "Yeah, okay. I'll check with Drake." After a split second of hesitation, I ask, "Do you mind if Tristan comes too?" I know it's risky, but maybe I can spend time with Tristan and keep Ashley happy at the same time.

She purses her lips, but she replies, "Yeah, sure. Invite whoever you want."

"Okay, cool. I'll see you tonight, then."

Her face brightens. "Okay. See ya."

"You wanna go bowling with me and Ashley and Tristan tonight?" I ask Drake during lunch.

He chokes on his Coke. "Ashley *and* Tristan?"

I shrug. "Yeah. Why not?"

"Man, you've got a death wish."

"Why?"

"You can't put Ashley and Tristan in the same room. Are you crazy?"

"Why? They're both my friends. If they want to be friends with me, they should learn to get along."

"I think you're treading on thin ice here. You know how Ashley feels about Tristan, and I can imagine he's not fond of her, either."

"How Ashley feels isn't my problem anymore."

"Well, what about Tristan? Is he okay with this little group therapy session?"

"I don't know. I haven't asked him yet. I don't think he'd have a problem with it. He knows Ashley and I are still friends."

He studies me for a moment, then shakes his head. "Yeah, count me in. I wouldn't want to miss the fireworks."

"Drake and Ashley want to go bowling tonight. You wanna go?" I ask Tristan as I drive him back to his house.

His eyebrows lift in surprise. "Ashley?"

"Yeah."

"Are you sure you want me to come?"

"Yeah. Why wouldn't I?"

"I don't know. I just figured she wouldn't want me around."

"You're my boyfriend. If she wants to still be friends with me, she's gonna have to put up with you, too."

"It's weird hearing you say that word."

"What? 'Boyfriend'?"

"Yeah."

"Well, that's what you are, right?"

"Yeah, I guess. It's still weird, though."

"Well, get used to it. Anyway, do you want to go?"

"I do, but are you sure it's a good idea? If Drake already suspects we're together, aren't you afraid that Ashley will find out too?"

"We'll just have to be careful, that's all."

He thinks for a second, then says, "Alright. What time are we going?"

"I'll pick you up around seven thirty."

"You're not staying?"

"No. I've got some errands to run."

"Oh. Okay." He looks disappointed.

"Don't worry." I smile at him. "I'll see you tonight."

At seven thirty, Tristan slides into the passenger seat. I hold out a small bouquet of wildflowers.

"What the hell is this?" he says.

"You said that if I wanted to get past first base with you, then I'd have to bring you some flowers. So here you go."

He laughs. "Are you kidding me?"

"You know, most people would be happy that their boyfriend brought them flowers on a date."

"Is this a date?" He takes the flowers from my hand and smiles as he looks them over.

"Yes. Just one where we're not alone and we can't act like we're on a date."

He chuckles. "Sounds romantic," he says as he tosses the flowers onto the back seat.

I grab his hand as I start to drive. "So I was thinking we need a game plan for tonight. Apparently, I don't know when I'm flirting with you so you need to let me know when I'm being too obvious."

"How?"

"We need like a signal."

He smirks. "You want me to hoot like an owl or something?"

I laugh. "No, I mean like cough or tug on your ear or something like that."

"Hmm, that could work. How about this for a signal?"

He lifts my hand to his mouth. He looks up at me through his eyelashes and seductively sucks on the tip of my middle finger. My jaw drops to the floor. *Holy shit!*

"You keep that up, I'm gonna wreck my car," I scold.

He lowers my hand and grins. "Sorry, I couldn't resist. Not after you bought me those pretty flowers and all."

"Well, if I'd known they'd have that kind of effect on you, I'd have given them to you a lot sooner!"

He laughs. Then he says, "I guess I could touch the back of my neck. Would that work?"

"What, as a signal?" I ask, confused. I'm still distracted by the feeling of his lips around my finger.

"Yeah."

"Yeah, okay. Works for me."

We pull into the parking lot outside of the bowling alley. I park as far away as possible from the entrance to allow us a little privacy while in the car. "You ready for our non-date date?" I ask.

He kisses me, then smiles and says, "Yep. Let's do it."

We get out of the car and walk toward the entrance. I try to keep a foot or two between us. Ashley's already by the door, and it looks like she made an effort to dress to impress again. She's wearing more makeup than usual, and she's wearing a close-fitting lavender shirt and a short black skirt. Her outfit isn't slutty, but it's definitely something to make a guy take notice. Tristan's eyebrows rise when he sees her, then he shoots me a sideways look. I sigh inwardly. I'm probably going to hear about this later.

"Hi!" she says to me.

"Hey," I reply.

Tristan doesn't say anything.

"Is Drake coming?" she asks.

"Yeah, he should be here any minute now."

"Okay, good. I reserved two lanes."

"Oh. Thanks."

At that moment, Drake's car pulls into the parking lot. We watch as he parks in the front row. He jumps out of his car and struts up to us. "Hey, how's everybody doin'?" He shakes my hand and pats me on the back, then does the same with Tristan.

"Hey, Drake," Tristan says.

Ashley's eyes widen when she sees how friendly Drake and Tristan are with each other. She clears her throat. "Shall we go in?"

She already got her bowling shoes, so she goes to pick out her ball while Drake and I make our way over to the shoe counter. Tristan follows a step behind. "Where are we going?" he asks.

"To get our shoes," I say.

"We need special shoes?"

"Haven't you been bowling before?" I peer into the cubbies to see if they have my size. Drake tries to flag down the shoe guy, but he's too preoccupied with his cell phone to notice us.

"No," Tristan answers.

Drake and I both turn to gawk at him.

"You've never been bowling before?" Drake says.

"No."

Drake and I look at each other, then break out into identical grins. "Should we tell him about the bumpers?" he asks me.

"Bumpers?" Tristan says. "What's that?"

It's tempting to let him try to hack it out without the bumpers, but I decide to go easy on him. I don't want him getting too frustrated on our secret date. Feigning reluctance, I say, "Yeah, we probably should." I look at Tristan and tease, "Since he's a virgin and all."

Tristan flushes. He avoids my eyes as he rubs the back of his neck. *Is he?* I wonder. Maybe he's embarrassed because he is. Or perhaps he's embarrassed because he's not.

The shoe guy finally comes over and takes our shoe orders. "They don't want us messing up their floors, so we have to wear their shoes," I explain to Tristan.

"Huh. That's kinda weird."

We receive our shoes from the counter, then walk past a handful of tables and down a couple of stairs to get to our lanes. In front of each lane, there's a row of plastic chairs, and in between the rows sit two computer monitors. After I get my shoes on, I pick out a couple of bowling balls from the rack by the stairs. I carry them over to where Ashley is standing by the ball return rack and set them down next to hers. As I press the button to lift the bumpers, she asks, "What are you doing?"

"Tristan's never done this before, so he's going to use the bumpers."

"Well, I don't want to use the bumpers."

"That's fine. I'll be in his lane. You and Drake can be in the left lane."

She hesitates as if she's about to argue, then she says, "Fine. Should I go get some drinks?"

"Uh, sure. Here, I'll get the first round." I pull out my wallet and give her some bills. "Why don't you get us a pitcher of Coke and whatever else you want?"

"Okay." She beams at me, then heads to the food counter. I look around for Drake, but it looks like he wandered off, too. It's just me and Tristan now. Well, him and me and about a hundred other people. I fight the urge to sit next to him and instead sit in front of the computer at the end of the right lane.

"Hey, Tristan, come over here," I call.

He walks up behind me, then rests his hand on the back of my chair and leans over my shoulder. I'm suddenly aware of how close he is. *What is with me tonight?*

"What's up?" he asks.

"What name do you want?"

"We can choose our names?"

"Yeah."

"Ummm . . . what do you think I should choose?"

I think for a moment, then I grin broadly. "Knight Rider."

He furrows his eyebrows, trying to figure out why I'd name him after a corny eighties show. Then comprehension dawns on his face and he barks a laugh. "Okay." He grins at me. "Go for it."

I tap it in. "Alright. What should my name be?"

He purses his lips as he thinks. "Tyler Durden."

I examine his face. The last time he made a *Fight Club* reference, it didn't work out very well for either of us. Is he referring to when I beat up Brandon Stover? What is he trying to say?

He smirks at me. "I know how much you like Brad Pitt."

A slow smile spreads across my face. "He *is* rather dreamy," I say as I type it in.

Drake comes up behind us and laughs when he reads the screen. "I didn't know you were a fan of the Hoff, Avery."

"I'm not, but Tristan is."

Tristan smiles. "Don't knock David Hasselhoff. He's an American icon."

"You just like to see him on *Baywatch* running around without his shirt," I tease.

He leans close to my ear and whispers, "I do have a thing for lifeguards."

My gaze follows him as he straightens up and turns away from me. He throws an alluring look at me over his shoulder as he walks back to his seat.

Drake taps my arm, interrupting my reverie. "Hey Avery, how do you work this thing?" He's sitting in front of the other computer, punching random buttons to try to erase the previous team's score.

Exasperated, I say, "Jesus Christ. How long have you been coming here?"

"Just shut up and show me what to do."

"Seriously, you're as bad as my grandma. Just press the start button."

"What start button?"

"Oh my God. It's right here." I point at the button that clearly says "start."

"Oh. *That* start button." He smiles as he presses his finger to the screen.

Ashley returns with a couple of pitchers. She sets them down on the table closest to our lanes. "You haven't gotten it set up yet?"

I swivel in my seat to look at her. "No. Bill Gates over here can't figure out how to use the computer."

"Do you want me to do it?" she asks.

"No! I got this," Drake says.

"Okay. I'll go get some cups, then."

"Do you need help?" Tristan asks as he moves to get up.

"No, I got it," she replies coolly as she walks away.

Tristan raises his eyebrows and looks over at me as he sits back down in his seat. I shrug at him. If she doesn't want his help, so be it.

"So now what do I do?" Drake asks.

I return my attention to him. "It's a good thing you're not thinking of pursuing a career in a missile silo. You wouldn't know where the red button was if it was staring you in the face."

We bicker until Ashley appears behind us. "You *still* haven't gotten it?"

"We were waiting on you!" Drake says. "What name do you want?"

"I don't know. What do you think, Avery?"

I shrug. "It's up to you."

"Okay. How about Allie?"

"Like bowling alley?" Drake asks.

"No. A-l-l-i-e."

Drake looks at me. I'm just as perplexed as he is. We look up at her and ask simultaneously, "Why?"

"From *The Notebook*," she says. "It's my favorite movie."

I glance over my shoulder at Tristan. He rolls his eyes at her back. I smile at him, then turn back to Drake. "Do as the lady says," I order.

He shakes his head as he taps on the screen. "*Okay*, but I would have chosen something more badass. Like 'Queen of the Undead' or something like that."

"You can still choose that," I say.

"Fine. Maybe I will." He types "KOTU" into his name slot.

I point at the screen. "'Queen' is spelled with a q, not k."

"K is for 'king,' jackass."

I laugh. "We ready?"

"Yep. Let's do this thing," Drake says.

Ashley makes her way to her lane to take her turn. I hop out of my seat and say, "Tristan, you're up first."

I follow him as he walks over to the rack to retrieve his ball. He picks it up and looks at me. I nod in Ashley's direction. "Watch Ashley first. She's pretty good at this."

Her lips curve in a smile. "Why, thank you, Avery."

She takes aim, then casts her ball down the lane. It stays in a straight line and hits the front pin, knocking down all the remaining pins except for one straggler in the very back corner.

"Good shot!" I say.

She grins and comes back over to us.

"Now she'll get a second turn to try to knock that last pin over," I say to Tristan.

Her ball shoots out of the hole on the ball return. She picks it up and strides back over to the line. She launches her ball and holds her breath. The ball hits the edge of the pin, sending it reeling across the lane. Ashley jumps and claps her hands as Drake and I both yell, "Ohh!"

She trots back over to me and Tristan. I smile and hold up my hand. She beams as she gives me a high-five, then she goes over to give one to Drake.

I look over at Tristan. He raises an eyebrow.

"She made it look easy. It's a lot harder than it looks."

I gesture for him to take his spot at the end of our lane. He walks over to the line, and I follow.

"Okay, so first things first. Don't cross this line." I tap on it with my toe. "An alarm will go off if you do."

"Seriously?"

"Yeah, seriously."

"Why?"

"I don't know. To catch cheaters, maybe?"

He laughs. "Do people really take this that seriously?"

"Some people do. There are bowling tournaments and bowling leagues, just like with any other sport. If you come during the week, you'll see a bunch of old guys in leather jackets who think they're hot shit because they can bowl a two fifty without breaking a sweat."

"What's the highest score you can get?"

"Three hundred. I usually clock in around one fifty, one sixty."

"Really? Is it that hard?"

"Yeah. I told you it's harder than it looks."

"So what should I do?"

I smile. "Well, first . . ." I step as close as I dare behind him and grasp his shoulders. "You need to be standing here," I say in a low voice as I guide him toward the middle of the lane.

He smiles over his shoulder at me. I think he's enjoying our close proximity as much as I am. "Okay. Now what?"

"Now," I say as I step to his side, "you need to make sure you're holding the ball correctly."

I take the ball from his hands and rotate it around, then gently grasp his right hand and guide his fingers into the holes. I glance up at his face. He's staring at me wide-eyed—this must be that puppy dog look Drake was talking about. Behind him, I see Drake smirk at me as he picks up his ball from the rack. I look back at Tristan and say, under my breath, "Tristan? Do you think I'm flirting with you?"

"Oh, shit! Right. Sorry," he mumbles with a guilty smile as he lifts his left hand to scratch the back of his neck.

I smirk at him. "I'm relying on *you*, you know."

"I'm sorry," he hisses. "I can't concentrate when you're around me."

At least I'm not the only one.

I smile and step back. Louder, I say, "Okay, so now you want to take a couple of steps and throw the ball like this." I demonstrate with my own arm. "It helps to point your thumb in the direction you want the ball to go."

"Should I just aim for the middle pin?"

"No, you want to aim over there." I point over my shoulder at the wall behind us.

"Smartass," he grumbles.

I grin and give him room. He exhales slowly as he concentrates on the pins at the end of the lane.

"Any day now."

"Shut up, Avery," he mutters. He takes a step and releases the ball. It bounces off the left bumper and crawls its way down the lane. After a decade, it knocks over a couple of pins on the far-right side and disappears.

He frowns as he looks back at me.

"So? What do you think?" I ask.

"You were right. It is harder than it looks."

"See? I told you. Let's go try it again."

While we wait for his ball to come back, we stand around and watch as Drake takes his turn. His ball rolls like lightning down the lane and knocks all the pins over with a satisfying crash.

"Wow," Tristan says. "How do you get it to go so fast?"

Drake struts up and replies, "Strength and skill, my friend. Something our friend, Avery here, knows nothing about. You want to learn from the best, you gotta learn from me."

"Tristan, don't pay any attention to this poser. He may know how to throw a fast ball, but he couldn't hit the side of a barn if it was two feet in front of him."

"Oh yeah? Tell that to those ten bowling pins I just knocked over."

"That was dumb luck. You couldn't make that shot again in a million years."

"I bet I could get more strikes than you."

"Alright, I'll take that bet. But are you sure you wanna get into more debt? You still owe me a steak and lobster dinner."

"I don't owe you shit. Let's do this: each spare is five bucks, and each strike is worth ten."

"What about split spares? That's harder than strikes."

"No, that's too complicated. Just strikes and spares."

"Okay. Deal." We shake on it.

Drake looks over at Ashley, who's been listening to us banter from her seat behind the computer. "Yo, Ashley!" he calls. "You want in on this action?"

"Yeah, count me in," she says with a smile.

"Good. We're gonna clean house on this loser," he boasts.

I point at him as I steer Tristan back to our lane. "We'll just see about that. You better go to that ATM over there and get your money ready for me. I won't be taking any IOUs from you anymore."

Drake grins at me as he trades places with Ashley.

"What's a split spare?" Tristan asks.

"Oh. That's when there's pins left on each side of the lane. It's really difficult to knock them over at the same time."

"Huh. That does sound harder than a strike. Do you get more points for it?"

"Nope."

"That doesn't seem fair."

I shrug. "Them's the rules."

He takes his place in front of the line. He takes a breath and throws the ball, with more force this time. It veers to the left again, but it doesn't hit the bumper. It knocks over the farthest pin on the left-hand side.

I beam at him. "Better."

"What do you mean, 'better'? I only knocked one pin over."

"Yeah, but you didn't hit the bumper this time. If we didn't have the bumpers, you wouldn't have gotten any pins last time."

"Oh. Good point."

"Okay, now it's my turn. Stand back and watch a true master at work."

He snorts, then steps back a few paces.

I grab my ball from the rack, then walk back over to him and give him a rakish grin. He crosses his arms and looks at me skeptically. I take a few quick steps and launch the ball down the lane. It hits the front pin dead-on and the rest collapse like dominos. I saunter back to him and give him a smug smile.

"Show-off," he mutters, but I can tell he's trying to restrain a smile.

"Your turn." I give him a half-bow and gesture for him to lead the way.

He rolls his eyes at me as he goes to retrieve his ball.

I strut over to Drake and rub my fingers together. "That's right, buddy. That's ten bucks already in the pot. You better start pulling out a line of credit with your bank, 'cause you're gonna owe me a lot more by the time this night is through."

"Uh, no, you owe me ten bucks, too, remember?"

"Whaddya mean? You got that strike before we made our bet."

"Doesn't matter. We're going with what the computer says, and the computer says I have a strike and Ashley has two spares."

"What?" I spin around and look at the monitor above my head. Sure enough, Ashley just scored another spare.

She grins at me as she passes by. "You owe me ten bucks now too, Avery. We're all even."

Huh. This competition may be harder than I thought.

After two games, Drake and I are still tied, and Ashley's not far behind.

"Alright, we need a tiebreaker," Drake says as he looks up at the monitor.

"We can play another game," I say. "It'll give Ashley a chance to get some of her money back."

She smiles at me.

Tristan pipes up. "Can we eat first?"

I look at him. "Yeah, you hungry?"

"Yeah, I'm hungry."

"Okay. Let's take a break, and then we'll have our final showdown."

Ashley nods and Drake says, "Sounds like a plan."

We head over to the food counter. I step back to let Ashley go before me. "Ladies first."

She flashes me a smile and steps up to place her order. After she pays, she heads over to the far side of the counter to wait for her food. I gesture to Drake for him to go before me, too. "Ladies first," I repeat with a smirk.

He rubs his eyebrow with his middle finger, but he steps forward anyway.

I turn to Tristan. "What are you getting?"

"Umm . . . I don't know. What's good here?"

"Well, we're in a bowling alley, so don't get your hopes up too high. But the burgers are edible and their fries aren't bad."

"I guess I'll try their fries, then."

"You don't want anything else?"

"No."

"Cheap date. I like that," I say with a smile.

His eyes widen in alarm. He shushes me and nods toward Drake's back. Drake didn't hear me, though. He's too busy flirting with the girl behind the counter.

"Come on, he's not paying attention. Here, watch." I look over at Drake and, in the same level of voice, I say, "Drake Williams is a moron and a shitty baseball player."

Drake doesn't react; he just keeps chatting with the counter girl.

I look back at Tristan. "See?"

He tuts and shakes his head.

Finally, Drake pays for his food and steps out of the way to let us place our orders. He shoots me a wink as he passes by me to join Ashley. I'm not sure what he means by it—he's probably just gloating that he found another poor girl to fall for his charms.

Tristan steps up to the counter and orders his fries. As he pulls out his wallet, I grab it from him. "Oh no, you don't! Your money's no good here."

"What? No!"

He tries to take it back, but I hold it out of his reach and tell the counter girl, "I'll have a burger."

She smiles as she rings it up. "That'll be seven fifty."

Tristan makes another grab for his wallet, but I hold it behind me and turn so my back is to the counter. I shove his wallet into my rear jeans pocket, then pull my own out of the other pocket. I toss it over my shoulder onto the counter and stand in Tristan's way so he can't get to it. "There should be a ten in there," I say as I smile mischievously at Tristan.

He folds his arms across his chest. "You gonna give me my wallet back, or do I have to call the cops and tell 'em you stole it?"

"You want your wallet? You're gonna have to come get it."

He flushes and rubs his neck with both hands. I grin shamelessly back at him.

"The change is in your wallet, sir," the girl says behind me, her voice shaking with laughter.

I turn around and grab it off the counter. "Thank you," I say with a conspiratorial wink.

She giggles.

"Okay, fine," he says as he follows me toward the pickup counter. "*Now* can I have it back?"

"Nope. You're just gonna have to get it back from me later somehow."

I don't turn around to see his face, but I imagine he's probably blushing.

Drake and Ashley get their food right as we get to them.

"Don't wait for us. Dig in," I say.

"Like we'd wait for you," Drake says as they go back to the table.

When they're out of earshot, I turn to Tristan. "Having fun?"

"I know *you* are," he replies with a smirk.

"Yeah, I am," I admit. "I might even make some money tonight. Which is good, because that two dollars I spent on your fries nearly put me in the poorhouse."

The girl sets our orders down on the counter. Tristan reaches for his fries, but I beat him to it. I grab both plates, and he shoots me an exasperated look. I wink at the counter girl again. She smiles and shakes her head at us.

Tristan follows me back to our table, where Ashley and Drake are sitting across from each other. I make a split-second decision and sit down next to Ashley. I figure that having Tristan sit next to Ashley would be a recipe for disaster. Tristan sits across from me and I slide his plate toward him. We both grab the ketchup bottle at the same time. He glares at me. I smile and lift my hand in surrender. A smile plays upon his lips as he shakes his head and pours ketchup on his plate.

"So Tristan, what do you think of bowling so far?" Drake asks.

"It's fun. It's harder than I thought it would be."

"How can you not have been bowling before?" Ashley asks. It's a legitimate question, but her tone is unmistakably condescending. I'm tempted to kick her under the table, but I restrain myself.

Unflinching, Tristan looks her in the eye and replies, "Some people don't get around as much as you do."

My eyebrows shoot up. Now it's Tristan I want to kick.

Drake's eyes meet mine, and a huge grin spreads across his face. I know exactly what he's thinking: *Fireworks.*

Ashley's eyes narrow into two dangerous slits. "Excuse me?"

Drake claps his hand on Tristan's shoulder. "I think that what my man, Tristan here, is saying is that he's not as *experienced* as you."

Tristan breaks into a smile that rivals Drake's. The two of them look exceedingly pleased with themselves.

Archly, Ashley says, "You guys are assholes."

Drake and Tristan both laugh. I can feel the tension in the air start to dissipate. Although I can't say I approve of them ganging up on her like that, I'm hoping that Drake's obvious support of Tristan sent her the message to back off.

"Hey Drake, did you tell Ashley you're going to the University of

Texas?" I ask, hoping to smooth things over.

"No, he didn't," she exclaims. "Oh my God, that's so exciting!"

I listen to them chatter on about their college plans while I eat. They're obviously looking forward to the whole college experience, but for some reason I can't drum up the same kind of enthusiasm. I glance at Tristan. For an instant, his eyes meet mine, then he looks down at his plate. I know what he's thinking about, because I'm thinking about it, too. We'll need to talk about it, and soon.

I finish my burger and wipe my hands with a napkin. Ashley looks over at me and says, "You've got some ketchup." She gestures at her mouth.

"Where?" I run my thumb down the right side of my mouth.

She giggles. "No," she says as she wipes the ketchup off the left corner of my mouth with her finger. She smiles at me as she wipes her finger off on her napkin.

Tristan's mouth twists with disgust. "I'll be right back," he mutters as he gets up from the table. He won't meet my eyes.

"Where are you going?" Drake asks.

"Nature calls." Without looking back, he stalks toward the restroom at the other end of the bowling alley.

I look down at the table and think quickly. "I gotta go, too. Carry on."

I jump out of my seat and follow him. The door shuts in my face right as I get to it. I shove it open. At the sound of the door creaking, Tristan looks over his shoulder. His eyes widen in surprise when he sees me. Before he can ask what I'm doing, I grab his wrist and tug him into the closest stall. I throw the door lock into place, then I pin his body against the wall with my own and kiss him urgently. He responds in kind, and we're a mess of tongues and hands and heavy breathing.

"Avery...!" he gasps as I hungrily run my mouth down his neck. He pushes my chest to make me stop. Breathlessly, I pull back to look at his face.

The words rush out of his mouth. "Avery, I'm not a virgin." He looks anxious, like he's afraid that this revelation will make me push him away with contempt.

I shake my head. "I don't care."

I crush my lips against his to cut off any arguments or second guesses. I need him to believe me when I say that I don't care about who he's been with or what he's done. It's not like I have a clean slate, either. He's with me now, and that's all that matters.

He wraps his arms around me and pulls me tighter against him. After several long seconds, I break off our ardent embrace. "We should go," I tell him. I can't help but smile at his flustered facial expression. His cheeks are pink and his eyes are smoldering with a sensual heat—there's no way he can go out there like this without raising suspicions.

"I'll go out first," I say. "You stay here a minute, then come out after me. Okay?"

"Okay."

I give him a last, rough kiss on the lips, then push myself away from the wall. I adjust my pants, then unlock the stall door and quickly shut it behind me. I hear a click as he locks it again. I glance in the mirror. My hair is a bit disheveled, but other than that, I look fairly normal. I straighten my hair with my fingers, then exit the bathroom. I stride back to the table and plop down in my seat.

Drake peers at me suspiciously. "Where's Tristan?"

I shrug. "I dunno. He must have fallen in."

Drake laughs and Ashley smiles. After about thirty seconds or so, Tristan returns. The additional time helped—his eyes are calmer and his face has almost returned to its normal shade. He sneaks a shy glance at me as he sits down, then quickly looks away.

Drake asks, "Everything come out okay?"

Tristan snorts. "Yes. Thank you for asking."

Drake grins.

"So you guys ready for round three?" I ask.

Drake says, "We don't have to have another round. You could just pay me now and save yourself the embarrassment."

"Big talk coming from . . . who are you again? Princess Peach?"

"It's King of the Undead, you bastard."

I laugh. "Alright, Your Highness. We'll just see who the last man standing really is."

"Oh yeah? Bring it."

"Yeah, that's right. Who's the king?" Drake gloats as Ashley and I hand over his reward money outside the bowling alley. By the end of the last game, he'd squeaked into the lead with one extra spare.

"Alright, alright. No need to rub it in," I say.

He grins as he shoves his wallet back into his pocket.

Ashley speaks up. "I should probably get going. I have to get up early tomorrow for cheer rehearsal."

"Yeah, me too," I say. "Well, not for cheer rehearsal, but you know . . ."

She smiles and gives me a hug. I avoid Tristan's eyes. She gives Drake a hug, too, then looks over at Tristan.

"See you, Ashley," he says without any sarcasm or disdain. I get the impression he's extending an olive branch for my sake.

She seems to accept his peace offering, because she politely replies, "Good night, Tristan."

Inwardly, I sigh with relief. It's nice to not have them at each other's throats, for once.

Ashley gives us one last smile, then turns and heads for her car. Drake sighs. "Well, sports fans, I guess that's my cue." He stretches out his hand. As he pulls me in to thump me on the back, he mutters in my ear, "I may be a moron, but I'm still smarter than you."

I shoot him a sharp look. *How much did he hear?*

He gives me a smug smile, then exchanges a handshake with Tristan. "Later, Tristan. You guys drive carefully." He throws us a wave as he trots back to his car.

After he pulls out of the parking lot, I glance at Tristan. "You ready?"

"Yeah."

We walk slowly back to my Honda. I don't want to take Tristan home, but it's getting close to curfew and I don't want to be grounded. When we reach the car, Tristan follows me to the driver's side. I stop and look at him suspiciously. He slides between me and the door, blocking me from getting in the car.

"What do you think you're doing?" I really have no idea what he's got in mind, but there's a playful smile on his lips that makes me want to find out.

He doesn't answer. He steps forward until he's almost touching me and slides his hand around my waist. For one wild second, I think he's going to make out with me right here in the parking lot, but then my hopes are dashed when he pulls his wallet out of my rear pocket. He holds it up in front of my face and says, "Got it."

I let out an indignant gasp. He grins back at me as he walks over to the passenger side and climbs into the car.

I drop into the driver's seat and turn to give him a scolding look.

"What?" he says.

"Tease."

"Oh, *I'm* the tease? You're the one who left me hanging in the bathroom!"

"Well, if I'd stayed any longer, Drake and Ashley would've sent out a search party, and then where would we be?" I say as I start the car and head out of the parking lot.

"That settles it, then. They're just not going to be invited to any more of our dates. Especially Ashley."

"She wasn't that bad, was she?"

"Not as bad as I thought. Though I did want to strangle her pretty little neck when she touched your mouth."

I laugh. "Listen to you, all violent all of a sudden. I'm afraid I've been a bad influence on you."

"I wasn't violent. I just had to go cool off for a minute."

"You aren't still jealous of her, are you?"

"No. Not anymore, at least. I figure if you still had feelings for her, you'd be taking her home right now, not me."

I reach over and grab his hand. "That's right," I say as I shoot him a smile.

He caresses the back of my hand with his thumb, then says, "You know she wants to get back together with you, right?"

"Tristan . . ."

"No, I'm serious. I can see it on her face. I'm only telling you this because she may try to come on to you, and you need to be prepared to deal with that."

"I don't think she'll try anything. She knows it's over between us."

"Well, you know her better than I do. But she doesn't seem to me to be the kind of girl to let things go."

When I pull up to the end of his driveway, he looks at his house and sighs. "I better go inside. It's late."

"Can I walk you to your door?"

"You want to?"

"Yeah, I want to."

He shrugs. "Yeah, okay. Oh, hold on. I almost forgot."

He turns around and pulls a daisy out of the bouquet of flowers sitting on the back seat. He smiles at me as he tucks it into his jeans pocket and pulls his shirt down over it. "Okay, let's go."

We walk side by side up the path to his door. The back of my hand brushes against his, and I feel an urge to hold his hand, but I know it's too risky. Even though it's late, there's no telling who might see.

He steps up onto the porch and I hang back on the walkway. The step makes him slightly taller than me—it feels strange to look up at him instead of the other way around.

"Thanks for inviting me," he says. "I had a lot of fun. Even with Ashley there."

"Yeah, me too. I'm glad it worked out."

"You coming over to study tomorrow?"

"I've got fencing and baseball, but I can come by after."

"I wish I could come watch."

"I know, but you have a promise to keep."

He grimaces. "Yeah, I know."

I smile. "Don't worry. I'll see you tomorrow afternoon."

"Okay." He bites his lip, then mouths, "I love you."

"I love you, too," I mouth back.

I grin at him, and he smiles shyly back. Then he says, "Good night," and turns around to go inside.

"What? No good night kiss?" I tease, remembering the last non-date date we had. Even though I want him to kiss me this time, I know he can't. Not out in the open like this.

He hesitates with his hand on the doorknob and looks over his shoulder. I give him a lopsided grin. "I'm kidding, Tristan. Good night."

He looks at me longingly for a moment, then he turns and takes two steps toward me. In the sexiest voice I've ever heard, he says, "Fuck you, Taylor," then throws his arms around my neck and kisses me with an intensity that knocks me off my feet. My heart soars, and I throw caution to the wind and kiss him back. Time comes to a standstill as we sway under the porch light, wrapped in each other's arms, in front of God and the whole world.

Then time fast-forwards, and I'm reluctantly brought back to the present when he gently disentangles himself and pulls away from me.

"Don't go," I whisper. I never want this moment to end.

He smiles. "I'll see you tomorrow," he promises. Then he turns and goes inside his house, taking my heart with him.

29

"How did your session go this morning?" I ask as I flip another page in my English book.

Tristan's sitting across from me on his bed, poring over what looks to be the biggest, most boring chemistry textbook of all time. I'm so glad I'm not in AP classes.

He shrugs. "It was okay."

"Oh yeah? Did you tell her about us?"

His cheeks flush pink. "Yeah, I did."

"Really?" It makes me happy that he took my advice and opened up to her. Telling her was a big step, not just for him but for our relationship as well. Even though Drake figured out my feelings for Tristan before I did, I still haven't admitted to him that we're a couple.

"Yeah, she asked why I didn't show up last week and I told her that I was spending time with my boyfriend. It was pretty funny seeing her reaction. It was like she was pissed at me and happy for me at the same time. I told her that I don't want it getting back to my dad, so hopefully she won't let it slip."

"Why? Do you think he'd have a problem with me?"

"Maybe. I don't know. He's such a two-faced liar, I don't even know how he'll react to things half the time."

"What do you mean?"

"He always makes these promises to me and he never keeps 'em." He deepens his voice. "Sure, son. You can come stay with me over the summer. Oh no, I forgot, you *can't* stay with me because my job is too goddamn important." He returns to his normal voice. "He's also a big fucking hypocrite. He tells his constituents that he's all for helping the poor, but he lives in this huge freaking house and throws money around like it grows on trees. I can't stand him."

"Why do you have a tattoo of his family crest if you hate him so much?"

"I don't hate him. Not really. He just pisses me off."

"Do you ever regret it?"

"What, the tattoo?"

"Yeah."

He shakes his head. "No. Even when I'm pissed at him, I know from experience that there are way worse fathers I could have."

I nod. "True."

He peeks up at me and tilts his head. "Do you have any tattoos?"

He's seen me without my shirt dozens of times, but then, there are other places I could get a tattoo. I close my book and set it to the side, then I lean in so close that we're sharing the same breath. "Hmmm, I don't know," I murmur. "You want to find out?"

His eyes widen. His lips part.

"*Hell, yes,*" he breathes.

I don't want to break away. I never will.

I have to breathe, though.

Tristan's heart beats erratically in my ear. I move my head up a little to let more air in.

"You okay?" he whispers, his hand tightening on my shoulder.

"Yeah. I'm good." The understatement of the century. I shift up until my face is even with his. "That was incredible," I whisper, nuzzling my nose against his.

His face is already flushed, but it darkens even more. "Yeah."

"Are *you* okay?" I ask, brushing his hair back from his eyes.

"I-I've never felt like this before."

"Me neither." It's true. I've never felt so close to anyone in my life.

I can't get enough of it, though. With tender kisses, I taste the sweat along his temple and down his jaw. He shivers as my lips tickle his neck on my way down to his chest. I pause when I get to his tattoo so I can trace the outline of it with my tongue.

"If you got one, what would you get?" he murmurs as he plays with a few strands of my hair.

"A great big rainbow across my face might be nice."

His chest shakes as he laughs.

"What about you?" I ask, grinning. "Would you get another one?"

"I'm considering it. I was thinking a sword. To go with the shield, and to remind me of you. So I'll always remember you."

I frown. "Remember me? You going somewhere?"

"No. I just figured, you're probably going off to college in a few months, and . . ."

"And what? You think I'm going to dump you?"

I raise my head to look at his face. The corners of his mouth droop as he nods.

"Sorry to disappoint you, but you can't get rid of me that easily. You're going to be seeing my ugly mug around for a long time."

"Really?" He still looks sad, as if he doesn't quite believe me.

I let out a small sigh. "Tristan, I love you. I want to be with you, always." My brow furrows. "You want that too, right?"

His eyes brim with tears. He nods and says, in a choked voice, "Yes."

I smile. "Okay, good." I lift myself and gently press my lips to his.

"Tristan?" a woman's voice calls.

Tristan stares at me, horrified. "Shit! It's Jeanine!"

We scramble to get dressed as quickly as possible. I can't find my belt anywhere. *Oh well, I'll look for it later.* Tristan finishes before I do, but his hair is a wreck. He rushes over to his chair and pretends to write something. I pick up my book just as I hear a soft knock on the door.

The door opens. I notice, too late, that I'm holding my book upside down. A tall, statuesque woman with dark hair walks in. She looks just as I would expect a politician's wife to look: dressed in a deep blue dress and high red pumps, with pearls around her neck, hair that looks like it's being held together by hairspray, and very long red painted nails.

"Tristan, I—oh!" She stops when she sees me sitting on the bed. "I didn't know you had a guest."

Tristan glances at me. "Oh, uh . . . Jeanine, this is Avery. Avery, this is my stepmom, Jeanine."

"Pleased to meet you," I say.

"Well! It's nice to finally meet one of Tristan's friends. You two studying?"

"Yes," we answer simultaneously. We avoid each other's eyes.

She looks at Tristan and her eyebrows come together. "Tristan, you look a little flushed. Are you feeling alright?"

"Yeah, I'm fine!" he squeaks. I have to bite my lip hard to keep from laughing.

"Okay, well, dinner's in half an hour. Avery, you're welcome to stay for dinner, if you like."

"Sure, that sounds great."

"Good. I'll let Betty know to set an extra place setting. Alright, I'll let you get back to your studying." She exits and shuts the door behind her.

Tristan falls forward and presses his forehead to the desk. I lean my head back against the wall and exhale slowly.

"Christ, that was close." He peeks up at me from the desk. "You think she noticed?"

"What? That you look like you just did *exactly* what we just did?"

His cheeks turn crimson. "Yeah."

"Let's just hope she has the eyes of a bat. Now, where the hell did I put my *belt*?"

I follow Tristan downstairs and through the French doors opposite the piano room into the dining room. Like the piano room, the furniture looks antique and is in pristine condition. The dining table is enormous, with at least twelve place settings, and is made of a beautiful deep cherry-red wood. In the back corner, next to a swinging door that I assume leads to the kitchen, there's a large cherrywood china cabinet filled with wineglasses and rows and rows of expensive-looking porcelain plates and bowls.

Tristan sits in the chair closest to the end of the table. As I pull out the chair next to him, a man with salt-and-pepper hair, wearing a crisp business suit and tie, walks in from the kitchen. Immediately, my eyes are drawn to his strikingly pale blue eyes—Tristan's eyes.

Mr. Chevalier stops in surprise when he sees me, but he recovers quickly. He smiles broadly and strides across the room with his hand outstretched. I accept his handshake and try to match his firm grip.

"Franklin Chevalier, at your service." He sounds like a used car salesman.

"Avery Taylor. Pleased to meet you, sir."

"I didn't know we'd be having a guest tonight. If I'd known, I would have asked Betty to make something special. Unfortunately, you'll be stuck with the regular, humdrum Chevalier fare."

"It's no problem, sir. I'm easy."

He looks down at Tristan and claps a hand on his shoulder. "Hello, son."

Tristan shifts in his seat and mumbles, "Hey, Dad."

"I'm going to freshen up. Be back in a jiffy," Mr. Chevalier says as he exits through the French doors.

I sit down in my chair and lean in close to Tristan's ear. "In a jiffy?"

He closes his eyes and shakes his head.

Jeanine walks in from the foyer and sits down across from Tristan. She smiles at me and says, "Avery, are you in Tristan's class?"

I shake my head. "We don't have any classes together this year. We were in home ec together in eighth grade, though." Out of the corner of my eye, I see Tristan look over at me.

"Oh," she says. "I didn't realize you'd known each other that long. I don't remember seeing you around before."

My eyes meet Tristan's. I don't know how much to tell her.

He speaks up. "We didn't really start hanging out until recently. He wanted to learn how to play the piano, and he asked me to teach him."

"Tristan's been teaching you the piano?" she says, even more surprised.

"Yeah, he's been giving me lessons after school." Then I add, "I hope you don't mind that I'm using your piano."

"No, not at all. I'm glad somebody's getting some use out of it." She smiles at us.

Mr. Chevalier strolls back into the room and takes a seat at the head of the table between Tristan and Jeanine. Right at that moment, a short flustered-looking woman comes out of the kitchen, laden with a tray of food. This must be Betty, the cook. Either she has impeccable timing or she was watching through the door to see when Mr. Chevalier sat down. Neither would surprise me.

Jeanine says, "Thank you, Betty. This looks delicious."

Betty nods quickly and says, "Yes, ma'am." She scurries back into the kitchen.

Mr. Chevalier looks around at us. "Well? Dig in!"

The "regular, humdrum Chevalier fare" turns out to be a beef pot roast, with buttered rolls and asparagus in a cream sauce. All of it is delicious. *I wonder how much they pay Betty.*

Throughout dinner, Mr. Chevalier talks animatedly with Jeanine about fundraisers and lobby groups and various politicians I've never heard of before. It's all over my head, so I just sit quietly and school my face into a politely interested expression.

During one particularly boring conversation about campaign contributions, I glance over at Tristan. He's staring at the wall behind Jeanine with a glazed look in his eyes while he eats. He's obviously no more interested in politics than I am. I smile inwardly. I could have some fun with this.

I reach over under the table and slide my right hand onto his knee. He jumps, then looks down at his plate to hide his face, which has turned red all the way up to his hairline. I grab my dinner roll off my plate and hold it in front of my mouth to cover my smirk. He drops his left hand under the table and places it over mine, but he doesn't push me away. Encouraged, I slide my fingers up and caress the inside of his leg. His eyes widen. He squeezes the back of my hand, obviously willing me to go no further. I heed his silent plea. I rotate my wrist and intertwine my fingers with his, then rest the back of my hand on top of his knee. I shoot him a quick smile. His head is still bent toward his plate, but he's looking at me out of the corner of his eye. He smiles shyly back at me.

Tristan's parents miss our exchanged look. They're too busy discussing the senate voting agenda to pay any attention to us. I'm not really paying attention to them, either, until I hear Mr. Chevalier say the word "gays." Suddenly, I become very interested in what they're talking about.

"We've been over it before, but there's more pressure than ever to put forth an amendment to address the marriage issue," Mr. Chevalier tells Jeanine.

"Didn't the courts already decide on gay marriage?" she asks.

"Yes, but now that the court makeup has changed, there's more of a drive to get it overturned. We won't be able to test it unless I introduce a resolution for an amendment. And if I don't, every God-fearing constituent will be calling my office about how I'm not doing enough to protect families."

"Wait," I say, confused. "You don't support gay marriage?"

He raises his eyebrows as he looks over at me. He'd probably forgotten I was sitting here. "Oh, I . . . I'm not against homosexuals. It's more complicated than that."

"What's complicated about it?" I ask.

"Well, if gay people can get married, then other people will want to get married, too. They'll ask to marry multiple wives, or dogs, or even children. It's a slippery slope."

Tristan squeezes my hand in warning, but I ignore him. "So you'd rather keep marriage to one man—one woman. That's what you're saying, right?"

"I'm not saying gay people shouldn't be able to be together. I'm not prejudiced."

"No. You're fine with them living together, as long as they don't get all the benefits that real married couples get." He opens his mouth to speak, but I cut him off. "What if it was your own son? What if Tristan wanted to marry another guy? You wouldn't want him to get all the benefits that your wife gets from you?"

I hear Tristan whisper, "Avery . . . ," but I don't look at him; I just continue glaring at his father.

Mr. Chevalier smiles a little. "I don't think that's going to happen."

I shrug and retort, "You never know."

Tristan bites his lip and stares at me, wide-eyed. Jeanine looks between him and me and comprehension falls across her face like a curtain. My heart jumps. *Crap. I shouldn't have opened my big mouth.*

Mr. Chevalier opens his mouth to argue, but Jeanine jumps in. "Stranger things have been known to happen." She turns to him and smoothly changes the subject. "For instance, did you know that Liza and Bill are getting a divorce?"

Her distraction works. Mr. Chevalier's eyebrows shoot upward. "No! I didn't hear about that. When did this happen?"

As she fills him in on the gossip, I relax in my chair. I hadn't realized how tense the debate with Tristan's dad made me. I look over at Tristan and mouth, "Sorry."

He squeezes my hand, then lets go. I go back to eating my dinner in silence.

After dinner, Tristan and I retreat back to his room. I sit on the edge of his bed and clasp my hands together. "I'm sorry, Tristan. I didn't mean to start a fight with your dad."

He sits down next to me. "I told you, he's good at pissing people off."

"So much for making a good first impression," I mumble.

"He's used to arguing with people. I wouldn't worry about it."

"I'm just worried that I said too much."

"I was surprised to hear you say all that stuff. About me."

I shake my head. "I shouldn't have brought you up. It just made me angry to think that he wouldn't be supportive of you if you and I decided to . . ." I stop. I hadn't expected to have this conversation yet.

"Decided to what?"

I gulp and look down at my hands. "You know. To get married someday."

I'm too afraid to see his reaction, so I keep my eyes trained on my fingers. He doesn't say anything at all. Quickly, I explain, "Look, I'm just saying someday. It's not like I have a ring in my pocket or anything."

"You're serious?" he mutters.

I shrug a little. "Yeah, I'm serious. I told you earlier, I want to be with you always."

"Avery . . ."

I look up at him. His face has turned an alarming shade of white.

"Are you freaking out?"

Shakily, he replies, "No, I'm not freaking out. I just never expected you to say something like that."

"Like what?"

"That you'd actually consider *marrying* me."

I look back down at my hands. "I'm not picking out tuxes yet, but yeah, I've considered it. I've been thinking a lot about my future recently. Where I should go to college. *If* I should go to college. What I want to study. What I want to be. I've been thinking about that crap for months and I don't feel like I'm any closer to figuring any of it out. But no matter what I do, I'd still like to be with you." I look up again and give him a lopsided smile. "If you'll have me, that is. You may not want to be with me if I end up peeling potatoes for a living."

He raises his voice. "You think I give a shit about that? You could be a goddamn sewer cleaner and I wouldn't think twice about marrying you."

My heart swells. I feel my face break out into a huge grin. "Really?"

He rolls his eyes. "Jesus, Avery. Do you even have to ask? Of course I'd marry you. In a heartbeat."

I beam at him. Even though I know we're only speaking hypothetically, it makes me indescribably happy to know that he feels the same way as I do. A funny thought crosses my mind. "Can you imagine the look on our dads' faces when they found out?" I say, chuckling.

"We don't have to tell them."

"What, elope? I might be down for that."

He shakes his head. "I can't believe we're talking about this."

"Why?"

"Well, let's see." He ticks off each point on his fingers. "Because we're in *high school*. Because nobody even knows we're together. And if anyone found out, we'd get our asses kicked. And because you are way out of my league."

I scoff. "This coming from someone who lives in a big-ass mansion."

He grimaces. "Money isn't everything."

"No, it isn't." Then I say, quietly, "I think Jeanine knows about us."

"What makes you say that?"

"She gave me a funny look when I said you might want to marry another guy. I think she figured out I was talking about me."

"Hmm. She did change the conversation pretty quickly."

"Will that be a problem for you? Her knowing?" The last thing I want is for our relationship to cause Tristan any more heartache.

"Well, there's nothing we can do about it now. But no, I don't think she'll say anything to my dad. She's actually pretty nice, for a stepmom."

I'm relieved to hear him say that. The more people he has in his corner, the better.

30

I RETURN HOME from Tristan's house, still giddy. As I turn the corner to go up the stairs, I hear my father's voice from the living room. "Avery? Is that you?"

I spin around and walk jauntily into the living room. "Hey, Dad. What's up?"

He smiles. "It's nice to see you in a good mood for once. I thought you might be stressed out with finals this week."

I shrug. "I'm not really nervous about it. Tristan's been helping me study."

His eyes narrow. "That Chevalier kid?"

I roll my eyes. "Yes, that Chevalier kid."

His jaw works, like he's grinding his teeth. "I told you before, son, you need to be careful about who you hang out with. And trust me on this, you don't want to be seen in the company of someone like him."

My good mood wanes. "Someone like him?"

"I didn't want to be the one to tell you this, but your friend isn't what he seems to be. I heard from some of the other parents that he'd been exchanging sexual favors for good grades."

My blood goes cold, then it goes boiling hot. *"What?* That is *bullshit!"*

"Watch your language!"

"You don't know what the hell you're talking about! Tristan gets good grades because he's smart, not because he . . . he . . ."

"Son, listen to me. Now, it may not have been for grades, but he was doing things he shouldn't have been doing. Especially since the teacher was . . . well, a much older man."

"Wait. Hang on. Are you saying that you'd like Tristan more if he'd been with a *female* teacher?"

"No, that still would be wrong. But it would be more . . . understandable."

I shake my head. "Nice. All my life, you've been teaching me about fairness and not jumping to conclusions about people, but now I see that you're a hypocrite and a bigot as well."

"Avery! I'm trying to help you, son."

"I don't need your help! I'm going to keep hanging out with Tristan, and nothing you say will stop me. Deal with it."

"When you're in my house, I expect you to abide by my rules."

"What *rules*? Do my homework? Fine. Don't stay out late? Okay. But I don't recall any rules about who I can and can't be with."

"Be with?" His tone drops. *Uh-oh.* "What do you mean by 'be with'?"

I bite down hard on the inside of my cheek. I wasn't planning on telling him like this, but it's too late now. I straighten myself up to my full height. "He's my boyfriend, Dad. I love him."

His mouth opens and closes several times, like a fish. His face turns a curious shade of purple. Before he's able to recover from the bomb I just dropped on him, my mother walks in the door.

"Hey, honey." She sees him, looking like a powder keg about to blow, and then turns to me, standing with teeth gritted and fists clenched. "What's going on?"

My dad finally gains his voice. "Your son . . . has a *boyfriend*."

Out of the corner of my eye, I see her look at me, but I don't break away from my father's glare.

"Tristan?" she asks.

Surprised, I look over at her. Her eyes are bright, and she smiles at me. Her smile is like the sun coming out after a storm, and it fills me with warmth. I relax my stance and unclench my fists. I smile back.

"You *knew* about this?" he snarls at her.

She stares coldly at him. "Avery, dear," she says without taking her eyes off my father, "please go to your room. Your father and I need to talk."

I retreat up to my room and shut the door. I shove my earbuds in, but I don't turn any music on. I pace around my room and listen to my parents yell at each other for what feels like hours. Telling them was the last thing on my agenda, and now that it's out there, there's no way I can take it back. *Shit. What am I going to do?*

Don't, I say to myself. Dad's the one who did this, not me. If he hadn't been so critical, maybe I wouldn't have had to hide it from him in the first place.

Before I can get lost in guilt, I turn on some music and try to drown out the voices rising from the floor below.

The next morning, I go into the kitchen to find my dad already sitting at the breakfast table. He doesn't say anything to me; he doesn't even look up from his paper. I can tell he's still upset, though, by the way his jaw clenches when I sit down with my cereal bowl across from him. I keep my eyes trained on my spoon while I eat. If he wants to give me the silent treatment, that's fine. Two can play at that game.

He finishes the sports page and sets it aside, then gets up and grabs his jacket from the back of his chair. He shrugs it on as he walks past me. I hear the front door open, then shut again. I can't help but wonder how long this will last. With the draft coming up, he can't pretend like I don't exist forever.

I throw my bowl in the sink, then grab my backpack by the door. As I'm reaching for the door handle, my mother comes into the kitchen. "Where are you off to?" she asks.

"I'm going over to Tristan's to study."

"Wait a minute, Avery. I want to talk to you about Tristan."

I groan. "God, Mom. Not you, too."

"Now, don't get upset. You know I like Tristan, and I think you are really cute together. But are you sure you want to start a relationship so close to the end of the year? You may not see each other very much after the summer."

"I know. We talked about it, and we're going to stay together, no matter what Dad says."

She sighs. "Your father didn't mean what he said yesterday. I think you just caught him by surprise, and it may take him a while to get used to the idea of having a boyfriend around the house. But deep down, he really wants you to be happy."

"Sure, he wants me to be happy, as long as it doesn't involve Tristan. He's never liked him."

"I know," she admits, "he probably would've preferred that you'd stayed with Ashley, but he knows that it's not up to him." Her eyes sparkle as she says, "I told him he should look on the bright side: at least we don't have to worry about you getting Tristan pregnant."

I flush as I laugh in disbelief. "You did not."

She jingles a laugh as she nods. "I did. I don't think he appreciated that, but it's true." Then she says, "That's not to say you shouldn't be using protection, though. Statistics show—"

"*Jesus*, Mom!" I hold up my hands. "Stop. I know. I get it."

"Okay. But if you need help getting condoms, I can—"

"Thanks, Mom. I think I'm good." My whole face feels hot.

"Okay, just making sure." She smiles at me.

Frustrated, I say, "Are you done embarrassing me?"

"*Yes*, you can go. Tell Tristan I said 'hello.'"

"I told my parents last night. About us."

I'd been trying all day to figure out how I was going to tell Tristan that I let the cat out of the bag, but every time I opened my mouth, the words got caught in my throat. I finally just told myself to grow a pair and come out with it.

Tristan looks up from his textbook. "You did? Are you serious?"

"Yeah. My father was saying bad things about you and I couldn't hold it in anymore."

"What did he say about me?"

I hesitate while I consider how much to tell him. I don't want to tell him any of it. I shake my head. "It doesn't matter."

"I want to know."

I sigh. "Tristan, I really don't think you want to hear it."

He closes his book and sets it on the bed next to him. "No, I really do. Tell me."

Reluctantly, I say, "He said . . . well, he mentioned Mr. Trawler."

Tristan looks down and nods to himself. "Figures," he mumbles.

I quickly apologize. "Look, I'm sorry my dad is such a douche."

"No, it's okay. It's nothing I haven't heard before. He wasn't there; he doesn't know what it was like. Richard—I mean, Mr. Trawler—was very . . . *persuasive*." His voice drips acid.

"What happened?" I whisper. I don't want him to stop talking, but I don't know if I want to hear this, either.

He hunches over slightly, but he doesn't wrap his arms around himself like he usually does whenever the subject of his past comes up in conversation. Instead, he clasps his hands together and says in a monotone voice, "When I started high school, I was still living with my mom and that jackass she called a husband. It was bad, then. He beat me just for looking at him. I didn't have any friends, so there was no one I could go to about it. The only thing that made me even remotely happy was music, and our school doesn't have a piano so I signed up for choir as an elective. Mr. Trawler . . . he said I was good at singing and encouraged me to take private lessons with him after school. I'd never had an adult take any interest in what I did—my dad was never around, and my mom didn't seem to care what I did—so I thought it was nice to have someone who was supportive of me. I started meeting with him after school, and we'd practice scales and vocal exercises. He praised me a lot and he'd bring me little gifts, like candy and sheet music and stuff like that. He became sort of a father figure to me. After a while . . ." Tristan looks down at his hands.

"Yeah?" I prompt in a whisper.

"H-he suggested that I come to his house for the lessons instead. Said it'd be more productive without people coming by to interrupt us, or some bullshit. Nobody ever interrupted when we were at school, but whatever. I was stupid and listened to him. His house was full of games and stuff kids like, which seemed a little weird since he didn't have any kids. I remember the first day I went over, he had this Nintendo console and I got so excited because I hadn't seen an original Nintendo in ages. He said we could play it if I wanted, so we did. He didn't even mention the singing lesson. When it was time for me to go home, he said I could have the Nintendo. I couldn't believe it. I couldn't understand how he could just give it to me, without a second thought. I asked if he was sure, and he said that since it made me happy, I could keep it. He said he wanted me to be happy. I think that was the first time anyone ever said that to me."

Tristan sighs. "So I took it home with me. He drove me to my house, and right before I got out of the car, he gave me a hug and . . . and kissed me. I knew that sometimes family members kiss each other, so I told myself that's all he was trying to do. Show me we were family.

"I went back to his house the next day. And the next, and the next. Sometimes we'd sing, sometimes we'd play video games. He always found a way to touch me in some way: put his hand on my shoulder, give me hugs, stuff like that. Eventually, he started . . . I don't know. It was really confusing. When I told him I didn't want to, he'd lay this guilt trip on me. Said I didn't appreciate him after all the nice things he'd done for me. That he was just trying to show me that he loved me. I tricked myself into thinking that he did love me, but I knew, deep down, that it wasn't love. He was just using me."

His voice catches. I don't say anything. What can you say about something like that?

After a heavy silence, he says, "One day, I was in Mr. Trawler's classroom after school. Veronica Little saw him kiss me through the little glass window on the door. She went and told Principal Johnson. Johnson showed up with Officer Gálvez and they escorted Mr. Trawler out. Johnson told me that Veronica had seen us together. He asked me about my relationship with Mr. Trawler, and I couldn't tell him. I couldn't tell him that I . . . that I . . ."

Tristan's face falls, and he starts sobbing uncontrollably. I can't take it; I can't stand to see him like this. I place my hand on his back, attempting to comfort him, but he flinches and moves out of my reach.

"It's my fault! It's all my fault," he cries. "I should have known better. If I hadn't taken those *stupid* singing lessons . . ."

"Don't say that. It's not your fault."

He shakes his head. "I let it happen. I should have stopped him, I should have *told* someone." He buries his face in his hands and cries harder. "God, I fucking hate myself. And now you hate me too, and—"

"What?" I say, stunned. "Why on earth would I hate you?"

"Because I'm stupid," he blurts. "And *dirty* and . . . and *worthless!*"

"Tristan, you are *not* worthless. And you're not dirty, and you're definitely not stupid. You taught me calculus, for Christ's sake."

He looks up at me. His eyes are bloodshot and tears are streaming down his face. I would do anything to make that pained, haunted look disappear from his eyes. I scoot closer and wrap my arms around him. He shudders violently. I press my lips to his hair and rock him gently back and forth while he cries against my chest.

Eventually, his sobs fade away and he feels limp in my arms. I don't want to upset him again, but this may be my only chance to get the truth. Quietly, I say, "Can I ask you something?"

"What?" His voice is muffled by my shirt.

"You didn't fall into the river, did you?"

He hesitates, then shakes his head.

Though I knew the answer before I asked, my heart drops. I squeeze him tighter. "Why did you do it?" I whisper.

In a tired voice, he says, "I just didn't see a reason to live anymore. I didn't want to sing or play the piano. It was like I was already dead inside. Nobody cared about me. I hated myself." He racks a sob. "I *still* hate myself."

"Hey." I lift his chin with my finger and look into his eyes. "You wanna know something?"

"What?" he asks weakly.

"I'm glad I pulled you out of the water that night."

"*Why?*" he asks, searching my eyes. The misery and self-loathing in his voice break my heart.

Softly, I reply, "Because I got to get to know you, and you're the most amazing person I've ever met. You're fun, and smart, and a wonderful musician. And I'm really lucky to be with you."

His face crumbles like he's about to cry again. Hurriedly, I press my lips to his to stop him from crying, but it doesn't work. Not completely, at least. His mouth trembles against mine and I can taste the salt of his tears on my tongue.

"I love you so much," he mumbles against my lips. His voice is choked with emotion.

"I love you, too," I whisper. I kiss him again, and he clings to me desperately, like a castaway clutching a lifesaver at sea.

31

We pull into the parking lot in the back of the school. We'd agreed last night that we would skip swim lessons today and sleep in, but I still insisted on driving Tristan to school. He hasn't spoken more than a few words all morning. Although he's calmer now than he was last night, I'm disturbed by the way he sits listlessly in his seat with his face drawn, staring out the window as if he's being haunted by specters that only he can see. A phrase from *Full Metal Jacket* drifts to the surface of my mind: *the thousand-yard stare.*

I turn off the engine and look at him, but he won't return my gaze. I lean over and kiss his cheek. He closes his eyes with a pained expression on his face. He doesn't say anything to me, he just unbuckles his seat belt and grabs the handle of his backpack between his feet as if to leave.

"Hey," I say as he reaches for the door.

He freezes with his fingers on the handle.

"Walk with me today."

Finally, his eyes meet mine. "Really?"

The Lifesaver

"Yeah. Why not?"

"Aren't you afraid of what people will say?"

I give him a half-smile. "Fuck 'em."

For the first time since he told me his secret, he smiles.

We get out of the car at the same time and head toward the entrance side by side. I reach down and grab his hand. He blushes and looks at his feet as he wraps his fingers in mine. Drake is loitering by the entrance again. His face splits into a wide grin when he sees us walking hand in hand. He whistles a catcall, which travels across the parking lot and causes people to turn their heads. I hold my head high and meet their stares, daring them to say something. Nobody does, but I can see the range of surprise and disgust and amusement on their faces.

"Well, would you look at this!" Drake says. "So Tristan, you finally got him to settle down, huh?"

Tristan peeks up at him and blushes again.

"Well, it's about time!" Drake says. He lowers his voice. "Listen, I'm happy for you guys. But there will be a lot of people who won't be. Good luck today, okay?"

Drake and I have been friends for years, but it's at this moment that I really see what a true friend he is. Knowing he's got my back makes me feel like I can take on the whole world. "Yeah. Thanks, Drake."

He thumps me on the back.

As we walk through the door, Drake calls from behind us, "Oh, and Tristan?"

Tristan looks back at him over his shoulder.

Drake points a finger at him. "You break his heart, I'll kick your ass."

Tristan smiles. "Yeah, that'll never happen."

Drake winks at me, and I smile.

I escort Tristan to his locker. The students in the hall shoot us funny looks, but I ignore them all. I casually lean against the locker next to his and watch as he exchanges his books and binders from his backpack. He keeps looking over at me and blushing. I smirk at him. "What? Am I distracting you?"

"Anyone would be distracted by that look you're giving me."

"What look?"

"That stalker look."

I laugh. "Should I not look at you anymore?"

"I didn't say that. I'm just saying it's distracting."

"No, *this* is distracting." I lean forward and kiss him on the lips. He drops his backpack. Three other people in the hall stop to gape at me. I laugh and say, "See? I told you," as he flushes and picks his bag off the floor.

"You're gonna get us suspended," he grumbles.

"Oh, come on, lighten up. You know people do way worse than that at school."

"Yeah, but they aren't you and me."

"So? If we get in trouble, then we'll sue for discrimination."

He shakes his head as he shuts his locker. "You're crazy, you know that?"

I shrug and grin. "I'm okay with that."

He rolls his eyes at me, but he smiles, too. I grab his hand and lead him down the hall to room 103.

When we enter the doorway, Mr. Smith glances up from his desk, then does a double take. His eyes linger on our linked hands as I walk Tristan to his desk at the back of the classroom. Tristan doesn't pay any attention to him, but I sneak a glance as I sit on the desk next to Tristan's. Without saying a word, Mr. Smith returns his attention to his paperwork. From across the room, I think I see the corner of his mouth turn up a fraction of an inch.

"How do you think Ashley's going to react when she finds out?" Tristan asks as he pulls his binders out of his backpack.

Crap. I forgot about Ashley. "Well, she won't be pleased, I'll tell you that."

He laughs. "I can just see her face now."

"Yeah." I sigh. "She probably won't want to be friends anymore."

"I'm surprised you were able to stay friends after your breakup anyway."

"Me too."

I glance up at the clock. "I gotta go. Don't want to be late." I hop off the desk and peck his cheek. "Have a good day. I love you," I say under my breath, but I'm sure Mr. Smith can hear me anyway.

Tristan's cheeks turn pink. "I love you, too," he says softly.

I strut toward the front of the classroom and say loudly, "See ya, Mr. Smith."

He doesn't look up from his desk, but I can tell he's trying to restrain a smile as he replies formally, "Good day, Mr. Taylor."

To my chagrin, Ashley's waiting by my locker when I arrive, looking ready to spit fire. When she sees me, she marches up and shoves my chest. "Are you out of your fucking *mind*?"

Word travels fast, I think disdainfully. People stop in the hallway to gawk at us. I know it would just make their day to see a big fight before first period. We can't have this conversation in public. She seems to know it, too, because she grabs my arm and pulls me into an empty classroom nearby.

I walk to the center of the room and turn around to face her. She slams the door shut and strides up to me, her eyes flashing. "Avery, what the *fuck*? Holding hands? With *Tristan*? You want to tell me what the hell is going on with you?"

"I don't know. Maybe his gay cooties rubbed off on me."

"I'm not joking, Avery."

"I'm not *laughing*, Ashley."

"This is ridiculous! I know you're not gay. You *can't* be gay, not after all the things you and I did together!"

"Did it ever occur to you that it's not about being gay or straight? Tristan gets me. I get him. We connect. End of story."

"What are you saying?"

"I'm saying I'm in *love* with him, Ashley."

She looks as if I had just slapped her. Her eyes brim with tears and her body starts to quiver. I suddenly realize that I didn't break her heart when I broke up with her. I'm breaking her heart as we speak.

"Hey . . ." I reach a hand out to console her, but she backs away.

"Just . . . just go," she says, her voice shaking.

"I'm sorry," I whisper.

With a heavy heart, I walk out the door, leaving her sobbing behind me.

I make it through first period without any problems. The other students throw me furtive glances and whisper amongst themselves, but nobody says anything to my face. It's second period—gym class—that I'm worried about.

Inside the locker room, I go straight to my locker without making eye contact with anybody. As I'm pulling my gym uniform out, I hear their voices behind me.

"Hey, look who it is!" Mike says.

"Taylor, you sure you're in the right place? The girls' locker room is across the hall," says Jamaal.

"Yeah, when were you going to tell us you were a cocksucker?" says Tom.

I sigh. "Cool it, guys."

"Cool it, guys," Mike mimics in a high-pitched voice.

I can't let them get to me. I know that if I react, it will only escalate.

"So where's your boyfriend, huh? What's his name? Kristen?" says Mike.

"Tell us, does he give good head?" asks Jamaal.

"I'll bet he does. We should call up Mr. Trawler and ask," says Mike.

They all laugh.

My blood starts to boil. I clench my fists.

"Maybe I'll give him a buck after school and find out for myself," says Tom.

They laugh again.

This has to stop. I can't ignore them any longer. I don't want to fight, but I can't go to Coach Barnes, either, because then I'd get a reputation as a pussy and that wouldn't do me or Tristan any favors. I turn around to face them.

"What about you, Taylor? What's your going rate?" Tom jeers.

"You couldn't pay me enough to come near your puny dick!"

Jamaal and Mike yell, "Ohhh!" and look at Tom, anxious to see how he'll respond to my insult.

His face turns red. He hops over the bench and gets up in my face. "What did you say to me?"

Behind him, I see Mike and Jamaal inch closer, ready to strike at a moment's notice. I look at the three of them and, for the first time, I regret having a locker in the corner. Although I'm tempted to start throwing punches, I'm outnumbered and I know it would just end badly for me. Not only would I get my ass handed to me on a silver platter, but I'd get kicked off the baseball team as well. I'm still not a hundred percent sure that I want to be in the Major Leagues, but I don't want to throw away all my chances, either. I have to try to defuse this situation.

With my body still tense and ready to defend myself, I relax my face into a lazy grin. "I may be a cocksucker, but I've still got my standards."

Mike and Jamaal laugh. Tom's eyebrows are still furrowed as he stares me down, but I can see the hint of a smile playing at the corners of his mouth.

He reaches up and roughly pushes my head to the side, messing up my hair. "Go fuck yourself, Taylor."

He turns away from me and goes back to his locker to change. I breathe a sigh of relief as the three of them bicker and tease each other as if I were never even there.

After class is over, I change back into my regular clothes as quickly as possible. I grab my backpack and start to make my way out the door, but Coach Barnes's voice calls me back. "Taylor. Got a minute?"

I turn around and step into his office. He's sitting behind his desk, shuffling papers.

"Yeah, Coach?"

He doesn't look up. In his low, gruff voice, he says, "Baseball is a man's sport."

I don't reply.

"The Majors don't draft fairies."

I feel the ground fall out beneath me. I'd expected slurs from jackasses like Tom, but this? I never expected this. Blood rushes to my face as I try to sort through the hurt and humiliation to find an

The Lifesaver

appropriate response. I come up short. There's nothing I can say to that.

He rotates his chair away from me, clearly dismissing me. I look up at the ceiling to blink back a few tears, then I sling my heavy bag across my back and plod a slow retreat out of his office.

I can't concentrate on anything during third period. I'm still reeling from my conversation with Coach Barnes. Never mind the epithet—could he be right about the Major Leagues? If the scouts found out about Tristan, would they pass over me for someone else?

I don't see why the scouts should care who I'm with. Being with Tristan hasn't affected my ability to play ball. I guess I can see why an all-male team might feel uncomfortable getting undressed in front of someone who's admitted to being attracted to other men, but just because I'm in a relationship with Tristan doesn't mean I'm going to come on to any of my teammates. None of the dozens of questionnaires I filled out asked about my relationship status or sexual orientation.

And yet . . .

It's a hard fact that the overwhelming majority of professional baseball players have been straight, or at least publicly identified themselves as straight. In the history of baseball, I can only think of a couple names of openly gay players, and even then, I don't think they came out until after their professional careers had already started. Would they have made it into the Majors if their preferences had been known up front? I know that there's been a push for sports teams to embrace diversity, but old prejudices die hard. Coach Barnes is proof of that. How many like-minded people will I have to face if I try to pursue a career in baseball?

Maybe this is why my dad was so upset when I told him. He'd

been cautioning me for months about being careful so as to not jeopardize my opportunity to go pro, and now he's probably thinking that my relationship with Tristan is the last nail in the coffin.

If the Major Leagues don't want me, then that's their problem.

I'm not giving up Tristan, and I'm not going to pretend anymore that we're not together. If that means I won't get drafted, then so be it. I'm done hiding.

I drop my lunch tray in front of Drake's and slump into the seat across from him.

"Soooo. How's your day going?" He gives me a knowing smile.

"I haven't gotten my ass kicked yet, so that's a plus," I grumble.

"Well, that's good to hear. Though I wouldn't get your hopes up too high yet. Ashley is on the loose and is looking for blood."

My heart sinks. "Really?"

"Yeah, man. Hell hath no fury. She already read me the riot act for 'conspiring' against her."

"What?"

"Yeah, she's totally paranoid! She claimed that I knew all along that you were cheating on her. I told her she didn't know what she was talking about."

My heart drops even lower. "She said I cheated on her?"

"Yeah. I told her you would never do that, but she wouldn't listen to me."

I rub my hands down my face. I don't want to tell him that she was right, that I fucked up, but I don't like lying to Drake. Especially not after he went through the trouble of defending me. Reluctantly, I say, "Actually, I kind of . . . did."

His mouth drops open. "Are you shittin' me?"

I close my eyes and shake my head. "No. I sort of got drunk and made out with Tristan the night before prom."

He blinks. Then he bellows a laugh, causing flecks of food and spittle to fly out of his mouth. I bury my head in my arms on the table. "God, I feel like such a *dick*," I moan as he laughs at me.

"Ohh, man." He gasps for air. "You're really a piece of work, you know that?"

I groan.

"Look, I won't tell her what you just told me. She already seems to know anyway, though how she found *that* out, I have no idea. Chicks must have a sixth sense about these things. But if I were you, I'd keep Tristan away from Ashley as much as possible. You think she's mad at *you*? You should hear the things she's saying about Tristan."

My head jerks up. "What did she say?"

"I tuned out most of it. But I'm pretty sure the words 'cock-sucking whore' were mentioned."

Now I'm pissed. "Are you serious? Tristan was right. She *is* a bitch."

"Are you really that surprised that she'd talk bad about him behind his back? We're talking about Miss Gossip Queen of the Universe here."

"But her issue should be with me, not Tristan."

"Come on, Avery, you know how these things work. When a guy dumps a girl for someone else, she's not gonna blame the guy. She's gonna unsheathe her claws and scratch the eyes out of the girl who stole her man. Or, in this case, the guy who stole her man."

"Nobody stole me," I mutter. "I dumped her. It was my decision."

"Yeah, but she doesn't want to see it that way. Think about it from her perspective. You were together for, what, a year? And then she finds out that not only did you rebound so quickly after you broke up, but you rebounded with a *dude*? What does that say about her? Of course she's upset."

"It's not that I didn't like Ashley. It's just—"

"You don't have to explain yourself to me. I see the way Tristan looks at you, and the way you look at him. But that's exactly why Ashley's hurting right now. She wanted to be the one you looked at that way. She's jealous of Tristan. She has been since you first started hanging out with him. That's why she's lashing out at him, not you."

"So what should I do?" I ask helplessly.

"Just don't let her get to you. Nothing you say to her right now is gonna change her mind about Tristan. But I wouldn't sweat it; she'll get over it eventually, and then she'll find other things to bitch about."

I push the food around on my plate with a fork. "I feel like if I can just get through today, then everything will be alright."

"Well, you're already halfway there." He smiles.

32

This has got to be the longest day of my life, I think as I watch the second hand inch around the clock. It's last period, and in three minutes, I'm finally going to get to see Tristan and get the hell out of this place. I'm nervous that our little act of defiance this morning has hurt him rather than helped him.

The bell rings. I jump up, grab my bag, and hustle out the door, trying to beat the rush of students in the hallway. I almost get to the end of the hall before a rough hand grabs my shirt and shoves me up against the wall. Brandon Stover. He puts his meaty arm up to my neck and pins me so I can't escape.

The students in the hall give us a wide berth. Some continue walking, averting their eyes and pretending they can't see what's going on. Most, however, have stopped to watch the show. My eyes dart from face to face: a few are anxious, almost all are excited, but not a single one of them looks like they're going to intervene on my behalf. I'm on my own.

"I knew you were a *faggot*," Brandon growls.

His arm is constricting my airway, but I manage to choke out, "Takes one to know one." I know I probably shouldn't antagonize him, but my ass is toast either way, so I may as well get in a few shots. Brandon is much bigger, stronger, and meaner than I am. The only reason I was able to beat him last time is that I had the element of surprise. He got the drop on me this time, though.

"I'm gonna kill you, you little fucker," he says in a low snarl. "And then I'm gonna kill your faggoty boyfriend, too. And you know what? Nobody will even care that you're gone."

A prickle of fear runs down my spine. He sounds like he really means it.

"What is going on here?" a deep voice booms. I look over Brandon's shoulder and see Principal Johnson standing there, looking livid.

Without taking his eyes off mine, Brandon removes his arm from my neck and takes a step back. I cough and put my hand to my throat.

"You two. My office. *Now*," Johnson says.

Brandon sneers at me, then turns and follows Johnson toward his office. People part to let them through. I follow slowly, trying to keep several feet of space between me and Brandon. I glare at his back as he struts in front of me. He looks more like a man on a stroll through the park than someone who's about to be condemned.

We walk into the front office. For once, Ms. Murray is at her desk. She looks up as Principal Johnson approaches her. "Kathleen," he says, "please call Officer Gálvez to my office."

Ms. Murray picks up the walkie-talkie near her keyboard and says a few words into the mic. Johnson turns to us and points at the chairs against the wall. I perch myself on the edge of the chair at the end. Brandon ignores Johnson and continues standing. A tic jumps in Johnson's cheek, but he doesn't say anything.

Officer Gálvez walks in the door.

"Juan, please keep an eye on Mr. Stover," Johnson says. "Mr. Taylor and I are going to have a little chat. Taylor, come with me."

Brandon's lip curls as I get up and follow Johnson into his office.

I take a seat in the small, uncomfortable wooden chair in front of the large desk. Something tells me that the choice of furniture in this room was not incidental. Johnson sits in the tall leather chair across from me and steeples his hands. "This is the second time you've had an altercation with Brandon. Is that correct?"

"Yes, but he started it."

"Do you want to explain to me what happened?"

"Yeah. I was walking along, minding my own business, and he shoved me up against the wall for no reason."

"What did he say to you? I couldn't hear him clearly."

"He called me a faggot and said he was going to kill me and Tristan."

"Tristan Chevalier?"

"Yes. Why are you interrogating me? Brandon's the one at fault here."

"I'm just trying to get the facts. If I'm going to expel Brandon, I'll need to provide sufficient justification."

"You can't just expel him. He belongs in jail!"

"For what? What crime did he commit?"

"He threatened to kill me!"

"Taylor, if I threw every hotheaded teenager who said they wanted to kill somebody into juvenile detention, I wouldn't have a student body left."

"I think he meant it, sir."

Johnson sighs.

"Could he at least be charged with assault?"

"You don't seem to be the worse for wear."

"I don't mean for what happened today. I mean when he punched Tristan in the gut."

"As I recall, you punched Brandon as well."

"Because I was defending Tristan!"

"Which is exactly why I suspended Brandon and not you."

I glare at him with exasperation.

He continues. "Brandon will be expelled. He won't be able to graduate, which means he'll have to retake senior year. It will look bad on all of his college applications, if, indeed, he's planning on attending college. It will have a very big impact on his future. That kind of punishment is nothing to be laughed at."

I grit my teeth.

He peers at me. "Brandon really seems to have it out for you and Tristan. Why?"

"He's a bully," I retort. "He wants to prey on the weak and vulnerable."

He lifts an eyebrow. "You don't strike me as either of those, Mr. Taylor."

"No. He wanted to get at Tristan. I'm not saying Tristan is weak, but he can . . . be vulnerable. I just got in Brandon's way."

"Tristan has had a hard time here," he admits. "The teachers look out for him as much as possible, but I can't have Officer Gálvez follow Tristan around all day long as a bodyguard. But it seems he found his own bodyguard." He gestures at me and gives a small smile.

He straightens up in his chair and assumes a more businesslike demeanor. "Alright, Taylor. You're free to go." His mouth twitches as he says, "Send Stover in here, will you?"

The Lifesaver

I step out of the front office to see Drake and Tristan leaning against the wall. Tristan's face is pale and anxious, and Drake looks just as worried. As soon as Tristan sees me, he rushes up and throws his arms tightly around my neck. I wrap my arms around him and squeeze him back. "Are you okay?" I ask.

He chokes a laugh as he replies, "Are *you* okay?"

I meet Drake's eyes. His face is full of concern. A few minutes ago, I was anything but okay, but now that I'm with him and Tristan again, I'm already starting to feel better.

I lean back to look at Tristan's face. "Yeah, I'm okay." I kiss him, and his anxious expression dissolves into a relieved smile.

Drake steps forward and claps me on the shoulder. I turn to face him, but I keep an arm around Tristan to keep him close. "How did you know where I was?"

Drake says, "I waited by your locker, but when you didn't show, I went to find Tristan. He hadn't seen you, either, and that's when we heard that you and Brandon had gotten into it again. We were afraid you'd been carried off on a stretcher, but then someone said they'd seen you go into the principal's office so we came over here."

"Johnson showed up before Brandon could really do anything. He's gonna be expelled."

"Good!" Drake spits. "That fucker should've been expelled a long time ago."

"Something tells me he won't care about getting kicked out of school. He probably thinks it'll add to his street cred."

"Who cares? As long as he's not around to use you as a coatrack, who gives a shit what he thinks?"

I laugh.

"So what do you want to do now?" Drake asks. "I already told

Coach Barnes we weren't coming to practice."

Surprise and relief flow through me. I don't think I could handle Coach Barnes right now.

Tristan speaks up. "We can go to my house."

"Oh yeah, Drake hasn't seen your humongous TV yet."

"Humongous TV?" Drake says. "I'm in!"

"Damn, Tristan! You must be loaded." Drake whistles as he kicks off his shoes and looks around the elegantly furnished foyer. Then he nods in my direction and says, "You know he's just using you for the money, right?"

His statement throws me for a loop. It never occurred to me that people might think I'm pretending to be in love with Tristan to get my hands on his parents' wealth. Wide-eyed, I look at Tristan. He's watching me with a suspicious frown. I flounder to find the words to say that will convince him I'm not a gold digger.

After a couple of seconds, Tristan shrugs. "That's okay. I'm just using him for his body."

He and Drake laugh. My cheeks feel warm. I'm not used to my best friend and boyfriend joking together at my expense.

"Come on, this way," Tristan says as he leads us back to the den.

Drake's jaw drops when he sees the impressive setup. "Dude! How can I not have been here before? Your house is awesome!" Then he glares at me and says, "Piano lessons, my ass."

I laugh. "Actually, I do take piano lessons, believe it or not."

"Uh-huh." He walks up to the cabinet under the TV and examines the array of game consoles.

"You wanna play something?" Tristan asks.

"Sure. What you got?"

While he and Tristan kneel on the ground to skim through the game titles, I take a seat on the couch and allow myself to unwind. I'm content to let them choose what we do; it doesn't matter to me, as long as I get to be around them for a while.

"We could play *Duck Hunt*," Tristan says. He looks back at me over his shoulder and gives me a wicked smile.

My heart skips a beat. *He does remember.* I return his grin and wink at him.

Drake doesn't see our exchange. "Nah, that game is boring. All you have to do is shoot at the middle of the screen and you get the duck."

Tristan laughs. "See, Avery? I told you."

After some back-and-forth banter between the two of them, Drake says, "Alright, I've got it: *Mario Kart*."

"Okay," Tristan says.

"Sounds good to me," I say.

Hanging out playing video games with Tristan and Drake has got to be one of the best stress relievers in the world. Between the jokes and smack talk and ridiculous attempts to sabotage each other, I don't think I've laughed this much in months. We get so caught up in the fun that we lose track of time and it's only after the windows have turned dark that Drake looks at his watch and says, "Shit! I was supposed to be home ten minutes ago. I gotta go." He shoots up off the couch and grabs his backpack.

"I'll walk you out," I say.

Drake exchanges a handshake with Tristan and says, "Later, bro."

"See ya," Tristan replies.

I follow Drake into the foyer. As he slips on his shoes, he looks up at me and says, "He loves you, you know."

I flush. "Yeah, I know."

He straightens up and points a finger at me. "You break his heart, I'll kick your ass."

I smile and shake my head. "Yeah, that'll never happen."

"Good to hear." He flashes one of his brilliantly white smiles before he opens the door and trots to his car.

I stand in the doorway and wave as he pulls away. After his taillights have disappeared down the street, I look out into the night. The warm yellow streetlamps dapple the road at regular intervals, and between them, the cars and grass and pavement are cloaked in the soft grays of dusk. I take a deep breath of the fresh spring air, and my senses come alive. Suddenly, the house feels small and constricting. I want to be outside.

I make my way back to the den. Tristan sits up and looks at me expectantly.

"It's nice outside. You wanna go for a walk?"

"Yeah, alright." He turns off the television and follows me out to the foyer.

We put on our shoes, then walk out into the night. He slips his hand into mine as we walk down the long driveway. It's such a freeing feeling to be able to hold his hand and not have to worry about who might see.

Without intending to, our feet take us to the bridge where we met. I lead him down the hill and we sit on the grass in the same spot where I dragged his limp body onto the riverbank. I swirl my fingers through the water. It's cool, but considerably warmer than it was the last time we were sitting in this spot. It may even be warm enough to swim in.

I take my shoes off and dip my feet into the water. Tristan sits cross-legged next to me and looks out over the river. The moon is almost full, and its light illuminates everything around us and makes the water shimmer.

"It's actually kind of beautiful, isn't it?" he murmurs.

"Yeah, it is."

We sit in silence for a few minutes, content to just enjoy the night air. I look over at Tristan. He's gazing up at the stars, looking more at peace than I've ever seen him before. He's so beautiful—I want to memorize every line, every detail: the way the light of the moon washes over his face, giving him an ethereal glow; the way his neck gently slopes as he looks up toward the sky; the way his lips curve in a small, contented smile rather than the sardonic one I'm used to. It doesn't seem possible that I didn't see how beautiful he was until a few short weeks ago. I should have realized it years ago, the moment I first saw him in my eighth-grade home ec class. *How could I have been so blind?*

He glances over at me, and his mouth quirks when he sees me staring at him. "What?"

"Nothing." I smile as I shrug. "Just admiring you."

He blushes and looks away.

"I didn't get a chance to ask you before. How did your day go?"

He chuckles. "Better than yours, I think. People made fun of me, but that isn't any different from how it was before. Actually, this turned out to be one of the best days of my life."

"Really?" I ask, surprised.

"Yeah. Going public like that? It meant a lot to me. I always figured you'd want to keep it a secret because it would hurt your reputation. Or people would make fun of you, or you'd get your ass kicked. I wouldn't have blamed you if you'd never wanted to be seen with me. But this morning . . . that took a lot of guts. I can't believe you risked all of that just to be with me."

"Yeah, I'm pretty sure my reputation is shot. People definitely made fun of me, and I almost got my ass kicked. And you know what? I'd do it all over again. And I will. Tomorrow."

He looks down at the ground and shakes his head. "I just don't understand."

"Understand what?"

He lifts his head again and searches my face. "*Why* do you love me?"

I stand up and brush the grass off my shorts. I pull my cell phone and wallet out of my pocket and hold them out to him. Bewildered, he takes them from me. I look down at him and give him a wolfish grin. "I'm just using you for the money."

I run two steps and, fully clothed, I leap into the river. I hear Tristan gasp behind me.

I swim out a few feet, then turn around and tread water. Tristan's standing on the shore, slack-jawed, looking at me like I've lost my mind.

"Well? What are you waiting for?" I call out to him.

"What? No! I'm not going in there."

"Yes, you are."

"I told you, I'm afraid of the water."

I roll my eyes. "Tristan, you've spent the last two months swimming in the pool. This is no different."

"It is different. The pool doesn't have a current."

"The current isn't very strong. You'll be fine."

He still looks worried.

"Come on, Tristan, weren't you the one who said to 'face your fears'?"

He glares at me while he tries to think of a comeback. He must not be able to come up with one, because after a moment he mutters, "Goddammit."

Feeling victorious, I grin as he kneels to take off his shoes.

"This is so fucking stupid," he says as he unties his shoelaces.

"Quit your bitchin' and get your ass in here."

"You better not make me drown again."

"Hey."

He looks up from his shoelaces. I can see a hint of fear in his eyes.

"Do you remember our first swim lesson?"

"Of course."

"What was the first lesson I taught you?"

"Umm . . . how to float?"

I shake my head. "Before that. Before you even got in the water."

He looks up at the sky as he tries to remember what I said. Then he smiles, and I know he's figured it out. "You said you wouldn't let anything happen to me."

"That's right. Now come here."

He empties his pockets onto the grass, then hops into the water. Before he reaches me, I say, "Race you to the bridge," and start swimming upstream.

"What? No."

"Come on, you need the practice. Besides, it's shallower over there."

"It's shallower on land, too," he grumbles, but he swims after me.

I stay close to him in case he runs into trouble, but he doesn't need my help. He's still not a fast swimmer, but his form is good and he controls his breathing well. *He's learned a lot*, I observe proudly.

When we reach the bridge supports, I grab his arms and pull them around my neck. I slide my hands around his waist. The water is shallow enough for him to stand so his head and shoulders are above water.

"You see?" I say. "This isn't so bad."

"No, it's not," he begrudgingly admits. "Though I don't know why we're doing this now. At night. Fully dressed."

I shrug. "That's how we met, isn't it? Swimming in our clothes in the dark? Though in your case, I'm using the word 'swimming' loosely."

He groans. "You're never going to let me live that down, are you?"

Suddenly serious, I reply, "Yes, I will. That's what I'm trying to do, right now. I saw you at your lowest that night. And right now, despite all your bitching and moaning, I'd be willing to bet that you're feeling pretty happy. I want you to have a chance to replace that night with a happier one."

He doesn't respond. His eyes glisten in the moonlight as he stares at me.

"You okay?" I ask.

Roughly, he says, "Christ, Avery. You're so fucking sappy sometimes," but I can tell that he's moved. I smile and pull him closer. He wraps himself around me, more than willing to accept the second chance I've offered him.

The water flows gently by us as we make love under the bridge. Together, we drive away all the painful memories of the past. I forget about Ashley. Coach Barnes. Brandon Stover. My father's disappointment. Tristan's scars. Him weeping into my shirt, confessing sins he never wanted to commit. His limp body and blue lips. All of that disappears until all that's left is us, here in the now and the future before us.

33

Early the next morning, I pick Tristan up to go to the community center. He hops into the passenger seat and gives me a kiss. "Hey, stud muffin."

I laugh. "Stud muffin?"

He shrugs and grins. "It's growing on me."

"Alright. Who are you and what have you done with Tristan?"

"Just drive," he orders, but he smiles when he says it.

"Yes, sir," I say as I put the car into gear.

He picks up the aux cord and plugs in his phone. As "We Will Rock You" starts to play, I turn the volume up loud. I drum on the steering wheel while he taps his foot to the beat. I can't believe how different this morning is from yesterday's.

We pull up to the community center, and I grab our bags from the trunk.

"So what are we going to do today?" he asks.

"How would you feel about trying out the diving board?"

His eyes widen. "Umm . . . Yeah, I guess I could give it a shot." He sounds nervous, but I'm glad that he's willing to try.

He follows me into the locker room. I set my bag on the bench and he goes into the next row, like usual. I shake my head and laugh. "Seriously?"

"A little modesty never hurt anybody."

"Oh, is that what it is? Or are you just afraid that if I see you get undressed, we'd never leave the locker room?"

"Yeah, that too."

I laugh.

He comes around the corner as I zip up my bag. "I forgot to ask you," he says. "Did you see Ashley yesterday?"

I heave a sigh. "Yeah, I did. She took it really hard. I kinda wish I had been the one to break the news, but she already knew by the time I got to her. I think you were right that she was hoping we'd get back together, 'cause she cried when I told her I was in love with you."

"You told her that?" He looks stunned.

"Yeah. Why wouldn't I?"

"I dunno. I'm just surprised, that's all."

I smirk at him. "It's not like it was a big secret, after people saw me holding hands with you in the hallway."

"I know. I guess it's just different hearing you say it out loud. Especially to her."

I shrug. "I've got nothing to hide. Not anymore, at least. If people don't like it, they can kiss my ass. Even Ashley." Then I grumble, "Though I do have to say that I wish she wouldn't say bad things about you. I may have to pull her aside and straighten her out if she keeps it up."

He scoffs. "Like anything she says could hurt me. As long as

The Lifesaver

you're with me and not her, I could give a fuck what she says to people."

"I still don't like it."

"If you want to defend my honor, then be my guest. Just don't expect her to back down. She's always hated me, even before you and I started hanging out."

"Yeah. I wonder why that is."

"Must be because I'm prettier than she is."

I laugh. "Must be."

We walk out to the pool. I don't even bother with the lifesaver and pool noodles anymore. I climb the ladder and walk to the end of the diving board, then turn around and gesture for him to follow. He gulps and climbs up the ladder. I hold out my hand and he walks slowly toward me, keeping his eyes on his feet to make sure he doesn't fall off. He finally reaches me and grasps my hand.

"See? It's not so bad," I say.

He gives me a tentative smile.

"The biggest lesson here is to hold your breath. You can dive or flip or do a cannonball—it doesn't matter, as long as you close your mouth *before* you hit the water. Another thing to keep in mind is that when you hit the water, some might go up your nose. You can always blow it out, but you might want to hold your nose when you jump in if it makes you feel better. I'm also going to be nice and tell you up front that hitting the water flat on your belly hurts. A lot. If you were anyone else, I'd just push you in and let you learn the hard way, but I'll go easy on you 'cause I kinda like you and want to keep you around for a while." I grin at him.

"Thanks for the tip." He smiles back. "So how *should* I jump in?"

I let go of his hand and stretch my arms wide. With a smile, I shake my head and say, "Any way you want."

I leap backward off the edge of the diving board and bring my arms above my head. I hit the water with a splash and let myself sink, then bring my arms down and kick until my head surfaces above the water again. I shake the water out of my hair. "Your turn!"

He stares apprehensively down at the water. I hear him murmur to himself, "Okay. One . . . two . . . three . . ."

He closes his eyes and pinches his nose with his thumb and forefinger. He takes a deep breath and hops off the board into the water. I cheer as he resurfaces and blinks the water out of his eyes. I swim over to him and kiss him on the lips. "Good job, baby. I'm proud of you."

He blushes and mumbles, "Thanks."

"You wanna go again?"

"Yeah, okay."

We take turns jumping off the diving board. Tristan's confidence grows each time, and before long, it looks like he's having just as much fun as I am goofing off and playing in the water.

After an hour or so, Tristan glances up at the clock on the wall. "They're going to be opening soon. You ready to go?"

"Umm . . . I think I want to do a couple of laps first. You go on ahead."

"Okay." He climbs out of the pool and heads to the locker room.

I take a deep breath and swim under the water from one end of the pool to the other. I love being in the water—I love all of its contradictions. How it resists my body's movements, and yet it feels so soothing to my skin as I push my way through it. How it tries to hold me afloat, even when it's weighing me down. How it sounds so loud and so quiet at the same time. How it can easily take away a life, but just as easily give one.

I swim a few laps, then reluctantly climb out of the pool. I'd much rather spend my day in this sanctuary with Tristan than go back to the cruel world we call high school.

I start to push open the locker room door, but then I stop when I hear a sweet, tenor voice singing. *That can't be Tristan. . . .*

Careful not to make any noise, I open the door and close it gently behind me. Tristan's washing himself off under the showerhead at the end, facing the wall away from me. I can hear him sing, "*. . . And pain is all around . . . like a bridge over troubled water . . . I will lay me down . . .*"

My heart swells. I may not be his therapist, but I know that this has to be some sort of breakthrough. I walk closer, then lean against the wall a few feet behind him so I can watch and listen without disturbing him. He doesn't notice me; he just continues bathing and singing to himself, as if he doesn't have a care in the world. *He really does have a good voice. It's a shame he's been holding it in for so long.*

My eyes start to burn as I'm overwhelmed by a mix of emotions: awe that he sings so well, even after all this time; anger at the injustice he's suffered; and, above all, a fierce pride that he's overcome another deep-seated emotional hurdle. I've never loved anything or anyone more than I love him right now, at this moment.

I step forward and wrap my arms around his waist. He jumps and breaks off mid-verse. "Jesus! You scared the crap out of me."

I chuckle. "I'm sorry. I didn't mean to scare you."

"How long have you been in here?"

"Long enough. I heard you singing, so I had to come over and listen."

"Hmph." He resumes soaping his arm in silence.

"Please don't stop. I like to hear you sing." I hug him tighter and murmur in his ear, "Especially love ballads."

He smiles. Hesitantly, he picks up the song where he left off. He sings softer than before, as if singing a lullaby. I lay my cheek on his shoulder and listen to his voice echo off the shower wall. He rests his hands over mine and leans back into me as he sings the final chorus. When he reaches the end of the song, neither of us move. Although the only sound I hear is the water flowing down around us, it feels like his silvery voice is still lingering in the air.

After a few moments of contented silence, I lift my head and rest my chin on his shoulder. "You're amazing, you know that?"

He blushes. "Why do you say that?"

"You just are. You've been really brave these last few weeks. Learning how to swim to overcome your fear of the water. Being with me at school when you know what people might do to you. Telling me about your past. You've been through so much, and you've handled it like a champ. I'm really proud of you."

He looks down and shakes his head. "You shouldn't be proud. I'm not brave, and I definitely haven't handled anything like a champ. The only reason I'm able to make it through each day is because of you."

"Don't say that."

"It's true. I'm a big wuss, you know that. I tried to kill myself, Avery. And if you hadn't kept pestering me, I would have tried it again."

"Do you still think about it?" I murmur.

"Not recently," he admits.

I breathe a sigh of relief and squeeze him tighter. "Good. I don't know what I'd do if I lost you."

"Oh, you'd get over it," he says dismissively. "You'd probably end up marrying a supermodel and having twenty kids just like you wanted."

"Don't say that," I say sharply. I whirl him around to face me, my voice rising. "Don't even joke about that! Don't you get it? I want *you*. I want to marry *you*! I don't *want* anybody else, I don't want *kids* with anybody else, and *I'd never get over it if you killed yourself*!"

His face is as white as a sheet. I've never been this angry with him before, and it looks like he doesn't know how to react. "Okay," he whispers. "I'm sorry."

Immediately, my anger dissolves. I sigh. "Come here." I pull him to me and hug him tightly. "I'm sorry I yelled at you," I mumble.

"It's okay. I liked what you said, even though you were yelling it."

I groan. "That shows you how romantic I am. Next time, I'll scream a sonnet or something."

He laughs. "Yeah, you could throw some furniture around while you're at it. Show me you *really* care."

I laugh, too. I lean back and hold his face in my hands. "I love you," I say, then I brush his lips to take away any remaining sting.

"I love you, too." He beams back at me.

"We should get going."

"Yeah." He sighs.

I release him so he can finish rinsing off and walk back to my bag. It's almost opening time and I don't have time to shower first. I dry myself off and get dressed. As I'm tying my shoe against the bench, Tristan appears beside me. He's already in his school clothes with a towel around his shoulders, holding his bag in one hand. "You ready?" he asks.

I straighten up and give him a mischievous smile. I grab both ends of his towel and pull him closer. "Not yet," I growl, then I kiss him on the mouth. Just at that moment, Jeremy walks in through the door right next to us. I freeze, my hands still wrapped in Tristan's towel, and look over at him. He stops and stares at us in shock. *Crap. This may be the end of our swim lessons.*

Jeremy crosses his arms and a big smirk stretches across his face. "Hey. No hanky-panky in the locker room."

I grin, then hold up my middle finger while I give Tristan a big, slobbery kiss.

Jeremy rolls his eyes. "I'll pretend I didn't see that. You kids better get going if you want to make it to school on time."

"Are you anxious about your test?" Tristan asks as I park the car in my preferred spot below the trees. He knows today's the day of my calculus final, the exam I've been the most nervous about.

I breathe out. "If I'm not ready now, I'll never be ready."

He smiles. "You're ready."

"Thanks for all your help this year. Sincerely. I don't know what I'd have done without you."

"Well, it's the least I could do after you saved my life."

I look at him in surprise. Not once has he ever expressed any gratitude for rescuing him. I've often wondered if he secretly resented me for reviving him and forcing him to live when he was so determined to die. Cautiously, I ask, "Are you saying you're glad to be alive?"

"I'm glad to be with you."

It's not the same thing, but it's close enough. I pull his hand up to my lips. "I'm glad you're with me, too."

He smiles.

"You ready to go in?"

He sighs. "Not really."

I smile sympathetically and kiss his cheek. "Let's go," I whisper.

He nods. We get out of the car. I grab my backpack from the back seat and sling it across my shoulder. I open my mouth to speak, but then I see a shadow slip from behind a tree and my words get caught in my throat. A strangled yell escapes my lips. "TRISTAN!"

He sees my panicked look and turns just in time. A baseball bat crashes into the roof of my car, only centimeters away.

I drop my backpack on the ground and leap onto the hood. I throw myself onto Brandon as he prepares to take another swing at Tristan. The force of the impact sends us both reeling to the ground. The bat clatters to the pavement next to us. We're a tangle of limbs and it's difficult to see as we both struggle to gain the upper hand. I quickly realize that I'm not going to win this fight, but he's not giving me an opportunity to escape, either.

Tristan's frozen to the spot, his mouth hanging open in horror. Brandon grabs my throat. I reach for the bat. It rolls beyond my fingertips.

"Tristan—" I choke. "Tristan, the bat!"

Tristan looks around wildly for the bat. He makes a mad dash for it, but Brandon beats him to it. He grabs it and slashes it at Tristan's legs. Tristan jumps out of his reach. Brandon takes a swing at me. I wince as he lands a blow on my back. He uses my moment of weakness to roll me off him. As he gets to his feet, I shout, "Tristan, run!" He has to get out of here, or it will be him next.

Tristan backs away a few steps, his eyes wide with terror. *Why isn't he running?*

Brandon raises the bat above his head. As it comes toward my face, I raise my right arm to block the blow. The bat hits my wrist. A stabbing, searing pain travels up my entire arm as the bone splinters. Tears jump to my eyes, and I scream. I cradle my shattered wrist and roll over onto my side, my body curled in agony. "Tristan . . . run . . . ," I gasp.

Brandon lifts the bat once more. Through my tears, I see Tristan's blurry outline sprinting away from me toward the school. The last thing I feel is relief, before the bat descends and everything goes black.

34

Through the fog, I think I hear Tristan's voice, but it sounds far, far away.

I try desperately to move, to get closer, but I can't. I'm alone in this pit of darkness, grasping for him, but I can't reach.

"... Avery ..."

I strain my ears to listen.

"I don't know if you can hear me," he chokes, "but I am so ... so *sorry*." He starts sobbing.

My heart goes out to him. I want to comfort him and tell him that everything will be okay, but all I can do is lie helplessly and listen.

"This is all my fault. This never would have happened if you hadn't met me. Your dad was right. Maybe everything would have been better if you had just let me drown."

I want to scream to him, to let him know that it's not true. My mind struggles violently against the fog, but it's no good ...

I'm trapped within my own body.

35

My dad argues with the nurse while I eat the bland hospital food. "He's been here a week already. You're saying he'll need his cast for another *six weeks*?"

"Yes, Mr. Taylor. At a minimum."

"When will he be able to play baseball again?"

"Dad," I say, but he shushes me.

"My son needs to practice. The draft is this month. He's going to be a baseball player; he can't be out of commission for six weeks!"

"Dad! It doesn't matter. I don't want to be a baseball player."

"What?" he says.

The nurse looks from me to him, then tactfully excuses herself and leaves the room.

"I don't want to be a baseball player," I say again.

He gapes at me. "Well, what *do* you want to be?"

Without stopping to think, I blurt out, "I want to be a psychologist."

Until now, I hadn't really given it serious thought. But now that I've said it out loud, I know that it's true.

"A shrink?"

"Yeah, a shrink."

"Why on earth would you want to be a shrink?"

"I want to help people, Dad! Understand them. Baseball is just a stupid hobby. I want to feel like what I do actually makes a difference to people."

He stares at me, not knowing what to say. At that moment, Drake appears in the doorway. "Knock, knock! Look who finally decided to join the land of the living! Hi, Mr. Taylor."

He ignores the look my dad gives him and walks up to the side of my bed. "Here," he says as he holds out a Taco Bell bag. "I brought you some real food."

I push my hospital tray away and grab the bag. "Thanks, man. I owe you one."

My dad glares at us for a moment, then stalks out of the room.

Drake pulls up a chair. "What was that all about?"

"Oh. I just told my dad I didn't want to participate in his grand scheme for me."

"Nice. How'd he take it?"

"I dunno," I mutter. "I'm sure I'll find out after you leave."

He looks around the room at all the floral arrangements and balloons. "Must be nice to have admirers. Oh, speaking of which . . ." He pulls a purple envelope out of his pocket. "From Ashley."

I shake my head. "You can throw it away."

"Aw, come on, man, don't be like that. She just wants you to know she still cares about you. Besides, there may be money inside."

"I don't want to think about Ashley right now."

"Fair enough." He tosses the card onto the nightstand.

"Have you seen Tristan recently?" I ask, trying to sound casual.

He shakes his head. "No. His parents pulled him out of school right after the incident. I swung by his house a few times. That was really intimidating, by the way. I thought for sure I'd be arrested just for standing on the porch. But nobody ever answered."

A lump forms in my throat.

"Hasn't he come to see you?" he asks, surprised.

"I think he came by once when I was still unconscious. I haven't seen him since I woke up."

Drake looks at me with concern etched across his face. "Look, I'm sure he'll turn up soon."

I nod. He pretends to notice an interesting spot on the wall while I wipe the moisture away from my eyes.

"Are you excited to be going home tomorrow?" my mom asks. She's still wearing her scrubs, but she took a short break to visit me.

"I'll be excited to get out of this bed," I groan as I adjust my position. My muscles have atrophied and I feel sore all over my body. She grimaces in sympathy.

"Your father tells me you want to be a psychologist," she says.

"Yeah, I do."

"That will require a lot more school. A lot more studying."

"I know, Mom."

"Okay. I just want to make sure you know what all's involved before you make up your mind."

"I've already made up my mind. It's what I want to do. I can handle it."

She smiles. "I'm so proud of you, honey. Look at you, all grown up."

I hear a commotion in the hallway. My mother looks out the door and frowns. "It never ends," she mutters to herself.

The sound of hurried footsteps and the wheels of a gurney go by. I catch bits of the nurses' anxious conversation: "Twenty minutes . . . attempted suicide . . . senator's son . . ."

My stomach drops. *Senator's son?*

I scramble to get out of the bed, but I'm so weak that I collapse as soon as my feet touch the floor.

My mother rushes to me and helps me to stand up. "Avery, what—?"

I don't stop to explain. I barrel my way into the hallway and look around to see which direction the gurney went. I see the back of a nurse disappearing behind an automatic double door. I run after her. My mother is yelling something behind me but I can't hear what she's saying—I can't hear anything except the blood pounding in my ears. I squeeze my way between the doors just as they're about to close. I hear voices coming from the first room on the right. The door is closing. I rush over and shove it open, knocking a nurse out of the way.

"You can't be in here!" she yells, but I ignore her. I have to see, I have to know.

The room is in chaos. Doctors are scrambling, grabbing tools and shouting orders. I take two steps in to get a better view, and suddenly my world—my whole *universe*—comes crashing down around me. All I see is him. Tristan. Covered in blood. Hands are grabbing at my arms, trying to pull me away, but I resist. I scream at the faceless hands to let me go, but they don't listen. Can't they see that he needs me? I have to reach him! I have to *save* him . . . !

36

I pace around my hospital room like a caged animal, biting the nails on my good hand. Nobody has told me a goddamn thing. It feels like I've been trapped in here for hours. *What the hell is going on? How can they* do *this to us?*

My father is the worst of them all. He's standing outside the door, holding me prisoner in here. I want to scream. I want to break open a window.

Before I can contemplate it, the door swings open. My dad's standing there, looking haggard, like he's aged a dozen years.

"He's awake," he says.

I halt in my tracks, the room spinning. "What?"

"They moved him down the hall. Your mother's looking after him. He's . . . well . . ."

"He's alive?" I gasp. The room is too blurry. I lean against the bed, trying to hold myself upright.

"Avery?" Dad says, hurrying up to me.

His strong arms grab my waist just before I fall. My heart is beating too fast, my muscles weak. A heaving sob bursts forth, racking my whole body. Then another, and another.

"Oh, son . . ." He tightens his hold on me.

"D-Dad, he tried . . ."

"I know. I'm sorry."

I grip on to his shirt, my palm slippery with sweat. *Did he do this because of me?*

He attempts to lift me up. "Do you need to lay down?"

"No." I try to regain my legs. "I want to see him. P-please."

His neck tightens. "I . . . I'm sorry, Avery. They're not allowing visitors."

I pull away from him. "*Dad.*"

"Here," he says, patting the bed. "Why don't you sit down?"

"*No.*" I take another step back. "I need to see him."

"Avery—"

"I'm the reason he's here."

Dad stares at me. "What?"

"I . . ." The words come rushing out. "I came out with him at school, and then Brandon tried to attack him, so I . . ."

Dad's gaze drops to the floor. "Shit," he mutters under his breath.

"I'm sorry." I burst into tears again.

"Oh, Avery." He looks at me and squeezes my shoulder. "It's not your fault."

"He doesn't know I'm okay, Dad. Please."

His eyes roam up to the ceiling. He lets out a long breath. "You're going to get me into trouble."

I wipe my nose on my sleeve. "What?"

"Come on. Let's go." He wraps an arm around my shoulder. "Can you walk?"

"Y-yeah."

Holding on to me, he steers me toward the hall. My legs grow sturdier the closer we get.

When we arrive outside a closed door, Dad stops and looks around. "He's in here," he mumbles. "Tell your mother I'm the one to blame."

I wipe my face. "O-okay."

He peers closer at me. "You want me to go in with you?"

"No." My guts shrivel inside. All the things I've done to him, and now he's helping me. "D-Dad, I'm . . . I'm sorry."

He pulls me into another tight hug. "Avery," he says with a sigh, "you have nothing to be sorry for."

It almost seems like he means it. I clench my eyes shut to keep more tears at bay.

He squeezes me hard, cutting off my doubt. "I love you, son," he murmurs in my ear.

The tears escape down my face. "I love you, too."

He holds me out at arm's length. "It'll be all right."

I use my good hand to wipe my cheek. "Okay," I breathe, wanting to believe him.

He lets go of me so I can face the door. Now it's actually time. *I can do this. I can do this,* I tell myself. *Please, let him be okay.*

Carefully, silently, I open the door.

The room is dim inside. The only light is from a window in the corner. My mom's sitting in a chair in front of it. As soon as she sees me, she stands up.

"It's okay, Mom," I whisper, waving my hands downward.

She takes a step toward me, but it's too late. Movement from the bed makes us both freeze.

Tristan *is* awake, his eyes bloodshot and teary as he looks over at me. Thick bandages cover his wrists.

All the air escapes the room.

"H-hey," I manage to croak.

His eyes widen as they travel from my head to my feet. "You're walking," he says in a gravelly voice.

Despite everything, a tingle runs down my spine when he speaks. "Yeah, I am," I murmur.

His face scrunches up.

"Oh, baby . . ." I drag a chair up next to the bed, but he turns away from me and starts to cry. I reach out to caress his arm, but at the last second, I let my hand drop to the blanket instead. "What's going on?" I whisper.

Before he can answer, Mr. Chevalier and Jeanine walk in. Mr. Chevalier stops in the middle of the room, taking in the scene, while Jeanine hovers behind him. "What is this?" he asks.

I stumble to my feet to face him.

"Avery?" he says, peering closer at my scars.

"Y-yes, sir. It's me."

His face blanches. "I didn't recognize you." He returns his focus to Tristan and goes up to the bed. "How's my kiddo?"

Tristan sobs harder.

"N-not good," I admit, following his gaze.

Mr. Chevalier sits down in the chair. Jeanine stands behind him and leans over his shoulder. "We were so scared, sweetheart," she says to Tristan.

"God, just leave me alone," he begs.

Mr. Chevalier looks up at my mom, his tie clasped in one hand. "What should we do?" he asks.

She shakes herself off, remembering her job. "A social worker will be here soon to ask a few questions."

"A social worker?"

"It's hospital protocol. They'll do an assessment to see if he needs to stay a few nights."

"No," Tristan yelps, looking back at his dad. "I don't want to stay."

Mr. Chevalier frowns. "Is there any way around it?" he asks my mom.

She twists her hands together as she looks between them. "I don't recommend it. It's for his safety."

"What happens if we don't?"

"The court may get involved. It's . . . messy."

"D-Dad . . . p-please . . . ," Tristan says.

"You need rest, honey," Jeanine says.

"I can't take this place," Tristan says to his dad. "I'm serious. *Please.*"

"If I may—" my mom says, but Mr. Chevalier holds up his hand.

He stands up as if he draws all his power from his feet. "Forget the court," he announces to the room. "I'm taking him home."

37

I CONVINCE MY PARENTS to check me out of the hospital so I can go home with Tristan. I'm fucking sick of the hospital anyway.

The Chevaliers don't know what to do, so they let me come along. Tristan slides as far away from me as he can in the car. I reach for his hand to reassure him, but he pulls away. "Don't," he mutters.

"Okay."

I almost can't breathe in here. The air in the car feels too stale. The sunlight outside is too bright, too cheery; it's obscene. *God* . . .

I was too fucking late. If I had woken up sooner. Not been so . . . I don't know . . . stupid. If only I had taken out Brandon—

Tears pop to my eyes. I should have been much faster. I should have been stronger. I cover my mouth and face the window, trying not to let anyone see.

When we arrive at the house, his parents get out of the car first. Tristan seems like he's not going to get out, but then he slowly opens the door after I do. I wait for him to go ahead of me up the path.

Mr. Chevalier fiddles with the keys and unlocks the front door.

"I'll call to schedule your next appointment," he says as we enter.

"I'm going to bed," Tristan says as he passes by him.

"We need to—" Jeanine says.

Tristan stops at the foot of the stairs. "What?" he says without looking at her.

"Remove any sharp objects," she finishes.

He gapes at her over his shoulder. "Are you serious?"

"And the sheets," adds Mr. Chevalier.

Tristan's face goes gray. "No."

I step forward quickly. "I'll stay with him."

"We still need to remove them," Jeanine says.

"I'll take care of it," I say.

Tristan glares at us. "Fuck you all," he says as he turns on his heel and heads up the stairs.

I follow him before he can lock me out of his room. He doesn't try to close the door on me, though. "Are you my jailer now?" he says as I enter behind him.

"Just . . . cooperate with me, okay?"

"Here. Take the fucking sheets." He starts ripping them off the bed.

"I didn't say it," I say as I watch them pile up on the floor.

"But it's you, coming to the rescue." He waves his hands in the air.

He may as well have stuck a dagger in my heart. I wait for him to lie down on the mattress before I sit cross-legged on the floor. "Why don't you want me to be here for you?" I ask.

"I can't stand you looking at me," he mumbles as he stares at the wall.

"Is it my face?" I ask, painfully aware of my bruises.

"No," he says shakily.

I gulp. "Then what?"

His voice lowers. "Don't act like you're not pissed at me."

My jaw hangs open. "I'm not pissed at you."

"You're lying."

My head swirls, completely untethered. "I am just so . . . so glad you're here."

"Jesus Christ," he mutters.

"To be honest, it seems like you're mad at *me*."

He picks at the mattress. "You don't understand."

"I don't. Why didn't you wait for me to wake up?"

"You have no idea what it was like seeing you like that. No fucking clue."

"So this . . . this was your solution?"

He picks harder at the mattress. "I was doing you a favor."

"You left me when I needed you."

He stops.

My neck gets sweaty. *I wasn't there for him either*, I remind myself. *God, how do we come back from this?*

"You don't need me," he says darkly. "I'm toxic."

"You're depressed. There's a difference."

He's silent for a moment, as if thinking about this. "I know I'm crazy," he finally says.

"You're not crazy, you're . . . challenged."

"Oh, that's better."

"That's not what I meant. I mean you have challenges. Who doesn't?"

He glares at me over his shoulder. "Don't patronize me."

"Patronize you? I saw you in the hospital, too, remember? I watched you die, baby. Twice."

He turns back to the wall.

Fucking hell, Avery. This wasn't supposed to be a competition. I wipe my eyes, which can't seem to stop leaking. "I haven't rescued you, Tristan. I . . . I may have helped you out of the river, but the rest you did on your own. You decided to live this long. You're strong. You're so fucking strong—"

"Please stop."

"I just want to see you keep doing that."

"You're asking me to suffer."

"It'll be okay."

"When? When will it ever be okay?"

"I-I don't know," I admit, my voice trembling.

He sinks lower into the mattress. "This is me, Avery. The real me. This is who I am."

"Okay, it's you. I still want you to stay with me."

"I don't think I can."

"Yes, you can. You can do anyth—"

"Stop."

"Just promise me you won't try again."

"I can't promise you that."

"Just not tonight. Please, not tonight. That's all I ask."

"Fine."

He goes quiet as the light in his window fades to black. I bite hard on my thumb and sob silently in the corner.

No. No, no, no.

I wake up sweating. It feels like my legs are tied together, buried underneath the ground. I kick violently until I realize it's just sheets wrapped around my legs. I chuck them off, gasping. *Blue sheets?* They seem strange but familiar.

Suddenly, I realize where I am.

"Tristan?" I jolt up off the ground. I can't believe I fell asleep.

Light filters through the window blinds at weird angles, illuminating the bed. It's empty.

"Tristan!" I yell, running out the door.

The bathroom door on the right is open. My shoulder knocks into the door frame as I slip through the entrance. Tristan's sitting on the closed toilet lid, staring at a toothbrush in his hand.

"What? I'm right here," he says, looking up at me.

I clutch my chest and slide down to the floor next to the bathtub.

He sets the toothbrush on the counter. "Are you going to do this every time?"

"Perhaps." I pant.

"You need a better hobby." He kneels on the floor next to me. "Here, let me see you," he says as he gently rolls up my sleeve to examine my shoulder. Goosebumps prickle my arm where his fingers graze against it. He doesn't react, though, as he takes a look at my skin. There doesn't seem to be a bruise, at least. His gaze flicks up to the scar on my hairline as he rolls the sleeve back down. "Your head looks better."

"I think Brandon knocked a couple screws loose."

His face whitens. "Don't joke about that."

"Sorry," I whisper.

He starts to sit next to me, but he freezes partway and looks up. "Dad."

Mr. Chevalier's standing in the doorway, watching us. "I made breakfast," is all he says.

Tristan and I stay quiet as his dad turns and walks down the stairs. I avoid Tristan's gaze as we stand up. We tread slowly after him down to the dining room, where platters of food await us on the table. It all smells good, but the thought of eating it turns my stomach.

Tristan grips the back of a chair as he surveys the table. "Is Betty here?"

"No," Mr. Chevalier says. "She took some time off."

Tristan's grimace deepens.

I pull out the chair next to Tristan and lower myself down. Mr. Chevalier waits for Tristan to sit too, then he puts his hands on both of his shoulders and squeezes. "I love you, my boy."

Tristan slumps forward until his forehead touches the table. "This is awful," he mumbles.

"It's just breakfast," his dad says as he goes around the table and takes a seat across from us.

Jeanine is also trying to appear casual as she passes around the silverware. She gives Tristan a fork, but not a knife. He doesn't notice, though, because he's more interested in the tablecloth. I take mine from her and pretend to pick at my food.

Tristan raises his head and watches as his dad fills his plate with sausage and syrup. I half expect his parents to have a conversation, but they stay quiet and listen to the clink of silver on plates along with us.

When Jeanine is almost done with her meal, she says to Tristan, "We booked an appointment for this afternoon. We can go as a family, if you like."

Tristan's gaze drops to his plate. "What family?" he mutters.

Mr. Chevalier's fork clatters to the table. "Don't talk to her like that."

Tristan's head snaps up. "I'm talking about you!"

Mr. Chevalier's eyebrows rise. "I've given you everything—"

"You give me nothing!"

"Tristan, calm down," Jeanine pleads.

The Lifesaver

Mr. Chevalier gestures around the room. "This house, this food—"

"It's all bullshit," Tristan says.

"We have a lot—"

"You aren't here. You know it's true, Dad. I'm just a trophy you put on your wall."

"Now, that's not—"

"Tell him." Tristan points from Jeanine to his dad. "Tell him how he forgets about me when he leaves."

"Sweetheart—" she says.

"I'm not your 'sweetheart.'"

I prop my elbows on the table and steeple my hands in front of my face. I wish I could melt into the floor.

Tristan's dad lifts his napkin off his lap and places it on the table. "I think we better call them now," he says as he gets up.

"No." Tristan juts his chin out. "I'm fine. I'm just telling it like it is."

Jeanine reaches her hands across the table toward Tristan. "If we *ever* thought we were hurting you . . . ," she says, her eyes tearing up.

Mr. Chevalier pauses and puts his hand on her shoulder.

Tristan quivers in his chair. I think I might implode.

"Please, Tristan," Jeanine says. "Let us get you some help."

"It doesn't fucking matter," he says as he looks away. "I've gone through this before."

"When?" Mr. Chevalier asks.

For the first time, Tristan seems to shrink in his chair. "Um . . . March, I think?"

Nausea gurgles up within me. I lower my arms, finally ready to admit the truth. "I'm sorry, sir. I should have said something."

Mr. Chevalier keeps staring at Tristan. "*Why?*" he asks.

"It was the same old shit, the same old . . ." Tristan's chin trembles. "Fuck . . ."

"You didn't tell your therapist?" Mr. Chevalier asks.

"No."

"But you went to the hospital?"

Tristan doesn't answer.

"No," I say. "I found him and, um . . . gave him CPR."

As this news sets in, Jeanine stands up. "You boys have seen too much. I'm giving you some chocolate."

Tristan and I both chortle in surprise. She walks to the kitchen and disappears behind the door. While she's gone, Mr. Chevalier sits heavily in her chair. He leans against the backrest and looks at us. "And how long have you been dating?" he asks, trying to sound normal.

The change in subject throws me for a spin. My face heats up.

Tristan twiddles his thumbs in his lap. "Uh . . . a while," he answers.

"I wish you had told me."

Before Tristan can respond, Jeanine comes back in with two large candy bars. She gives one to me and hands the other to Tristan.

"Thanks, Jeanine," he mumbles.

She stands behind him and rubs his back.

I tentatively open my wrapper and take a tiny bite off the corner.

Tristan opens his, but he just stares at it. "I, um . . . I'm really not hungry," he says, blushing.

"It's okay," she says as she runs her fingers through his hair. "Is there anything else you wanted to talk about?"

"Um . . ." He reddens more. "Not really."

"That's okay. You can go back to sleep or . . . or do whatever. We'll be here."

We both look at each other. He nods slightly, so I set my candy bar down. He puts his on his plate and gets up. As we head to the doorway, Mr. Chevalier takes Tristan's bar and breaks a small piece off for himself and Jeanine.

When we get back to Tristan's room, Tristan closes the door partway. "I shouldn't have said those things," he mutters.

"I think you were brave. I mean, you said some stuff that wasn't true, but you stood up for yourself."

"What stuff?"

"You have to know that they love you."

He clenches his fists as he looks at the floor. "Shit."

"It's okay, Tristan. They'll forgive you."

His gaze wanders to the sheets. "I don't know what I'm doing," he says as he goes over and picks them up. He hesitates, then holds them out to me. "I'm sorry I threw these at you yesterday," he says under his breath.

My throat closes up. "Don't mention it."

I accept them and walk over to the closet to look for a laundry basket.

He sits on the edge of his bed. "I don't know why I can't stop hurting everyone," he says, toeing at the ground.

"Maybe mention it to the therapist, I guess."

"That's it? That's the magic cure?"

"I don't know. I don't know anything anymore. I thought . . ." My eyes well up suddenly. There he is again, lying on the hospital bed, his skin white and his arms red. *I almost lost him. Maybe I've still lost him.* I drop the sheets and sag to the floor. "I'm sorry. I'm sorry," I say, holding my knees and rocking.

He stands up in alarm. "What's going on?"

"I messed up. I . . ." The image won't leave. I can't control it.

"Avery . . ." He kneels next to me, his face pale. "Don't do this, please."

"I'm n-not . . . I'm not trying to."

He sits down. "Jesus Christ, I'm an asshole."

"It's not you, it's me."

"What do you mean?"

I take his hand. He doesn't pull away this time. "I just want you to sing," I cry, waving his hand for emphasis. "I want you to play piano with me. I want to be able to just fucking swim, a-and have sex, and hold your hand whenever I feel like it and not be called a faggot or fucking killed for it. Like, why is that so hard?"

His fingers twitch. "Yeah."

"But I can't do any of that without you, and I . . . I should have stopped him. Why didn't I stop him?"

He grimaces. "Because I couldn't get you the bat."

"What?" I almost drop his hand. "Is that what you think?"

He avoids my eyes.

"Tristan, no. You were perfect. You were perfect," I say, stroking his knuckles. "It was me. I . . . I wasn't . . ."

"There wasn't anything else you could have done."

"That's not true. I fucking goaded him. He tried to kill us!"

His frown deepens. "He wanted to kill me first."

"He would have killed me in a heartbeat, whether you were there or not. He told me so, the day before. Before the principal's office." My voice cracks.

Tristan hangs his head. "At least he's in jail now."

"Yeah. Yeah. Shit, I'm sorry." I release him and shudder. "I shouldn't unload on you like that."

"You're human."

"I know. This is what I'm like, too." I sniff and stare at the floor.

He stares at the same spot, as if processing it. "So you're . . ." He exhales. "You're really not mad at me?"

I manage a weak smile. "Do I look mad at you?"

"I thought . . . I mean . . ."

"What? That I'd blame you?"

He nods.

"No, baby. It wasn't your fault. I swear."

His voice lowers. "I really thought it'd be better if . . ."

I swallow. "Well . . . it wouldn't." I rub my face. "God, this is so fucked. I really didn't want you to die because of me."

"I didn't want you to die because of me either."

"Well, we're still here. Isn't that the better option?"

His neck turns red as I fix my gaze on him. He plays with the carpet in front of him. "You sure you . . . still want to be with me?"

"Of course," I whisper.

The blush spreads to his ears. "And you still want to have sex with me?"

I choke on a laugh. "That's what you got from all that?"

"I mean, it stood out."

I chuckle again. "Yes, I know. I'm down bad," I say, nudging his side.

He wipes his mouth, but it seems like he's hiding a smirk. "I think I need to check you into therapy, too."

"I would," I say, serious again. "If you want me to, I would."

His hand drops to his lap. He purses his lips, but then he says quietly, "Alright."

38

This therapy thing is a lot harder than I thought. Every day is something else I need to face about myself.

At least I don't have to deal with high school anymore. Principal Johnson waived my exams, so I was able to graduate without them. It's kind of a shame I wasn't able to test what I learned, though.

Tristan didn't seem to care. The school offered him a waiver, too, even though he didn't technically attend there anymore. He told them to go to hell, but they mailed him a diploma anyway.

I don't know what we're going to do when college starts, though. It's looming in front of me like a big fucking dead end. Drake texted me last night to let me know he's already packing, and it nearly sent me into a spiral. How am I going to do this on my own?

Even Ashley let me know she'll be leaving soon. She texted me the other day while I was home, and it made me feel guilty enough that I opened her card. On the front was a picture of Snoopy hugging a dozen Woodstocks, and on the inside she had written:

I am so sorry! I hope you're both okay.
♡ ♡

It made me break down into tears. I debated whether to show Tristan, but then decided he needed the support more than I did. He chewed his lip as he skimmed over it, then said, "That was nice," and handed it back to me as if it hadn't made any impact at all. I never told him about her text. I don't want him thinking about college any more than I am.

The one small reprieve is that we still have a couple of weeks to go before it happens. Grateful for another hot sunny day, I scan the parking lot in front of the clinic. I finally got my cast off this morning, and the skin is almost reflective where the tan doesn't reach. I stretch my fingers to test out the muscles and glance once more at my phone. *Where is Tristan?* He was supposed to pick me up after his therapy session.

Before I get too anxious, his BMW pulls up. I hide my relief as I step off the curb and open the passenger door. On the seat, there's a small bouquet of daisies.

"What's this?" I ask as I pick them up to sit down.

"It's for you," Tristan answers. He's wearing a short-sleeved shirt, one I haven't seen him wear in a while.

"Thanks." My heart unexpectedly swells at the gift. I sniff the flowers, then set them on the dash.

He tosses his hair out of his eyes, but his cheeks turn pink. "How was it?" he asks as he starts to drive.

"I feel naked," I say, showing him my shriveled wrist. "How was your session?"

"She wants me to practice breathing exercises. Like that ever helped."

"I kind of like them."

He glances at me. "You would."

"You know what I learned at mine?"

"What?"

"That I have a Napoleon complex."

He laughs out loud. "You do not."

I grin. "Yeah, I do. I think I'm big but I'm actually really teeny."

"Well, I guess that tracks."

We stop at a light. Staring at the flowers, I ask him seriously, "So does it really not help?"

He frowns. "What? Therapy?"

"Yeah."

He rubs a finger on the steering wheel. "Well, I haven't killed myself yet, so there's that."

I breathe out. "Yeah. That's the best outcome we could have."

He reaches over and takes my hand, a hint of his former smile returning. "You don't have to worry right now," he says, wagging my fingers back and forth.

I suppress a smirk. "Okay."

"So, which way?" he asks as the light turns green.

I close my eyes. "I dunno. Surprise me."

"Got it."

The engine revs and we jet forward. I feel the rumble in my chest through the leather seat. We pick up speed, and my breath shortens. I grip the corner of the seat as we go around turns.

"You okay?" he asks on a straightaway.

"Yeah." The air rushes through the window, ripping away my voice. I can feel it in my guts, my soul, the wind of summer. It's terrifying sometimes to close my eyes, but I'm learning to trust him.

After several minutes, the feel of gravel bumps along under my feet. The engine shuts off and Tristan says, "We're here."

I open my eyes to see the Sonic. I raise my eyebrows. "You're hungry?"

His face is suspiciously flushed. "I want to try something first," he says as he opens the door.

Confused, I step out and follow him to the grassy area behind the building. My heart's already beating wildly at the possibilities.

He stops in the middle of the field and turns to face me. "Okay, push me," he says.

I almost snort. "What? No."

"Come on, push me." He taps my foot with his toe.

"No, this is stupid." Heat rises to my neck. Here in the broad daylight, anyone could be an audience.

"What? Are you chicken shit?" he teases.

"Why are you doing this?"

"I want to see if I can." He pushes lightly on my shoulders.

"I don't like this," I say as I block a second advance.

He grabs my arms and pushes them against my chest. I laugh despite myself as I stumble backward. "You're going to break my wrist again."

"No, I'm not." He grins and leans in harder, careful not to handle my wrist.

We stand deadlocked for a moment, swaying side to side. I hook a foot around his ankle, and he lands on me as we tumble down in a heap. We both laugh.

"We'll have to practice that," I say as he shimmies off of me.

"Yeah." His cheeks turn darker. He sits back on his heels in the grass. "I have something else to show you," he says as he helps me sit up.

"Oh, yeah?"

"I wasn't going to tell you, but you'll find out soon enough anyway." He leans forward and lowers the neckline of his shirt.

I suck in a breath. "What the hell?" On his chest, peeking above the shield, there's a glistening new tattoo. A sword.

He sits back and pats his shirt in place. "Yeah."

"What the hell?" I say again. Tears prick my eyes. "Is . . ." My mind races. "Is this a goodbye present?"

"Huh? No."

"What did your therapist *say* to you?"

"This isn't about her."

"Tristan. Fuck." The tears won't stop coming.

He shifts uncomfortably. "I wanted you to know."

"This means so much to me. I can't . . ."

"Are you okay?"

"I can't . . . I don't . . ." I look up at the sky, then at him. "I don't want to leave you," I moan.

His eyes widen. "You're not leaving me."

"Yes, I am. I'm going to Middleton, and . . ." I curl forward until I'm in his lap.

He wraps his arms around me. "I love you," he whispers, his lips touching my hair.

"I love you, too," I cry.

He squeezes me. "You're going to live your life."

"My life is with you."

"I know. We can be in two places at once."

"Fuck. I know." I sit back and wipe my eyes. "You sure you don't want me to stay?"

His mouth trembles as he frowns. He cups my face with both hands. "Avery, go to college. This is your future. You can do it."

"But what about you?"

He lowers his hands and shrugs. "I'll be here. An hour away."

I look down and pluck a few blades of grass. I want to ask if he's telling the truth, but I don't want to start a fight. Instead, I mumble, "You'll call me if you want me?"

"Yes," he says softly.

"You know I'll be bugging you for help on my homework."

He stops my hand. "I wouldn't have it any other way."

I take a chance and meet his gaze again. His eyes are bright with a kindness I never thought I would see. The wind picks up, and it smells like freshly mown grass and Sonic hamburgers. Before I can speak again, he reaches up to touch my lips. He's so handsome, so . . . real. His scars show faintly pink in the sun, but he isn't trying to hide them. Instead, he leans forward and kisses me, with the leaves rustling high above us. And, with that, I allow myself to hope. Hope that he'll still be here, as promised. Hope that, despite our dark days, we'll have better ones, like this. Hope that he'll forgive, just like I've been learning to forgive myself.

I don't know what's going to happen next year. Anything could happen at any time. Hell, we may do things we regret this very day.

But it can't be worse than what we've already seen. And if we made it through this, well, then maybe . . . just maybe . . . we will find a way to live our lives.

Bridge over Troubled Water
Words and music by Paul Simon

When you're weary
Feeling small
When tears are in your eyes
I will dry them all
I'm on your side
When times get rough
And friends just can't be found
Like a bridge over troubled water
I will lay me down
Like a bridge over troubled water
I will lay me down

When you're down and out
When you're on the street
When evening falls so hard
I will comfort you
I'll take your part
When darkness comes
And pain is all around
Like a bridge over troubled water
I will lay me down
Like a bridge over troubled water
I will lay me down

Sail on, silver girl
Sail on by
Your time has come to shine
All your dreams are on their way
See how they shine
If you need a friend
I'm sailing right behind
Like a bridge over troubled water
I will ease your mind
Like a bridge over troubled water
I will ease your mind

988 SUICIDE & CRISIS LIFELINE

Acknowledgments

First and foremost, I have to thank Eve 6 for writing "Friend of Mine," without which this book would not have been possible. And yes, I do like the heart in a blender song.

Second, and more importantly, I need to thank my husband, Justin, for standing by me throughout this journey. You made a good investment, baby.

I would also like to thank:

My work colleagues for their enthusiastic support over the years. Special shout-out to fellow author Loretta Veney for answering my endless questions about indie publishing.

Jane McClanahan, my first (and most patient!) reader, and her lovely daughter, Erin. I owe you both a box of tissues next time we meet. Thank you for sticking with me and my story.

My alpha readers Brona Mills, H.R. Booth, Erin Srivastava, Sam Barclay, Marisa Urgo, Luna Nightingail, and Linda Dell'Angela. I learned so much from you. Thank you for the swaps and the advice.

My beta readers and writing partners-in-crime Tonia Markou, T.M. Delligatti, Ambrose Hall, and the rest of the Scrib crew. You all know what it means to me. Floralfang forever!

My extremely kind editor, Gary Sunshine.

My creative cover designer, Lena Yang.

Hal Leonard and Columbia Pictures for graciously permitting me to quote from their works.

Kathy Kitts for setting this fledgling author on the right path.

My parents for surrounding our house with books.

And you, dear reader. You are loved. It'll be okay.

About the Author

C.N. Steinhour was a traveler at a young age, being the military brat of two Air Force veterans. She eventually settled in Virginia to marry her high school sweetheart. When she's not writing, she can be found tickling the ivories or cuddling with her gentle rescue cat. You can visit her online at cnsteinhourbooks.com.

Made in the USA
Middletown, DE
13 July 2025